PRAISE FOR

"K. Bromberg always delivers ... ...onally
intense, sensual romance . . ."

—*USA Today*

"K. Bromberg makes you believe in the power of true love."

—#1 *New York Times* bestselling author Audrey Carlan

"A poignant and hauntingly beautiful story of survival, second chances, and the healing power of love. An absolute must-read."

—*New York Times* bestselling author Helena Hunting

"A home run! *The Player* is riveting, sexy, and pulsing with energy. And I can't wait for *The Catch*!"

—#1 *New York Times* bestselling author Lauren Blakely

"An irresistibly hot romance that stays with you long after you finish the book."

—#1 *New York Times* bestselling author Jennifer L. Armentrout

"Bromberg is a master at turning up the heat!"

—*New York Times* bestselling author Katy Evans

"Supercharged heat and full of heart. Bromberg aces it from the first page to the last."

—*New York Times* bestselling author Kylie Scott

"Captivating, emotional, and sizzling hot!"

—*New York Times* bestselling author S. C. Stephens

This is a work of fiction. Names, characters, organizations, places, events, and incidents are either products of the author's imagination or are used fictitiously.

Copyright © 2019 by K. Bromberg

All rights reserved.

No part of this book may be reproduced, or stored in a retrieval system, or transmitted in any form or by any means, electronic, mechanical, photocopying, recording, or otherwise, without express written permission of the publisher.

Published by JKB Publishing, LLC

ISBN-13: 978-1-942832-20-1

Cover design by Helen Williams
Cover Image by PeopleImages
Formatting by Alyssa Garcia at Uplifting Author Services

Printed in the United States of America

ALSO BY K. BROMBERG

Kelly—
Own your
wild !
K. Bromberg

Then YOU happened

NEW YORK TIMES BESTSELLING AUTHOR
K. BROMBERG

Kelly,

Our love,

xoxo,

K. Bromberg

This book is dedicated to the broken ones:
To the person with a broken heart.
To the reader whose trust has been broken.
To the woman feeling broken because she lost sight of who she was for a moment.

You're not alone.
Keep your heart under lock and key.
Keep your trust guarded
Keep your chin up.

One day this will all be just a memory.
The hurt.
The lack of confidence.
The loss of self.

Hopefully you will rediscover your own resolve as you watch Tatum stand her ground.
Hopefully Jack will help you realize that trust can be given again.
Hopefully the two of them will give you hope that love can be found again.

You found parts of me I didn't know existed
and in you I found a love
I no longer believed was real.
— j. iron word

Prologue

"You walk out that door, Tatum Valor, and you might as well leave your last name here when you do."

I stare at my father—at his stern face and too-proud posture, at his gray eyes, which are the same color as mine, and the hurt in them—and see the life he wants me to lead. One that matches the Waterford crystal vases strategically placed around his dining room—pretty to look at, serving no real purpose, and displayed simply to let others know how successful the Valor name is. I glance out the front door to Fletcher's truck parked across the street. His head is bent forward as he looks at something on his phone, and all I can see is a future with him. No reprimands to act like a Valor. No leashes holding me back from pursuing the things I want to try and fail and try again without embarrassing the family name. Nothing but the blissful unknown stretched out for miles before Fletch and me. Nights full of laughter and love as I help him fulfill the dreams he's had since he was a little boy, and I figure out the woman I am and who I want her to become.

Excitement swells as my obstinance holds fast.

"What are you going to do, Dad? Disown me?" I snort. "I'm a grown woman who can make her own decisions, thank you very much."

It's his turn to make a noise, and it sounds one hundred percent like disapproval. "Ah, to be twenty-three and think you have all the answers." He takes a step toward me, the chuckle he emits anything but humorous. "You don't know a thing."

"What do you think, I'm incompetent? I graduated college at the top of my class. I traveled Europe for a year on my own. I seemed damn capable of making decisions for myself then. I was—"

"Doing all of that with *my* money paying your way."

His words are cold but honest and rub me the wrong way because he's right and there's nothing I can say to refute him.

"True, but your money always comes with strings."

"Just as your last name does." We wage a visual war in the room that holds so many memories for me. Family gatherings and celebrations. Holidays and laughter. Traditions done the Valor way. I wish I could see the good times through all the disappointment and anger billowing around us. "And it's not as if you complained when you were enjoying the benefits that either of them had given you."

"This is ridiculous," I mutter when he just keeps staring like I'm going to wither under his scrutiny like the little girl I used to be did.

Then the fear of the unknown creeps in as his threat lingers.

Is it the threat itself or the worry of doing wrong by him that the threat brings? Or maybe it's then going against him part when I've always danced to his tune.

There's no way he'd disown me if I left.

Would he?

The dead silence eats at me, and the certainty I felt when I walked in here to tell him I was leaving dissipates. I'd assumed he'd be angry but that he'd get over it.

I'm not sure if he will.

Not now.

"I meant what I said. You walk out that door . . ."

Tears well in my eyes because the decision a twenty-three-year-old must make between family duty and self-fulfillment is never an easy one.

"You don't mean that," I whisper when I meet his eyes, more than afraid that he actually does.

"If you think I'm going to pat you on the back and congratulate you while you throw everything away . . . you're crazy."

"Throw everything away?" My voice rises in pitch and I don't care that I just committed a cardinal sin in this house—raise my voice to my father. "Maybe I'm just growing up and want to see the world. Maybe I need to find my place in it. Maybe—"

"And maybe you've met a man who tells you all the right things so that you're blind to all the wrong things about him."

My shoulders square in response. "You'll say anything to keep me here. The question is, *why, Dad*? Don't you want your kid to go out and spread her wings? Don't you trust the wisdom you've given me to make the right choices?"

"I'm looking at the choices you're making and not trusting much of anything at the moment."

Screw you.

The words want to fall from my lips but don't.

"He's a boy, Tate—"

"*He's a man.* We're not teenagers—"

"And yet you're acting like one by throwing away everything you've worked for, all of your talent, all of your hard work, by being with him."

3

"I thought you said *my hobby* was a waste of time." Every time he told me my photography was taking away from real hobbies runs through my mind. "Now, all of a sudden, when it's in your favor, you tell me I'm talented. Why?" I ask, disbelief marrying with the anger coursing inside me.

"It was never a waste of time . . . but you spent two years in one of the top photography programs in the country."

"Going to Yale was your requirement, not mine—"

"And then you spent the last year working your way around Europe to build your portfolio—"

"For what, though, Dad? So I could come home and you could tell me who I should date? Who I should marry so I can give you the most desirable offspring and keep you in the right circles so I don't embarrass you?"

"Stop acting like a child, Tatum."

"Then stop treating me like one!" I shout, frustrated and furious and disappointed this hadn't gone a different way.

My father crosses the room and looks out the front window. He stares at Fletcher's truck, and I know all he sees is the dented fender and the faded paint, not the quality or the character of the man behind its wheel.

"You working on your craft is more important than anything."

"I will be working on it."

"Not in some Podunk town. You should be here in Baltimore where you have the right resources and the right connections and—"

"And where you can tell me what to do and who to associate myself with?" I sneer. "This is total bullshit."

"That's enough!" His voice thunders, and when he turns to meet my eyes, the vein in his neck is bulging and his jaw is clenched. "You want to just throw away everything you did for the past seven years? All that education and talent? Your future?"

"You don't understand . . ." My words hit him and fall flat, his expression unwavering.

And I know that if I spend one more night in this house, I'll suffocate. Adventure I can find easily, but the strings attached with having Valor as a last name, the pretenses I must continually maintain, kill every ounce of creativity I have.

That, and there's Fletcher.

"I'm warning you. If you walk out that door . . ."

"But I love him!" Fear begins to tinge the exasperation that owns every part of me.

"You don't have a clue what love is yet. How can you?" His voice resonates with anger as my mom presses a trembling hand to her lips. Somehow, she knows—*like I do*—that there is no going against the wishes of Renquist Valor III without a life-changing fallout.

"You don't get to tell me how to feel."

"Like hell I don't," he thunders as he points to Fletcher's truck and my suitcases lying in its bed. "Do you think he's going to be with you when the money runs out? Do you think that, when times get tough and the pipe dream he has of breeding horses falls flat, he'll still love you? Men like him are all the same. They take and take and then take some more. It's all fine and dandy when your mommy and daddy are helping foot the bill, but sweetheart, how long do you think he'll stick around once mommy and daddy say enough is enough?"

"When did you become so judgmental? When did people who didn't have money become less than us?" I shake my head and realize I no longer idolize the man standing in front of me. In fact, I hate him. "You're not being fair."

"I'm not? You think I don't know that you poured some of your monthly trust payment into fixing that heap of his out there? You don't think I know you plan on using your money to help him buy the land and the horses and everything else he needs to prepare for failure? I may be old, Tate, but I'm far from stupid."

My hands fist and teeth grit as I hold back the words I want to scream at him: it's my money; I can do what I want with it.

But I don't say a thing because he won't hear me. He's already made up his mind.

"Dad—"

"I wish I'd listened to my gut and never let you ride," he says the sentence like one big swear.

"Why? Because the stable hand I met at the country club isn't good enough for me?"

"You're goddamn right he isn't!" I jump when his fist slams onto the table at his side, my mom's beloved Kosta Boda vase rattling as her yelp fills the room.

I glance to her and taste the bitterness of her rejection. How can she not step in and defend me? How come she isn't telling my dad he's wrong?

"It's a hard lesson to learn, and I hate that I even have to teach it to you . . . but if you walk out that door, that's it. The money you have in your savings is yours, but your trust fund is cut off. There will be no calls home asking for more. There will be—"

"So that's the leash you're strangling me with to stay? You'll cut off my trust fund in the hopes that I'll come crawling back begging for money?" I huff out a laugh, part disbelief that he said it and part gratitude over the huge transfer I just made from my trust account to my personal savings account.

"Yep."

"And then, of course, you'll give me the ultimatum that, if I want my money, then I have to leave him?"

"No worries there. If the money runs out, he'll already be gone." My father's voice is barely a rumble of sound, but it's deafening to me.

"And if you're wrong?" I shake my head and cross my arms

And when I cross the driveway and climb into the truck beside Fletcher, I can't look at him. I can barely breathe let alone think, so I say the one thing I can, "Drive."

One

JACK

Six years later

It's pretty enough.

That's my first thought when I sit on the initial stretch of gravel driveway and stare at the expanse of ranch in front of me. The split rail fence stretches farther than I can see on both sides of me. The main house has a worn brick exterior, pitched roofline, and a covered verandah that wraps around its front. The pastures are green, and the stables large enough, but where the house looks worn, they *feel* more neglected than they look.

Drive the car, Sutton. Walk the walk, and talk the talk. Fulfill the promise you made, and then get the hell out of Dodge with a clear conscience and maybe a few months of vacation before you have to step into shoes you never expected to fill.

I glance up at the entrance, take in the sign hanging from the wood arch that says *Knox Ranch,* and notice the broken hinge of the opened gate in front of me. There are two cameras with frayed electrical cords and cracked lenses positioned on either side of the

"I don't associate with people who lie," I muse as I lean against the railing behind me.

"Then what in the hell are you doing at the bar in town? They all lie and you're listening to them, right?"

Touché.

"Why'd you tell me to come out here, Knox, if you already knew you were going to fire me the minute I showed up on your porch?" I ask, curious about her when I shouldn't care.

"Why'd you sit in town and listen to the rumors, believe them, before you ever even met me? Shouldn't your boss be given more respect than that?"

"I don't believe rumors, but they aren't lies if they're true." I shift on my feet, the wood of the porch creaking beneath me. "And respect is earned, not expected."

This woman. Hell. If her spite wasn't so damn frustrating, it might be a little attractive.

"Why are you still standing here?" she asks.

"Good question." I wondered the same thing. Turning my back to her, I take in the dead flowers and weeds overflowing the planters positioned around the porch and let my eyes skate over the paint peeling on the railing on the verandah.

But I know why I'm here.

I know what guilt feels like as it weighs you down so heavily you'll do anything—even deal with a woman like Tatum Knox—if it means you just might get to lift it off your shoulders.

It's a goddamn emotional tug of war, and I'm not quite sure which side I want to win.

"You hired me to get you more business," I say when I turn back around. "You think potential clients are going to be eager to buy a horse when they stroll up here and see this?" I motion to the first set of pots. "How can you be trusted to keep horses healthy when you can't even keep flowers alive?" I give a slow shake of my head in displeasure, causing her to scowl.

"If you're trying to win my favor, you're going about this all wrong."

"Winning your favor is the least of my worries." I cross my arms over my chest and just hold her glare for glare. "Forget me being able to secure quality studs to breed. Screw me getting the ranch new clients under a long-term contract. What you really need more than anything is a ranch manager who is worth a shit."

"Is that so?"

"It is." I nod. "By the looks of what I see, he's not managing shit. Your hired help isn't pulling their weight. Your feed isn't being housed properly. You have fences that seem to have been broken for some time. And I haven't even started on the horses. For a ranch that survives by selling its foals, it doesn't look like you have nearly enough pregnant mares out there, which is something you mentioned during our phone interview."

Those eyes of hers narrow.

Hit a nerve now, did I?

"I didn't realize I asked your opinion."

"You didn't have to. I give opinions freely." I smile, but I do it to piss her off.

Truth hurts, doesn't it, sweetheart?

I recall the comments that were made in town.

"That Tatum woman doesn't fit in here."

"She supposedly works on the ranch, but come on, what rancher has the beautician come out on the regular to do her hair and nails? She's probably the gopher. Or the trophy groomer. There's gotta be a reason why she runs all the employees off. She's probably worried word will get out that she doesn't know what in the hell she's doing."

"The sheriff's up there weekly. There's one complaint after another about her substandard care for the horses. No one in town dares buy one. They don't trust that they're in good health."

"She doesn't deserve the land she owns. No wonder the Destin twins are pissed and want it back. She and her husband have done nothing but waste their opportunity with that ranch."

"Do I need to call the sheriff to have you removed?" she asks.

"I hear you two are good friends with his regular visits up here and all." The tendons in her neck strain as she tries to hide her temper. I'm trying to push boundaries so that I can walk away from this place with the lie set in place that I really tried to make this work but failed.

"It's Texas, Mr. Sutton. No one will think twice if I shoot you for trespassing." She smiles sweetly. "We like to protect what's ours and know we won't be questioned for doing so."

"Ah, but you're not from Texas, are you?" I ask, uncertain why I feel the need to keep bantering. "From what I gather, the citizens of Lone Star don't really claim you as their own."

I'm a prick for pointing out the obvious since I'm probably more welcome in this town than she is, but I can't figure out how she lives here, has set up a life here, and yet, no one really seems to know her.

Maybe it's their not knowing her that's earned her the vitriol.

Then again, all she has to do is open her mouth and their point's proven in the first few sentences.

"I don't care what the people in town think of me, let alone anyone else, really." Another tight smile. A throw of her thumb over her shoulder. "Should I go prove to you I have the shotgun locked and loaded, always on the ready . . . just in case?"

"You talk a good game, Knox, but you know damn well that, if I leave, ain't no one else coming to help. I don't believe the bullshit in town, but others will. No paycheck is enough to put up with your attitude. Not a one."

"Good. Be on your way then."

The dismissal in her tone this time sets me off. It gives me a temper to feed off, a reason to get pissed and walk away.

19

"Thanks for proving you're exactly how I thought you were going to be." I tip my hat as her eyes narrow with confusion. "Enjoy losing your ranch to the bank."

"Go to hell. I'm not—"

"It seems to me that's what you're angling to do anyway."

"Good. Go."

"I will."

Fury and anger and failure course through me as I turn from her and start toward the steps, as I force myself to walk away from the woman with storm clouds in her eyes and defiance in her voice.

I'm ten feet from my truck when her voice rings out.

"Jack."

It's the way she says my name like a woman wanting to hold it all together while fearing she isn't going to be able to. That single syllable is full of defiance and fear and confusion and determination.

There's something about her I can't peg.

Something that's pulling me in that's just as strong as the promise I made and my need to keep my word.

Something that I hate myself for wanting to explore.

I turn to where she stands on the top of the steps, staring at me across the distance with one hand on her hip and the other shielding her eyes. Her expression is stoic, no reflection of the tinge of desperation that just rang out in her voice.

And yet, my name felt like an olive branch extended in a war zone. One that's only going to be offered for mere seconds before it's snatched back.

Walk away, Jack.

Walk the fuck away while you can.

Instead, I take a step closer, twist my lips, and look around, wondering why I'm not taking the out when I can.

Because I made promises, that's why. Duty and defiance war against each other within me.

I take another step toward her.

"You can't expect anyone to successfully sell your brand and this place when it looks like it's been neglected." She starts to speak, and I just keep on talking. "How many people do you have on your staff?"

"One."

"*One?*" I laugh. "Funny. You have forty horses here. How many people besides the *one* ranch manager do you have on staff?"

"If you don't count good ol' eighty-one-year-old Sylvester who stops by and helps now and again, it's just one."

"Sylvester?" I ask. "Should I assume he's how you know I've been in town for a few days?" She nods and twists her lips as I try to fathom how she only has one employee. How she manages all of this that way. Then again, she isn't exactly a ray of fucking sunshine either. I can only imagine how pleasant she is to work with and for. "Well, fire the *one*. He's not doing his job. Tell him he's been replaced."

"Replaced?" Her chuckle is low and condescending. "By whom?"

By whom? Definitely the upper crust of New England.

"By me."

Her laugh rings louder now, it's long and rich, and it is followed by a shake of her head. "I've already fired everyone who can be fired. Thanks for letting me know how to run my ranch, though."

"Your ranch. Your problem," I say, noting how moments before it was her husband's ranch but, now that she's defending it, it's hers. "You said you needed to sell more horses this year. Rebuild and revamp by breeding and selling. Pick up some key clients who might create repeat business. Maybe even sell a rodeo circuit champion or two," I say. "Increase profits in general, right?"

Tatum just stares at me as indecision fights over her features. The need for help against the want to stand her ground.

"I don't think I heard you wrong, did I?" I continue. "Feel free to go at it alone, but from what you told me, you need the help to turn a profit and stay afloat. I can help with that. Or you can tell me to walk away, taking all my experience and connections with me, and you can keep doing what you're doing."

Stubborn pride or guaranteed success.

Your call, princess.

Her body tenses, and her teeth grit. "There are other people I can hire. No worries there."

"The question is, will they work for you?" I snort. "Next time someone comes out, you might want to mention to them they're going to be fighting an uphill battle trying to promote a ranch this size without any help."

"Running the ranch is my responsibility. Selling the foals was supposed to be yours."

"So the rumor mill is true, then. You won't take qualified help even when it's sitting on your front porch."

"Qualified doesn't mean *quality*."

I just lift my brow and smirk at the dig. "Tell me something. Did you fire your help or did they quit?" That wipes the look off her face. "I have twenty bucks on they quit. I've been here no fewer than ten minutes, and you've insulted me more times than I care to count. I heard you were difficult to work for. Criticizing how someone does something when you don't know how to do it yourself doesn't exactly win you any respect. You have a smart mouth and a bad rep. Being easy on the eyes and having an Ivy League education doesn't mean shit in a town like this . . . especially when you throw it around and look down upon those who have less."

And almost as if on cue, a neigh sounds off in the distance. The sound of a familiar friend I can relate to in this hostile environment.

Two

TATE

Bring this place back to life, my ass.

I don't know how long I stand and stare at the dust his tires kick up as it dances through the sunlight.

How about stop sitting at the bar listening to rumors, huh? How about not believing the lies told and meeting me first? How about giving me a chance before they poison you to who I really am?

That cocky grin. Those chocolate-colored eyes alit with humor because, even though I told him he wasn't, he was right . . . so right in so many ways. Still, it was worth every damn word of that fight. His sarcasm, which hit all the right notes at all the right times, like nails on a chalkboard to my ears and sledgehammer to my ego. The truth he threw around was so much closer than anyone could ever imagine because I'm doing everything I can to keep my financial trouble a secret. I've been doing everything to prevent the vultures from circling while they wait for me to lie down and die.

The town knowing the truth would only help them run me out

of here, and that's the last thing I want to give them—victory and satisfaction.

I think about what he said, focusing on the emotions he evoked and not on what it felt like to have a man standing on my porch challenging me. The slight flutter in my belly when those dimples showed. The uptick in my pulse over the flex of his biceps beneath the cuffs of his shirt.

I was supposed to hate him on sight.

Sylvester's warnings about seeing him in Ginger's bar the past few nights talking with the locals were supposed to be enough of a warning to send him packing.

Too bad, because I'd wanted to hire him up until Sylvester told me. The last thing I need is for another employee to blast what's going on at my ranch all over town like the last one did.

I learned my lesson. Never again.

I was supposed to hate him on sight.

Instead of hating him, though, I watched him as he sat in his truck at the edge of the driveway. As he drove slowly toward the house, looking here and there as he took in the fence and pasture and house. When he climbed out of his truck, it was as if I'd been sucker punched squarely in the gut.

When our eyes met for the first time.

When his body tensed, his eyes widened, and the slightest hint of desire crawled through them a moment longer than would be normal, allowing me to notice it.

My plan to lay out my reasons calmly went out the window because I'd felt that slightest hint of desire too. The notion I had that I was going to explain to him that I had to trust who I hired, and that I simply didn't trust him, got lost in that momentary lapse of concentration.

In my head, I'd had it all worked out. I'd spout off to him, and he'd wave a hand in the air—maybe even lift his middle finger—as he walked away without a second thought. He'd save me the trouble and the heartache of getting attached to another ranch manager only to learn they were in town badmouthing me and telling everyone my secrets again.

In my mind, the whole scenario would have been over in mere minutes.

But damn it, he stood there with his pride bristling and his smile smug as I was a bitch to him. And the more I spoke, the more he dug in as if something were keeping him here. Something that made him fight for a job that was way beneath his qualifications.

I should have been asking myself why he would do that, but I was so determined to hate him on sight that I didn't.

So, I fought him. I was rude and nasty and scared as hell because I wanted to hire him—knew I needed to hire him—but am so gun-shy after hearing Sylvester tell me who he was sidling up to in town that I pushed him away.

And now that the dust from his departure had settled, I couldn't help but feel as if I'd made a monumental mistake.

Being about to lose my farm is not exactly what I'd call having things handled.

But Jack's comment and Sylvester's warning marry together and ring through my thoughts, telling me I did the right thing.

He is arrogant and cocky and *handsome* and qualified and *tall* and is willing to stand up to me when most people don't even talk to me these days.

"Christ." My shoulders sag under the weight of that choice, and the humid air is suddenly suffocating me.

It's how I've felt day after day, month after month, for the last year because I've done all of this myself. I have thrown myself into the thick of things—feeding and grooming and tracking estrus cycles—and have learned to do Fletcher's job all on my own. When he was alive, all he'd let me do was the trivial stuff, and I'd become the window dressing to all the hard work everyone else did. It was all he allowed me to do.

All because Fletcher didn't want me to get too close to anyone. He didn't want me to hear the whispers among workers about how the *jefe* was down in the bunkhouse placing bets with money he didn't have. How on the breeding trip he'd just gotten back from, he'd spent more time in the sports bar, hedging his bets and unbeknownst to me, losing everything we had, than he'd spent at the stables, ensuring breeding success.

By the looks of it, moments of weakness are all you seem to have.

"Prick," I mutter, hating Jack for no other reason than he called me out on failing at the ranch. Okay, there was also a bit of dislike that he'd walked away when I really needed him to stay. Not that I blame him after the way I'd acted.

I pinch the bridge of my nose, knowing how crazy I sound, and yet, simply being too exhausted to care.

I've been busting my ass, trying to make this work and having to figure things out as I go. God forbid, anyone in this town ever offer any advice other than to tell me I should sell and move back to where I came from.

And I'm the cold-hearted bitch who's too good for them?

The thought grates harder than the stacks of correspondence from the bank inside and the voicemails filling my phone that tell me I'm about to lose my ranch.

I storm through the house, feet stomping on the hardwood floors in an attempt to try to make myself feel better. Isn't that the best part about living alone? You can do what you want, and there is no one there to tell you that you're overreacting.

But I am.

Because all I hear are Jack's criticisms and all I see is that taunting smirk on his handsome face. I bet he can't wait to run back to Ginger's Bar to tell everyone how much I'm failing or how I don't even know how to store my feed correctly.

My temper rages like a damn inferno within me. My insecurity about if I'm doing this right and my stress over always having bill collectors at my throat probably aren't helping, but Jack's criticism on something so damn simple sets me off. Gritting my teeth, I pass closed door after closed door—memories I'm not sure I want to remember or erase contained behind the slabs of wood—as I walk down the hall, push out the back door, and head toward the stable. I only have one goal, which is to prove him wrong.

I'm out of breath when I reach it. The bales of hay are stacked neatly inside, the bags of feed dry but lying haphazardly on the floor beside them. The color-coded buckets for grain and supplements are on the floor where I threw them when I saw the text from him saying he was on his way.

"Screw you, Jack Sutton," I mutter as I grab the first fifty-pound bag of feed and drag it to its proper location.

One bag after another, I do my best to stack and arrange them despite their weight and my small stature.

There is no satisfaction in the work, no release from the pain still burning bright inside me, and no reprieve from the chaos that the upending of my world started well over a year ago.

I do the tedious task.

The work I never thought in a million years I'd have to carry out is my only focus.

It's either I do it or I lose the only thing I have left—this place. I gave up everything else already.

I hate you, Fletcher.

The refrain fills my mind as I force myself to ignore the sadness that comes with it. The life I thought we had versus the life we really lived. The all-encompassing truth that follows right behind it, which is that I walked into our marriage knowing what I was walking away from without ever imagining that some five-plus years later I'd be standing alone.

Shoving away the first tear that slips down my cheek, I pretend like hell that the hole in my chest isn't real when I swear it is. It's been there ever since Sheriff Chatsworth rang my doorbell and said the words that will forever be etched in my mind.

"There's been an accident, Tate."

The shattering of my heart was different then, though. I was mourning the loss of my husband and best friend. Little did I know how my feelings for him would change when the truth came out. Little did I know how my world would be forever different.

I hang my head down to try to catch my breath, shove away the anger, and I remind myself that I won't give up, that I won't lie down without a fight, not even when it feels like that's all I've been doing for the past year. Fighting. Willing. Surviving.

Because maybe Jack Sutton was right.

I need help. This place needs help—more than I can give it all by myself. If I plan to keep it, I don't have any other choice than to get some. That means I'll have to continue to ignore the gossip in town and how the Destin twins and Jed from the feed store seem to thrive on spreading it.

None of them know just how long it has taken me to slowly climb out of the hole Fletcher dug us into. They have no clue that it's taken me countless hours of sweat and tears, of questioning and blaming myself, to get the ranch and its finances to where they are . . . or that it's still nowhere near enough.

I'm still on the verge of losing everything.

I'm not sure that I'll ever get back above water, but I'll never give up.

The part of me that walked away from her family for a man she was desperately in love with needs to prove that it wasn't all for nothing. That I can take the dream my husband failed to attain and make it not only my own but also successful.

That I can show the citizens of Lone Star I'm not who they say I am.

That I can prove that I'm more than just a trophy wife.

Another small part of me yearns for the ignorance and oblivion in which I used to live, and I shake the thought away by hefting another bag of feed that's almost half my body weight.

It's hard to live in a place where there are so many things that remind me of him—his footprints in the concrete we poured outside of the stables, the fence rail that is still broken from where the horse spooked and he fell through it, our last name carved in the rail on the porch, the bed I sleep in—and not get bogged down with them all.

Not to hate as fiercely as I thought I loved.

Not to question my judgment when before I trusted blindly.

I use the back of my hand to try to shove the tears off my face, but I know that, even with dry cheeks, I'll still feel the defeat that is seated deeply in my bones.

A horse neighs out in the paddock, and the sound forces me to move because standing here sure as hell isn't going to fix a damn thing.

"No rest for the weary," I murmur as I pick up the pails and head over to the washbasin.

Channeling all of my frustration into scrubbing the stubborn residue and grime off the buckets, I tell myself not to think of him.

The problem is that I'm not sure which *him* I'm referring to: Fletcher, who brought me to Lone Star and lived a lie with me, or Jack, who thinks he can just show up and tell me what to do and how to run this place.

"Christ, Tate. You *are* losing your mind," I say with a laugh because I know Jack said none of that.

None at all.

And yet, that's what I heard in every single nuance of his tone, in just that lone lift of his eyebrow.

Jack wins, and my thoughts, the brunt of my temper, and the obstinance that goes hand in hand with my pride turn their focus to him.

Screw you, Jack Sutton.

I can do this by myself.

I have been.

So, I scrub until my arms ache and my hands hurt, and when I'm done, I feel no better for the time put in. Hell, the damn horses aren't going to care if there's a stubborn speck of mud on the inside of their pail. They aren't going to care if the water I add to bind the supplements to their feed is lukewarm or cold.

They aren't going to care about any of it.

And that's when it hits me. How could Jack have seen any of this when it's all inside the stable? How could he pass judgment on how my feed is stored when he never ventured this way in the first place?

I watched his every step from the moment he stepped out of his truck.

All six foot plus of him with that dirty-blond hair that curled at the back of his neck and the swagger he walked with. My eyes were on him until he strode up to my porch and set those chocolate-brown eyes on me.

And I thought I was in control of this situation right up until he played me like a damn fiddle.

"The feed isn't stored properly, my ass," I mutter.

I was firing him, and he was arguing with me, and hell if he didn't work me up so much that I fell for his bullshit accusation.

Hell, he's probably sitting in Ginger's right now, telling them all how he put me in my place and I didn't even know it. They're probably laughing at how I'm running around the ranch like a chicken with my head cut off, trying to fix all the things he mentioned so that no one knows.

Screw you, Jack Sutton.

I hang my head and laugh with only the horses to hear. I laugh until tears fill my eyes and my stomach hurts because isn't this par for the course? Isn't this how I've felt since Fletcher died? Like I have everything under control when someone else is there to remind me that I don't?

If I didn't think I'd gone crazy before, now I certainly do. Laughing and crying and hating and regretting.

I shake my head. *Well played, Jack.* Even though I hate him, I still have to admire him for having the last word.

Three

TATE

"It's time to sell her."

I pinch the bridge of my nose and close my eyes at the sound of my accountant's voice on the phone at my ear.

The day is hot, and my quick respite inside doesn't offer much reprieve from it.

"Have we come to that?" I whisper, already knowing the answer.

"I'm sorry, Tate. I've held off calling you for as long as I could, but yes, it's come to that."

"Fuck." The word is more for me than for her, but I say it anyway.

"Pretty much," she agrees. "I've been making calls left and right, trying to have the mortgage company get you another extension, but you've already had one and so they're not too keen on it even after that last chunk you paid."

"That last chunk came from the sale of a yearling. I won't have any new foals for a few months." I withhold the groan because there's nothing I can do.

"The plus side is that, even if they technically start the fore-closure process, you have about six months to figure out what's next."

I hear her but shake my head as I walk down the hallway, my feet needing to move. "There is no *what's next* for me. You know I put all my eggs in one basket." But my gorgeous Ruby flickers in my mind. She's my derby horse, which really has no business being here on my quarter horse farm, but I love her with all my heart.

"How'd that new guy turn out? Maybe he can help you turn the place around."

A nervous chuckle falls from my lips. "Don't ask."

"That good, huh?"

"Does it matter? I'm damned if I do and damned if I don't." I bite the inside of my lip, and I'm more than grateful that she remains silent so I can work through everything in my head. "I need him to help me here so that I can ensure a successful breeding season, but I can't afford to pay him a salary."

"You have to spend money to make money," she murmurs.

"This coming from an accountant who's calling to tell me I need to sell my derby horse or risk losing my ranch because I can't pay my mortgage." I'll lose my house. The only things I have left to my name. "That's rich."

"You could always swallow your pride and . . ."

"And what?" I ask. "Sell off the equipment I need but that isn't a necessity? Done that. Pawn my jewelry? Did that months ago. You already know this. I just—"

"I know. I admire you and your damn stubbornness more than you could ever know." The line falls quiet, and I hate that I steel myself for what I know is coming next. "I meant you could call them. You're their daughter. Words said in the heat of the moment are never truly meant."

Emotions clog in my throat as I think of the one time I did call. How the phone was hung up on me. How I was reminded, without so much as a word being spoken, of how I made a choice . . . and it wasn't them. Of the disgrace I brought to the Valor name by running off and marrying the country club's hired help.

"Not an option." My voice is resolute even if my feelings aren't.

"Okay. Then since Ruby's your biggest asset besides your physical property, which you've told me you won't sell off, then you have to consider selling her. It will give you enough money to get by until the new foals are ready to be sold."

"I can't just put a for sale sign on her and parade her around town."

"Why the hell not?"

I sigh deeply and lean my head back against the wall behind me. "Because I don't want them to know."

"Who to know? The town? Screw them, Tate. They haven't once been concerned about you so why are you suddenly worried about what they think of you?"

"You wouldn't understand."

"Try me."

Thoughts collide and emotions whirl, and I feel stupid even giving them a voice. "The last thing they need is something else to gossip about. Between the increased prices I'm charged on supplies and bogus complaints lodged with the sheriff's office and ASPCA about my treatment of the horses, they have enough. All I can think is that the Destin twins are either trying to push me off this land with their bullying or they're trying to devalue everything I have with rumors so that when prospective buyers come to town, all they hear is great stuff about Hickman Ranch and shitty stuff about mine." I shift my feet and shake my head. "That's why I don't trust anyone to know what's going on."

"Wouldn't it just be better to cut your losses and leave, Tate?

Sell it to the damn Destin assholes and get the fuck out of that town that sounds like misery inside a sinkhole?"

"Misery inside a sinkhole?" I laugh the words out and appreciate her humor.

"Well, not the actual place, per se, more the shitheads in town."

"Would it be the easiest thing? Sure, but . . . this is all I have left. There are no savings. There is nothing. And deep down, a part of me wants to make it work so I can give the ultimate fuck you to Fletcher for what he did to me."

"He's dead, honey. He'll never know." Her chuckle is soft.

"But I'll know." My voice is soft, and my eyes burn with tears. "I let him manipulate me for *years*, Sheryl. I let him take everything I have, including my money, my trust, and my sense of self. I need to get that back. If by making this place succeed, I'm able to find a bit of the old me again, then it's worth all of this." I look to my left as Ruby neighs out in the pasture. "Besides, it isn't as if I have anywhere else to go. If I sell this place, every penny I'd make on it would go right to the bank. Then what? I'm homeless and broke? If I stay, then at least I have a roof over my head a little longer and something to actually try to make this work."

"Tate." My name is a warning at best.

"I know, I know. It hasn't worked this far . . . but it's been better than it was. It's taken me almost a year, but I finally dug out of all the holes he put me in other than the mortgage and home equity line. That's my last hurdle to jump before I can be out of the proverbial red."

"Selling Ruby will help with that." Her voice is quiet, and her words settle like a lead weight in my stomach. I wish I could shut out every single one of them, but know I can't.

This is my reality.

This is my robbing Peter to pay Paul.

This is what Fletcher has reduced me to.

"Fine. Yes. I know," I utter. "I have to go."

And when I set the phone on the bathroom counter, I sink down onto the closed toilet seat and shut my eyes.

Ruby. There is so much history with her. She is what helped to pull me out of my darkest depths I sank to after I found out what Fletcher had done. She has been my only friend here in Lone Star for so long, and now I feel like I'm betraying her by even talking about selling her.

I stand, and when I pass by the mirror, I force myself to look at it. To look at myself.

"How much longer are you going to do this, Tee?" I ask. How much longer can I hold on? Do I even want to?

I don't allow myself to look away from my reflection, from the doubt and exhaustion in my eyes. Or to deny the grit and determination that lingers at their edges.

"One year. Give it one more year."

I'm not sure why tears well in my eyes. Maybe it's because I'm so damn exhausted that I can't figure out how I'm going to do this alone for another year. Or maybe it's because I need to. The drive in me to prove that I didn't give everything up—my family, my passion, years of my life—only to end up with an empty bank account, bad credit, and a guarded heart.

Regardless, I mean it when I make the promise to myself. If my word is not good with myself, then who in the hell would it be good with?

Gravel crunches on the road outside my window, and my shoulders sag when I see the cruiser kicking up dirt as it pulls down the road.

"Fricking great," I mutter, already knowing what he's here for. I give myself one last look in the mirror, promise again to give myself one more year, and then head out to see if my assumption is correct.

I already know it is.

When I step off the porch, my lips are in a welcoming smile as Rusty Chatsworth exits his cruiser. He slides his hat on and makes the leisurely stroll up my driveway to where I stand, his eyes looking here and there as he goes.

"Must be a slow day in town, Sheriff, if you came all the way out here to pay me a visit. Let me guess, the Marx brothers are out of town so they can't cause trouble?"

He chuckles, his soft smile lighting up his dark blue eyes beneath his broad-brimmed hat.

"The Marx brothers are getting older now, Ms. Knox. One has a girlfriend and the other has joined the local 4H club and spends all of his time with his swine." He tips his hat my way while I try to fathom how the two snot-nosed kids Fletcher said got caught swiping candy from the local market can be old enough to have girlfriends. "And yes, it is quite a slow day, but isn't it always in Lone Star? It isn't late enough for the drunks at Ginger's to be falling out of their bar stools and it's too early for the kids out joy riding to do just that . . . so yes, it's a slow day, indeed."

Rusty sounds much older than his thirty-two years, but I guess that's what comes from listening to your dad your whole life.

"Your father doing well?" I ask.

He nods. "As good as retirement can be expected. I think he misses the feeling of importance that wearing the badge gave him, but he's managing just fine."

I had no idea that Rusty Sr. had retired, but the way his son says it, I should have. I smile to cover my surprise. "Does that mean he's driving you crazy and constantly asking about the town happenings?"

"Yes, ma'am." Rusty moves across the driveway, his eyes taking a curious glance around the ranch, and I wonder what it is he sees. Does he still see Fletcher Knox's ranch or does he see Tatum Knox's attempt to keep it afloat?

And I'm not quite sure why I care but Jack Sutton's words

from the day before hit a nerve that I want settled.

"What can I do for you, Rusty?"

He hooks his thumbs in his utility belt and shifts his feet some before meeting my eyes. "Another complaint has come in on the ranch."

"Christ. For what this time?" I ask with a part chuckle, part sigh of exasperation. "How can there be any complaints about my care when there isn't a single person who's been up here to see otherwise?"

"Not a one?"

"I think I'd know, and I assure you no one was up here who looked close enough to have a valid reason to lodge a complaint."

He draws in a steep breath and nods. "I have to investigate it all the same."

"Seriously?"

"Seriously," he says, slipping his sunglasses on. "So, you haven't had anyone come up here and cause you trouble?"

Jack was here, but he seemed like a straight shooter, not some asshole who would call in a petty complaint as a way of getting back at me.

But he has been hanging out at the bar.

"Nope. Can't say that I have."

"What about that Jack fellow. The one who's in town for the job?"

Definitely been at the bar.

"The complaints have been happening well before he got to town. I mean, I don't really know him, so I can't say for sure, but what reason would he have to say anything?"

Besides the fact I ran him off and he mentioned the complaints himself.

Shit.

"Did you hire him?"

"No."

"There's reason enough right there. He traveled quite a way to interview."

"He told you that?"

"No. Haven't met him yet . . . but rumor at Ginger's is that he did."

"Hmm. Love those Lone Star rumors." I sigh. "What was the complaint this time? You know I'm not starving the horses because you already checked on that complaint two months ago. You know they have the best medical care because Doc is your friend and she'd tell you otherwise. Besides, when that complaint was lodged last month, I showed you all of my vet bills so you knew that was false. Should I keep going through all of the grievances that have been filed and that you've debunked or can we just assume this one is just as baseless? Because, honestly, this is getting quite ridiculous."

"It is." His eyes take in the ranch slowly.

"When are they all going to get over that damn article? It wasn't meant how it was taken. I wasn't bad-mouthing Lone Star. I wasn't showing them how much better I was than them. Christ," I mutter, "if they don't want people to think they're small-minded, then they need to stop acting like it."

"We may be simple folk here, but we don't take being insulted lightly." He holds his hand up when I start to argue. "I know. You didn't mean any harm by the article, but opinions have been formed."

"And, apparently, they can't be unformed." I sigh in frustration, and Rusty nods without expressing an opinion. "The complaints are bullshit, Rusty. You know that. I know that. I'm not going to let them push me out, and I'm not going to tolerate being harassed."

"I know." He shifts his hat from one hand to the next and then places it back on his head. "But I still have to investigate all the same. The anonymous caller stated that you have a lame mare that you aren't getting the proper care for."

I laugh. "Apparently, I have a lot of lame mares considering less than half of them are pregnant."

"So I've heard."

Of course, he's heard. Everyone's probably heard about how Tatum Knox took over her dead husband's ranch and doesn't know how to run it any better than her husband did.

Just another thing for this damn town to gossip over. Just another instance where they think Karma has worked her magic.

I look down at my scuffed boots and then back up at him. "What is it you need so you can go back to doing the real crime fighting?" Sarcasm laces my tone, and I don't try to hide it.

"Do you mind if I take a look around?"

"Be my guest."

Rusty walks down toward the stables, poking his head here and there. Pushing open doors to see what's inside. He pauses briefly to talk to some of the horses, his hand automatically sliding up and down their noses in greeting before he passes on to the next one.

"See anything amiss?" I ask when he seems to have reached the end of his half-assed search. "All horses standing? Fed? Healthy?"

"Everything looks good to me. You've got some great-looking ladies out there." He lifts his chin to the pasture where a few of the mares are out roaming. "You're thin on stock, though," he says, reminding me of those first few months of chaos after Fletcher died.

When I was so lost in simply trying to get through the next second, the next moment, the next day because I'd been so swamped in grief that I let my storage rooms almost run bare. And then, just when I thought I might be able to breathe again, I was hit with the truth about what Fletcher had done. I was forced to figure out just how in the hell I was not only going to make it through the next day but also how I was going to keep this place afloat.

"You planning on bringing some new mares in here or are you going to keep some of the foals when they're born so you have more to work with going forward?" he asks, his tone genuine, as if he's interested in my future plans. All I really hear is the reminder of just how few horses I'm housing, which is nowhere near enough to maintain a breeding ranch's standard.

"I'm working on figuring all of that out. Finding someone who can come in here and tell me if it's better to keep the foals or to sell them and use the money to secure better bloodlines. Obviously, what we've—*I've done* in the past hasn't worked, so we'll see. Regardless, I need more mares for breeding. I need to build up my stock . . . my reputation"

"But more horses mean more work and more work—"

"Means needing more staff." I lift my eyebrows, trying to figure out where he's going with this. I laugh disbelievingly and cross my arms over my chest. "Hell, Rust, maybe this is fate's way of telling me I don't know shit about being a breeder and I need to just sell this place and walk away." My chest constricts at the thought.

"And let them win?" Rusty slides a glance my way with only the slightest turn of his head. It's the first and only time I've ever heard him say anything close to supportive. "You don't believe you should do that anymore than I do."

I shrug, a little surprised and a lot relieved. "It doesn't matter what I think. It isn't as if I can do anything right these days."

He rests his arms on the white railing and purses his lips as he looks out at the horses in front of him. The whole perfect picture is framed by the trees behind them. "Permission to be frank?" he asks without taking his focus from the pasture in front of us.

"This isn't the army. You don't have to ask to speak."

"True, but it isn't my place either."

I stare at his profile and wonder why it seems as if I'm spilling my soul to Deputy Chatsworth. Maybe because he's the first person in forever besides Sheryl who actually seems like they understand.

"What is it, Rusty?"

"You've pissed a lot of people off."

"Tell me something I don't know," I joke.

"Quite possibly, you've got some disgruntled employees."

"Hence, why they no longer work for me."

"True, but *no one* works for you now. You've run them all off."

I open my mouth and then shut it to cut off the immediate rebuke on my tongue. To explain that I could be the best employer in the world and it wouldn't matter is pointless. "When a person can't do the job right, they get fired."

Or when I can no longer trust them because they talk a little too freely in town about what's going on here at the ranch.

He takes his time responding. "Yeah, but they all seemed to do a good enough job for Fletcher, right? He gave them the reins to do their work. So, obviously, they were good enough."

Good enough that they hid Fletcher's secrets from me too.

"Mmm." It's my go-to response because how do I explain what it's like not to be able to trust anyone anymore? How do I tell anyone that my husband not only gambled away every last penny we had but also leveraged our property in the process? How do I explain what it's like to be hated by every single person in town—first because of a misinterpreted article and then because my husband blamed our unpaid balances on me, convincing our local vendors that I was the one who held the purse strings? How do I begin to describe that the townspeople weren't the only people he screwed over?

More importantly, how do I say any of that and not have red flags go up and have people start to question whether Fletcher's death was a suicide instead of the accident they ruled it as?

"Look, I know Fletcher made a lot of promises to people and was a bit arrogant, but man, people liked him."

"Your point?" I ask, a headache brewing behind my temples as my thoughts crash against the misinformation guiding his words.

"From an outsider's standpoint, it appears as if it's *you* who seems to be the problem."

I chuckle in discomfort because what in the hell am I supposed to say to that? "I'm assuming that isn't a compliment."

He sighs as he struggles to find the words. "You deserve a chance here. I'm only saying these things because I want you to succeed."

My laugh is louder, more disbelieving, this time. "At least one person in this town does."

There's sadness in his ghost of a smile. "You have to stop trying to do this all yourself. It's impossible. You need to hire more—"

"I'm doing the best I can." It's all I can say without letting the frustration I'm hiding manifest into the tears threatening to well in my eyes. "I tried to make everything right. I tried to . . . I don't know. All I know is that by paying everyone back, it—"

"It looked like you were happy your husband died so you could cash in on his life insurance and pay off your debts."

"Yeah. And doing the right thing and paying those debts did nothing to change how everyone thinks of me." I don't hide the tears or the hurt from etching into the lines of my face. My smile is reticent, and my soul is exhausted from caring what they all think.

"You need to win the town back over if you hope to survive—"

"I've got it handled, but thank you," I cut him off, not needing him to tell me what to do when I've done more than I should only to be rebuked time and again. By ranch workers. By accounts in town. By what feels like freaking everyone. No matter what I do, nothing makes anything better or easier and I don't have the energy to keep trying.

"Being stubborn isn't going to help, you know?"

"Permission to speak revoked," I joke.

He laughs, but the look of concern never leaves his eyes. "How long has it been since you've had anyone on the payroll?"

Too long.

"I have help. Sylvester comes up a couple of times a week to do what he can. Supplies are on delivery for me. Good ol' Amazon. Feed is on a regular delivery from Lone Star Feed. Doc comes up on a schedule or as needed," I explain and am grateful for them because it allows me to avoid running errands in town so I don't have to venture there. I shrug. "I don't need someone full time."

"And what about help with the horses? The feeding, the exercise, the mucking of stalls . . . all of the daily work that's way more than enough work for one woman? I know Sylvester helps, but he's limited in his capabilities."

It sounds crazy coming from his mouth, almost as if he's trying to shine a spotlight on how much my life has changed in the past year. As if he's flicking the thin thread I've been hanging on to while waiting for the upcoming breeding season so I can prove I'm not a failure.

"I'm getting by as best as I can."

"So I see." He shifts on his feet and adjusts his hat again. "But the calls about the welfare of your horses, Tate. Someone seems to be mighty pissed off at you to keep lodging baseless complaints."

"Being pissed off at me is far different from being concerned about my horses, which are healthy and well taken care of. They'll get over it."

This is why I don't go into town. This is why I stay here where I don't have to listen to unsolicited opinions and unwelcome judgment.

"Hmm."

It's his only response, and if he does it to make me ask what it means, it works. "*Hmm?*"

"Just that I'm only the first step."

"First step?"

"Yeah. I'm the first rung on the ladder. Who knows who else this person or persons may be calling and complaining to? Are they creating a legal record as recourse to try to get you shut down if they aren't successful in running you off?"

"Rusty." His name is a sigh of disbelief, but it isn't anything I haven't already thought of before. Hickman Ranch on the opposite side of town used to warn Fletcher of encroaching on their territory. The Destin twins and their protests to us buying the land when we moved here. So many sharks in these waters.

"I know you as best as you let anyone know you, Tate. I know you're up here busting your ass all by yourself and that even if ranching isn't your first love, you wouldn't hurt a damn fly." He tilts his head from side to side. "But the rest of the town doesn't see what I see when it comes to you. They've never taken time to. Lone Star is a small town. You know that better than most. One mistake, and you're judged. People talk, exaggerate, and pretty soon, the rumor becomes someone else's version of reality. Then by mistake number two . . . you're vilified."

"What are you getting at?"

"While your husband ran up accounts and promised the moon while not delivering or paying his debts, you stayed like a queen in your castle, living that high life of yours." I grit my teeth at the misconception but don't react. "Then Fletcher goes and dies, and it appears as if you act like nothing has changed. Rumors fly that you're still out taking those photographs you take. You still avoid town. You still think that you're better than Lone Star. Maybe people just don't know what to think, so they just fall into line with the gossip."

It's a circular argument that I'll never win.

"And maybe they're all just chauvinist assholes who can't

49

handle the thought of a woman running a ranch and a successful breeding program," I counter.

Where his words should ignite my temper and put me on the defensive, all I can do is shake my head. I'm so damn tired of all of this that I can't even find the effort to care anymore.

Even if I did, nothing would change the minds in this town.

Nothing.

I've tried.

"Look, I appreciate the pep talk, but—"

"You have to win the town over. Plain and simple. Fletcher may have charmed the pants off everyone with his promises to bring notoriety to Lone Star by breeding winning rodeo horses . . . but he stole your property right out from underneath the Destin twins by offering way over the asking price. Family roots run deep here in Texas and this here was their great-grandpapa's land. That was the first mistake . . . and not delivering on those pie-in-the-sky promises was the second one. People here don't take kindly to those who don't follow through on their word."

"And both of those things should have fallen on Fletcher's shoulders, not mine, but here we are."

The purse of his lips is slow, and his sigh is audible. His blatant silence when it came to the rumors in town about what exactly Fletcher did is noticeable. "Comments like that aren't going to win anyone over . . . and technically, it was both of you."

"Don't you see that what you're telling me doesn't matter because I can't change any of it? You tell me not to give up but then turn around and tell me that the only way to make good on what Fletcher did is to leave," I counter.

"Just telling you like it is. You guys never caused me any problems out here. You have a highly desirable piece of land. I'd hate for someone to run you off it with all these threats. The best way to combat that is to make a name for yourself. One that Fletcher was unable to. Hire someone who knows their shit to help. Get customers to come here from all over to buy your foals. No one will run a successful woman out of town when she's bringing Lone Star some notoriety."

I keep my eyes fixed on Ruby. Her legs are painted in spots of white and her muscles ripple beneath the surface with her every movement, putting on a subtle display of the winning blood coursing through her veins.

"She is a beauty," he murmurs

"She sure is. She was Fletcher's pie in the sky, sired by a Kentucky Derby winner, but after coming here and realizing how unrealistic breeding her was, he settled on quarter horses."

"Smart move," he says, stepping back from the fence, his shoes crunching on the gravel as he heads back to his cruiser without another word.

Even after his engine fades into the distance, I still stand against the fence.

Memories swirling.

Hope fading.

Uncertainty swelling.

Determination unwavering.

Four

TATE

I'm being ridiculous.

I need to get out of the truck.

Drumming my fingers on the steering wheel, I look around at the town I've lived in for more than five years, really looking at it for the first time in what feels like forever. When I'm here, I typically drive through it from one end to the other, only stopping at the vet's office to get a refill on medication or the feed store for their unwelcome hellos and an extra something for the horses.

Safe zones. The places I know that won't cause a scene or more drama. The places I know will do business with me.

The first few times I came to town after Fletcher died come to mind. How I thought I might get an ounce of sympathy because my husband had just passed away—selfishly, I maybe even thought I could use it to my advantage to soften the perception they had of me or dim the criticism on the piece I wrote for *the Texan Registrar*.

I was expecting a second chance and what I got was more like a blindsided tackle that knocked me on my ass and put a cowboy boot on my throat. Owners asked me to leave their stores. Others approached me on the street and made a scene by asking me when I was going to pay my bills. People shouted, yelling about how dare I drive up in my fancy SUV when they'd been struggling to make ends meet for months because my husband had short-changed them or screwed them over.

It was then that I realized why Fletcher always kept me corralled at the ranch. It wasn't because he wanted to protect me from the cattiness of the townspeople like he had said before. It wasn't because he didn't want me stressed out by their sneers, which could affect my chance of becoming pregnant again.

No.

Not in the least.

Fletcher talked me into believing—*convinced me*—that he was protecting me when, in reality, he didn't want me to learn just how thoroughly he'd been digging us in to debt and screwing people over. He knew that the first person who approached and questioned us would cause a shitstorm he didn't want to ride out. I'd demand to see the finances I had trusted him with. That I'd see the credit cards he'd maxed out or that we were a few months behind on our mortgage payments. I'd explode over the home equity line of credit I thought had a zero balance when instead it was well over two hundred thousand dollars and climbing.

Then I'd know the truth.

For some reason, Rusty's words hit me hard as I sit in the truck under the warming Texas sun. His unsolicited opinions about how I need to change the narrative. His comments about how I need to try to somehow prove myself again.

Maybe it's sitting here looking at this town I fell in love with when we first moved here with its quiet, homey charm that won me over and made me want to buy the ranch on the outskirts of town. Maybe it's wondering how life would be if I could have some friends or support in this damn place.

I study the boutiques that have sprouted up along Main Street, at the fancy salon that takes up four storefronts, at the abundance of cars in parking spots when it isn't tourist season.

Life has moved on while I've been sequestered and withering away.

"Get out of the truck, Tatum," I grumble, suddenly self-conscious, thinking of my reflection when I forced myself to look in the bathroom mirror last night after my shower.

I know they will all be able to see the hollowness in my eyes and exhaustion weighing down on my shoulders and the uncertainty in my expression. The brassiness of my hair and my roughened palms. My body, which used to be lithe with taut muscles, now looks tougher and bulkier but unhealthy and gaunt all at the same time.

"You have to start somewhere," I say as I open the door of my truck and slide out of the seat.

With a deep breath, I step onto the sidewalk. My sunglasses hide how my eyes flick left and right and take in the fresh coat of paint on all of the storefronts and the signs hanging from the streetlights that highlight different events coming up for Lone Star: the county fair, 4-H parade, and the next high school sports game.

It's a delicate dance being here in town. If my head is held too high, I'm the bitch who thinks she's better than them. If I look down and avert my eyes, then I've been defeated and am guilty of everything they've accused me of, which tells them they've won.

Neither is the truth, but at the same time, neither is a lie.

Before I have a chance to lose my courage, I beeline it for the salon.

"Welcome to Fiona's, how may I help you?" the perfectly styled lady says from her seat behind her shabby-chic reception desk.

"Yes, I called earlier about getting my hair trimmed and colored. Tatum Knox." Her eyes whip up, telling me everything I already knew.

That I was the topic of conversation around here after I called earlier.

She recovers quickly. "Yes. Of course. I have you booked with Fiona herself. If you'll follow me, we'll get you started."

Stares follow me as I move through the expansive salon, which reminds me so very much of the kinds I used to go to when I was younger. When my life was about debutante balls and who was dating who.

"Here you go. Fi will be right with you," she says, and I breathe a sigh of relief when I see that her chair is in the back corner of the salon and that no other stylist is around her.

"Tatum Knox. Blessed be," Fiona's distinctive voice calls to my right when she sees me. "You're actually among the living now. Talk about a sight for sore eyes."

Fiona bends to where I'm seated and wraps her arms around me in a hug that is as unexpected as her warm welcome. When she steps back, my smile is instantaneous despite my jittery nerves.

"Hi."

"*Hi*? That's all you have to say to the woman you are letting down by letting all of that brassiness rent space on that head of yours? What? You don't write. You don't call. You let gray hairs grow and cancel appointments."

I sit there and look at her, uncertain how to exactly voice my reasons, which are only justifiable by my standards. "Um . . . uh—"

"Such nonsense," she says as she grabs my hand and squeezes. "I don't care why you kept canceling, all I care about is that you're here. That you've finally shown that gorgeous face of yours." She pats me on the shoulders. "Now, let's get that mess on your head fixed up so you can feel like your old self again. You might still look great, but darling, I can make you look fabulous."

I laugh, and for the first time since getting out of the truck, I feel as if I can breathe. "I missed you."

She puts the cape on and squeezes my shoulder again. "I don't get a chance to miss you at all. Hell, you're still the talk of the town even when you're not here."

"Jesus." I roll my eyes, loving that she's still the same and they haven't poisoned her opinion of me yet. "That bad?"

"Nothing is ever as bad as it seems. Just be glad they're still talking."

We fall into small talk as she adds color to my hair. She doesn't once demand to know why I pretended not to be home the last time she came out to the house for my regularly scheduled appointment. She doesn't ask about the ranch or the horses or where in the hell I've been over the past year.

All she says is that it's good to see me.

All she talks about is the town happenings to catch me up to speed.

All she does is deflect anyone who wanders by to see if they can get any information to gossip about.

"Your scars are looking great," she murmurs absently as her hands massage my scalp in the washbowl.

My hand goes instinctively to the white lines on the underside of my jaw and lower part of my neck. The screech of brakes and utter fear that held me hostage return momentarily as if the car running me off the road happened yesterday, not two years ago.

"I used the concoction you told me about." I meet her eyes as she leans over me, her hands still rubbing in circles. "That, and they've faded with time."

"Time fades all scars. Even the ones we can't see," she says with a wink and squeezes the excess water from my hair. When she helps me sit up to wrap a towel around it, the other clients sitting near the bowls glance my way before texting furiously.

"You'd think you were royalty the way these ladies are burning up their phones," she jokes when she begins to trim.

"It's ridiculous."

"It is. Fletcher was a dick. No one else in this town will say that to your face, but you know me, I will. Ginger might too. But, I'm sorry, you're better off without him."

The part of me that isn't used to having any sort of support fights back the tears. "I know, it's just . . ."

"Hard? Shitty? Hurtful? Yeah, it's every single one of those and a whole slew more, but in this town, women don't stand behind women. They only hide behind their husbands." She says this just a touch too loudly as she snips two inches off my hair. "Good thing I've had enough husbands to know they aren't worth standing behind."

Her laugh sounds off in the brightly lit salon. One of the reasons she's my ally is because the people here have judged her just as harshly. If it weren't for the fact that she's the best stylist in town, they would treat her as they treat me.

As if her husbands never screwed anyone over and whatever they did was her fault.

"So, you were out and about taking photos the other day?" she leads. How did my walk out on Old Sawmill Road last week become town news? Rusty mentioned it too. Is it a crime to need a few minutes to myself with scenery other than the ranch? The irony is I didn't have my camera on me. The fact that someone added that detail shouldn't surprise me. "Honey, people in this town know the minute you step off your land. Get any good shots?"

"Don't play that off," I say, not bothering to correct her. "What are they saying now?"

"Nothing you need to care about."

"Seriously, Fi. What is being said?"

She smiles tightly, the lines at her eyes crinkling in a way that tells me she isn't going to tell me because she's protecting me. It's the same look she'd give me when she'd come out for her house calls to do my hair and knew what was being said about Fletcher in town but didn't want to let me know.

She holds her finger up before switching on the blow-dryer, and I know the moment is lost. There's no way she can shout over the sound and not let everyone else in the salon hear her.

So, I sit with my thoughts. I let the doubt own me, and the want to just get the hell away from here is just as strong as my need to prove them all wrong. That I'm nothing like my husband. That I'm nothing like the woman they've made me out to be.

The question is, do I believe it or am I turning a blind eye because I'm afraid to know the truth?

"And voila!" she says as she switches the blow-dryer off and unfastens the cape from around my neck. "As good as new."

I laugh. "Far from it, but—" I stare at myself in the mirror. At my hair, which is a couple of inches shorter but looks completely different. At the shiny color that has replaced the dull flatness I walked in here with. At the little bit of life in my eyes. "It's a start."

"Damn right it's a start." She pulls me into a hug so that her lips are close to my ear as she whispers, "I miss you. I gave you space because you asked for it, but I'm sick of giving it. Next time I come visit you at the ranch, I'm not going to let you pretend not to be there. I'd love to see your gorgeous face more than once every few months as you pass through town."

My cheeks flush with emotion as I struggle with how to respond. "You might, but no one else does."

"*Pshaw.*" She waves her hand my way. "So what? Between the article and your husband, you're doomed for life? Don't give them the satisfaction, girl. Get out and live, Tate, or life is going to pass you by."

I meet her eyes and wish that taking her advice was as easy as she makes it seem, but it isn't. It never has been. I walked away from everything I'd ever known for a man who I thought would be my everything. And he walked us into a town, a life, and a lifetime that I'm now stuck in alone.

"It's easier than it seems."

"Everything is."

"How much do I owe?" I ask to try to change the topic.

"It's on the house."

"Thank you, but that's not necess—"

"You can pay me back by introducing me to your new ranch manager." She laughs and wiggles her eyebrows.

"My new—what?" I look around as if the crystal chandelier above holds the answer to her question.

"Long. Lean. Hotter than fuck. That Jack is a nice piece of eye candy to admire . . . and, uh, imagine other things about too."

The image of Jack standing on my porch, arms crossed over his chest, and a smirk on his lips flashes through my mind.

"He's not my manager—"

"Why the hell not?" She smacks a hand against the counter. "Everyone knows why he's in town. Even the women who hate you are rooting for you—if not a little bit jealous—and the men are hating him already."

"I doubt anyone is rooting for me," I counter. "And he isn't my—"

"That's not a good enough reason." She props her hands on her hips and really hears me for the first time. "If you're not coming into town because you're afraid of what they're going to say, you sure as hell can be *coming* at home."

"Jesus, Fi." I cough the words out.

"We've established that Fletcher screwed you. Sure, you loved him, but I'm pretty damn sure he ruined that after you found out what he did to you. Why is it a bad thing to hire a man who might work you just as good in the sheets as he works on the ranch?" She raises her eyebrows as I sputter for a response. "C'mon. You know that passed through your mind. Then you got angry for thinking it. Then you denied that you ever thought it."

I stare at her with my jaw lax and my eyes wide.

"It's called moving on. We've all been there. Hell, I've been there six times," she says, referring to her failed marriages. "I know everything you went through was a hundred times worse than what I did so the guilt must be astronomical, but screw the guilt. Have some fun. Ride the cowboy."

I bite back my laugh and suddenly turn sober. "Wait, is he telling people he's working at the ranch?"

She just smiles and shrugs. "It isn't what a man says"—she winks— "but what a man does that matters."

"Meaning?"

"He's stayed here in town well after you told him you didn't want any. I'd say that's a man who's willing to weather a little woman's wrath, and nothing's wrong with that."

"I don't even know what to say."

"Oh, look. My next client is here." She offers a sly smirk. "I need to go assist her," Fi says as she rushes to the doorway. I'm about to call her bluff when I see her helping an octogenarian through the salon.

So, I stand there awkwardly because the ease I had with Fiona disappeared when she did. I glance around and meet the eyes of another stylist, who looks my way and then averts her attention just as quickly.

Heat creeps into my cheeks, permeating every part of me like a firestorm and making the room feel as if it's closing in on me. My heart starts to race, and I struggle to draw in a breath.

The panic attack hits me out of nowhere.

I used to have them all the time after Fletcher died and I'd found out about everything. They used to hold me hostage, curled in a ball, for hours on end, but I thought I'd shaken them.

I look frantically for the bathroom and run toward it the moment I see it, knowing I'm just adding more to the gossip mill.

With the door shut and my hands braced on the counter, I close my eyes and focus on my breathing. On hoping that I didn't just cause a scene over nothing and calming myself down.

On forcing myself to relax.

And just as fierce as the panic attack is my fury at myself.

It takes everything I have to meet my own eyes in the mirror. Sure, my hair looks better than it has in months, but nothing else does.

The hollow look still haunts my eyes. The straight line of my mouth still looks tense. The weight on my shoulders is still unbearable.

Who is this woman who is a mere shadow of herself?

When did I let this happen?

I never cared what they thought of me—correction, I told myself I didn't care what they thought of me. Fletcher only reinforced it by keeping me separated from them.

So what am I going to do about it?

Tears burn and well and my knuckles turn white as I grip the edge of the sink. As I struggle to control my emotions and let the anger at myself burn away the doubt and the insecurity and discord I've allowed to be sewn into the very fabric of who I am.

This is no way to live.

None.

The epiphany that I need to make a change has been staring me in the face. I know that if I really mean the promise I've made to myself, that I'm going to turn things around, then I have to start with myself.

The sound of my sigh fills the small space, but it's the alarm bell I need to wake myself up.

"No more, Tate," I whisper harshly, not wanting to give the people beyond the closed door anything else to talk about. "No. More."

I take a moment more to wipe the beads of sweat from my face, pinch some color into my cheeks, add a touch of lipstick I found in the recesses of my purse, and then I leave the salon with a fake smile as if I'm perfectly fine.

With clammy hands, I force myself to walk through town, past the posters announcing the high school's latest production of *Annie Oakley, and* beneath the banners on Main Street that announce the county fair is headed our way this summer. Even the old timer's sitting in Hal's Donut Shoppe with their coffee cups empty, their donuts long gone, and their opinions filling the air, are different.

Life has moved on. I may still be stuck in the ruts that lead the way out to the south end of the ranch where Fletcher was buried, but life has moved on.

Am I terrified?

Hell, yes.

But of what though?

Of living.

The acknowledgment hits me out of nowhere. Pair it with Jack's bold statements the other day, mix them with Rusty's comments about how I need to win the town over, and throw in Fiona's words about how I should take advantage of a new ranch manager, and it's the perfect storm to shake me awake when I've been sleepwalking through life.

So, when I spot Jack's truck parked in the lot next to Ginger's, a surge of confidence washes through me. It's matched with temper too, but the longer I stare at it, the more I realize all of these feelings, these realizations, within me came to life the minute he stepped on my porch.

The minute he somehow entered my life.

Five

JACK

"When's your next gig?"

Pursing my lips, I take my time studying the beer Ginger just placed in front of me before glancing over to the man. His hair is red, his freckles coat every inch of his skin, and for a giant of a man, he moves with a surprising ease behind the bar. His smile is genuine, and his laugh tugs at the corners of my mouth when he lets it loose.

With a shrug, I lean back in my chair and think about the daunting prospect of returning home and facing the shitstorm I left behind, but I welcome his question. I've been in and out of here for the past week, mixing with locals and listening to the town gossip, but Ginger has steered clear of me. I just can't figure out if it's because he's one of the few in town who actually like Tate or because he just doesn't care to get to know me.

"Six months," I finally answer.

His whistle sounds out and draws looks from a few other patrons in the bar. "That's a long time without pay."

"It is." I nod like a man who has to worry about money would and nod in greeting at the man who slides onto the barstool beside me. It isn't as dark and dank as most bars I've been in and the atmosphere is chill. The patrons mostly pretend to keep to themselves while listening to what everyone around them is saying, and from the few meals I've eaten here, the food is better than most bars I've visited.

"Where's it at?"

"Back where I came from," I reply, purposely being vague.

"And that isn't a good thing?" he asks.

"Depends on who you ask," I say with a snort as I take a long tug on my beer. Some days I miss the endless fields and the comforts of home, and other days, the responsibilities that come with my name are like lead weights.

"You gonna hang out here in Lone Star until you've got to get there?"

A noncommittal shrug is my answer.

"The boss lady still not hiring you?" He lifts a chin to the front of the bar as if the Knox Ranch is just outside.

"You know how it is."

I let my finger run over the label on my bottle, thinking about how small towns really are funny things. All the people want you to do is gossip so they can side with you to your face and then bullshit about you behind your back because you spoke ill of one of their own.

Tate, however, seems to be the exception to that rule. I've heard the rumors of how people talked ill of her to her face as well as behind her back.

"She's a mixed bag no one can quite figure out . . . so, I'd say yes, I know how it is . . . but I don't. No one does, really."

"So, people just hated her on arrival?" Sounds pretty damn ridiculous.

"Huh," he says and twists his lips as if he's gauging how much to say. "She's never fit in here. She can don the Wranglers and Ariats, but looking the part and being it are two different things." Ginger waves to customers walking in the door. "We'll just say she didn't make a good first impression, and after that, it went downhill."

"What did she do?"

"Oh, I don't like to gossip," he says, but his eyes tell me he can't wait to.

"I've never met a bartender who didn't have a pulse on his town before," I egg on.

A sheepish smile plays at his lips. "She was some kind of photographer. Fancy education. Wealthy family. Nose stuck up in the air at our blue jeans and boots while she wore her designer threads."

"She wasn't wearing her designer jeans when I met with her," I say, having no idea why I'm defending her.

"Maybe that's because she showed her true colors and was knocked down a peg."

"Come again?"

He holds up a finger as he pours another drink and slides it across the bar to another customer before turning back to me. "She was into photography and was writing a travel blog or something like that. She decided to do a piece on Lone Star."

"That bad?"

"That's putting it nicely."

"What was the problem?"

"She definitely has an eye for photography. The pictures they posted of hers were incredible. It made this town look way better than it really is—majestic even. But the article?" He shakes his head. "That article was the nail in her coffin before she even stepped foot in the grave, if you know what I mean. One sec."

Ginger tends to a customer at the opposite end of the bar as I pull out my phone and search for the article. The Wi-Fi sucks, and it doesn't download before he comes back. "I can't remember the gist, but she tried to pull it off as if living here was a step back in time. And, honestly, she's right. Sometimes it is like that, but the people here are a proud people and they didn't take to it very kindly."

"And the problem with that is what?" I ask. "Don't most towns like to be described that way? Quaint and idyllic?"

"Yeah, but there was something about the *way* she phrased it . . . almost as if she were mocking us or looking down on us for choosing to live life like this."

"So, basically one person made a comment that they were offended and the rest of the town jumped on board." I snort, not surprised but still disappointed in people I don't even know.

Ginger eyes me as if he can't figure out if he likes me or hates me for the comment. "Something like that."

"And there was no going back, right?" Growing up in a small town myself, I've seen it before. Shit, Tate could make all the apologies in the world, but once the tide turns, there is no turning them back. Sure, she might have phrased something wrong, but . . . *Christ.* "Everyone makes mistakes."

"True." He lets the word hang. "Personally, I didn't find much fault in what she wrote, but I'm in the major minority. Add in her husband coming in here and buying that ranch right out from underneath the Destin twins, and no one really gave them much of a chance."

"You mean a normal real estate transaction?"

"To outsiders, yes. But to those who live here, that there land had been their families for generations."

"Then it would have been passed down to them in a will," I argue with common sense. "If it was for sale, then it was up for anyone to take it."

His smile says otherwise. "Fletcher came in here and paid way above the asking price for that land. Rumor has it he stalled the sale by greasing some of the realtors' palms so they would hold off on taking the twins' offer and then swooped in and stole the land right out from under them."

Hence the bitterness. Why it was aimed at Tate and not the sellers of the property was beyond me. The old owners had every right to say no to Fletcher's offer if they wanted to keep the property with local owners. Though, I know better than to point that out.

"Is that rumor or is that truth?"

The opening and closing of his mouth says he doesn't exactly know.

"That isn't her fault."

"No, not when you look at it in pieces, but when you look at the whole, it is something a lot of people won't overlook. She stopped coming into town after that article. People went to her at the ranch—hair, nails, shopping—hell, who knows what else. But she made it known that she thought she was better than the rest of us and that was the start."

"Surely, there were other reasons."

Like maybe she knew how much you all hated her and didn't want to deal with it?

"Well, when you're paying extra for people to tend to you and buying new cars and trailers while also maxing out accounts and never making payments on them, people don't take too kindly to you."

"So, she's shit at running the finances?" I ask, trying to see where he's going with this.

"Nah, it was Fletcher who was doing that. Her good-for-nothing husband who dealt with the accounts, but she had to have known what he was doing, which makes her just as bad."

I tuck my tongue in my cheek, lean back on my stool, look

around the bar, glancing between the couples at tables with their young kids, the businessmen in their slacks and cowboy boots, and the men on their lunch breaks between transporting livestock.

I understand these people and the simplicity of working with your hands on the land. The way someone looks at you when you walk in somewhere with cow shit still stuck on the heel of your boot, not because you forgot but because you were too damn exhausted to remember to wipe it off.

If what Ginger says is true, I'd probably hate her too.

Then again, I can also relate to Tate, and I'm not sure if I own it or reject it.

"So, is that why her ranch is in dire need of help?" I ask. "No one likes her enough to work for her?"

"That ranch is a mess because her husband didn't know his ass from a hole in his head. He was shit at picking studs to breed. Like absolute shit." He throws his towel down and wipes the bar top. "He had a good enough head to keep the place above water, sell what needed to be sold, but that was about it. One of the horses he sold died. Another was quite sick. People don't take kindly to spending hard-earned cash on damaged goods."

I chew the inside of my lip as I glance at the images that finally pop up on my phone. Ginger's right. Knox did make this place look majestic. I don't know shit about photography, but the lighting and angles and what-the-fuck-ever other terms photographers use make Lone Star look like a little piece of lost America. Turbulent skies over idyllic pastures and symbols of time gone by: red-white-and-blue flags, Radio Flyer wagons, cowboy boots, and apple pie.

I pull my focus from my phone and force it back to Ginger.

"People are saying she's to blame for the horses' deaths?"

"Nah. But a ranch that produces sick foals doesn't exactly win any recommendations."

I take a slow draw on the neck of my bottle and nod. "True."

"I'm assuming that's why she brought you here. You any good with breeding and such?"

Another slow nod as I think of home. Of the endless acres filled with livestock and my duties in overseeing it all.

"I can hold my own."

"She see your references?" he asks.

"You vetting her employees for her now?" I counter. No one needs to know shit about me. Not who I am. Not where I come from. Not shit.

Ginger's chuckle is more miffed than amused. "Nah. Just curious. You seem like you might be worth your salt."

His eyes say he feels differently, but I'm not offended in the least. I don't have to prove myself to anyone in this town.

"Why can't she keep anyone on staff?" I ask.

He chuckles, his eyes flitting around the room before coming back to meet mine. "Supposedly, he paid ranch hands double what everyone else would."

Seems there was a lot of paying too much for things on Fletcher's part.

"*He* being her husband?"

Ginger nods. "Some say it was so they'd keep quiet about the things going on there. Most did, so no one really knows for sure. After he died, I guess she went into a rage over something and fired them all. She's tried hiring others, but they don't stay for long because she won't pay what he was and other places pay more. Something like that."

"Is that your official Lone Star warning that I should steer clear?"

"That's for you to decide, man. If you like a challenge"—he throws his hands up— "then be my guest."

So many rumors. I'm sure some are warranted while others . . . not so much.

Tatum was all defiance and defeat mixed with uncertainty and obstinance when I'd met her, so I'd put the split at fifty-fifty.

"But if you're going to stay, I suggest you keep to your six-month stint."

"Why's that?" I glance up at the television where a baseball game is underway—the Austin Aces against the Los Angeles Dodgers.

"This isn't the life she wants. I give her one more season before she cashes out while she can and makes a new life for herself."

"The six-month time frame was my doing. Not hers. I have other obligations I need to fulfill." I clear my throat to make a point. "And who says this isn't the life she wants?"

Ginger chuckles as he serves a beer down the line to a man who looks like he doesn't need another drink. "You've spoken with her, right? Hostile. Nasty."

"Determined?"

"Don't look now," Ginger says, "but you just stood up for her."

I shrug as I take a long pull on my beer.

"Five-plus years is a long time not to turn a piece of land, a business like hers—with a goddamn derby horse on it, no less—into a successful breeding operation," he muses.

"For most of that time, it wasn't her running it, though," I argue on her behalf while keeping the little tidbit he just dropped tucked away.

She has a derby horse? Why isn't she breeding it?

He slides a beer across the bar to his server and gives me a wink. "You learn how to read people standing behind a bar," he says.

"Thanks for the heads-up. I'll keep that in mind."

"One more thing. No one in this town wants their name affiliated with failure." He leans close and lowers his voice for dramatic effect. *Jesus fucking Christ, does he ever shut up?* "Nobody likes a long shot, man, and the Knox Ranch is the long shot. No. People around here like the sure thing."

I chuckle in response to this small-town bullshit nonsense. Fucking hell, it's no wonder the poor woman is struggling.

They like the sure thing.

Running my thumb over the Coors Light label, I give the subtlest shake of my head, wondering how much of what he said holds any weight.

"I have a hundred of those beers you're holding that say you can't salvage what's left of that ranch," he says and wipes his hand on the rag tucked in the side of his waistband. "I'm all about defying convention, but you can't do that when you don't know the ropes. And she sure as shit doesn't know the ropes. Hell, she'd do best if she took the offer she was given a while back to sell it so she can go live that hoity-toity life it seems she was born to lead. Give us back our land and . . ."

And by the rest of the heads turning, I can guess who just walked in the door—the woman who's been the bar owner's main topic of conversation for the past god knows how many minutes.

I don't turn around. Instead, I let the silence eat up the space until all that's left is the sounds from the televisions around us.

"Well played, Jack." Tatum's voice rings through the bar.

"Can't fault me for seeing if you actually pay attention to criticism." I chuckle more to irritate her than anything and am quite surprised that she did.

"Tell me one reason why I should hire you."

I run my tongue along the inside of my cheek and take my time responding. "Because I'm exactly what you need. I'm your *sure thing*." I turn around on my barstool slowly.

And there she is.

I ignore the punch in my gut that seeing her again delivers. Her hands are on her hips, and there's that fire I admire in the jut of her chin. There's clear determination in her stance as a bar full of townspeople watch her and listen to her every word.

"That didn't answer my question." Those storm-cloud-colored eyes of hers lock onto mine with the lift of one of her eyebrows. "Sure things rarely pan out."

"Then you shouldn't hire me," I say with an indifferent shrug. There are only seconds for me to decide how to play this before I fall into the same trap Tatum did when she moved here—the one that leaves me hated in town because of misperception. "Besides, I've been warned about the ranch . . . about you. No skin off my nose to walk away."

"I didn't figure you for a quitter," she murmurs with disdain.

"You want me. You don't want me." My chuckle hums through the uncomfortable silence in the bar. "Indecision seems to be a real problem of yours. That, and your temper. No wonder you can't seem to keep a single person on staff. I'm not your husband. I won't kowtow to a woman like he did. You need to learn some manners, *Ms.* Knox."

"Manners get you nowhere."

"Neither do demands."

Yet, there is something about the pride in the set of her chin, the humiliation edging the gray of her eyes, and the harsh bob of her throat as if she's wondering if she should stand her ground or turn and run that gives me pause. Her even being here despite the crazy rumors about her almost has me admiring her strength. She has to know what they all think of her, and yet, here she is, full of false bravado, insecurity, and determination.

It's those things that should tell me to run the other way like the goddamn wind, but they are the same reasons I didn't keep driving after I convinced myself that I'd somewhat fulfilled my promise to my father.

"Well?" she asks, one eyebrow arching as her chin quivers. Vulnerability laced with obstinance. "You still think you're the right person to get the ranch up and running to speed? You still think we can run a better breeding program than Hickman Ranch like you claimed we could?"

Ah, she came to play. Throwing in Hickman while everyone listens puts me on the spot. The embellishment of my words and pitting me against the other successful ranch on the opposite side of town is nothing more than a challenge. Her throwing it down in a bar full of people gives me no other option than to say yes.

If I turn it down, then I'll be labeled as a man who doesn't hold to his word, which might be even worse than how they'd labeled her.

Does she even realize that she just put an even bigger target on the ranch's back?

"I'm a glutton for punishment," I mutter as I throw a ten on the bar top for Ginger and rise from my stool. "Outside." It's all I say to Tatum, and she bristles from my command as I stride past her and head out the front door.

As I walk into the bright sunshine of the parking lot, I debate how long it'll take her to follow me.

Not if.

I know she will.

She needs me too much. Not just on the ranch but also as an ally in this fucked-up town full of quaint charm and rampant rumors.

Right on cue, the door shuts and the sound of her feet on the pavement echoes off the concrete buildings around us before stopping behind me.

I give her a minute to stew and to figure out everything in the world she's fucking angry at so she can direct it at me. She needs to have one more reason to push me away, and I need to give myself one last chance to walk the hell away while I can.

"Well played, Knox. Well played," I murmur her own words back to her.

"You're not the only one who needed to make a point."

I finally turn to face her, and she has her arms across her chest, her jaw is clenched, and her eyes are narrowed. The woman looks both impatient and irritated.

And goddamn it . . . *she's beautiful*.

Like that fucking matters.

"You asked me out here. Was there something you wanted to say?"

"I wanted to show you exactly how this relationship is going to go. I give orders, and you follow."

"You're an ass."

"Tell me something I don't know." I shrug and take a step toward her. "Let's get one thing straight. You need me. You—"

"I don't need—"

"If you didn't," I say, cutting her off and infuriating her further, "you wouldn't have sought me out in Ginger's and made a show out of trying to prove you wear the pants in this relationship."

She opens her mouth and then proceeds to shut it when I lift a lone brow in challenge.

"But you know this town better than you think you do. You know they're judgmental assholes who think only men can ranch and breed and that maybe . . . just maybe, hiring a man like me, who they've already taken a liking to, might be in your best interest," I say, full well knowing her little comment inside might have just damaged that likability factor some. "So, like me. Don't like me. I don't give a fuck. You need me to help run your ranch and to help change the tide of opinion, and you know it."

"Charming," she mutters through gritted teeth, but I know I have her. They may think she's a haughty bitch, but I see the scared lady who's running on instinct and grit and scraps of hope.

"I know. Charm is a rarity for me, so enjoy it while it lasts."

Ginger's patrons are trying not to make it obvious that they are craning their necks to see what's going on outside the windows, and I turn away from them.

"And what's in it for you?" she counters.

"For me?" I laugh and bite back the first thing that comes to my mind as I take a long look at her because she definitely is not hard on the eyes. "I'll, uh, get to hone my skills."

She angles her head as she tries to figure out what I mean.

"I thought you were at the top of your game. Now you tell me your skills need honing. Which is it, Sutton?"

"You'd be a fool not to hire me."

"Why's that?"

Because I'm a Sutton.

The words almost slip. My birthright almost exposed in a place where no one needs to know my business or who my family is. One more crumb possibly dropped as to why I'm here.

"Because you just would be. Sending me away is not a mistake you want to make." A muscle in her jaw feathers as she bites back the retort I can see glaring in her eyes. "Good. Now that we have that settled, let's set some rules."

"I'm the boss," she says in a soft, even voice that sounds like controlled temper and mistrust all rolled into one.

"In theory and name, yes."

She bristles. "In everything."

I give her a half-cocked smile, letting her know how wrong she is. "You may have busted your ass to keep that place afloat, but we both know something had to have been mismanaged. You have no staff, very few foals to sell come season, and you're running that place on a shoestring budget when you need a hell of a lot more than that to be successful. Hell, I admire you for trying to figure out the ins and outs of this world based on things you overheard from your husband, but I already know them." I take a step closer to her. "I'll work your ranch, Knox. I'll get what needs to be repaired, repaired. I'll get your mares pregnant with the next batch of foals to sell. I'll make your name and horses known in the places it needs to be known in order to get some customers who don't know a thing about the bullshit the people in this town spew about you. On top of that, I'll even try to get that derby horse of yours a stallion because we both know that foal could net you a pretty penny. Regardless, we do this my way. My rules. My—"

"But—"

"Not your turn." I hold up a hand and take a little bit of joy in watching the shock on her face. "You ran that place into the ground, even if there were extenuating circumstances. You want to learn how to do it, then be prepared to step in and get your hands dirtier than they've ever been. I'll gladly teach you, but I won't take attitude and I won't be the punching bag for your temper while I'm trying to rebuild it."

"Go to hell."

"Seems to me like you've already been there and back. You can either let me help you or you can keep doing what you're do-ing." I shrug. "Your choice."

We stand in the early afternoon sun as a war over who is more stubborn rages between us.

"Fine." It takes everything she has to scrape that small contri-tion from her.

"Good. Room and board—"

"Absolutely not."

My laugh is long and low, and I just stare at her with a shake of my head. "It's a deal breaker for me."

"Same goes here."

"What are you afraid of? That you might actually end up liking me? That I just might show you how to make your ranch work?" I take another step toward her. "You need me on-site. You need me there in case something goes wrong with a horse in the middle of the night. You need them comfortable with me considering I'm the one in charge. I assure you there's enough air up there for us both to breathe and not get in each other's ways." My grin is a taunt for her to test me. "I live there or my offer is off the table."

"Your offer?" she asks as she coughs through a laugh.

"My offer." I nod. "You can have it one of two ways. You can keep your failing ranch that you run all by yourself because no one else will work for you . . . or you can let me run the ranch and make it what it should be. *On my terms*. Your call."

Six

TATE

Two duffel bags.

That was all he had.

What kind of man plans to move to my ranch, run it for the next six months, and only brings two bags of personal items with him?

Two bags?

Is he married? Divorced? A player? Hell, is he even who he says he is?

The thoughts fire off as I tell myself not to watch him from my perch on the porch. I should be focused on my dwindling finances, which are listed on spreadsheets on the table before me, but curiosity rules my mind.

It doesn't help that Fiona's comments run circles around my own thoughts.

I glance toward the bunkhouse and the shadow that keeps passing in front of the window every few seconds. I can only imagine what he's doing in there. It isn't as if he has many belongings to put away. Maybe he's on the phone with his lover or telling someone how crazy he is for agreeing to work here.

And yet, I keep watching.

I keep questioning if I made the right decision in inviting Jack Sutton to work here, to be a part of my life, to know my business.

I keep wondering if he will even be able to save my ranch and home.

One glance at the total listed at the bottom of the spreadsheet is a stark reminder of what's left of my savings.

At some point, the dream of running this ranch stopped being only Fletcher's, but I don't know at which point it started to be mine. Is it my dream, or is it my chance to prove to everyone else that they are wrong? Can my motivation be spite? To prove to a dead person exactly how it can be done without cheating people and to show an entire town that I'm stronger than they think I am?

Maybe it's more personal than that. Maybe it's my need to know that I didn't give up my family, my career, and my possibilities for nothing.

Will simply saving my ranch from foreclosure give me that, or do I also need to make sure it's a raging success before I feel as if I've found whatever in the hell it is I'm trying to find? Closure. Confidence.

Blowing out a breath, I lean back in the porch chair, rest my head along its back, and look up. Stars light up the night sky, and I stare at them until they blend into the darkness. The tumult of emotions that never seem to stop whirl around me, but this time, they're different. Sure, the anger over what Fletcher did will always be there and so will the sense of loss I felt when I found out that everything I had believed in was a lie. There is even a bit of understanding that, while he might have loved me, loving someone doesn't mean I have to accept being screwed over and left to clean up the other person's mess.

But there's also a guarded curiosity.

Is Jack Sutton what I need right now? Not only to fix my ranch but also to help me learn how to run it myself?

Perhaps it's a bit of all of them.

An echo of laughter floats across the country silence. I'm so used to the rustle of trees, the neigh of horses, and the sound of my thoughts, that a man's deep tenor as he laughs at something is alien to me.

It feels weird to have a man living on-site again. Sure, I've had ranch hands on and off, but they went to their own homes at night. I haven't let them live here because I didn't want to share space, hear them, see them, or run into them while I was sitting on the porch in my pajamas at eight o'clock at night with only the ache of loneliness as my company.

It's only been four hours since Jack followed me up here, signed the contract, and started getting settled, but the change in atmosphere is noticeable. Undeniable.

I squeeze my eyes shut but force my hands to relax their grip on the arms of the chair.

Six months.

That's all it is, Tate.

One hundred eighty days before his contract expires and he's gone and I'll know if I . . . *what*? If I've saved my ranch and have turned some kind of profit? If I'll be forced to walk away as a failure?

Hell, even if I save this place and prove everyone in town wrong, I'm not sure if I'll stay. The thought of living with Fletcher's ghost isn't something that really appeals to me.

I shake my head as uncertainty circles and watch the small window above the shower light up as he moves into the bathroom.

"Work, Tatum. Get back to work," I mumble as I grab my papers and head inside, but not before one more glance his way.

Seven

TATE

One cluck of a tongue is all it takes for Willow to fall in love with him.

That's all it takes for her to saunter over to him, lower her nose, and nuzzle her forehead against his as he whispers sweet nothings to her.

Gracie and her all-black flank with the diamond of white on her forehead is even easier for him to schmooze than Willow. She sees the attention he is giving to Willow and fell into line: tail swishing, ears falling apart, a neigh sighing from her mouth.

Then there's my thoroughbred Ruby, Fletcher's pride and joy, who prances some at the sight of Jack.

Looking at her hurts, but the decision I made when it came to her hurts even more. So, I focus on Jack instead. On how irritated I am at him because all he has to do is talk to them to win them over while I have to pull out every stop.

I'm standing just outside the stable, watching him. The grass is wet, and steam rises off it in the early morning sunshine, a promising prelude to a warm day. In short, it's a beautiful and poetic morning to watch my horses get to know him while I personally bristle every time I hear his voice.

Fletcher used to laugh at me as I called the horses over and over, bribing them with apples and carrots and affection, only to have them walk over to him. After he died, their desire for my comfort was even less. It was almost as if they knew he was gone and blamed me. They refused to eat. They fought my direction or urging every chance they got.

They weren't sick. They just didn't like me. Still don't, not really.

Watching them cozy up to Jack and playfully vie for his attention has me choking on an odd sense of betrayal.

Just like a female to fall for a sexy voice and a nice ass.

Not this female, though.

Gracie dances as Jack moves out of the ring and into the stable area before reappearing a second later, leading Ruby by her bridle.

"Jealous girl," he croons to Gracie as he lets go of Ruby, her coat glistening in the sunlight. She bows her head a few times and whinnies at the sound of his voice.

"You could at least play hard to get," I grumble as I turn my back and start to head back to the house. A man gives them attention, and they preen from it.

"Who was that?" Jack calls over his shoulder, making me stop in my tracks and turn to face him again.

"Who was who?" I feign ignorance about who was in the truck that kicked up the dust on the driveway a half hour ago and step toward the fence. "Oh, the man? Wrong address."

"He sure stayed a long time if it was a wrong address." He tips his hat up off his forehead with a finger. "Was the envelope he handed you for the wrong address too or was he serving you papers?"

"Wrong address." It was actually the process server who was in the right place, and the envelope he hand delivered to the correct person was from my lender.

Sheryl warned me it might happen and that it was standard procedure, but it didn't make it any less jarring to be receiving them.

"Usually, lawsuits are served like that?"

Or foreclosure notices.

"He was at the wrong address." My voice rises with each word.

"Huh." The sound carries across the breeze but doesn't convince me that he believes me, but he purses his lips and nods before turning back to Gracie, letting it go for now.

Still, with each passing second, my cheeks heat and anger rises. Embarrassment from actually being served and anger over him watching it all happen are both clear emotions in me.

It's none of his damn business, and I'm not sure why he feels as if he has any right to ask about who stopped by.

I stare blindly through the tears welling, my hands beginning to hurt with how hard they are gripping the railing in front of me, but it stings.

All of this stings. The unforgiving bank and Jack with the damn horses that like him on the spot but that still somewhat hate me.

"You gonna stand there all day and watch me, or are you going to come learn something?" Jack calls out as another gust picks up and I have to shield my eyes against the dust it brings with it.

"My ranch." I shrug and push the hair off my cheek.

His chuckle is low and even as he angles a glance over his shoulder, his dark brown eyes are unrelenting when they meet mine.

"This is how it's going to be?" He shrugs as he takes our all white mare, River, by the reins. "Suit yourself."

"I will."

"Good." Another chuckle. Another shake of his head. Another slow rub up and down her nose as he continues walking her around the ring. "It isn't worth getting upset over, you know?"

"What am I upset over?"

"It seems as if you're pissed that the horses like me, which, to me, would seem to be a bonus considering you hired me to take care of them."

"And?" I shift my feet and wait for the point he's trying to make known, but he doesn't continue. He walks River a bit more before reaching into a bucket and handing her a piece of apple while praising her.

It's hard to want to hate him when he's nice. It's hard to want to trust him when I know he went into town last night and did who knows what at the bar.

"If you're going to stand there and watch, you might as well help. Grab Willow and brush her down for me, will you?"

"Fine. Sure." Still angry but happy to have something to do besides sulk, I climb the fence, and my boots thump when I land. Within seconds, I have Willow by the reins and am leading her toward the gate that leads into the shaded area outside the stables where the grooming supplies are.

"You know, we could hire someone else to do that, right?" he calls out as I shut the gate at my back. "Most ranch owners aren't the ones responsible for that task."

"I'm not most ranch owners," I counter instead of asking him why he suggested I do it in the first place.

"You most definitely are not," he murmurs so quietly that I can just barely make it out.

I set to work on Willow, running the brush in one hand followed by my bare palm of the other over the strong muscles playing beneath her coat. I find an odd solace in the work. In the repetition. In taking care of something that truly needs it.

Here and there, she leans into me when I hit a sensitive spot that feels good to her.

Jack's clucks and praise to the other horses slowly become background noise as I let the mindless task become a sort of meditation that both relaxes and soothes me in the simplest of ways.

The gate at my back clanks open and shut as Jack goes to grab something. My guess is more treats, but I don't turn to look. Instead, I listen to the beat of his boots on the concrete floor as they grow faint when he walks away and then louder as he returns.

And just as the gate clanks open, another gust of wind hits, swirling inside the alcove where I have Willow hitched. The blast of air picks up a plastic shopping bag that had been shoved in a bucket to save it for a later use and throws it up.

Before I can intercept it, the bag flutters against Willow's face, and she spooks. With the handle of the bag freakishly looping over her ear, she rears up on her hindquarters and a loud cry falls from her as she bucks to get it off.

"Woah, girl!" I shout as I try to avoid her landing on me at the same time I try to pull the bag off her face.

Right as I'm within grasp of the bag, she rears up again, but this time, she turns toward me as she comes back down.

Seconds pass in what feels like snapshots of time—fast and furious.

Jack pulling me back from her front legs. The tether rope coming loose from where I tied it. Willow running toward the dead end of the stables, bag still attached to her ear as she bucks and thrashes her head.

His hands are on my shoulders as his head lowers so his eyes can meet mine. "You okay?" he asks, and when I fail to find words around the adrenaline surge, he gives me a shake. "Knox? Are you okay?"

"Yes. Sure. Fine." But my words sound anything but sure when I get them out.

Willow's neigh, frightened and freaked, followed by the slam of something breaking cuts through the fog and has both of us running. We find her cornered in the stables with the bag still on her ear. She apparently kicked a stall door so hard that it swung open and was pressing her into a corner with its weight.

I reach her before Jack does and focus on opening the door and getting the bag off so I can calm her down, but just as I get my hand on the door, Jack pulls me back.

"What are you—"

"She's gonna hurt you if you do that. Kick you into the hospital. She's freaked out, and that goddamn bag spooks her more and more every time she moves."

"That's why we have to get it off her!" I shout the obvious, frustrated that we're talking about it and not doing it.

"I'll keep the door pressed against her, you climb on the inside of the stall and remove it. She won't be able to hurt you that way."

But she'll still be able to hurt you.

The thought glances through my mind as Jack pushes his hands and weight against the door to try to keep the frightened horse where she is. But the gate would never be able to protect him if she decides to let loose again.

I step on the rail so I have a better position, and Willow jerks her head as I try to grab the bag. "C'mon, Will," I croon as I let her settle a bit before I go to try again, but when I do, I get the same result.

She's more freaked and the bag moves violently only to spook her more. My concern for her safety is growing.

I adjust my feet in the rails for more leverage while soothing her with soft words, but she's still jittery and unpredictable.

Just before I go to reach toward her again, Jack's voice fills the air. Its tenor is deep, its tone is melodic, and his words are bluesy.

Stunned, I glance over to him to make sure that's really his voice. His hands are still pressing against the gate, his head tilted down so I can't see his lips, but it's clear that the strong voice that echoes off the concrete floors is coming from him.

The words might be about someone who has lost their heart, but they somehow soften the fear in Willow. Her feet stop moving. Her head begins to lower. Her muscles relax.

I reach out and remove the bag as soon as I can, and she doesn't even flinch. She just lowers her head farther as Jack slowly opens the gate, relieving its pressure from her hindquarters. He continues singing as he places his hand on her rear, running it slowly up her back toward her neck before petting the length of her nose, and then resting his forehead against it. They stand inches from me, in the depths of the stable, while he soothes her with his presence. He takes a startled animal scared of something beyond her control and calms her with words she doesn't understand but actions she can.

I hate that I'm mesmerized by the sight of it.

I dislike that I wish it were me who had that type of super-power to calm Willow.

Even more, I hate that I want to hate him. Despite struggling with accepting his presence here on the ranch, hate is an impossible emotion when I know I'll always remember this. Jack Sutton crooning to a petrified horse to calm her.

The thought replays over and over as he gets her to begin to move. His voice is softer now, the compassion just as poignant as he leads her out into the paddock where the other horses are all waiting and curious as to what her shrieks were all about.

All I can do is stand there and watch him with them, taking in the tenderness of a man who comes across as anything but gentle.

The singing turns to humming as he takes the bucket of halved apples and, one by one, holds a piece to each horse. Each one a reward for their calmness. Each one a bribe for it to continue.

My feet move closer without thinking. I rest my forearms on the top rail, set one foot on the bottom rung, and watch, mesmerized as they stand and wait for him to pay them attention.

"It isn't my fault most females are taken with me." He flashes me a grin that shows perfect teeth.

Arrogant prick.

I smile because, for some reason, this banter is what I need to calm my nerves over Willow's freak-out and Jack . . .well, Jack saving me from being hurt. I struggle with admitting that I needed anyone to save me.

"I'm not most women."

"If you were, I'd already have won you over." This time, he looks at me over a sea of ears and manes and studies me with an intensity that's unnerving.

"What?"

"You could say thank you?"

"Thank you?" I snort.

"Mmm-hmm."

"For what?" I ask when I know the answer.

"For saving you. For helping you calm her. For giving you something good to look at while you make up reasons why you hate me so much."

"You're insane." I push back off the rail and shake my head as if it will help me reject the fact that he is just that handsome. "And you should thank me for the job."

"So you don't think I'm good-looking? It's a simple question, Knox." He tilts his head to the side and gives me another disarming grin as he slides a hand up River's neck. "You can still hate me and think I'm sexy."

I glare in response.

"There are those daggers again." He laughs and presses a kiss to the horse's nose. "You mind telling me what in particular I'm doing to piss you off, or is it a permanent thing and you're always angry?"

All the reasons I'm angry these days, all the ways I harbor resentment, flit through my mind, and I know not a single one is his fault.

"Just you."

"Is your attraction to me that hard to fight? I'm sensing it is."

I fight the smile and lose as I bark out a disbelieving laugh. "That's exactly it. You're right. I can't resist you."

"See? Don't you feel better now that you got that off your chest?"

"My chest is perfectly fine. My chest is . . ." My voice drifts off as I realize what I'm saying, and the lopsided smile he offers me says his mind went right there too. "You're an asshole." The words come out in a laugh.

"So you've said."

No apologies. No nothing. Just a man standing there with a sweat ring around the neck of his T-shirt, his biceps stretching at its cuffs, a singing voice that quite possibly could make a woman weak in the knees, and a smirk that unnerves me more than I'll ever admit.

"You're still admiring me, Knox," he teases. "The ladies here are getting a bit restless with jealousy."

"Are you dismissing me?" I snort in disbelief.

"Last thing I need to be is micromanaged."

"Last thing I need is for you to be arrogant."

It's his turn to snort and take a step toward the railing where I stand, the horses stepping apart for him as if he silently asked them to. He mimics the stance I had moments ago, tips the front of his hat up, and lowers his voice so I'm forced to take a step closer to hear him. "You pay me for arrogance. You pay for the sure thing. You wouldn't be getting your money's worth if I were any other way."

"Whatever," I mutter as I take a step back to gain some distance from him. The sudden chills that chase over my skin from the deep tenor of his voice don't diminish with the extra foot or two.

"I'm sure you have work to do."

"I do."

"Good."

"Then I'll go do it." But it takes me a beat longer to actually take another step back and break the hold he has on my gaze.

Just as I turn on my heel, he says, "I'm glad you didn't get hurt, Knox."

My feet falter and my head drops just a bit before I nod slightly and then continue walking to the house.

I wanted to roll my eyes at him.

I wanted to argue and tell him he's an ass and his arrogance doesn't do a damn thing to win my favor nor do I find him attractive in the least.

Hell, I wanted to thank him for saving me from getting trampled.

Instead, I stomp up the steps to the house, vibrating with a restless energy I can't quite understand.

When I was younger and felt this way, I'd lace up my running shoes and just go. Take off for miles until the feeling settled and my head was clear. When we first moved here, I'd grab my camera and get lost in capturing the perfect image. After Fletcher died, I'd throw my suit on and go swim laps in the pool till I couldn't do one more stroke.

After I was thoroughly exhausted from swimming myself ragged, I'd slip below the surface of the water and scream at the top of my lungs to alleviate all the hurt and betrayal that was eating me alive inside.

It's been a while since I felt as restless as Jack being here makes me feel.

And, damn it to hell, I think everything that just happened might have won a little piece of me over to liking him.

Just a little bit.

It's the singing.

It has to be the singing.

Eight

JACK

She moves like a force to be reckoned with. Stroke after measured stroke, she cuts through the water with a determination that is part admirable, part intimidating.

Standing on the edge of the deck, I watch her as the sun begins to set in the west, slowly painting the sky with oranges and pinks.

I came to ask her about Ruby's feeding regimen and the breeding schedules that I couldn't find in the stack of papers she handed over to me. Ever since Willow spooked this morning, though, she's avoided me. Maybe I've done the same since singing isn't something I share with most people, and Tate is now part of that small number.

Hell, I came here to ask her questions about doing my job, but all I want to do is watch her.

Now all I want to do is try to figure her out.

She does some kind of tuck when she hits the edge and pushes back through the water. I try to find something else to look at, but the rest of her backyard is sparse. There isn't any patio furniture for entertaining or umbrellas for guests to gather under to beat the late afternoon Texas heat. Besides the pool, there is a barbecue that looks like it hasn't been used in ages, a plastic chair that her towel is draped over, more flower pots filled with dead plants, and a dilapidated dog house that hasn't seen a dog in a long time.

So, when I turn my attention back to her, I blame it on boredom instead of intrigue. Her movements are fluid and confident and natural. When she's on the ranch and with the horses, she pretends to be just this sure of herself, but there is an underlying insecurity over whether she is doing the right thing. It's slight but there, and I wonder what exactly that husband of hers did to her to cause it.

The question is why do I care?

Trust.

That's what it all comes down to, and for the fucking life of me I'm not sure why I care so much if she trusts me . . . but I know that I hate that she doesn't.

Feeling like an ass for standing here watching her, I take a step in retreat. But it's the minute my back is turned that I hear the sound. The muffled scream beneath the water.

I whip back around, afraid for her safety, and spot her on the bottom of the far end of the pool as if she's sitting there, body still. Each air bubble that breaks the surface releases part of her scream into the air around me.

Each one relieving only what I can assume is a tiny bit of her stress.

Each one helping to bring her slowly back to life.

Unsettled, I watch her when I know I need to leave. I tell myself that it isn't my problem and that whatever she's screaming about is because of something that happened way before I showed up here. That whatever she's hurting from isn't my fault.

"Not your place to care, Jack," I mutter when every part of me wants to step forward and ask her why she's sitting at the bottom of her pool screaming.

As I retreat, the sound carries with me.

The sound eats at me.

The sound all too familiar to the one that fell from my own lips when I found out my father had died and I wasn't there. My scream that said I was too damn selfish to stop my own life and give in to his requests for me to come home and so all I was left with was to fulfill the promise I made him instead. My shout that expressed how I felt knowing I'd missed the chance to see him one last time and let him know that I loved him with everything I had.

I know that sense of loss that makes you want to scream until you lose your voice, and I'm not sure why I'm surprised to see it in Tatum Knox.

The woman has ice in her veins.

At least, I thought she did until I heard the cry for help in her screams.

Nine

TATE

The strength in his hand as he holds the reins. Each muscle defined. Each white scar highlighted by the light.

Click.

Those brown eyes as he looks up at me from under the bill of his hat.

Click.

His broad shoulders as he hefts a bale of hay over the fence into the corral.

Click.

His swagger as he moves toward me. The dust his boots kick up almost like a haze around his legs as he walks.

Click.

His lips framed in the lens. His stubble a dark shadow against his tanned skin. The feather of the muscle in his jaw as he fights whatever it is he's going to say.

Click.

"Put the camera down, Tate." Jack's voice is a deep rumble that washes over my skin and makes me look up from the finder.

"Why? What's wrong?"

"Nothing's wrong." He strides the rest of the way to me and takes the camera from my hand. "It's my turn to take some of you."

"No way." I pull the Canon away from him, but he's stronger, faster, bigger, and he is able to get his arms around me without much of a struggle.

Not that I struggled very hard against the familiar heat of them. The undeniable strength in them. The smell of sun and shampoo on him. All of these things hit me about the same time as Jack's lips slant over mine.

His tongue slips between my lips, and every part of me heats and aches and melts into the familiarity of the kiss. Into the sense that he gives me that everything is going to be all right.

"Wait a minute!" I say, ending the kiss and pushing against him playfully. "Do you think your lips are going to distract me enough that I'll get on the other side of the lens?"

His laugh rumbles through his chest as he rests his forehead against mine. "Tate." He sighs my name so that the warmth of his breath feathers over my lips. "I'm about to distract you a whole lot more than that."

I AWAKE WITH A START. My heart is in my throat, and my hand drifts to my lips as I take a minute to allow my brain to catch up and my pulse to calm down.

Real.

It seemed so damn real.

Real and peaceful and *normal*.

How is that possible when everything about Jack Sutton riles me up? He's strong-armed his way into my life, my ranch, and my business, and now he's invading my damn dreams.

"Fiona." I groan her name, knowing her comments were what got my imagination going and caused this dream.

That has to be it.

Still, I dreamed about photography. I dreamed about it when my muses haven't been seen or heard from in years. Sure, I've picked up the camera and headed out to the pond, begging to be inspired, needing to get lost in something other than the ranch's day-to-day routine, but I've always put the camera down after taking one or two photos. After each of those impulsive outings, I was left feeling emptier than I was before because the one thing I used to count on, getting lost in my art, was no more.

Of course, it doesn't help that I feel as if my subconscious is betraying me by suggesting that Jack could be my new muse. Nothing like a dream like that to whack me over the head and tell me to stop resisting Jack's help. That deep down my mind was telling me that letting him in might be a good thing for the ranch's success and for me to learn to trust others again.

I'd rather focus on *that* revelation than the kiss that lit every single part of my body so brightly the ache still burns . . . even if it was a figment of my imagination.

It was a dream.

A kiss in a dream.

That's it.

Plus, I only dreamed it. My subconscious chose to speak to me that way because it's been over a year since a man has touched me.

It knew I would wake up and hear it.

Too bad I still feel it.

Needing to shake it from my thoughts, I sit up in bed, prop my pillow behind me, and grab my book from the nightstand.

But after staring at the page for way too long and never seeing the words, I realize what's bugging me so much. It's that everything I've ever loved began with my seeing it in snapshots like art playing out before me: the first time I saw Fletcher, the first time on the Mediterranean, the first time I laid eyes on Ruby.

And how does Jack play into all of this?

Click.

"Christ," I mutter before giving up on the hope of reading, sliding back down under my blankets, and forcing myself to fall back asleep. The last thing I need is for my brain to start suggesting that the dream could really happen.

Or, worse, for more snapshots to fill my mind.

Only I can't fall asleep. Every time I close my eyes, it's as if I can feel the heat of his body against mine and taste the flavor of his kiss on my tongue.

It's maddening and arousing, and as much as my previously dormant libido flutters to life, I need to stop thinking about this.

About him.

I shove up out of bed and out of my bedroom.

The house is quiet as I walk through it, the pad of my feet the only sound, but I welcome its silence and darkness. It feels as if muting any kind of outside distraction is my only goal these days. It's a sad thought since I used to have so many goals, so many dreams and desires.

Photography. It used to be my life, my passion, and a way to show others the beauty they could see if only they knew where to look.

And now, as I run my hand over the door that leads to the room that used to be my studio, I feel the hum beneath my skin for the first time in years.

Fletcher robbed me of that. First with his anger at how I pissed off the citizens of Lone Star when I wrote that article and made life harder for him. Then it was because money was tight and he needed me to help out more on the ranch even though he barely let me do anything. When I could find a moment to sneak away to shoot, he would become enraged. Back then, I didn't know it was because he didn't want me talking to anyone in town. I didn't realize he was afraid that if I did, someone would confront me and tell me about the overdue accounts and mounting debt.

The anger and rage he'd fly into every time I grabbed my camera became too devastating.

The fights became not worth it.

So I gave up.

And like everything else I had previously cherished in my life, I gave up photography to keep Fletcher happy.

Twisting the knob, I push open the door and steel myself against the onslaught of emotions I know will come when I see the space again.

And they come. The tsunami fueled by rage, betrayal, loss, and pain hits me the minute the room comes into view.

The photos of things I loved about Fletcher that had been hanging on my mock clothesline across the far wall are torn into pieces and thrown around the room. Images that depicted a life of happiness and honesty but unbeknownst to me covered up a marriage based on deception and lies. The ones I ripped from their frames and hangers that I tore up in dramatic flair to try to do anything I could to relieve the hurt I felt when I'd learned what he'd done, what he'd hidden, and what he'd cost me.

Photo after photo and memory after memory of a life I thought we shared.

The desk is a mess of unedited prints that I was amassing for a future photobook project. A ceramic figure he'd bought me still lies shattered where I'd thrown it to the floor. The small satisfaction in its crunch was fleeting and only left me with a mess I haven't cared to clean up.

Our wedding photo still sits beneath the splintered glass of the frame. A day I thought held so much promise despite the absence of my parents or anyone else for that matter.

Just the two of us.

The two of us in a shotgun wedding at city hall.

That was all I thought we'd needed.

I glance around again, and the destruction tells me how very wrong I was.

How had I missed the deception before the day I lost my mind in here?

A brand new camera sits on the workbench. It's the only thing not broken. It was Fletcher's apology for smashing my other one "on accident" in a fit of rage after a major sale fell through.

I'd let him talk me into believing he was crushed over the long-term loss it would bring and had forgiven him for his outburst.

It's the only thing untouched because it was the only thing I still gave a shit about.

My destruction is visual evidence of what happened when I found that not only did my husband max out every credit card we had but that he'd also squandered away what I'd still had of my savings account from before my father cut me off. The small stash that I kept on the side for just in case was gone, and I hadn't even known.

This is the devastation I wrought after I found out my parents were right.

This is the realization that I was used. Sure, the love I felt might have been real, but the trust and security were nothing more than a smoke screen.

This is what the loss of the hopes and dreams I thought I was going to spend the rest of my life chasing looks like.

I give my studio one last look before retreating the two steps I had walked in and shutting the door again.

Tears salt my lip, but I don't wipe them off as a broken laugh shreds my throat.

It's almost cruel that I woke from a dream about one man I don't want to want only to be reminded of the dream shattered by the only man I ever wanted.

"How about neither. How about neither are, were, or will ever be a good decision," I mutter as I walk down the hallway on the way back to my bedroom. But when I pass a window and look toward the bunkhouse—at the darkened night beyond and the moonlight that seems to give the shadows a life of their own—my feet falter as the light inside flickers on.

My breath catches when I see a silhouette cut across the doorway. For the briefest of moments, I think that it's Fletcher and not Jack, my mind brought back to the months before his death when he spent more time there than at the main house, working late into the night.

Or, rather, making bets with his bookies.

Fletcher is dead, I remind myself.

But Jack's truck only rambled down the road and its headlights cut across my bedroom wall a few hours ago when he came back from wherever it is he goes every night when he clocks out. How in the hell can he already be up?

But he is. And I watch as he reaches for the bar braced in the doorway and slowly pulls himself up, pauses, and then lowers himself.

He does the pull-ups with an ease that's impressive but with a determination that seems as if it's a penance. One after another. Over and over. There is no break, just a punishing cadence that gives the impression—even across the distance—that he's agitated by something.

Curiosity has me watching him and asking myself questions I say I don't want the answers to, knowing that's a lie.

Latent desire has me not turning away, my dream a not-so-distant memory that holds me captive just as securely as the man himself.

I *could* turn away.

I *should* turn away from the muscles rippling in his shoulders as he moves or the moonlight that reflects off sweat on his torso with each pull-up and then measured release back down. His body in tune as he demands physicality from it.

But I don't.

Because I wonder.

And I question.

Would it be so bad to have a man like Jack Sutton for a lover? Would it be wrong to want to lose myself in someone simply so I can maybe find myself again?

It would be the worst mistake I could ever make because it would mean I didn't learn from the first time I'd made it. After all, wasn't the need to find myself one of the reasons I followed Fletcher in the first place? He offered me a way to be free of the restrictions of my parents so I could be me. He promised a future where we could raise our child with unconditional love.

I scoff.

Yes, he offered that, and what a pretty lie it had been.

I need to stop watching and go to bed.

Succumbing to the exhaustion from exerting himself for the past however long it's been, Jack puts his feet on the ground and braces his hands on his knees to what I can only assume is to catch his breath.

Way too many complications to add him to the mix.

I jump as my refrigerator icemaker kicks on and then close my eyes and laugh at my own nervousness. When I open them again, I find Jack standing, back straight and head angled just slightly to the side. It feels as if he's looking straight at me.

A gasp sneaks past my lips before I freeze, quelling the urge to duck away from the window.

I know there is no way he can see me since the room behind

me is so dark even my silhouette would be hard to make out. Yet, he still stares in my direction through the darkness, and I still stand where I am, staring back as chills climb over my skin and prick my scalp, pulling it tight.

I'm not sure why I stand here like this in the early morning hours with an invisible connection across the distance that I'm not even certain is real, but I do. And then, as if he doesn't understand it either, Jack gives a subtle shake of his head before disappearing into his house and shutting the door.

I need to stay damn clear of him . . . at all costs.

Ten

TATE

I know he's behind me.

Even if his shadow didn't cut the bright sunlight the open stable doors welcomed in, I'd still know he was there.

Because he's been everywhere over the past few days.

If he's not in the ring letting the horses get to know him, he's in the stable organizing it to his liking while irritating me by putting things in places different than I'm used to. When he's not hammering something somewhere, fixing whatever it was I obviously didn't, he's dropping schedules and ideas on my desk in the form of Post-It notes because I'm never around long enough for him to talk to me.

He's even in my thoughts when I don't want him to be simply because he has to be.

Jack freaking everywhere.

So much so that I've been feeling claustrophobic in my own house, on my own land, as I try to navigate to anywhere but where he is while also having to work with him in some capacity.

We've worked in silence when we were forced to be near each other, him asking what's wrong in that confident yet playful way he has while I assert that everything is fine.

This is all because I decided to give him the job.

No. It's happening because I decided to let him in and use the situation to figure out how to trust again.

Strictly for the ranch that is.

The anger I have derives from something else. I know it despite how vehemently I try to deny it.

It's because every damn time I look at him, I'm reminded of his gentle way with Willow the other day, his spectacular voice, and the incredible way he kisses.

And then I feel ridiculous all over again because who gets embarrassed by a kiss that happened in a dream? Who tries to tell themselves it means nothing when they had the same damn dream again last night?

It's ludicrous at best, asinine at worst, and frustrating all around.

Of course, the dream comes rushing back to me now as I feel the heat of his stare on my back. I pretend he isn't there and continue to measure the supplements for each horse so I can mix it in with their grain.

"Are we ever going to talk about this?" Jack finally asks, the dirt beneath his feet crunching on the concrete floor as he shifts his weight.

"Talk about what?" Nonchalant. Unaffected. My attention still focused on what I'm doing.

"About why you keep avoiding me."

"I'm not avoiding you."

He chuckles, and the deep rumble echoes off the wall so that it hits my ears twice and makes it seem as if he's everywhere. "Yes, you are. Now, what seems to be the problem, Knox?"

"My name is Tatum. Or Tate."

"*Or Knox*," he says, pulling me to glance over my shoulder at him for the first time. His silhouette is haloed by sunshine, and there's the slightest of smirks on his lips.

Click.

Jesus. Get a grip.

"I'm working here. Shouldn't you be doing the same?" I snap, irritated at myself for wanting to take his picture.

"I am. Part of my job is communicating with you, and you are sure as hell making that more than hard to do."

"I thought we were doing just fine. I handle the feed and grooming. You handle the horses and everything else we agreed upon in that fancy contract you signed. So, as long as we stay out of each other's ways, we'll get along perfectly."

His shadow against the wall in front of me moves as he takes a step closer. "Works for me, but I can't do my job properly because we have yet to sit and talk about the breeding schedule or the budget for stud fees. The—"

"I trust you to handle it."

He emits a low, disbelieving chuckle. "Handle what, exactly? A little direction would be nice. A budget would be a good start. Information about who's already been bred with who would also be helpful. But hell, if you're giving me carte blanche to do as I please, I'll just shoot for the damn moon and find a Thoroughbred for Ruby—"

"That isn't what I said!" The words tumble out in a panic. The stud fees that Fletcher used to quote have my throat closing up. There's no way I can afford anywhere even close to them. More importantly, Ruby's up for sale. The last thing I need is her getting pregnant and losing the only way I have to keep this place afloat. I scramble with what to say, with how to tell him I don't even have enough money to pay him let alone exorbitant stud fees. "Leave Ruby out of this."

"You said you trusted me, though." He flashes me a smile and then tilts his head in thought. "Why is it you get so irritated with me? One minute, you're fine, the next, you aren't. It'd make this working environment a whole lot easier if you just admitted you liked me and told me I'm doing a good job." He takes a step closer to me. "In fact, fantastic would be an even better adjective to use."

"Fantastic?" I ask with a lift of my eyebrows and a shake of my head. When he takes another step toward me, I want to take one in retreat but am unable to with the counter at my back.

The dreams come back to me. The feel of his body against mine. The taste of his kiss on my lips. The featherlight touch of his fingertips over my skin.

The settled feeling I had from his presence during them is almost overwhelming.

He leans forward and lowers his voice, that cocksure grin irritating and attractive all at the same time. "Yes, *fantastic*."

His voice right now doesn't help me forget anything at all.

"You're staring at me," I finally say after a few seconds have passed, and I'm more unnerved than not without anything pertinent to say.

"And?"

"And don't you have work to do?"

"Sure do." Another megawatt smile meant to irritate me. "But until you start filling me in on the details I need to do it, then I'm just going to follow you around"—he crosses his arms over his chest, leans his hip against the wall, and simply holds that smile as steadfast as his gaze— "and stare at you like you do me."

"I don't stare at you."

I absolutely do.

His laughter is his answer. "Most women have a hard time resisting the jeans and the hat." I begin to speak, and he cuts me off. "I know. You are not most women." Moving a step closer to me, he takes the scoop from my hand without asking, and begins to measure the supplements. "But I'll grow on you. Pretty soon, you won't have any other choice but to like me." His shoulder rubs against mine as he leans forward to pour the supplements into Sky's bucket. "Next thing you know, you'll be daydreaming about me."

"Give me the scoop," I say through a laugh with a swipe of my hand, but he holds his hand above his head, which makes it impossible for me to reach.

"Nope. Not until you talk, Knox. We can't make *this* work— the ranch, that is—until you get me up to speed on all its problems."

"You've seen all the problems. In fact, you don't hesitate to point them out every time you find a new one."

He gives his head a measured nod, but his eyes don't waver. "There are always problems no one can see. Those are the ones that will ruin a ranch . . . pull it under. Last time I checked, you not trusting me *is* one of those problems."

I bristle at the truth in what he just said . . . and lie. "I trust you."

"Nice try, but lip service isn't going to do shit. You won't give trust, but you expect it. That there is a problem."

"You don't know what you're talking about."

"I don't?"

"No." I raise my voice and stand on my tiptoes to reinforce my denial and hope that it hides the fact that I'm on the defensive. Really, I want to refute everything he's saying simply because he's right.

"Then we'll do this another way," he says and takes a step back, his words confusing me. "You're doing this all wrong."

I bark out a laugh of disbelief and pretend the condescension in his voice and the rebuke doesn't sting. "What do you mean I'm doing this all wrong? The ranch? You're the one doing *everything* wrong," I say calmly while my pulse pounds in my ears.

"Define *everything*."

"The horses. The schedule. The—the . . . just everything."

"You mean the schedule you refuse to talk to me about? That schedule?" His chuckle grates on my nerves. "Why don't you tell me specifically what I'm doing wrong with the schedule and then explain to me how you normally handle it so I can correct the error in my ways?"

I want to stomp away and leave him to enjoy his sarcasm all alone, but I end up narrowing my eyes and glaring at him instead.

"You changed the routine."

He swears under his breath. "How would I know I changed it if you never gave me one to follow in the first place? Let's see. I've tended to the horses, I've put in calls to past associates, trying to cash in IOUs to get some of them out here to look at us as a breeding partner, the stables are getting a much-needed facelift, and the farrier was out here today. For not knowing the routine, I'd say I'm doing pretty damn *fantastic*. Forgive me if I'm not adhering to *your* routine, but they're always easier to follow when they aren't imaginary."

"You can add knocking that condescending smirk off your lips," I say and hold my hand out for him to give me the scoop back.

"Should I use my invisible pen to add it to the imaginary schedule?"

"It's time for you to go and work now and to stop badgering me. I'll get you the lists and schedules and whatever else you want by tonight," I say, making the offer purely to get him and his charming smile out of my face because it's so much easier to ignore my dreams when he isn't in my line of sight. "Is that acceptable?"

"It's fantastic."

"Jesus," I mutter.

"Just face it, Knox. You're head over heels in love with me." He finally smiles, dimple winking and those eyes lighting up as he takes a step toward me, holding the scoop to his chest. "You can't be near me because you want me, and you can't talk to me because you get all flustered and tongue-tied."

"There is nothing about you I find attractive," I lie.

He places the scoop in my hand but doesn't let it go when I try to take it. "It'd be much easier and a whole lot less distracting if I could say the same of you." He lets go of the scoop and dips the tip of his hat in an aw-shucks kind of way. "But I'm not one to lie."

Our eyes hold across the short distance as his comment floats through the air and fades like the dust specks dancing in the sunlight.

"That won't work, you know?" I say.

"What won't?"

"You trying to charm me every time you want something. I know your kind, Jack Sutton, and I'm not impressed by them."

"Is that so?" He shifts on his feet and adjusts his hat before re-crossing his arms over his chest. "And what kind is that?"

"A man who uses his good looks and smooth words to get his way with people. A man who turns on the charm to disguise it."

His eyes darken and then narrow. "Just like you're the woman who keeps living her privileged life . . . fiddling while Rome burns down around her?" he counters, making me want to scream that he knows nothing about me or how I live or what I've been through for the last year. A small part of me is shouting about how that was his point, but I tell the voice to shut up. "And if by good looks and smooth words, you're implying I'm like Fletcher, I suggest you not infer that again." That muscle in his jaw feathers in contempt.

"I'm not the woman you think I am."

He twists his lips and stares at me in a way that feels like he is seeing right through me. It's unnerving and unsettling, and I force myself not to look away because his silence is telling me that maybe he thinks I am.

I'm not sure why that bugs me. Why I want him to see me as someone different.

"I'm not even certain you know who that woman is either," he says. Before I can process what he means, he continues, "Tell me about the complaints lodged against the ranch. They're talked about but no one seems to know what they are or who's making them. Any clue?"

"They're baseless and not relevant in the grand scheme of things."

"I beg to differ." His Adam's apple bobs as he studies me. "This is the part where you try to trust me, Knox."

Heat flushes my cheeks as I struggle with how to do this, how I start to let someone in. "I'm trying."

"That's all I can ask." He nods and doesn't call me out on the panic he can probably see swimming in my eyes.

"What do you want to know?"

"For starters, who's making these complaints and why? What exactly did Fletcher or you do to the people in town that earned you that look every time either of your names is brought up?" He shakes his head. "If you paid off all of your accounts in town with his life insurance benefits like rumor has it, what in the hell are you sinking your profits into? I know you said there hasn't been a ton of foals, but Christ, Knox, where's the money going?"

Each question is like a blow to the face, and by the time he finally falls silent, I might as well be lying on the floor bleeding. I steal myself against the pain the answers to his questions bring and glare at him.

"What I do with my money is my business. How I make it, how I spend it . . . my business. Last I remember, I kicked you out of here on day one for listening to the town gossip mill." It's my only defense and a shitty one at that.

"Your money is my business. Did you forget that you hired

me to make you more of it? I have to know what you have and what the budget is for me to make this magic happen." He grabs a handful of hay off the bales stacked beside him and throws it to the ground as if everything he said wasn't hard for me to hear. "It seems you need to be coddled. Not my style. Fletcher may have spent hours stroking that ego of yours, but rest assured, I won't."

"Screw you."

"I wasn't aware that was part of my contract." His laugh is loud and rich and irritating. "Fighting the whole world isn't an option, so it seems you have decided to constantly pick a fight with me. Is that what this is? Kick me out. Ask me to stay. Not give me the tools I need to do my job so you have someone to blame?"

"This conversation is over," I say through gritted teeth.

"Nah, we're just getting started," he says with a laugh and a smack of his hands, "because we're finally getting somewhere. I'm finally figuring you out. I'm finally understanding why every couple of days you sink to the bottom of your pool and scream at the top of your lungs because you don't think anyone can hear you."

I just stare at him, feeling more naked, more vulnerable, than I have in what feels like forever.

Having to deal with what Fletcher did, how what he did made me feel, is one thing, but I learned my lesson. I told myself I'd never let myself feel that way again, and yet, something as simple as Jack seeing me in my weakest moments gets to me.

"You're a bastard." My voice is barely audible as the shame and hurt course through me. "Get out. I didn't invite you on my ranch to take shots at me left and right." I point to the door of the stable, wanting space, needing distance.

"Why are you constantly on the fucking defensive? Can't you see that all I'm trying to do is to get you to talk? All I'm trying to do is to get you to trust that I'm going to try to help you." He blows out a frustrated sigh that I can hear but that I can't process being the cause of. "I'm on your side, Knox. I'm—"

"No one's on my side." My voice is soft, even . . . raw with a vulnerability I hate. "I learned that the hard way."

Eleven

JACK

She looks like a little kid who's lost.

Her eyes are wide, and her voice is soft but determined. Fuck if I don't feel like an ass for slipping that I'd seen her in the pool—that I'd seen her in a private moment as she worked through her own shit.

But it's out there, so I can't take it back.

All it's done is make her push me away harder and shut down faster. This is the second time I've seen her do this, so maybe it's her natural defense mechanism? Guilt or anger or insecurity, I'm not sure, but blocking me out isn't going to do her or this ranch any good.

Sure, maybe she had it easy when she was growing up. Maybe when she first met Fletcher, the world was in the palm of her hand, but the hurt I see in her eyes right now is deeper than a spoiled primadonna throwing a tantrum because her husband died and now she has to get her hands dirty with work.

It's more than that.

And I need her to see it.

I need her to realize this is hers now.

Not Fletcher's.

"I'm not on your side?" I ask. "I'm not here trying to turn your horseshit into diamonds for you?"

I stare at her proud shoulders and petite body, at the gray in her eyes and the wisps of hair that curl around her cheeks, at the swell of her breasts through her tank top and the tight fit of her jeans around her hips.

And I wonder how I can want her and not really like her at the same time.

Her unique beauty is undeniable, and I'm not sure I'd ever want to tame her temper or mood swings.

"I've been busting my ass nonstop for a year to try to make this work. I know I hired you to help, but it seems you spend more time questioning me than anything."

"Maybe if you'd answer the questions, I'd stop asking them."

"What's the question this time?" She asks, but I doubt she'll answer the one I'm going to ask.

"What's your end game?"

"My end game?" she asks, that fire of hers faltering momentarily.

"Yeah, your end game. What is it you hope to get out of this? Make the ranch successful and sell it off? Make it profitable and live out your days here with a new husband and the two point five kids? Walk away in a month without a glance backward? What?"

Confusion flickers across her face followed by determination, but she doesn't respond.

"You ever run a breeding ranch before? Have you ever even been to one before Fletcher bought this one?" I ask, switching gears.

"What's your point?" Her hands are on her hips, and her lip is curled up in anger.

"How'd you learn to do all of this?" I point to the pasture beyond the stable and to the feed scoop in her hand. "If you never learned how to do all this, then how do you plan on succeeding?"

"He taught me a few things. Others I picked up from watching the hands we had. Some from research on the internet. I'm doing the best that I can."

"How do you know you're doing it right?" I push.

There it is . . . the look I knew she'd give me.

Insecurity, nice to fucking meet you. I've been waiting for you to show, waiting for her to acknowledge that you're why she's continually sabotaging my success.

So I push harder.

"Just how do you know you're doing it right? Is it Fletcher's fault you weren't more prepared? Will it be his fault if this ranch fails? Will it, in part, be his achievement if it doesn't?"

"I've got work to do." She glares at me.

"It was Fletcher's dream, wasn't it?" I ask, ignoring her comment.

"This conversation has nothing to do with him."

"Doesn't it?" I chuckle and push her buttons again. "He brought you here and then screwed you over. No one would blame you for walking away. No one would blame you if the ranch failed. Hell, sell off the horses and give them a better life on some other ranch and you can move on."

She growls out in frustration, and when I smile at her response, I swear to god she balls up her hands to punch me.

At least that would be more cathartic than screaming under water.

Does she not see what I see?

"You give up your dream to chase his, didn't you?" I take a step closer, and the fisting of her hands doesn't relent. "Photography, right? You gave up all that creativity you thrived on to live this lifestyle. I bet that wasn't part of the bargain when you moved here. I bet that wasn't something you thought would happen."

"Him dying wasn't part of the bargain either, but it happened," she says with a chill to her voice. "And you don't get to waltz into my life and act as if you know what's best for me and for my horses."

There you are, Tate. Good to see you again.

"You invited me in, though, didn't you?" My smile is mocking.

"Let's get something straight." She jabs her finger in my direction. "I don't have to explain to you that this sure as hell was his dream, not mine. Not in the least. But after every single thing I've been through, maybe I want to prove to myself—to my parents, who wrote me off; to the judgmental cows in town, who do nothing but talk shit; to my dead husband, who screwed me over—that I'm nothing like they think I am. That I can succeed. That I can make this place what he never could. Then maybe, just maybe, everything I lost in the process might have been worth it."

Our eyes hold and question and challenge before she turns back to the grain in front of her. But all she does is grip the edge of the counter and breathe in the truth she just allowed herself to voice.

My voice is soft when I speak to her back. "Don't look now, Knox, or you might stop questioning yourself and realize you've kept this place afloat. *You.* Not Fletcher. Not the people in town. Not your parents. *You.* So, the next time someone asks you to defend what you're doing, stand behind it. Don't let them tell you you're wrong, even if you're secretly questioning if you are. You own this place now. You've been running it. *You fucking defend it.*" I take another step closer and give a quick shake of my head she can't see. "You want to fight? You want to go scream in the deep end of your pool? Be my fucking guest. But remember who you are. Remember that this is your dream now and you're going to fight like hell for it." I take a step back. "I've got work to do."

Twelve

TATE

Discord still rides like a tidal wave through me as I stalk my ass down to the bunkhouse. It has been this way all afternoon, ever since Jack told me to keep standing my ground.

For the first time in forever, I swear to God something other than despair fills me. I'm not quite sure what it is, but I'll take it.

If giving Jack Sutton what he wants will help prolong this feeling, then I'll do just that, I'll give him everything I have. I'll kill him with kindness in the form of breeding schedules and bloodline histories on our horses.

"Jack!" I shout as I approach the bunkhouse, a box full of enough binders and spreadsheets that his eyes will cross after studying them heavy in my arms. "Jack!" I kick the front of his door before setting the box down on the porch.

"Yeah?" he calls from somewhere on the side of the house.

And right as I turn the corner to go tell him what I've left for him, I run smack dab into him. Since he had been jogging toward me when we collided, he knocks me backward with his momentum.

I land on my back with a thud.

And he lands right on top of me.

Every long, lean, hard, shirtless inch of him.

The strangled cry that comes from my mouth has so much more to do with the assault on my senses than the shock of our collision.

"Well, shit." He laughs in that easy manner of his that tugs on the latent desire in me I want to ignore as it vibrates through his chest into mine.

"Oh. Sorry. I mean—"

Then a split second after he pushes off me and before I can sit up, he squats beside me, eyes intense. "I guess that's as good of an apology as any," he says with that lopsided, boyish smile of his.

"Apology?"

"Relax, Knox." He clasps my hand in his to help pull me up. "I was teasing you."

"Yes. Of course. I, uh . . ." I forget what I was going to say because he's standing there shirtless and I want to look but don't want to admit that I want to look . . . "Yeah. That."

"That?" He chuckles as he runs a hand through his hair, each and every one of his muscles, which I'm not supposed to be noticing, are suddenly impossible not to look at. "What's that?"

I clear my throat and point to the box on his porch he can't see, his shirtless torso distracting me more than I'd like to admit. "That's it. The box, I mean. It's what you asked for."

He steps around me to peek around the corner, giving me an unhindered view of all the striations in his shoulders and back. "I've asked for a lot."

He faces me and lifts a lone eyebrow when it takes a second for my eyes to snap to his instead of his body.

"Yes. You do. You bet. I'll get some for you."

He bites his lip with his smile still playing at the corners of his mouth. "You will?"

"Mmm-hmm."

I nod because I have no clue what I am agreeing to but can't seem to get my brain to work.

"Good thing, then."

"Yes. Definitely."

"So, when should we plan it for? Tomorrow night? The day after?"

"Wait—what?" I ask, suddenly wary.

"Dinner." That damn smile of his causes things to stir in my belly that I haven't felt in years.

"Dinner?"

"Yep. I said I liked steak and potatoes, and you said you loved to cook and were excited to finally have someone to cook for."

"You're insane." I push against his chest in jest but then realize what I'm doing and yank my hand back. "I did no such thing."

"Yes, you did," he says as his eyes sweep down the length of my body. "Here." I jump as he reaches out and dusts something off my hip. "You had some dirt. My fault."

"Yes. Sure."

"See?" He laughs, and it's such a welcome sound when it isn't that haughty, know-it-all tone he normally uses. "You just agreed again to dinner later this week."

"Whatever." I wave both of my hands at him. My own smile so wide my cheeks hurt. "The box has the breeding lines and blood schedules inside it."

"You mean bloodlines and breeding schedules?"

"Yes. That."

"Do I make you nervous, Knox?"

"Of course not," I say as I almost trip over my feet in my haste to take a step backward.

"Uh-huh."

"It's just been a long day. It's just been . . . you know how it's been."

"I do." He takes a few steps toward the front porch and bends over to pick up the box. "Should I pick up some steaks when I head into town tonight?"

"Jack." His name is an exasperated sigh.

"If you're cooking, it's the least I can do."

"Sure." I roll my eyes. "I'll get right on that."

"Cool." He nudges the handle on his door to bring the box inside as I stare at him, mind spinning.

"So that's why you go into town every night?"

"What do you mean?"

"Earlier today. In the stable." I hook my thumb over my shoulder as if he understands it means when we were fighting. "You talked about the rumors about my finances. Is that where you heard them? Do you go to the bar to catch up on the latest gossip about your boss?"

Careful, there, Tate. You sound like a conceited, controlling woman with comments like that.

"Why assume I'm at the bar?"

"I didn't mean for it to sound like that." Nerves lace the edge of my voice. "What I meant was—"

"I'm not out to get you, Tate. I promise I'm not going into town to try to get dirt on you."

"Of course, you aren't," I say, feeling like such an idiot. "I didn't mean for it to sound like that." *Why am I so tongue-tied all of a sudden around him?* "What I meant—I just . . . never mind."

"Who says I don't head into town because I'm a shitty cook

and need to eat?"

There's an intensity to his stare that I can't make myself look away from. It's almost as attractive as that little ghost of a smile that plays at the corners of his mouth. "There's always peanut butter and jelly."

"A man can only live on so many PB&Js, Knox."

"True."

And just when I'm certain this conversation is over, Jack takes a step back toward me and says, "I go to town every night—sometimes the bar, other times the diner—because the pulse of a small town is always felt in the people around you. Who's doing what. Who's screwing who. Where you can catch a break." His smirk is a slow smolder as his eyes take a long minute to skim lazily over my body, feeling like a trail of fire heating my skin, before meeting mine again. "That, and it's a hell of a lot easier sitting in town each night than sitting here, knowing you're less than two hundred yards away looking like that."

"Oh."

There is no ignoring the intention in his eyes or the innuendo of his words.

"Good night, Knox."

Jack pushes the door closed behind him, but I stand there for a quick second, trying to decide what he meant.

And how exactly it makes me feel.

Thirteen

JACK

"What in the hell are you doing there, Jack?" My sister is as confused by the notion as I was when I packed my shit and headed here.

"Drinking a beer." I glance around at the evening crowd in Ginger's. The regulars are here, but there seems to be more people than usual tonight due to some barrel racing competition a town over.

"You jackass. Not the bar you're sitting in . . . the town. Lone Star. Why are you there?"

"I'm not explaining this again to you."

"Why? Because you don't want me to tell you that you're on the crazy train taking a job there? Or that you punched that ticket twice by adding on working for *her*. The promise you made was null and void the minute he died, Jack. You being there isn't going to do anything to change that. Finish your beer, then go back and pack so you can come home. We need you here."

"Lauren—"

"You have shit here to straighten out that needs your attention more than she does. I can't do this on my own. I can't run and manage and—"

"You can manage for six months, Lauren. I'll be back before the calves are born and the real work starts. I did this on our down time . . . or as much of a down time as the ranch has. I'm keeping my word, Lauren, to both you and dad." I take a sip and watch a couple walk through the door, knowing the promises I made and the amends I need to follow through on so I can find the peace I've struggled with, aren't things she'll understand. "This is something I need to do."

"Jack." My name is a drawn-out sigh.

"You wouldn't understand." How could she? She'd been so lost in her bottle back then, so consumed, that there is no way she could have known what kind of standards my father held me to and the reasons I bolted the first chance I had. She's ignorant to the life choices both of those things have led me to make.

"It's me you're talking about. Epic screw up kid while you were off conquering the world to try to make your own name."

"Conquering isn't exactly what I'd call it." Escaping is more like it. Escaping from the relentless pressure to be who he needed and not who I wanted. "You believed Dad was as sick as he said while I shrugged it off. You were there for him when I wasn't." It's barely a whisper, which the crowd eats up the minute it's out of my mouth, but I know she hears it. Her silence in response says it.

"Talk to me, Jack."

"You ever hear people say they need to get back to basics? That they need to figure out why they loved it in the first place?"

"What's the *it* you're referring to?" she asks as I nod at Ginger and the bottle of beer he slides in front of me.

"Ranching. The horses. When it was nothing more than simple schedules and the day-to-day. When your hands were dirty and your body was exhausted by the time the sun set. Building something up instead of tearing it down," I say. "Before it became a burden, an obligation, and a privilege to be a Sutton all at the same time?"

I think of everything I chased and everywhere I went so I could be anything other than a Sutton. I put so much into trying to escape the thumb he wanted to keep me under, only to be pulled back in.

"I came here to keep my word to Dad, but I'm finding out that I needed more than that."

"What is it that you need that you can't get here?"

I blow out a breath and shake my head she can't see. "I'm still trying to figure that out."

"If it's forgiveness you're looking for, he already gave that to you, you know. Dad wasn't mad at you for not dropping everything and coming back," she says softly, and the guilt hits me just as hard now as it did when she told me he'd fallen asleep and hadn't woken up. "He knew you had to go and figure yourself out before the world started to expect things from you simply because you're his son."

I swallow over the lump of emotion that seems to magically appear the minute I think of him. The hardass man I hated, only to figure out when it was too late how much I really loved him.

"Guilt's a nasty bitch to live with, Lauren."

"It's hard for me too. I was here and saw him like that. I'll have that image in my head the rest of my life while you are mad at yourself because you don't. I'm not sure which one is better, so why don't you come home so we can live with the guilt together?"

The softness in her voice tells me she's crying again, and I fucking hate that. I hate how his death has ripped our family to shreds. He was the rock. Now we're just . . . rubble. I also know that she means what she says. If I go home, she'll give less to her kids to make sure I'm okay, which is the last thing I need. Her changing her life for me when I probably wouldn't have changed shit if she'd asked me to would only pile on more guilt.

I'm too selfish. Too much of a bastard.

This is part of my promise to him, though. The Knox ranch is killing two birds with one stone. Figuring out how to run that place on a shoestring budget so it can thrive instead of letting a bigger ranch swallow it is my own demon to fight.

Figuring how to make amends in my own way.

Dealing with someone else's problems.

Tate's problems.

"Jack-Jack?" Lauren says, using the nickname she gave me forever ago.

"Yeah. Yes. I'm here." My sigh eats up the silence on the line. "Just distracted, is all."

"Tell me about her."

My smile is instant. The scowl just as fluid right after. Isn't that Tate though? A smile and scowl mixed with everything in between.

"She's off limits, you know that, right?"

"Why would you even think to say that?" I ask.

"Your silence. That's what made me think to say it."

"Lau—"

"Don't Lauren me, Jack. I know you better than anyone . . . and that silence after I asked you to tell me about her spoke volumes."

"She's complicated." And gorgeous and frustrating and so much I can't figure out.

"You like complicated."

I bark out a laugh at her insanity. "And you like to snoop."

"See? I told you that you liked her. You talk when you don't care. You clam up and accuse when you do."

"I assure you there is nothing there."

But I remember the feel of her body beneath mine earlier. The

127

heat of her skin. The nerves edging her laugh that fueled my need to leave the ranch and head to Ginger's before I made a colossal mistake.

Like knocking on her door.

And what kind of dick does that make me out to be?

"Last thing this family needs is you falling in love with her and never coming back home."

My laugh is loud and draws looks from those around me. "When's the last time I fell in love with someone other than myself?"

"Spoken like the true asshole you are." She falls quiet for a beat. "I still don't agree with you doing this, but I can hear something in your voice. Maybe this is what you need—the time there helping with the ranch, *not her*." She laughs. "So, do what you need to do. Just promise me you'll be back."

Five months plus some change. Christ. The countdown feels like a noose around my neck and a blessing all the same.

"I will." I gave my dad the same assurance and then didn't hold to it. "I know what's expected of me. You don't need to worry."

"'Kay. I love you."

"Love you too."

When I end the connection, I take a long draw on my beer with my family front and center in my mind.

The game playing on the flat screen drones above my head. The bar chatter ebbs and flows. Ginger's laugh rings out more often than it doesn't.

So much noise, so many people, and yet, I'm lonely as fuck and brimming with regrets.

"Is it true?"

I glance to the woman who just slid into the booth next to me. She's tall, her top's as low as it is tight, and her eyes are hungry for attention.

"Depends on the question," I say without giving her another look.

"Name's Violet."

"Mmm." I keep my head forward, eyes focused on the game that I really don't care about.

"You the new man up on the Knox ranch?"

"You wouldn't be asking if you didn't already know, now would you?" I lift a lone eyebrow and receive a coy smile from red painted lips in return.

"You going to be the one to save that bush league ranch?"

And who the hell are you?

A person walks up and tries to insert themselves into someone else's business if for no other reason than to start trouble. She's definitely looking to start something.

"It's got good bones," I murmur as I turn my attention back to the game and bring my beer to my lips. "All it needs is personnel with a little more experience, a lot more foals, and some of the clients I've been hired to bring on board to say yes. Oh, and winning the clients over from Hickman wouldn't hurt either. Quite a few are taking interest," I say, the last statement about our local competition a lie, but it sets the stage for the town to know we're here to play hardball.

Her slight double take is expected, and I bite back my scoff. Within an hour, the inhabitants of Lone Star will know I'm vetting some high-dollar owners who might possibly sign a contract with the Knox Ranch. Could be rodeo, could be barrel racing, could be a lot of things, but I don't tell her anything more.

It's all about perception. Defining it. Containing it. Perpetuating it.

"And your background?" Violet asks, suddenly way more interested in who I am than what's in my pants.

Who am I kidding? By the way she keeps adjusting in her seat so her knees brush against mine, she's still interested in that.

"I've dabbled in breeding here and there. Lots of time as a ranch hand. Some as a stable manager." I offer a tight smile. "But mostly acquisitions."

I neglect to tell her I'm also part heir to one of the largest cattle ranches in the States. Sure, breeding cattle is different than horses, but that might draw attention to me I don't want.

"Where you from?"

"Here. There. A bit of everywhere."

"True cowboy, then." She laughs.

"Through and through."

I turn my attention to a group singing happy birthday in the far corner. I know she's waiting to see if I'll buy her a drink. I know because I've watched her work the room over the past two weeks, only recently setting her sights on me.

Snippets of conversation float my way when the singing and clapping are over.

"The Donaldson's struck oil. Now, how about that? Who knows what's beneath that land of ours."

"Did you see Gaylord sold that heifer for a grand? A grand? It was worth a whole shit-ton more than that. He must be hurting."

"Jesus, this server is slow. Can't a man drown his sorry ass in a beer without begging?"

None of them hold my interest any more than Violet does.

"If you're planning on staying, then you'll get used to all of us." Her laugh is seductive and throaty and would do things to most men . . . but I'm not most men.

"I'm sure I will." Disinterest definitely doesn't deter her.

"Don't worry, Sugar. If you're like everyone else who's worked up there, you'll be down here nightly so you can manage to stay there as long as possible. Hell, why be alone with her when you could be down here getting warm with us?"

"Who said I was looking to get warm?"

Violet pushes my beer toward me and taps the neck of her empty bottle against it. Her eyes never move from mine. "Every man likes warmth."

"You ever meet Knox?" Might as well ask.

"Him or her."

"Both."

"Him. Fletcher could charm the panties off every woman and have every man inviting him over to their table for a drink." Her smile tells me she has memories I probably don't want to hear about. In addition to everything else he did, it wouldn't surprise me if cheated on Tate too.

"He was a charmer then?"

She nods, and my opinion of her, of this town, diminishes a bit more. Where they see charmer, I see snake-oil salesman. "Never really interacted with her. She ran the finances while he worked the horses. From what I heard, she never paid accounts. She never cared how it affected the families who owned the businesses. Typical snob who comes from money—always worrying about herself and not the little people like us."

"Hmmm." It's all I say as I lift a finger to the bartender, silently asking him to bring us fresh drinks. It's the least I can do.

"The husband even got in a fight with Jed at the feed store over it before he died. Huge shouting match out in the street. The owner was asking for payment because he was getting hit with fees or something. I don't remember the words, but Fletcher said he was going to make her pay it and offered a certain percentage of interest for the trouble."

I trace the image on the beer bottle and try to figure why, in a town like this, men would take to another man like Fletcher, who seemingly allowed his wife to lead him around by the balls.

That doesn't sit well with me.

Either that, or Tate has duped me.

"And you know us women, we don't take too kindly to other women who treat good men like cattle—brand them, cut their balls off, and treat them like a piece of meat. You know, like it seemed Tate did to poor Fletcher," she explains, her voice never changing from its seductive drone.

My laugh is loud on purpose just so everyone looks my way. "Seems to me like you've got an active imagination."

Her smile widens and voice lowers. "You want to head out of here so I can show you just how active it is?"

"Thanks, Violet, but not tonight." Or any night, for that matter.

"Okay then . . ." She runs a hand up and down the length of my arm. "When you're looking to leave there, I could help you get a job in oil. They're more than plentiful around here if you know the right people."

"I take it you're the right people?"

"I'm a lot of people." She slowly slides out of the booth, smile still coy and expression still playful as she presses a napkin into my hand. It no doubt has her number on it.

"What's this?"

"Just getting a feel for the water, is all."

Hell if I haven't been treading for way too long to know what it already feels like to slide under the water's surface before begrudgingly fighting my way back to its top again.

"How's it feel?" I ask.

"A little chilly at the moment, but I was just getting my toes wet. I have a feeling it gets warmer with time." She offers me a wink and a soft chuckle before turning her back, hips swinging as she heads back to wherever she came from.

I blow out a breath and turn back to the game that I don't care about.

Fletcher sure snowed this little town. Either that or Tate really is who they say she is.

My money's on the former.

Hands down.

I lift my finger and ask for another drink before I'm halfway through the one I have.

Fire.

Beauty.

Pain.

Fucking Tate.

I'm going to need it if I have any hope of preventing myself from doing something I'm more than certain I'm going to regret.

Like knocking on her door.

Fourteen

TATE

Panic rifles through me as I stumble, still half asleep, to find out who is pounding on the front door. Groggy as I may be, my adrenaline has spiked to the point in which I can feel my heartbeat in my throat and all I can think is that the lights that hit the windows moments before weren't Jack's, but Rusty's.

"There's been an accident."

I keep hearing Rusty say those words and reliving the feeling of the bottom dropping out from under me as I struggled to comprehend him.

Boom. Boom. Boom.

"I'm coming," I yell to whoever it is. Flustered and so wrapped up in the memory that holds me hostage, I don't even look at who is on the other side of the door before flinging it open.

"Jack!" I gasp in relief when I see him standing there. His hair is mussed, and his jaw is clenched, but it's his eyes that knock every sense of panic out of my head. They're intense as they pin me motionless, and anything else I was going to say dies on my lips.

"Who ran the finances here?" No greeting. No hello. Just a stone-cold expression and a demanding question as he pushes his way past me and into my house.

"What are you—Jack?"

"I asked you a question. Who ran the finances when Fletcher was alive? You or him?"

I stare at him, my thoughts bewildered. "He did."

His eyes are dark as they study and judge and question. "You didn't know?"

"Know what?" Alarm bells are sounding off, but I can't ignore them this time around, so I let them blare in the background.

"The overdue accounts in town. Did you know about them? Why didn't you pay them? Did you—" He steps closer to me. The foyer is dark and the only light being from the kitchen at our backs, but his determination is undeniable. "Why didn't you pay them?"

"I didn't know about them. He ran the finances. He had the passwords to everything. He—"

"And you never asked? You never paid your own bills?"

I laugh in unease. "I'm not—I didn't used to be detail oriented with stuff like that. When I left home, I sucked at it and just let him handle it." I shake my head, hating that I have shame heavy in my belly. I'd been so complacent and naïve that I never bothered to try to handle my own finances. After the first payment I missed because I was so distracted taking pictures of all the new scenery to remember, I hadn't wanted the responsibility, and that's on me. "I didn't know about the late accounts until the first time I showed my face in town after Fletcher died."

"Who ran the ranch?"

"We did."

"The day-to-day, who ran it?"

"I don't understand—"

"Just answer the goddamn question, Knox!"

I flinch and hate that, for the briefest of seconds, he sounds like Fletcher used to in those last few weeks, which is to say demanding and agitated and nonsensical.

"*We* did. He did the major stuff like the breeding schedules and stud fees and payroll. The . . . the day-to-day," I say, flustered and confused.

"And your role?"

I try not to get my feathers ruffled at his tone. He has no idea how completely inadequate I always felt or how Fletcher didn't let me do anything when all I wanted to do was more.

"I exercised the horses. I groomed them . . . but other than what I learned from hearing the guys talk or watching them work, I didn't know much else than that."

"You lived here for years, and you think I'm going to believe that you just sat idly by the whole time?"

"I wasn't idle. I was sneaking out when I could to do photography on the side."

"Of what?"

"Ranch life and landscapes. Things I had planned on putting in my portfolio to someday try to open a gallery with."

His head angles to the side momentarily as he chews over what I've said, as he decides whether I'm lying or not.

"How did you think you were getting supplies?"

"What do you mean? Like feed?"

"And groceries and everything else. If you weren't going into town, everything was being delivered, right?"

"Yes." I draw the word out because he just answered his own question so I'm not sure he needs more.

"Why didn't you go to town for them?" There's something in his tone—in what he's looking for—that almost feels like, if I say the wrong thing, he's going to walk out and never come back.

I hate that the thought makes me panic.

What the hell happened?

"Fletcher didn't like me going into town alone. He was paranoid about something happening to me. But—"

"So why didn't he go with you?"

"Stop cutting me off!" I shout, which kind of shocks him so that he steps back. He doesn't speak or even try to apologize. He just stares at me with an unrelenting desire to have answers to questions I don't understand why he's asking. "I didn't realize that Fletcher asking me to stay here was really him *controlling* me until after he died. He had me convinced he was protecting me from the people in town—their judgment and harsh words—and I was dumb enough not to question it." I shrug, feeling like an idiot as fresh shame settles over me like a well-worn jacket from the back of my closet. "He told me stories about how he was treated in town. How people still made comments about the stupid story I wrote. How the Destin twins were still upset about us getting the ranch. He made it seem like it was just easier if I stayed here. He convinced me, and I believed him."

"So, he locked you up here like Rapunzel, but instead of putting you in a tower, he put cameras on the gates to watch your comings and goings?" he asks sarcastically, and my spine stiffens, his comments making me feel stupid and compliant. He snorts. "I have a hard time believing the woman with a blazing temper and loaded shotgun would ever put up with that kind of shit."

I despise that every part of me agrees with him but knows that unless he was in that moment, unless he had been so worn down mentally that he believed the mistruths he was being told, he couldn't ever truly understand.

My throat tightens as I force a swallow over the lump in it. I should just nod and tell him I agree because he's right.

But I was a different person back then. A person who saw the signs but was too afraid to speak up. A woman who saw the hints that her husband's explosive temper was more than just the stress of trying to make this place thrive. A wife who wanted to believe that the long nights he spent in the bunkhouse were because of work or that he really did *accidentally* leave his phone there instead of leaving it on purpose so that I wouldn't see or answer his calls.

A spouse too afraid to speak up and face the truth because I was held captive by my decisions.

"Right, Knox?" he says my last name like a slur. "Why didn't you leave then, huh? Why didn't you—"

"You want to question me. What about if I want to question you?" I say, my mind scattered as I try to shove away all the emotions his accusations have drummed up. "What kind of man takes a six-month contract to work as a ranch manager? What kind of man gets turned down for a job but sticks around town just to wait to see if the owner will change her mind? Who are you, Jack?"

"You know everything about me you need to know. It's all there in my resume." His nonchalance does nothing more than push my buttons and not in a good way.

"I know your history—a breeder, a trainer, a guy with connections, but I don't know shit about *you*. You could be an axe-murderer for all I know."

His laughter rings through the house. "That's it. I prey on single female ranchers. I stay with them for a month, put up with their temper and defensiveness, and then decide to kill them. That's exactly who I am." He shakes his head and takes a step forward while I take one in retreat, my ass hitting the accent table that lines the wall behind me. "Is that enough of an answer?"

His lips barely move when he says the last sentence, and for some reason, when the scent of his shampoo or cologne or whatever the hell that fresh scent he wears hits my nose . . . I have a hard time remembering that I'm angry at him.

I have a hard time forgetting that I'm not supposed to be attracted to him.

"Why Texas?" I ask, my eyes flickering between his lips and his eyes and then back again.

"Same thing could be asked of you." His voice lowers to a deep tenor that is nothing but seduction when I don't want to be seduced.

"Because that's where Fletcher wanted to move to." I draw in a shaky breath. "You?"

"A friend of a friend of a friend of a friend. They knew I needed a change of scenery for a bit. There was a death in my family. Someone I was close to, but I didn't get back in time to see him."

"I'm sorry."

"Mmm." He nods, and I hate seeing the pain that fleets through his eyes, but the minute I do, it's gone. "Anyway, the friend of a friend of a friend . . . they told me about this woman who needed help but who had run everyone off."

"And you thought that sounded like an easy job?" I murmur with a smile because his words didn't piss me off even though a minute ago I was ready to explode on him.

He takes a step closer, his own lips curved up in a ghost of a smile. "Exactly. Nothing like a challenge to take my mind off things."

"Why are you here?" I ask again because gut instinct tells me there's something more to it.

"The same reason you are."

"So, your husband dragged you here and then died, leaving you with a world of shit to clean up?" I joke.

He snorts. "No. I misspoke. Definitely not for the same reasons." His expression softens, easing the lines around his eyes and relaxing the set of his chin.

"What are your reasons, Jack?"

"I'm keeping a promise I made to my father."

"And what do I have to do with that?" I ask.

His lips twist as our stares hold for a beat. "Nothing really. It's—It's complicated." He scrubs a hand over his jaw, and the scrape of it over his stubble fills the room. "Maybe I'm just escaping everything that's expected of me and trying to figure out who the hell I am before I have to get back to it."

His words hit me to the core, and even though I have no idea what he means, I feel like we have found a tentative common ground. We both feel a bit lost and need to regain a bit of control.

We get each other. It sounds stupid and is even more ridiculous to feel that way . . . but I can't explain it—I do.

"Enough about me, Knox." He breathes the sentence out as he tucks a strand of hair behind my ear. There's something about Jack Sutton that calls to me, and it's so much more than learning how to trust again.

"Jack?" I murmur.

"Hmm?" He darts his tongue out to wet his lips.

"What happened tonight? Why are you . . . I don't understand why you're—"

"Because I need to make sure I'm right in my thinking."

His eyes dart down to my lips then back up to my eyes as his fingertips trace a line down the side of my neck until his palm rests on my shoulder. I want to know what he needs to be right about, but his hand is stealing all my focus. The warmth of his skin and the possessiveness in his touch have my body reacting, aching, wanting, needing.

"If I'm right"—he brushes his thumb back and forth over my collarbone as I force myself to remember to breathe—"then I can do what I've thought about doing all damn night."

"What's that?"

He looks toward the door for a split second, as if he's making a decision, and then turns back to me.

"Jack?" His name is a plea because I hope he wants to do the same thing I'm terrified of and thrilled about at the same time. "What is it you've thought about doing all night?" My murmured words reverberate through the sexual tension that's palpable.

"Get you out of my goddamn system." Then his lips crash onto mine and his hand fists in the back of my hair as he holds my head right where it is.

React.

Feel.

Savor.

The second his tongue demands to taste mine, my breath catches.

My body freezes. My hands and heart are statues as I try to process what's happening, as I let him chase away the uncertainty that wants to creep in.

I don't want to think. All I want to do is feel anything other than the doubt and the worry and hate that have consumed me for the past year. With his lips on mine and with such intention in his touch, I know I could get lost in these feelings.

The scrape of his stubble against my chin. The roughness of his fingertips on my bare arms. The taste of beer on his tongue. The humming noise he emits in the back of his throat that rumbles against my lips.

To feel. To ache. To want.

To run my hands up his chest and fist in his shirt.

To remember nothing but the last caress of his tongue.

To want him to kiss me slowly.

The moment I sink into the kiss completely and allow myself the possibility that I could deserve this, Jack tears his lips from mine with a groan that's part desire, part regret.

His hands are on my shoulders as his eyes close momentarily.

"This isn't . . ." He takes a step back, a grin of disbelief on his lips and desire lacing the edge in his eyes. "You deserved better than that."

When he retreats another step, I want to reach out and pull him back toward me, but better sense stops me before I make an ass out of myself.

It was just a kiss.

But the smile curling up his mouth tells me he wanted it as much as I did.

Of course he did. He's the one who initiated it.

I giggle, which sounds stupid and causes a blush to heat my cheeks. I know I look like an idiot, but he just kissed me—like kissed me, kissed me, and I don't even know what to do next because it's been so long since anyone made me feel this way.

He takes another step back. "I'm gonna go now, Knox."

No. Stay.

"My name is Tate." I can't remember if he's ever called me it, and my commenting on it is the only sliver of sanity I can seem to grasp on to.

"I know what your name is."

"Then why do you always call me Knox?"

It's his breath that stutters this time. "Because it reminds me that you're another man's."

If his voice and eyes and presence and that kiss weren't so mesmerizing, so all consuming in this darkened foyer that is clouded with everything about him, I might laugh. I might roll my eyes and shake my head.

But he's here, and I can't think of anything other than how much I want him to be here.

"I don't belong to anyone, Jack." My voice is a ghost of a resolute sound woven between the pounding of my pulse in my ears.

When his eyebrows lift and his smile widens, there is a boyish quality I never would have expected etched in the lines of his masculine face.

"Next time, I'll remember that."

"Will there be a next time?" I ask before I can bite it back, and I end up almost as embarrassed by the hope in my tone as I am desperate for him to kiss me again.

A shake of his head. Another step back. "I was wrong."

"About what?"

I hate that he's reaching for my doorknob.

"That wasn't nearly enough to get you out of my system."

My cheeks hurt from smiling as he opens the door, revealing the moonlit sky behind him.

"Then why are you leaving?" I ask as I twist my fingers together and shift on my feet to abate the sweet burn between the apex of my thighs.

"Because it's your move, Knox. When we sleep together, it isn't going to be a mistake. That's one word I never want to hear pass over your lips when it comes to me. I will never be a mistake . . . but right now, you aren't sure if it would be or not. I want you to be sure."

"Oh."

His lopsided smirk pulls higher on one side. His dimple melts parts of me that are already heated enough.

"Your move," he murmurs as his eyes do a slow sweep down the length of my body.

I nod, afraid to speak because my body is desperate for his touch and every part of me wants harder than I have in as long as I can remember, but he's right.

"'Night, Jack."

"'Night, Knox."

Fifteen

TATE

I use my vibrator for the first time in forever that night.

As I reach for it from the depths of my nightstand drawer, I can't help but understand why Jack goes to the bar every evening. It's hard as hell to want a man who's within walking distance and not be able to have him.

If I feel this way after one kiss, it's going to be torture over the next however long it is until we kiss again.

The thought puts a goofy grin on my face.

Instead of giving in to the temptation and acting like a teenager who can't control her hormones, I lie in bed, close my eyes, and relive every single thing about that kiss.

The scent of his skin.

The taste on his tongue.

The groaned hum of approval.

I keep my eyes closed as I slide my fingers between my thighs. I'm already slick with arousal as my fingertips circle over my clit.

The groan this time comes from my own lips, but I still hear his in my ears as I turn on my vibrator and touch it to my sensitized flesh.

I hear the rumbled tenor of his voice as he says my name, making my nipples tighten beneath my thin tank. When I see the desire in his eyes as he lowers himself over me, my legs tense and I begin to move the toy in circles. I feel the fullness as the length of his cock pushes into me. My breath begins to labor as I work my nerves into a frenzy and fantasize about what he'd feel like moving inside me. I imagine what his body atop of mine would feel like and wonder how he'd sound . . . what he'd look like as he came.

My body detonates into a thousand pulses of pleasure. Blissful warmth and heightened sensitivity followed by heavy pants and quickened heartbeats.

But it's Jack on my mind.

It's Jack who I want.

It's Jack who I plan to have.

Sixteen

TATE

The thunder rumbles in the distance, and the sky is gray with clouds building upon one another, but it doesn't stop me from riding.

I need the breeze in my hair.

I need the distance stretched out before me.

I need the dreams that have haunted me—good and bad—to clear my head.

I need to forget the threats from the lender earlier today on the phone and Sheryl's urging me to call my parents to ask for help.

Hell, I need to get laid by Jack.

It's my laughter that carries loud and carefree above the rush of the wind in my ears and the pound of Ruby's hooves against the ground. There's a freedom in acknowledging that I'm a woman who wants sex and intends to have it.

There isn't any shame, and it doesn't feel as if I'm contemplating cheating on Fletcher.

It's just a decision made and the anticipation of an orgasm given to me by the hands and lips and body belonging to Jack Sutton

We run at top speed over the terrain without a destination other than to get there fast. Each step allowing me to drown a little more out.

My past.

My future.

And just be.

And I try, I really do, but every few seconds, flashbacks of my past sneaks back through. Fletcher's anger. His carefully chosen words on why I should stay close, and my suspicion that maybe my accident *really wasn't an accident.*

"C'mon, Rubes." I dig my heels into her side to spur her on even though she doesn't need it. She already knows what to do. The need to run is coursing through her veins just as sure as her blood is.

Memories flicker through my mind as quickly as her feet do across the ground.

Happy beginnings and wedded bliss giving way to the stress to succeed and financial strain. Late night lovemaking dissipating into cold sheets beside me as he worked in the bunkhouse so as not to wake me up.

Sweet nothings replaced by harsh words, and excuses made to explain away the changes in him or between us. Justifications that he was simply trying to make this work. That he was under so much pressure to succeed since our budget was tight and money was running thin.

Thunder rumbles overhead and startles me from my thoughts. It's only then that I realize there are tears staining my cheeks. It's only then that I realize how much hurt and pain and guilt I've kept pent up.

But it's the letter.

The goddamn letter that I don't even have to have in front of me to know every word written in it.

Tatum,

By the time you get this, I'll be gone.

I'm sorry. You deserve better than a letter telling you I can't do this anymore. You deserve better than a husband who can't seem to make things work. You deserve the man you thought I was but couldn't seem to be.

My leaving has nothing to do with me not loving you. Quite the opposite, actually. It's that I've let you down. All my promises have fallen flat. Everything I told you we'd make of this life, I've ruined or lied about so much that I don't have the courage to face you and explain the what or why. To apologize that I wasn't enough. To tell you we're in over our heads and it's all my fault. To tell you that, no matter how much I love you, I can't fix the mistakes I've made.

I'm sorry I wasn't enough. Then again, I've never been enough for you. I thought I could be, but I was wrong.

I thought I could hide all of this from you, but I can't. I thought I could protect you from knowing . . . but I failed.

I'm leaving so you can have a chance at a better life.

Next time, you'll do better than me.

Next time, you'll find someone who keeps his promises.

Next time, you won't give up everything you love for someone else.

Next time, he'll give you what you deserve.

Next time, you'll be able to find someone who deserves the love you give.

Next time . . .

I'm sorry. Know that you were who kept me hanging on. It was your love I took for granted. I just can't go on like this.

-Fletch

RUBY SENSES SOMETHING is wrong because she slows as the sobs wrack my body. As I hunch over the saddle horn and wrap my arms around her neck, I let myself feel all the hate and regret and guilt.

I'm so sick of caring.

So sick of worrying.

Next time.

The phrase haunts and heals me.

Rusty swore Fletcher's car crash was an accident. Distracted driving, he called it. But that letter told me it was suicide. That note was telling me goodbye.

How do you hate someone because of the clusterfuck they left you with when they hated themselves enough they took their own life?

How do you hate them when you still love them? And then, how in the hell do you rationalize that when every part of you is fighting day-in, day-out to wade through and survive and over-come a life in ruins?

Ruby's feet dance beneath me. Her innate nature to comfort displaced and uncertain as I sob, letting out the loneliness and frustration and shame that have been trying to eat me whole.

The thunder rumbles again. The gray clouds stacking one on top of the other look like how my emotions feel inside me. Violent in nature, unexpected in their power, and yet, I've been here long enough to know we won't get any rain today.

There will be no release.

Not from the clouds in the sky anyway.

As I stare up at them with the tears drying on my cheeks and the hitches in my chest subsiding, I realize how right Jack was about so many things. I did let my dreams die for Fletcher's. I let his become mine, and I need to find my own again. I need to take control and get them back.

I've tried my hardest to keep the ranch afloat, to keep it out of foreclosure, and to slowly claw my way out of debt, but I also stopped living in the process. My life became about saving all of this and becoming consumed by anger instead of carving out pieces to enjoy for myself.

And one of those pieces I want to carve out is Jack.

I want to sleep with him.

My laughter bubbles up again, and I know I should be worried that I'm crying one minute and laughing the next, but I'm not. Jack Sutton was also right when he said that I didn't want it to be a mistake.

I just want it to be whatever it is.

However it happens.

Cue the panic.

The worry that I've forgotten how to do it.

Damn insecurities.

"Don't think, Tate. Just do."

So, I close my eyes, hold tight to the reins, kick Ruby's flank, and push her to gallop so that we fly back toward the ranch as I try to let it all go.

As I try to figure out how to find myself again.

As I figure out how to learn to live again.

And maybe dream a little too.

"DID YOU HAVE A NICE RIDE?" Jack's voice startles me, and my heels dig into Ruby's flank, causing her to rear up on her hind legs.

A strangled cry falls from my lips, and I grip the saddle horn to stay on her as Jack rushes forward and grabs the reins I wasn't holding.

"Easy girl," he croons. "Easy there." He continues until Ruby calms some, her anxious hooves stop moving, and she takes the apple he somehow had on him.

"It's the thunder. It spooks her. It . . ." I fall silent as his eyes meet mine from over the top of her ears. There's amusement in them. Restrained desire.

"That's twice now," he says, referring to Willow and her plastic bag incident, and steps beside us so he can run a hand down Ruby's neck to her shoulder. "Next time you take off, you should probably tell someone." His fingertips hit the curve of my knee and skim the top of it.

"I know how to ride, Jack. I'm more than capable." A nervous chuckle falls from my lips because all I can focus on are those fingers of his and how I want them on me.

"No one said you weren't. You have to stop jumping on the defensive anytime someone tells you something, Knox."

"And I told you my name isn't . . ."

"As of right now, it is." His comment is simple, but his gaze, which travels the length of me as I stand in my stirrup to dismount, says a thousand unspoken words.

The slow curve of his smile is a seduction in and of itself.

The thunder cracks just above us, and Ruby rears up before I can get ahold of the horn, and I'm launched off her and right into Jack's arms.

If it weren't so scary and startling, I probably would have laughed at the romance-novel-worthy set-up Ruby just gave me.

But I don't.

Because our bodies are pressed together, our breaths are labored, and time feels as if it moves in slow motion.

Seconds feel like minutes as we stare at each other; the impending kiss something I can all but already feel.

"Third time is definitely a charm," he murmurs, the heat of his breath hitting my lips.

"Looks like you got yourself thrown from a horse there, Tatum," Sylvester's voice comes out of nowhere, and I shove back from Jack. My eighty-one-year-old helper smiles crookedly as he moves toward us.

My jittery hands move as if to pat myself down and make sure I'm okay.

But I know there's only one thing right now that's going to fix the nerves, and that is the man whose warmth still lingers on my skin. The man whose knowing smirk is angled my way.

"Yes. It's the thunder. You know Ruby," I blather.

"Aye. She's a fickle girl," he says, stepping right into the space between Jack and me as if he didn't just see how closely we'd been pressed together. He runs a hand up and down her nose as we both watch, letting the sexual tension ease.

Pat down over, I roll my shoulders and wince.

"The rain bugging your shoulder?" Sylvester asks.

"What's wrong with your shoulder?" Jack asks, eyes narrowing.

"Nothing." I brush it off and turn to get ahold of Ruby's reins.

"She was in an accident a few years back. Driving right out there if you can believe it," he says and points to the front of the ranch. "She had just made the turn at the end of the road and was about two hundred feet or so from turning into the ranch. Some drunk yahoo almost hit her head-on. She swerved. Crashed," Sylvester relays.

"It's nothing big." I shrug, hating any kind of attention when it comes to the accident or the rumors it caused. According to Fiona and her gossip, everyone in town was convinced that I'd crashed on purpose because I wanted attention and Fletcher wasn't giving me enough. Hell, they are probably still convinced of it.

"Nothing big? Fifty miles an hour into a ditch is more than nothing big. Broke her shoulder in a few places when the car rolled. Pins and everything in there," he drones on when all I want to do is end this conversation.

"Shoulder's fine, Syl." I offer him a tight smile and go to open my mouth when Sylvester continues.

"Had some bad cuts. That's what them scars on her chin and neck are from," he continues.

"Those are fine too. You can barely see them," I say, desperate to get the attention off me.

"Was the other driver hurt? The drunk?"

"Just like a drunk driver to escape unscathed." Sylvester snorts. "Never even veered off the road. The asshole spun out and kept going. They had a BOLO out for a dark, four-door sedan, but nothing came of it."

"Probably some kid. Got the shit scared out of him and straightened up," I murmur, but the terror of that night is still as fresh in my mind as the night it happened. The bright headlights swerving toward me. The jerk of my steering wheel as the edges of the pavement grabbed my wheels and pulled my car over. The crunch of metal. The hiss of pain. The smell of destruction.

Jack watches me though. "You let me know if you need help lifting stuff."

I wave him off. "I've been doing all the heavy lifting around here for some time now. I think I can handle it just fine."

Jack doesn't look convinced.

"Mr. Sutton?" I don't recognize the voice, but before I can ask who the heck is on my ranch, Jack glances over his shoulder.

"Yeah?" he says as a man who looks to be in his late teens, early twenties walks out from the stables.

"Who's that?" I ask immediately.

"That's Will," Jack answers, and I swear by the look on his

face as he studies my reaction, he's waiting for me to be on the defensive again.

I am, but I bite my tongue and try to hide it. "And he is?"

"I'm here to help get everything done." He tips his hat my way and grins as if his baby face weren't smeared with dirt and his jeans weren't speckled with remnants of hay.

"Everything?" I repeat, looking at Will before turning back to Jack. "You didn't have me approve—"

"He said you'd be mad," Will interjects, making Jack fight a grin.

"He did, did he?" My hands are on my hips as I lift my eyebrows at Jack. He just smirks, his dimple showing, and crosses his arms over his chest.

"He did." Will takes a few steps toward me as he stutters over what to say. "But I'm a hard worker, and he hired me on a temp basis. I'm new in town so I don't know anything about anything and—"

"And Jack told you to say that?" I ask.

"No," Sylvester says as he takes a step forward, always the peacekeeper. "I did." He nods, slow and steady. "He's a good kid, Tate. He needed some work. We needed some help so I told Jack about him."

I meet all three pairs of eyes, feeling as if I just walked into a planned intervention and hate the feeling.

"Jack." His name is a command as I nod at Will and Sylvester before walking away, expecting him to follow.

His footsteps fall behind me, and I wait until we're out of earshot before I turn to face him.

"This isn't a power play, Knox," he says before I can get a word out.

"Excuse me?"

"You heard me." He leans his ass against the railing at his back and hooks the heel of one boot in the bottom rung. Willow walks around behind him, nudging his shoulder, and he absently puts a hand up to rub the underside of her neck as his eyes lock on mine. "This isn't a power play. I'm not trying to assert my dominance or take your place or, god forbid, know what I'm doing."

"That isn't what I was thinking."

He smiles with a soft shake of his head. "Yes, it was." There is something in his eyes I can't place, and it doesn't make me uncomfortable, but it . . . it makes me feel as if he actually cares. "You're sexy when you're angry. You know that?"

"What did you say?" I ask, his words throwing me for a loop.

"You heard me." His tongue darts out to wet his lips.

"Look, Sutton." He lifts a lone brow, but I smirk. Two can play this game. "I married a man who tried to deflect me with his charm. I won't fall for it again."

That has the flirt melting away from his expression. "Watch it, Knox. I told you not to compare me to your husband."

I snort. "How can I not? You hired a man without even asking me if it was okay and then try to flirt with me so I drop it."

"Last I checked, I am the ranch manager."

"And I'm the owner."

We wage a battle of visual wills as the humidity thickens in the air around us. Sylvester laughs in the distance. There's a clatter of something against a trough. Willow brays behind Jack.

But we just stand in the paddock with the world moving on around us while I try to remind myself that I'm learning to trust him.

"There's nothing I'm going to do here that will harm this ranch."

"Trust is hard for me," I murmur. "Letting more people in to judge me, to gossip about me." I bite the inside of my lip as he pushes off the rail and takes a step toward me. "It's happened before."

"And you fired them." Jack angles his head to the side, his voice gentle, his features soft. Those chocolate-colored eyes of his try to understand, and where I expect to find judgment, I see compassion. "You have to start somewhere."

I nod, not trusting my voice to break and betray how nervous the idea makes me.

"We're coming into season. Will is helping me get everything up to speed, checking all the mares and charting them for me as well as helping with all the day-to-day. It's a busy time, and we're already behind the eight ball."

"I know but—" I try to find the right words when I already know them but pride is getting in the way of letting me say them. "I can't afford—"

"He's interning," Jack says. "He is studying at the junior college and needs some hours for hands-on experience. I told him if he does a good job, then maybe this can become something more. By then, we should have more of a steady income, foals on the way, and I can train him to take my place when I leave."

When I leave.

It's no surprise that Jack has a contract with an expiration date on it or a life to return to . . . but, somehow, he's become an everyday normal in the short time he's been here.

"Thank you." I hate the sudden vulnerability I feel, and my temper riots to combat it. "You still should have cleared it with me."

He chews the inside of his cheek, his stare his only response.

"Jack?" Will calls from somewhere in the stables. "When you get a minute, can I ask you a few questions?"

"Be right there," Jack says over his shoulder. "He's a good kid, Knox. Not everyone's out to fuck you over . . . especially not me."

I nod because the want to trust, the want to believe, the need to be able to do both feel so foreign after being so guarded for so damn long.

Jack begins to walk past me but stops so that my shoulder and arm are against the front of his chest. When he leans closer to me, the mint on his breath hits my nose. "I use charm to deflect your temper. Subdue it," he murmurs. "Not to deflect the truth. I won't lie to you, and I sure as hell won't screw you over." He takes a step back and tips his hat, grin slowly sliding back onto those lips of his. "Well, not unless you want me to."

And just like that, Jack Sutton wins me back over in a way no one ever has, by calming my temper and by soothing the insecurities planted by the hand of someone else.

Seventeen

TATE

"Fiona?" I stare at her standing on the verandah as if she owns the place, and my feet falter.

I don't have anyone visit for months, and in one day, I have Jack and Sylvester bring the new kid Will in and now Fiona has shown up.

"I know I did not do that hair of yours so it could be thrown up in a pony like that and forgotten about." She puts her hands on her hips in contempt, but her bright pink lips curl into a smile. "Come take a break for a few minutes and keep me company."

I know I should get to work since my ride already ate up two hours of my productivity, but I know there is no way I'm going to forgo visiting with her.

Before my boots finish clomping on the stairs, she has her arms around me and a shrill laugh is filling my ears.

"Look at you. You have color in your cheeks for the first time in forever." She steps back and moves her sunglasses off her nose so she can look closer at me. "Hmmm."

"Hmmm?" I laugh. "That's all you're going to say to me?"

"For now, yes."

"Take a seat . . ." My voice trails off when I notice the porch chairs have been suspiciously turned from their normal position looking at the scenery to be facing the stables. "Fi?"

Her coy smile tells me where her thoughts are. "Here," she says as she opens a cooler and pulls a bottle of white wine from it. It's already opened, which would explain the glass already half drank sitting on the table.

"How long have you been here?" I ask.

"Long enough to enjoy the scenery," she murmurs and then lets out a hum of appreciation, her attention toward the stables.

"Of course, you have." Without looking, I plop down onto one of the chairs.

Fiona's hair is perfect, her manicure fresh, and her blue eyes vibrant and alive.

"What's in that?" I ask, pointing to the pink bakery box she must have brought. I haven't eaten since the banana I grabbed before taking Ruby out on our ride four-plus hours ago.

"Muffins."

"Muffins?" I repeat because there's something about the way she says it that has me drawing my eyebrows together.

"I figured you already had the stud, so why not get the muffins to go with him?"

"Jesus," I bark out through a laugh, but hell if it isn't what I need. "Did you—"

"Yes. I did say that." She shrugs unapologetically. "It isn't exactly fair for you to keep him corralled up here all to yourself."

"He's a grown man who can come and go as he pleases."

I don't catch the innuendo until it's out of my mouth, but the quirk of her eyebrow tells me she sure as hell does. "Stud muffins like that"—she lifts her chin out to where Jack is working on something—"are more than easy on the eye and hard to come by." It's her turn to laugh. "Let's hope he's hard and the coming part is easy."

My mouth is agape as her suggestive chuckle echoes around the space.

Jack is showing Will something on the clipboard in his hand. They're squatting on their haunches with their backs to us and their heads leaned forward. I can assume it's our charting system for feed and exercise and medicines, but I'm not looking at that.

I'm looking at Jack's broad shoulders and perfectly showcased ass, the way he talks with those strong hands of his, his forearms flexing with each motion.

I keep picturing the look in his eyes the other day when he put me in my place.

When he told me the things I needed to hear that seem to be on repeat in my mind.

"Mmm-mmm-mmm," Fiona murmurs, and when I look her way, she meets my eyes. "You're telling me you haven't hit that yet?"

"I don't even know what to say to you."

"Men have been talking like that for years. It isn't a crime to be a woman and talk about a man how they talk about us." She takes a sip of her wine and keeps her eyes on mine from above its rim. "He's like a seven-layer dip. Sexiness layered upon a good body atop attractiveness—"

"That's the most absurd analogy I've ever heard."

"It can be absurd all you want so long as you get to the *layering* on top of each other part." She winks, and I bring my own glass to my lips because I have no words.

The wine is crisp and sweet and welcome, and even though I know I'll probably regret it later when I'm tired and sluggish, I take another drink.

"So?" She draws the word out.

"So?"

She is fighting her smile like a little kid trying to contain a secret. "So, how are things?"

"Good. Better."

"I bet they're better." Her laugh carries down to the men and Jack waves in greeting as Will shields his eyes to look our way before turning back to his work. "My, oh my, the man grew a goatee."

"Fiona." I'm not sure why her name comes out as a warning, but it does. Maybe it's because I don't want her to say what's been on my mind late at night. Then again, maybe I do.

"My third husband had one. We'll just say the feel of it between my thighs is the only fantasy I've ever had that he stars in."

"Never been with a man who had one."

"See? It's fate. He's just the man to break your goatee cherry."

"Goatee cherry?" I almost spit out my wine.

"C'mon, Tee. You know me. I'm part shock-value, part truth, and always pro you get yours."

After that, she doesn't ask anything else about things between Jack and me, though. Even with as forward as she is, I think she knows this is uncharted territory for me that I need to wade through on my own.

Instead, we fall into small talk. My plans for the ranch. How Rhonda Fitz was pissed at her husband so she got drunk at Ginger's and drove her car through the front of the Post Office. How I'm in desperate need of a manicure. If I'll attend the Lone Star charity event of the season this year.

The sun slowly moves toward the west as we sit and polish off the first bottle of wine and decide to have a sip or two of the second one.

"So, how's he working out?" she asks and lifts a piece of huckleberry muffin to her lips.

I exhale a long, audible sigh that speaks for itself, but the wine has me smiling like the cat that ate the canary. "He's frustrating and a know-it-all and . . ." The man can kiss like there's no tomorrow.

"And?" she prompts while her eyes flicker between the stable and then back to me.

"And what?"

"You like him, don't you?" My wine glass halts midway to my mouth as I contemplate telling a bald-faced lie with the truth. Fi points at me. "Don't you lie to me. It's written all over that gorgeous face of yours."

"You got a second, Knox?" Jack catches me off guard because I didn't notice him walk this way. A slow, sinking part of me knows that this whole situation is about to make me uncomfortable on so many levels. Between Fi's forwardness and Jack's tell-it-like-it-is attitude, I'm certain I'm in over my head.

"Talk about a tall drink of water," Fiona murmurs appreciatively under her breath, her eyes roaming the length of him. I sit up, suddenly feeling like a kid caught ditching school, and set my wine glass down.

"Yeah. Sure. What did you need?" I ask.

"She was just playing hooky for a bit," Fiona says, her Texan accent suddenly becoming a little more Southern and a lot more seductive. "You gonna get mad at her for that?"

"No, ma'am," Jack says as he walks up to the foot of the ve-randah and tips his hat in a way that I swear only happens in old-school western movies. His grin is wide, and his eyes crinkle at the corners.

There's an unexpected thrill that shoots through me, which I blame on the wine I've consumed but is really because I've already decided I'm having sex with him.

"And who might you be?"

"Jack Sutton," he says, his boots clomping on the wood as he walks toward her to shake her hand. I swear that, if I didn't know any better, she holds out her hand for him as if she's hoping that he'll kiss the top of it, which he doesn't.

Still, I'm startled by the small streak of jealousy that fires through me.

"Fiona Camden." She bats her lashes. "Such a pleasure. Is my girl here behaving herself? She's been known to have a wild temper."

I roll my eyes.

"Now, I wouldn't know about that." His tone says the opposite of his words.

"Life would be so much easier if you tamed it," Fiona says.

"What are—"

"*Her wild* is one of her best parts," Jack says, looking at me for the first time since stepping up here. But it's the look that he gives me—eyes intense, expression sincere—that knocks me speechless.

Even more so, it leaves Fiona in the same boat as he studies me and she stares at us.

I scramble for something to say. Anything. "You needed me? You said you did. What did you need?"

Jack's smile widens at my nervous rambling. "How's the wine?"

"It's fine—I'm not—Fiona—"

"Girl, will you listen to yourself?" Fiona says through a laugh as she slaps a hand on her knee, her own wine sloshing over the side of her glass. "You do not need to apologize for a little mid-afternoon drink with a friend. Does she now, Jack?"

"Not in the least," he murmurs, looking back to Fiona, and I finally feel like I can breathe when he does. "Everyone needs a little release sometimes."

"That they do," Fi agrees.

"I didn't mean to interrupt." He sets the bag he had been holding down and then raises his arms to lift his hat before resettling it on his head. Neither Fiona nor I miss the flex of his biceps.

"Interrupt away," Fi says, garnering another smile from Jack.

"You're a troublemaker, aren't you, Mrs. Camden?"

"That's Ms., and yes, I just might be."

"Everyone needs a friend who is," he says before turning to me as if remembering I'm still here listening. I'm still busy trying to get over his *her wild is one of her best parts* comment. "I need to schedule some time with you to go over a few things."

"Things?"

"Breeding schedules," he says. "The mares are starting to show signs that they're getting close to heat, so I want your approval of which studs to line with which mares to ensure success."

"And how exactly do they show it?" Fiona asks.

His chuckle is like sandpaper over my skin but in all the good ways. The twist of his lips and shake of his head says he isn't walking into Fiona's trap. "We'll just say that when a female is in heat, any cowboy worth his salt knows it."

"Mmm. And how do you go about picking the right stallion?"

"Animal attraction is something you can't deny." He turns to face me again, eyes holding amusement but darkening with something else. "Tomorrow perhaps?"

"Yes. Sure. I'm free in the afternoon."

"You can go over it now if you want," Fiona interjects. "I was just getting ready to head out."

His smile is slow and lazy as it spreads over his lips. "No need to. I have to go take a shower."

"A shower?" Both Fi and I say in unison. I'm sure she's imagining his slick muscles in the shower while I'm wondering why he's cutting out of work early.

Ha. Who am I kissing—kidding, I mean kidding. Oh, forget it. I'm imagining the same thing she is.

It must be the wine.

It has to be the wine.

"Yes. Shower." He grabs the bag he just put down and moves it to the table next to me.

"What's this?" I ask, my head slightly spinning as everything about Jack assaults me. Dimples. Eyes. *Him.*

"Steaks."

"Steaks?" I squeak out.

"Mm-hmm. You said you were going to cook me dinner, Knox. I brought the steaks. Now I'm going to go take a shower because it's rude to show up to dinner sweaty and stinky when someone has taken the time and trouble to cook for you."

His smile says he has my number.

Mine says he's a smug bastard.

"You were serious?" I laugh because, clearly, he was. My pulse is suddenly racing at the idea of us sharing a meal together.

Alone.

"As a heart attack." He takes a step back and purses his lips to see if I'll call chicken, which I don't. "See you in about an hour." He turns to Fiona. "It was a pleasure meeting you, ma'am. I hope to see you around here more often. Tate's laughter is a rare thing, but it's been ringing out over the ranch all afternoon. That's because of you."

With a nod, Jack turns on his heel and heads down the stairs, giving both of us a perfect view of his ass and strong shoulders as he moves toward the bunkhouse.

"If you don't screw that man, Tatum Knox, there is something definitely wrong with you," she all but sings under her breath.

"And how exactly am I supposed to respond to that?"

"Say, yes. Say, what the hell, I deserve it. Say, *I deserve him.*" She murmurs something under her breath that I can't quite make out and pulls my attention to her because daydreaming about Jack is how I got in this mess in the first place. "And I love how he calls you Knox."

"I hate it."

"Why?" she asks.

I shake my head as if it isn't important. It is kind of silly that I want to hear him say my name so I know how it sounds on his lips.

"I mean . . . what do I . . ."

"What do you do now?" she asks. "You take your glass of wine and strut that cute little butt of yours inside. You primp and shave and lotion and spritz every crack and crevice of that body because, let's face it, you want him to explore all of those places. You want to feel his goatee in all of those places." She winks and mock shudders as if she's the one experiencing it. "You wear something casual but not ranch-y. You let that hair down and do simple makeup. You know, because you want him to notice but you don't want to look like you tried too hard or care too much."

My laugh is laced with nerves. "But he works for me, Fi. Isn't that a big enough problem in and of itself?"

"Yeah, but he'll be gone in, like, what? Four months? Five months?"

"Something like that."

"Perfect. A little something to get over Fletcher. A man to make you realize you deserve better and show you a hint of what else is out there. It's actually ideal since there isn't the option of long-term ties."

"It's one dinner. No one said anything about long-term anything or a relationship."

"But you wondered about it. It's all you've ever known, so it's natural to be scared of entering into something that is the opposite." She reaches out and pours the rest of the bottle into my glass. "Sex. An action. A verb. Don't overthink it."

"I told myself earlier today that I was going to own it. Own this. But it's so much easier said than done."

"True, but so is seducing a woman at the same time as asking her to cook you dinner." She clucks her tongue. "But I just watched a man tell you that you're cooking his dinner, and we *both* swooned. Either we're that gullible or he's that good."

"He's that good," I say.

"Then he'll probably be good at everything else too."

And it's those words, the ones I needed to hear that make me laugh louder and longer than I should.

They also tell me what I already know.

I'm having sex tonight.

Holy shit.

Eighteen

TATE

"You said the other day that someone died, and that's why you needed a change of pace. Do you mind my asking who?" My sudden need to know more about him stepping in the way of what comes next.

His chewing falters momentarily, and he takes his time finishing his bite before leaning back in his chair. There's something in his expression, almost as if he's questioning whether or not he should tell me.

"It was my father."

My heart clutches for him. I think of my own father and how love doesn't overshadow what he did. Much in the same way I feel about Fletcher I guess.

"I'm sorry."

"Thanks." It's all he says, and I give him a few moments, thinking the conversation is over but hoping maybe he'll give me a bit more of himself. "He was a tough old bastard. The two of us were oil and water. Butted heads more than anything. I was . . ."

When his sigh crawls across the space, the regret in it is audible. "I was stubborn. He wanted me to stay and help him. He wanted me to bend to his every will, and I refused."

"What did he do?"

His smile is soft, his eyes have a distance to them, but he looks down to what's left of his steak when he speaks. "Horses. Cattle."

"Was it a big ranch?"

"Nah." A quick shake of his head is followed by him taking a sip of his wine. "I felt smothered. Undervalued. I wasn't a ranch hand, I was his son, damn it, and didn't I deserve the respect of that? I did everything I could to win his approval while others just walked into his world and got it."

The raw honesty in his voice is heartbreaking. The regret and hindsight he learned in time palpable.

"Like who?"

"My sister. My brother."

"I can see how that would be hard to grow up with."

"It was. I had a sister I resented because he was always consumed with her and her problems and I was sick of being overshadowed by that. When my brother was still alive, he brought his own set of issues to the table." He twists his lips and nods retrospectively. There is a big part of me that wants to know what happened to his brother, but I'm not going to ask.

"I'm sorry," I repeat.

"Thanks. I don't know, maybe I wanted to prove that my dad was a dinosaur and his ways were archaic. Maybe that I was better than him. But . . . horses are horses. Cattle are cattle. The land is the land. Sure, there will be advances in technologies and methodologies, but in the end, those three things remain the same."

"I think we all go through that phase." I know I did and can still replay that last conversation with my parents verbatim. It never gets easier either.

"Yeah." He pours more wine in both of our glasses. "But he was from the generation that thought boys were always supposed to act like men. His rules were brutal, his punishments for breaking them even more so. My sister could do no wrong when I could do no right."

"Did you ever go back to visit?"

"When my sister screwed up, I'd be summoned back. He was too busy with the day-to-day and would make an excuse for me to return home so I could fix what he was tired of fixing."

"Your sister . . . what . . ." I don't want to pry more than I already am, but I'm trying to understand him and maybe trying to find answers myself too.

"Alcohol is her poison of choice. It was how she coped with our mom skipping out when we were kids."

"I'm sorry, Jack."

"It is what it is. My dad wasn't exactly the most faithful man, and she got fed up with that. Or, at least, that's what she said. Personally, I think she felt like she was too good for the lifestyle my dad lived and too selfish to want to be strapped down with kids. Too bad she didn't realize that before she had us, huh?"

My heart hurts for the little boy who had to go through that as well as for the grown man who I'm sure is still affected by it.

"He didn't remarry?"

"No. It's probably for the best he didn't."

"So, you just left and never went back? What about your brother?"

His eyes hold mine for a beat as he works through his thoughts in that measured way he has.

"I went back, but things between my father and I were always strained." He shrugs, focusing on my first question. "So, I went back less and less. I made excuses as to why I couldn't make the trip. Of course, I regret those decisions now because I know he was trying to teach me how to be the man I needed to be to deal with what life was going to throw at me."

"Jack—"

"No. I deserve the guilt. Sometimes, when you make decisions when you're young, you stick to them when you're older even when you shouldn't so that they weren't made in vain. Pride can be a nasty bitch. It was in my case." He takes a bite, and I move my dinner around on my plate because he's hitting closer to home than I'd like to admit.

His description of how he felt when he'd visit even more so.

I think of when I lost the baby. I had been six months along and I was scared and sad and just needed my mom. Sure, I was still new on my adventure with Fletcher, but I was so homesick and so lonely that I'd tried to call her. She picked up.

Then my dad hung up on me.

But she never called me back.

Nursing a broken heart from both the loss of my baby and the official loss of support from my mother, I still spent months checking the missed call logs, hoping maybe she would call.

She didn't.

And I hate my dad for that.

"He got sick. He didn't tell anyone until it was too late for anything to be done to save him. My sister called me to come home." Pain flickers through his eyes as he clears his throat. "I—I was in the middle of a huge deal. A transaction of sorts. I was trying to be the big wig throwing his weight around—"

"What was the transaction?"

His attention stays locked on the slow swirl of wine he creates in his glass. "I was buying a ranch, taking advantage of the owner of a small ranch that was going belly up by throwing him a shitty bone from a rich landowner. I knew from the start that the buyer was essentially going to take everything that rancher's family had worked decades to build and dismantle it."

His gaze lifts to meet mine, silently asking me if I understand things he hasn't even said. I twist my lips, and my hands tighten on the stem of my glass.

"Yeah, Knox. You heard that right. I was screwing the little guy for the sake of the big guy. I thought I was making a name for myself, so when my dad called, I assumed my sister had fallen off the wagon, and he just wanted me to come home and clean up her mess again." His throat bobs. "He wasn't playing."

"Oh, Jack," I say, the break in his voice killing me. The pain on his face is so raw and unguarded that I reach across the table and squeeze his hand. I'm actually surprised that he lets me.

"When I finally took the call from my sister and she was sober and crying and begging me to come home, I knew it was serious. We talked as I ran through the airport to try to get to him. I made him every promise he asked for just so he'd hold on a little longer, but he died before I could get there. I was young and so stupid to think I was too good for him and his ways . . . and he was old and too stuck in his ways to see that all I needed was a bit of freedom before taking on the responsibility that came with the name Sutton."

"Don't you think he knew? Don't you think he was proud of you?" My voice is soft, laden with compassion as I voice words I often wonder about my own father.

He clears his throat and nods. I give him a minute to gather himself before he continues. "He let me roam when I needed to. He let me make mistakes so I could learn without stepping in. He let me live out from beneath his shadow, and I didn't realize it until it was too late to thank him for it."

"And now?" I ask.

"And now his ranch is mine and Lauren's, who's my sister, and we have to figure out what to do with it."

"Is that where you're heading when you're done here?"

He nods and takes his time placing his fork atop his knife on his plate. "Yeah. It'll be the busiest time of the year on the ranch then. The place could run by itself really, but it needs someone to lead it all. That and I promised Lauren I'd be back." He runs a hand over his jaw and purses his lips. "It's going to be hard . . ."

"How so?"

"I'll acknowledge the one thing I've never really done before—that I am proud to be a Sutton. That I am proud to be his son."

I shift in my chair, my feet accidentally bumping his beneath the table, and let the heaviness of the conversation settle.

"Why here, Jack? Why me?"

"I told you. A friend of a friend of a friend . . . and because of karma." His voice is barely a whisper, his eyes taking their time to find mine.

"Karma?"

It takes him a moment to respond. "That transaction I brokered didn't sit right with me. Sure, I made good money off the knowledge I exploited, but when I stepped back, when I went home and looked at how hard my dad had worked for everything just so I could have it one day, it really hit home." He leans forward and taps his wine glass to mine. "I needed to make right with what I did to the other rancher . . . with a lot of things, really. I needed to help someone save their ranch instead of help the sharks take it."

Tears well in my eyes because he has no clue how long I've been keeping the wolf knocking on the door at bay or how much I really do need his help, even if I've only just admitted it to myself.

"Hey." He squeezes my hand, and I draw in a deep breath. "I'm not a bad man, Knox. I'm just trying to find my feet and figure out who I am."

"And are you getting closer to figuring out who Jack Sutton is?"

"A bit. He's a man who needs to get back to basics and who

needs to remember what his dad taught him—that horses are horses and cattle are cattle and land is land and it isn't all that complicated so long as you respect them. A man who should have walked away from this place and the woman with a fiery temper and *wild* streak who lives here but who just couldn't seem to . . ." The undercurrent that has hummed all night sparks to the surface. "And now doesn't want to."

Nineteen

TATE

Nerves rattle through me.

I wash one dish after another, more cognizant of the weight of Jack's stare than I ever have been before.

But what happens next? How does one go from a serious conversation at dinner to what we both know is going to happen now that the meal is over?

"You can at least let me help," Jack says.

"You bought the steaks." I glance over my shoulder to where he's leaning back, arm over the chair beside him as the finger of his other hand runs over his bottom lip. His shirt is dark with the cuffs rolled up to his forearms. His hair is styled with gel and looks darker than it normally does.

He cleans up well. Very well.

"Technically, you cooked since you grilled them too. I didn't do much, so doing the dishes is the least I can do."

"Humph."

"And that sound means what exactly?"

"It means I'm not complaining about the view right now."

The sponge I have on the plate in front of me falters, and a nervous laugh falls from my lips. I try to cover its obvious sound with an unladylike snort. "You mean a woman in the kitchen cleaning the dishes? Don't expect the barefoot or pregnant part, Sutton."

"Nah, I couldn't give a rat's ass about the dishes." There is shuffling at my back. "Just the woman standing there, *Knox.*"

I know he's right behind me. I can sense him before his fingers graze over the nape of my neck and shift my hair to the side.

When the warmth of his breath feathers over my skin, every part of me freezes.

And aches.

And wants.

"Jack?" His name is a breathless syllable as he reaches around me and turns the faucet off.

"Hmmm?" he murmurs, and although we aren't even touching, I can still feel the rumble of it.

When I turn, he's inches from me and makes me aware of everything: the nearness of his lips, the wine on his breath, the warmth of his body. The anticipation is almost tangible in the air around us.

"My name is Tate," I whisper in the silence.

"I know what it is."

"Say it."

His smile is slight, but his eyes are loaded with the same desire that has been rioting through me all night.

When I opened the front door to see him standing there in a button-up shirt and genuine smile. The expression on his face—eyes wide, lips lax, fingers itching to touch—when he admired the simple maxi dress I threw on.

When he took the bottle of wine from me, hands closing over mine and holding it there longer than is normal before pulling it away.

When he eyed me across the dinner table, the conversation giving way to the sexual tension.

"Is this what you want?"

I nod.

"Tell me," he says, his fingertips trailing down my bare arm, goose bumps chasing in their wake.

"Jack." It's a soft moan as his hand slides to the small of my back.

Kiss me.

"Tate."

It's the only word he says before his lips crash against mine and he pulls me flush against him.

Where the last time I hesitated when he kissed me, this time I dive right in. I allow my hands to run up the plain of his chest to his shoulders to thread through the hair at the nape of his neck.

My lips take hungry sips against his. My tongue demands more with each graze against his. My nipples harden and ache as his hands find their way to cup my breasts.

The moan I release is a reflex I can't help, and I tighten my hands, which are still fisted in his hair.

"Christ, Tate." His groan pulls on every nerve in my body to want more, to need more, of him.

I'd say it's the copious amounts of wine I drank that has given me this heady buzz, but I know the way I feel has nothing to do with the wine and everything to do with Jack Sutton.

Absolutely everything.

Maybe the wine just let me lower my guard so I could relax enough to enjoy the moment.

And maybe it gives me the courage to say, "I want you, Jack."

He nips my bottom lip and pulls on it before he leans back. When his eyes meet mine, they're a mixture of desire and patience that I'm not sure how he controls because every part of me itches to touch and taste and take more.

"I've wanted you since that first time you threatened to shoot me." His chuckle rumbles against my lips as they meet mine again with a lot more urgency and a little less finesse than before.

This time, they tell me they aren't stopping.

His fingers grab the fabric of my dress and inch it up until he can slide his hand beneath it and cup my ass.

Moments pass in an assault on my senses.

His hips grind against me; his cock hard and tempting. My nails dig into his shoulder through his shirt. His mouth laces kisses down my neck to tease and taunt the soft spot on the underside of my jaw. My hips press against his, needing so much more than a hard dick through soft clothes. His hand yanks my leg up to his hip and holds it there while his other slips beneath the lace of my panties.

And then he touches me.

Holy shit.

My body lights on fire when his fingertips run over the bud of my clit and then slide into the wetness below.

We both groan when he tucks two fingers into me, and our lips meet again, his tongue darting in and out of my mouth in perfect cadence with his fingers.

"Fucking hell, Tate," he groans into my mouth as my fingers work clumsily on the buttons on his shirt.

It's hard to concentrate on anything other than the sensations he's pulling from me, but I want his skin. I need to feel it, see it, run my tongue over it.

Lose myself in it.

In him.

He takes his hands off me to shrug out of his shirt before trying to dive back in again, but I stop him.

I'm crazy for doing it because I can feel my body already burning the fuse and lighting its way to detonation . . . but I put my hands on his shoulders and just look at him.

The toned torso. The sun-kissed skin. The scar running over his left pec. The happy trail at the base of his abs.

"Tate?" he asks in a husky voice as he tucks a piece of hair behind my ear.

Forcing a smile to work through my sudden nerves and insecurities, which are running rampant, I focus my attention on unsnapping the button on his jeans.

Then tugging down his zipper.

And then on the size of his cock when he shoves his pants down and it springs free.

It feels like it's been forever since I've been with a man, not since Fletcher died, and I hate the riot of emotions that try to fight their way to the surface.

I don't want to acknowledge them or think about them because they have no right to appear in this space and time.

So I reach out and encircle his dick with my hand as I press my lips to his, using Jack to help me through this.

To take something I want—to have sex with a handsome man. A moment where I don't have to think about anything other than him or my own need.

His groan that I swallow with my kiss is a good start.

The way Jack pulls my dress over my head in one fell swoop a close second. How his eyes scrape over every curve of my body, the swell of my small breasts now bared for him, and the blue lace underwear I miraculously found in the back of my panty drawer an even better third.

But it's the way he spins us around and clears the few things left on the kitchen table with a swipe of his hand before laying me back onto it that wipes all thoughts from my head.

"It'll take too long to find the bed," Jack says as his lips find mine again, his smile curved on them.

His lips taunt me as my hips lift to beg him for more. His tongue slides down my neck as his fingers skim up the inside of my thigh, my breath hitching when he pulls my panties off. His mouth sucks on my nipple as he pushes apart my legs, the cool air hitting my most sensitized of skin. He only stops touching me long enough to put a condom on, something I didn't even think of but find oddly sexy watching.

Then his gaze fuses back to mine as his hands grip my hips. "Now, where were we?" he asks playfully and pulls me to the end of the table so that my thighs are parted around his hips and his hard length is lined up perfectly to me.

"Mmm," I murmur as I reach out and scrape my fingertips over that delineation of muscle in the V at his hips. His abs flex at my touch, his dick jerks slightly, hitting my inner thigh.

"Tell me what you want, Tate," Jack says as he presses the head of his cock into me. My body stills, my breath catches, my muscles tense, and we both groan, moan, whatever you want to call it so that it's the only sound that fills the room like a soundtrack for us to begin this intimate dance to.

My eyes close. My hips lift.

"Tell me what you need, Tate."

You.

This.

Me.

Now.

But I don't speak. I can't. I'm swamped with emotions as Jack Sutton bottoms out within me and then stills there as my body accepts and wraps around him.

When the sensation overwhelms me, it's my mewl that tears through the room, matching the pleasurable, burning ache that's rioting through my body.

It's my hands finding his where they are on my thighs and grabbing on to them.

It's my hips that lift to tell him to move. To pull out. To push back in. To grind against me until it feels so good I can't think. I can't speak. I can't open my eyes because all I want to do is absorb every single damn thing he's making me feel.

The nerves I had are obliterated by the sensations Jack is battering me with. One after another as his lips and teeth move along my collarbone and his hips and dick work between my thighs. And the noises he makes—the guttural groans and hisses of pleasure— are an aphrodisiac in and of themselves.

"You feel incredible," he murmurs, breath heating the skin beneath my jaw as his fingers possess and grip my legs before he pushes himself up.

My eyes flash open as he brushes his thumb over my clit, a strum to ignite the embers he left smoldering there. But there's something about meeting his eyes like this—in the dim light of the kitchen with his dick in me and fingers on me and his gaze telling me he wants more—that unnerves me in a way I can't describe.

Too honest.

Too real.

So, I close my eyes and tell myself to let the heat building within me take hold. I want to let Jack overpower my shyness and command that surge of energy and pleasure and bliss to ride through my veins and slam into me so hard that it knocks the breath from me.

"Jack."

And it does.

My hands grip the edges of the table.

"*Jack.*"

My back and neck bow.

Like a battering ram I run whole-heartedly into.

"Jack!" I moan as every part of my body is struck hard and fast by relentless lightning.

I tighten my legs around him as my body shudders, my breath turns to a pant, and my world goes white hot. I pulse around him until I hear my name on his lips . . . until it turns into a groan.

Until Jack is struck by the same damn lightning.

Twenty

JACK

ook at me, Tate.

I grunt as I punish myself. One pull-up after another. The damn refrain a punishing cadence I keep tempo to.

Look at me.

The words that filled my mind with each grind into Tate's body. The same one I repeated with each pull out.

Look. At. Me.

Then all thoughts were lost to the orgasm that tore through me, wave by obliterating wave.

But I think of the words now, of my need for her to see me, watch me, and connect with *me*. Sure, she moaned my name, but she wouldn't fucking meet my eyes. I hate that I wonder if her eyes were closed because she was thinking of Fletcher as I was fucking her when all I wanted was for her to be thinking of me.

My hands are sore. The burn in my arms the only release as I repeat the movement. Over and over.

"Wait. You're leaving?" The look in her eyes matched the tone in her voice—confused, uncertain . . . rejected.

I won't be a mistake.

Those were the words that ran through my head but were so very different from the ones that I said to her. *"It's probably best this way, Tate."* A tight smile, a soft kiss on her lips, and then a step back when all I wanted to do was dive back in again. *"We blurred a lot of lines tonight. You need to make sure you're still okay with this. With what just happened."* Another brush of lips before I slid my hand over her hip and let it come to a rest on her ass. *"Sleep in tomorrow. You might have a hell of a headache from the wine anyway."*

My shoulders ache, but I force myself to remember why I walked away. Of why I had to. Of what the fuck I just did.

But the ache doesn't do shit to erase the hurt that was in her eyes or the war that waged over her features as she kissed me one last time and then closed the door.

My chest burns. My breath is harder to catch. My heart is pounding in my ears.

"Jack. Son. I need you to come home. There are some things I need to tell you. About your sister and your brother."

That first phone call my Dad made to me. Who knew it would be the one that would start this whole goddamn ball to roll down the hill and lead me here?

My muscles scream with an ache that can't even begin to rival the one in my chest or the emotions I felt—still feel—after all was said and done.

The need to outrun or outdo the memory of that day is still burning strong.

But it's the guilt that eats at me. Why I felt it then and why I couldn't give a fuck less about it now.

"Jack-Jack . . . I'm so sorry. Dad died."

My arms falter on the pull-up. My strength wanes as I am hit with the emotions of that day. I'd been in the airport, rushing to get home, with my phone to my ear in the middle of hundreds of people trying to get somewhere and feeling as if I were lost.

It was as if I had lost something I hadn't realized I needed.

All the hatred I held on to was gone.

All the rebellion had no purpose.

All the love I felt for him would never be known.

At least I had the chance to though.

At least I was given that.

Twenty-One

TATE

I hate that I wait for the sound of his engine and that I expect to see his truck's headlights flash through my bedroom window as he heads to the bar.

I hate that I wish he would have stayed tonight and that he was probably right. We're adults who work together and need to keep working together. We won't be able to do that unless we are on sure footing despite the desire still burning beneath the surface.

I love that, even as the night burns into the morning, his truck never starts. Its lights never cause shadows to dance over my walls.

I love that, for the first time since Jack has come here, he doesn't go to the bar.

As I sink into sheets that used to smell of my husband, I replay the events of the night and dream of another man instead.

And I'm okay with that.

Twenty-Two

TATE

"You needed to talk about schedules?" I ask when I enter the stable. The butterflies that have been flittering with anticipation of seeing Jack again are in full flight.

When he looks over to me from where he's teaching Will something, I know he feels the same way I do.

Unsated.

Satisfied.

Wanting more.

So many contradictions at the same time.

The slow spread of the smile on his lips does more than should be legal to my insides. The subtle soreness from the sex we had last night is forgotten as the sweet ache of wanting him again spreads throughout my body.

"Good morning," Jack's voice rumbles.

"Morning, ma'am," Will says, and it takes all that I have to look his way and smile.

Because it's Jack who owns my attention as I remember what the rasp of his goatee feels like against my skin. What his fingertips can do. What his cock can accomplish.

"Did you have a good night?" Jack asks with a lift of one eyebrow and amusement loitering in the chocolate-color of his eyes.

"No complaints here," I say, and I'm sure my cheeks flush because I swear I'm wearing a neon sign above my head that reads: This girl had great sex last night. "What about you two?"

"Homework's always a good time," Will jokes.

"Television. A workout. A good dinner. Can't complain either," Jack says, but when Will looks down to what they were doing, Jack flashes me a megawatt smile followed by a wink that erases any and all awkwardness I had feared would be between us.

"Schedules?" I ask as I suppress my own grin.

"Yes. Will and I are coordinating with a local ranch as well as a few from farther away to get quotes so we can keep the bloodlines from becoming too linear."

"That's always important," I muse as I step forward and look at what they have worked up. Austin is about two hours away. Dallas two. Oklahoma four.

I twist my lips and worry about the logistics and the costs associated with his proposal. And then, of course, the veterinary bills, having to pay Jack his salary, and not having sold Ruby yet . . .

The sigh I emit is one reflecting serious concern.

"This is extensive," I murmur, silently adding everything up.

"And much needed after looking at how the breeding was handled before. You need to go outside."

I meet Jack's eyes over the paperwork, and for the first time ever, I truly trust him. Blame it on the sex or the conversation last night or whatever works, but I feel like he really is out for the good of the ranch.

"I know." I twist my lips and take a step back. "It's just going to take me some juggling on money to make it all work."

"As is expected. If it helps, I do have a few of the owners of the studs who are interested in keeping the foal. Some are willing to hold off on your payment for the stud fee so long as, upon the delivery of a healthy foal, you deduct the fee from the purchase price."

I can't remember anyone ever offering this to us in the past. "I don't understand," I say even though I do.

"It's good to know people," Jack says nonchalantly, as if he has no idea he's just secured the ranch a future income without me having to outlay any cash on the front end. "And I'm working on a deal that might secure things on a consistent basis."

Apprehension smothers any hope that might attempt to take hold. Fletcher used to say much the same thing, but instead of questioning Jack about it, I review his income projections on the sheet. I also try to work through how I'm going to stay afloat for the next twelve months until those foals are born. Sure, I'll have the income from the current batch of foals that will be born soon, but that's only if I can sell them.

And then if I don't sell them, if I don't—

"Hey, Will, can you go grab that binder on my desk?" Jack asks, interrupting my thoughts.

We both watch Will's long legs eat up the space, and the minute he's out of earshot, Jack lowers his voice. "We'll figure out the in-between, okay? I know that look on your face, and I'm working on it."

I refuse to meet his eyes and nod, feeling slightly overwhelmed. The high of last night is replaced so easily by the worry of today and the constant apprehension over how I'm going to make the finances work.

"Here you go," Will says, saving me from having to face Jack.

"Thanks," Jack says.

"Is that all?" I ask, needing to go groom the horses and use the time to figure out everything.

"Yeah." Jack's voice is gentle where it had been almost harsh in the past. "Wait. There is one more thing. The feed that was delivered yesterday . . . is that the same quantity and mixture you always order?"

"Yeah." My response is cautious as I look between the two, hating the tingles I'm getting on the back of my neck from it. "It's on a schedule from Lone Star Feed. Why? What's going on?"

"Nothing," Jack says with a shake of his head as he closes the binder with all the breeding info and grabs his keys from his pocket. "I'll be back in a bit. I have to run into town."

There's something in the way he makes the comment—an underlying anger I don't understand—that has me chasing after him as he strides out of the stable.

"Jack. Wait up. Where are you going?" He doesn't wait for me, forcing me to run after him. "Goddamn it, Jack! Tell me what in the hell is going on."

I grab his arm and yank on it right as he gets to his truck. When he turns to look at me, his face is a mask of measured fury that has me stepping back momentarily.

"They're cutting your grain."

"Cutting it?" I ask because I have no idea what that means, only that he's livid about it.

"Yeah. Cheating you by adding the cheapest filler to your high-end grain." He yanks open the driver's side door of his truck.

"You knew this and you were going to leave without telling me." For some reason, it's easier to focus on him than on them. "Don't you think I had a right to know?"

"This is where you trusting me comes into play," he says with a subtle nod. Where my voice is shrill, his is even as can be.

"But—"

"You hired me to manage the ranch, now you need to let me do my job, Knox." He climbs in and slams the door with a reverberating slam, his elbow resting on the open window as he looks at me, the harsh lines etched in his handsome face slowly softening.

"How did you—I mean, what makes you think we're being screwed?" I ask still trying to wrap my head around it all.

Jack's usually stoic expression struggles against the anger I can see fighting its way through. "I've suspected it for a while but wasn't sure until just now. The pellets varied so much from one batch to the next, but I needed to get a new shipment to confirm it. I wasn't sure if your records were off because of an honest mistake, a past employee who was pissed about pay and skimming product, or possibly even you. Hell, you were learning as you went for the most part, so I was waiting to get our first full shipment so I could know for sure."

"Those assholes," I mutter and shake my head, feeling both dumbfounded and duped. My judge of character questioned once again, my ability to trust outright tested anew. "I don't even know what to say."

"Will saw it right away. It was good to have him here for that," Jack explains.

"Christ," I say as I turn my back and step a few feet away from him so I can work through my thoughts and emotions on this.

Bracing my hands on the top rail and a foot on the lowest one, I hang my head and try to wonder how I could have missed this.

"Don't beat yourself up about it, Tate," Jack says as I hear the truck door open and the crunch of his boots on the gravel before he steps up beside me, his posture mimicking mine.

"I should have seen it. I mean, all this time I've been paying a fortune for the top-of-the-line shit while I've been getting bottom of the barrel crap." I blow my bangs out of my eyes and shake my head, mentally chastising myself. "I did call them months ago to ask why there was such a color variation in the pellets I'd received. There'd always been some, a few light brown pellets amid all the dark brown ones, but the mixture was beginning to change with each delivery so that there were more of the lighter ones. They told me it was a new supplier they were using and that it was all mixed together in the silo. I should have known better."

"Don't do that. Don't doubt yourself. Remember what I said to you. This is your ranch, you fucking defend it . . . even when you don't know the answers."

"But why, Jack? To hurt the horses? To get back at me for Fletcher?" Questions run through my head faster than I can process them, but the most prevalent one of all is the hurt I feel. The betrayal. *The everything.*

"Because they can." Jack turns and looks at me. "Because they're assholes. Because, for some reason, they have a hard-on for you and want you to fail."

"They were the first ones I paid back in full after I found out about the outstanding balances. I don't understand."

"You're a female, and assholes like to screw women over to feel like they're bigger men," he says. "That, and as sad as it seems, you're an outsider and this Podunk town doesn't seem to take well to outsiders."

I roll my shoulders and angle my head up to the blue sky above.

"I'll take care of it, Tate."

"And then what? They can laugh that I'm too dumb to have questioned more and high five each other because they were right and it took a man to point it out?" I fight the tears of frustration I don't want to well. "I'm sick of running and hiding, Jack."

I jump when his hand slides to the small of my back. The jolt is a kneejerk reaction, but his hand there has me realizing just how much I miss having someone to talk to when things got tough. Just how much I miss having someone wrap their arms around me to tell me everything is going to be all right.

"Get in the truck."

Twenty-Three

JACK

"Y**ou want to explain to me why I should believe a god-damn word you say?"

It takes every-fucking-thing inside me to keep from knocking his teeth out, but my forearm is pinned to his chest, my temper a riot of anger as he sputters in much the same way my brother did the last time he tried to extort money from me.

This is all too ironic. All too much of a clusterfuck of coincidence that I shake my head and sneer at the asshole.

His eyes are bugged. His breath is labored and stinks of the bag of Doritos he has hidden behind the counter. The sweat ring on his T-shirt that he tries to pass off as high dollar but is a knockoff grows.

"Believe the rumors they say about me, Jed. Believe them and realize this is your chance to do the right thing before I take pleasure in doing all the wrong things," I threaten without a fucking clue as to what the town is saying about me.

This is where keeping my mouth shut has come in handy.

"I swear. It's just . . . it was . . . an honest mistake." Spittle flies as he sputters, and I'm so pissed it doesn't even faze me.

"An honest mistake?" I ask with a laugh. "If it were an honest mistake, *Jed*, then why did you threaten to call the cops the minute I walked in here, huh?"

"I swear. If you'll just give me a second, I can explain."

"Maybe that's how you should have started this conversation rather than taking a swing at me before I ever said a word."

I fist a hand in his shirt and shove him back against the wall before I take a step back from the spineless son of a bitch.

He's the personification of guilt. How he came out from behind the counter the minute he saw me. How, when I asked him why the Knox Ranch was being screwed, he threw a punch as if I didn't see it coming a mile away. How he threated to call good ol' Rusty and charge me with trespassing. How he is still claiming it was an honest mistake without so much as checking an invoice first. He knows damn well what he's been doing.

Fucking unbelievable.

And Tate's been dealing with all of this on her own? She's been managing pricks like this? No wonder she hides up at the ranch.

The owner of Lone Star Feed is still standing there, probably trying to figure out how he can punch back at me and get out of this situation. His eyes dart over my shoulder to where Tate is standing at the doorway, arms crossed, back against the wall, expression completely unaffected by what she's seeing.

The fight to get her to stay in the truck was futile, so I compromised, agreeing to let her come in so long as she stood nice and quiet while I worked.

"I'm waiting." I raise my eyebrows and drum my fingers on the counter beside me.

"It was an honest mistake."

"So you've said."

"We-we have a new employee and he made a mistake on your order." His eyes flicker to Tate, to the side door where the stockroom is, and then back to me.

"Oh, so the person you're pinning this on is back there? Should I go talk to him?" I take a step toward the stockroom, but Jed puts his hands up to stop me.

"He's just a kid. Like I said, it was an honest mistake."

I twist my lips and look down for a sec as if I'm actually buying the bullshit he's spewing. When I look back to him, my eyes are hard, my face impassive.

"So, how new is he? I mean, if this has been happening for some time, you'd think, being the owner and all, that you'd have corrected it. Or at least called the customer and apologized for it."

He blubbers for an answer he doesn't have.

"Look, I get it." I lower my voice, good cop now in effect. "Her old man owed you money. He hurt you and your business, maybe even your finances, so you're getting back at him by screwing over his widow."

He shakes his head emphatically. "I told you, it was a mistake."

The bell rings, signaling a customer coming through the door, and we both turn to see two guys standing there. Jed's face turns red as he stutters. "We're closed temporarily. We—I—business meeting."

"Is everything okay, Jed?" the man asks, his shoulders squaring as he reads the situation.

"Should I ask him about his grain?" I murmur under my breath so Jed hears it, and the sudden jostle of his head tells me I just scared the shit out of him

"Yeah. It's fine, Kenny. Just sorting some stuff out," Jed says. "We'll be open in a few."

Kenny nods, eyes wary as he ushers his friend back out of the store but not before staring at Tate for a second.

"What's wrong, Jed? You didn't want me to ask Kenny about his deliveries? He owns the place up off the south end of Jergens, right? I'm sure he orders a significant amount." I take a step toward the counter where a log of deliveries is sitting on a clipboard. "In fact, why don't I contact all of these customers and tell them they should check their feed because it might not be up to par." When I reach out to grab the clipboard, he yanks it out of the way.

Wouldn't have thought he could move that fast.

"Look—"

"Or maybe I should head over to Ginger's and ask—"

"That isn't necessary—"

"I hear Raelynn's looking for new customers. Hell, she might be two towns over, but she's willing to deliver. I think I'll let her know she should expect some new customers. All it takes is one phone call for the word to get out."

"Leave my customers alone!" he shouts, losing his cool once again.

"Why? I think all of Lone Star should know you're shorting your customers. How many more 'innocent' mistakes have you made?"

"That isn't—"

"But it is—"

"It was only Knox!" he finally shouts, done with the back and forth.

And the minute the confession is out, the minute he realizes I got what I wanted, which was him so worked up that he forgot to keep his lies straight, his eyes widen and his lips fall lax.

"Yep. You did just say that, Jed. Loud and fucking clear." My chuckle reverberates through the room, and a part of me wants to glance toward Tate, but I don't. Instead, I take a step toward him as he takes one in retreat.

"I didn't—I mean . . ."

"Save it. Come clean and admit that you've been cheating her, switching out some of the expensive grain she's been paying for with the cheap grain made from who the fuck knows what because you thought you could get away with it? And you've been doing it for a hell of a lot longer than one month." I cross my arms over my chest, lean my hips against the counter behind me, and just stare at him.

"It won't happen again." His voice is barely audible, and his words do nothing to fix the problem.

My chuckle says as much. I lean in and keep my voice low and even when I speak. "And if you don't believe the rumors about me, then you should believe the ones about Tate. They're all true. She's a ruthless businesswoman who was burned by her asshole of a husband. Her reputation is already shot to hell in this town, so she doesn't give a flying fuck about damaging it further by taking a cheating son of a bitch like you down. She has the records, invoices, pictures of the grain, and witnesses to back her up." When I take a step back, I wink and flash him a grin. "This town might like you, but they don't like being screwed out of their hard-earned money more."

His Adam's apple bobs before he clears his throat, eyes flicking between Tate and me.

"The question is . . . what are you going to do about it to make it right, Jed?"

Twenty-Four

TATE

My cheeks hurt from smiling, my mind reeling from what Jed Bateman just agreed to.

"Did he really say that?" I ask, so stunned and so relieved that I can't really process it.

"Top-of-the-line grain for a year"—Jack glances my way as he flicks his blinker on and flashes me a grin—"free of charge."

I close my eyes and lean my head back against the seat as relief washes over me. This is huge. Bigger than huge. Not having to pay this will allow me a sliver of breathing room when it comes to my bills. I might be able to get current on one or two of the ones I'm behind on.

Or I could let those bills stay where they are and try to catch my mortgage payment up.

Not having to pay for the feed and grain for a year is like free money . . . and that's something I can't remember the last time I had.

I fight back the tears of relief that burn behind my closed lids, and when I finally collect my thoughts, I realize Jack's truck has stopped.

When I open my eyes, I find that we're in a parking lot and he's studying me, a ghost of a smile on his face.

"Sorry. I needed a minute," I murmur as if what just happened wasn't real.

"Take all the time you need." He reaches out and squeezes my hand and keeps it there.

I shift in my seat to face him, my need to say this suddenly very important. "Thank you for doing that."

"You don't need to thank me, Knox."

"But I do. I . . . before—" My sigh fills the cab of the truck as I try to put my thoughts into words, as I try to explain to him the things he probably questions. "I never liked to rock the boat. I never wanted to make waves before."

"And now?"

"And now I'll capsize the damn boat if I have to in order to stand up for myself."

"So I've experienced." His voice is quiet, almost hovering on admiration. "*Why?*"

It's one word but it's so loaded with curiosity that I'm not sure how to answer him.

"Because I gave everything up I'd ever known for him. My family. My security. The life I wanted to lead and, I don't know . . . I lost who I was. The *person* I wanted to be. The person I was." I twist my lips and look out the window toward the little boy with a balloon on his wrist being carried by his father, wondering how I ever let myself do that.

"You'll find her. I'm certain of it."

"I've learned from my mistakes. That I'm too proud to walk away, but at the same time, I'm petrified to take steps toward the life I thought I wanted."

"You're fearless, Tate." He half laughs, half snorts. "Stubborn as hell but fearless."

The veneration in his voice has me swallowing over the lump it formed in my throat while the last part has me laughing.

"Thanks. I guess."

"I'm going to rely on you to keep being both."

I turn back to him. "What do you mean?"

"This deal I'm working right now. It's going to ruffle some feathers in town." He hits his thumb against the steering wheel a couple of times as he looks around. "Rumors are that the Steely Brothers aren't thrilled with the quality of the horses they've been getting from Hickman Ranch. I plan to woo them over our way."

"The Steely Brothers as in—"

"Yes, as in the largest broker of barrel and bronco riding horses in the nation. We have quarter horses, and I intend to convince them ours are better than Hickman's."

"Oh." Caution edges the sound as my insides slowly soar, the hopes I held back earlier this morning finding a leg to stand on.

"It's nothing set in stone, but I sold one of the shareholders a ranch a ways back, and . . ."

"And what?" I ask, but he just shakes his head and laughs to clear the faraway look from his eyes.

"Nothing. I just wanted to let you know that things here in town might get worse before they get better."

"It isn't as if I'm not used to nasty, Jack."

"Yeah, but we're messing with one of their own here."

"I understand. I'll be ready for it."

"Good. But you're going to have to do the one thing you aren't too fond of."

"What's that?"

"Open your ranch up to the Steelys. They're going to want to inspect it. They're going to want to see if it's suitable for them to come and bring their studs during the month to be on standby for when the mares are ready. You're going to have to let them in when you normally shut everyone out."

I chew my lip and stare at him because that doesn't sound like the protocol I remember Fletcher following. Studs don't travel to mares, the mares travel to them, which is a big reason I have been so concerned about the cost.

"How did you finagle this?"

"Because I'm that good." He flashes me a grin that could melt my panties right off, but I have a feeling it's to distract me. I sense that Jack Sutton might have a little more clout and power than he says he does.

That begs the question, just who is he?

"Jack. This isn't normal. I don't understand why a big customer like Steely would take these measures when they are the ones in control."

He leans over and gets close enough that I can smell the shampoo in his hair and see the flecks of gold in his irises. "Because I can sell anything when I believe in it . . . and I believe in you."

My sigh fills the cab of the truck because, as much as that's a believable response, it still doesn't answer my question.

"Enough of this. C'mon." He slides out of the truck without giving me a chance to respond, and I follow suit before he can come around to open the door for me.

"What are we doing?"

"Taking a time out."

"A time out?" I ask.

"You have to celebrate even the small victories when they come, Knox." He places his hand on the small of my back and directs me to the front of the shopping center. "And we just got a small victory."

I let him lead me around the corner to where the old diner with crappy food and even worse service is, and I almost pull him to a stop and tell him that I refuse to eat there, but then I freeze. The diner is gone. In its place is what looks like a bar with a marquis that reads Axe's with a three-dimensional axe as the apostrophe on the sign.

"It's the new hot spot—if there is such a thing in this town." He winks and ushers me to the door. "Work hard, play hard, right?"

"I have a million things to do at the ranch—"

"Stop thinking about work," he says with another smile and another tug on my hand. "Just humor me."

Next time.

It reminds me that I need to stop. That I need to make this the start of all of my next times.

It's hard to think of this simple moment in time with Jack as a new beginning, as a the first step toward my next time—especially because nothing long-term is going to happen between Jack and me—but I have to start somewhere. I have to at least try.

"Fine."

"Fine?" He raises his eyebrows and knocks me over with a shy grin that gives me pause.

"Yes. Okay."

The whoop he rewards me with makes me laugh as he steps to open the front door for me.

The bar's decor is industrial ranch house with iron pipes and dark wood. The bar is on one side and there are designated throwing alleys on the opposite side of it. It's busier than I expected for a mid-afternoon, and a few Lone Star residents who are seated at tables glance our way when we enter. I exhale a breath when they turn back to their business instead of staring at us.

Within minutes, Jack has us on an open throwing lane.

"Who thought alcohol and axes were a good mix?" I ask as

Then YOU happened

he stands beside me to try to show me the best technique to throw one.

"No clue, but if you don't correct your shoulders, you're going to give that man next to you a Mohawk." I gasp in horror, but then he steps up behind me to give me more direction.

My breath catches when he places his hands on my shoulders and presses the heat of his body to my back.

If he is trying to make me concentrate harder, this is not the way to go about it. Every brush of his body against mine, each whisper of touch from him, has me reliving his body on mine—in mine—last night and throwing an axe is the last thing I'm thinking of.

"Like this," he murmurs, his hands and arms shadowing mine as he mimics a throw so I understand what he means.

"Yes. Okay. Sure. I've got it." I try to step forward, to gain some distance, but he stays put.

"Do you always ramble, Knox, or is it only reserved for me?"

I glance over my shoulder, hating and loving that he makes me feel like this. Flustered. Seen. Heard. Admired.

"I'm not. This is just . . . unnerving."

"Unnerving?"

"More like distracting, and if I'm distracted, I'm going to be looking your way and accidentally throw it so . . ." I eye the empty space behind him for him to step into and give me distance. "There are certain parts of your body that I'm sure you're overly fond of."

"I didn't hear you complain about those parts," he says coyly, the grin on his lips telling me he's not complaining either. The way his eyes drink me in tells me his mind is there too.

Aware that people are most likely eavesdropping on our conversation, I stand there, axe over my head ready to throw and question how to answer that question. I'm his boss and we had sex but I don't know what, if anything, that means. I've never done this.

The sex before a relationship thing, so how exactly is one to act?

When we're at the ranch, it's one thing. But here, in public . . . I'm not sure.

And I think Jack sees the panic in my eyes because he just stares at me above the rim of his beer as he takes a drink and redirects the conversation away from everything that is in my expression. "Point the axe that way, Knox." A wink. A lean of his hip against the wall to the side of me. "Throw it. I promise it's therapeutic."

"But what if I accidentally throw it too late and it hits my leg and cuts it off?"

"Christ, woman." He chuckles with a shake of his head. "Then you'd be a peg-leg pirate, and that isn't a good look for a rancher, so I suggest you don't do that." I laugh. "Try it."

With a deep breath and a little yelp of fear, I let the axe fly.

It hits the wood with a *thump* and falls to the floor with a *thud*. "Shit." I reach back to grab another one. "I want to try again."

And this time, when the axe hits the outer edge of the target and sticks, I let out a whoop of satisfaction.

Twenty-Five

JACK

"Wasn't it therapeutic?"

Tate stares at me above the rim of her wine glass, eyes alive, and cheeks flushed as she nods. "It was."

She looks back over to where there is some kind of competition going on. Who knew there were axe-throwing leagues? When I follow her gaze, I catch sight of the two jackasses who've been sitting in the corner paying more attention to us than anything else in here, but pay them no mind.

It's her I'm drawn to.

It's the smile that widens on her lips and the wisps of hair that've fallen out of her ponytail. It's the tension that has eased from the set of her shoulders, and the way she's had enough to drink that she's stopped caring about what everyone else in this bar thinks of her.

Even with all of that, the only thing I keep thinking about is last night and how fucking bad I want to have her again.

Only in a bed instead of on the table.

This time I want to taste her pussy.

This time I want to demand she look at me so she knows it's me who's buried deep inside her.

Christ.

I shift in my seat to adjust for my dick getting hard.

"Thank God, they kicked us off the lane for"—she waves her hand in indifference to the teams of men lined up to compete— "whatever it is that has those men looking way too damn serious. It is not safe for me to throw an axe right now." She holds her empty wine glass up as her laugh rings out. "Cheap date alert, right here."

"That's something that probably isn't best to advertise too loudly," I say jokingly.

"Not like any of them would step within five feet of me." She snorts.

And I'd kill them if they did.

The thought comes out of nowhere at the same time as a cheer goes up to our left. Someone has hit the highest point marker on the target, and I'm grateful for the distraction so I can shake the thought away.

Where the hell did that come from?

But when I look back to her, I know exactly where it came from.

God, she's fucking beautiful, incredible . . .

I lift my finger to the waiter for another round of drinks because I'm pretty sure I need it right now.

"Hey?"

Tate's voice draws my attention back to her even though my mind hasn't stopped thinking about her. "Hmm?"

"Where'd you go?"

"Nowhere." I offer a tight smile.

"Tell me something about you that I don't know." The unexpected question throws me.

"Something about me?"

She bites her bottom lip and nods like an eager kid.

"I thought I was invincible when I was younger."

"Don't we all?" she murmurs as she rests her chin on her hand and leans forward.

"I tried my hand at bronco riding."

"You did?" she asks, her eyes widening as she tries to take a sip from her empty glass and then giggles.

"I did." I lean back. "It wasn't pretty."

"No?"

"No. The scar across my collarbone is a reminder of the end result. A hoof to the chest is never a good thing."

She winces and runs a hand over her own in sympathy. "What made you try something like that?"

I was hurt and rebelling and trying to live up to expectations that I'd never reach. Doing something rash to thumb my nose at my dad seemed like a good idea at the time.

"Stupidity," I say through a laugh. "Quid pro quo." Her eyebrow lifts in acknowledgment. "Why don't you do photography anymore?"

There's a falter in her body language that tells me this is a touchy subject.

Good. It should be. If the images she posted in the newspaper were any indication of her talent, then her putting the camera down is a damn travesty.

"I do sometimes." She looks over to the competition where a huge cheer just went up. "Did you see that? He—"

"Uh-uh, Tate. You are not skating out of answering this question. You have serious talent. Your pictures should be on a wall somewhere."

"I wouldn't go that far." Her lips say the words but her eyes have a flash of regret or maybe *resentment* in them.

"What happened? Why did you stop pursuing it?"

"I had some opportunities, but Fletcher needed me on the ranch."

That's such bullshit, but I bite back the comment about what a crap move that was on Fletcher's part.

Look at me, Tate.

My refrain from last night hits my ears and has me gripping my beer bottle a little harder than I should be.

"Needed you?" I ask as politely as I can. "Because taking photos took too much time away from grooming horses and playing the part?"

Her fingers flexing is the only sign she gives me that what I said was accurate.

My own fists clench in response. My own temper fires at the thought.

"I had some galleries interested in my work. I had some companies who wanted to purchase some." Her voice is barely a whisper but the shame in her tone rings through loud and clear.

"What happened?" I would put money on the fucker's ego being more important than his wife's dreams. It had to be about him. His successes were his. His failures were hers.

"It was bad timing. They called, but I had just lost the baby and—"

"Jesus Christ, Tate." I scrub a hand through my hair and feel like the asshole I am for pressing. "I'm sorry."

Her smile is tainted with melancholy when she offers it with a slight shrug. "It's okay. It's life. It happens."

I reach out and grab her fingers atop the table. "Yeah, it happens but it's still horrible. I don't even know what to say."

"There's nothing to say. I was six months along and . . . then I wasn't." Her voice is soft and loaded with a sadness I know I can't chase away so I don't even attempt to. "Besides, it was a long time ago."

"Did you try again?"

She twists her lips and stares back out the window for a beat before speaking. "The timing was never right after that. A part of the reason I left home was because of the baby and when she was gone, life kind of became about making the ranch work. Another mouth to feed and hospital bills weren't exactly what we needed." Her smile is tight when she offers one, and it tells me that a baby might not have been what Fletcher thought was right but was what she still wanted.

"Even so . . . I'm sorry."

"Anyway, where were we? Photos and the people who wanted to buy them?" she asks, obviously not wanting to stay on the subject, and I nod. "It was shortly after we lost her when they called, and instead of letting me drown myself in work and spend hours getting lost in light and depth and shadows and filters like I wanted to, Fletcher decided it was his chance to make me a part of his world."

"But what about your world?"

She looks down at her fingers twisting on the stem of her glass, regret heavy in her slumped shoulders as her teeth worry over her bottom lip. "I had just walked away from everything I had ever known for him and for the baby we no longer had and for the dream he wanted to chase. There was no going back. Call it stubborn, call it stupid, but I wasn't giving my parents the satisfaction of knowing they were right."

Call it *her wild.*

I nod as I glance around, giving her a moment to gather her

thoughts as I wonder what her life would have been like if she hadn't met Fletcher.

"Look at the pair of us," I say. "Two kids who ran away from their parents to rebel against their expectations but were both too stubborn to admit they were wrong."

"Look at the pair of us." Her smile is soft and genuine, and fuck if it doesn't tug on parts of me that don't need to be tugged on.

Our eyes hold despite the chaos ensuing around us, and it takes everything I have to look away.

To break whatever hold it is this pixie-sized woman with a heart ten times bigger seems to have on me.

"You should start taking pictures again. How you view the world through a lens is something you should share."

"How would you know how I see the world?" she asks cautiously.

"I saw the article you wrote and the pictures that accompanied it. Your words were perfectly fine, but your photos . . . now those were phenomenal."

I swear there are tears in her eyes, but she blinks them away before I can make sure. "Thank you, but . . ."

"And," I say before bringing my beer to my lips, "you should do this more often."

"What's that? Bare my soul?" She laughs at her own joke but I know it's just to deflect.

"Relax. Celebrate." I shrug. "Smile."

Her expression falls and eyes grow quiet. "I haven't had a reason to." The moment is suddenly heavier than either of us expected, and she scoots her chair back abruptly. "Bathroom. I need to go. I think I should. Yeah. I will."

I nod because there's that fluster again. There's her wild that she doesn't even understand she has.

And fuck if I know what to do with either of them.

The buzz of my phone has me pulling it from my pocket and sending the call to voice mail. I'll call my sister later. When I look up, the two assholes from the other side of the bar are standing across the table from me.

They're big boys—shoulders broad, arms crossed over their puffed up chests, and sneers on their faces. A couple of pissed off cowboys is not what I need right now.

"What can I do for you gentlemen?" I ask, my tone one of indifference.

"You having fun?" The dark haired one asks, his goatee barely moving when he speaks, and his eyes are shadowed by his cowboy hat.

I purse my lips and look around as if I'm assessing the bar. "Yeah. The place could use some better music and a few more choices in beer, but for the most part, it'll do." I offer a smile that says fuck you.

"And how about Tatum. Will she do, too?" The bald one says, confirming that their glares from across the room had something to do with the two of us.

"No complaints here." I angle my head to the side, trying to figure out if these guys are here defending poor Jed or from Hickman Ranch. After the blow I landed on them yesterday with Steely suspending his contract, I'm not quite sure which one it would be. "And you are?"

"Concerned citizens."

"Ah." I draw the sound out. The Destin twins, then. "Thank you for your concern, but it isn't needed."

"How about you keep your nose out of her business." Baldy's smile is anything but sincere.

I lean back, cross my arms over my chest, and scrunch my nose. "If it's her business, shouldn't you do the same?"

"We look after our own here."

My laugh is loud and draws attention of those around us, which is what I intended. "Your own? Seems to me you left Tatum on her own to fend for herself after her husband died. If you were looking out for her, why didn't you lend a helping hand at the ranch? Why didn't you step in and teach her what she needed to be doing to make sure she had enough foals to sell off come spring? I mean, those are all things someone would do if they were looking out for someone, right?" I prop my boots on the chair across from me as if their threat doesn't bug me one bit. "But you weren't looking out for her, were you? You're just like every other asshole around here and would rather her lose everything . . . now, why exactly is that?"

"If she thinks things have been rough for her, she hasn't seen anything yet. You should probably talk her into selling," the dark-haired guy says, crossing his arms over his chest to mimic my posture, and probably to make sure I see the size of his biceps.

"And you should probably kiss my ass."

I get the reaction I expect, which is clenching fists and testosterone flaring, and they bump into the chairs across from me to reinforce their bullshit threat. "Who the fuck do you think you are?" Goatee Man growls.

"More than you can handle." I take my time unfolding my legs and standing to my full height, which puts us eye to eye and renders their attempt to threaten me by towering over me non-existent.

"It isn't smart to test us," Goatee Man says.

"I think you have this all backward," I say, taking a step closer. "It's you who shouldn't be testing me." I take a sip of my beer to draw out everyone's attention, to make sure that the rest of the crowd who isn't following the competition is taking notice. "You have no goddamn clue who you're messing with."

"Ranch hands don't worry us," Baldy warns.

But my laugh rings out loud and clear. "You keep thinking that's all I am, and I'll keep trying to figure out who the fuck sent you two assholes because you and I both know you're standing in front of me threatening me for Tate's sake. So, tell me, did Jed send you to make sure we don't tell everyone he's been shorting Tate out of the grain she paid for? Is he afraid others might start checking their orders a little more closely? Oh, no. You must be from Hickman, then. It must suck when another credible horse ranch threatens longstanding relationships you have with huge clients because you rested on your laurels and got lazy." The muscles in their jaws clench, and their eyes bore into mine as I offer them a lazy smile and a go-fuck-yourself glare right back. "Not that? Hmm. Is it her land in general you're trying to run her off? Rumor over at Ginger's is that Fletcher stole that land right out from under the nose of a pair of brothers who thought they deserved it. That wouldn't happen to be you two, now would it?"

"You don't know who you're messing with."

"Another empty threat." This time I smile even wider. "Can I buy you a drink?" I hold my finger up to our server. "You look like you could use it. What'll you have?"

"You've been warned."

"So have you."

They walk off just as Tate gets back to the table, and all of the people slowly turn their attention back to the contest.

"Dare I ask why everyone is looking at me like they saw a ghost?"

"That part I told you about things getting a little rough before they get better?"

"Yeah?" She swivels her head on her neck and looks around.

"The first warning shot was just fired over the bow."

"Let's hope you shot back with a much bigger gun."

I throw my head back and laugh, hoping the two fuckers hear it.

I hope they know we won't be intimidated.

And when I look back at her, the only thought that fills my head is just how bad I want to kiss her.

Right here.

Right now.

Stake my claim so every other asshole in this town not only knows she's taken but also knows she's protected.

I fight the urge that owns me because I don't need to shield her. The damn woman is strong enough on her own. That much I know for sure.

But it's her lips I want.

It's her moan I want to earn.

And fuck if that isn't a problem.

Twenty-Six

TATE

For some reason, I look at the ranch through fresh eyes when we drive through its gates.

Maybe it's because I'm looking at all this land and possibility through the haze of hope, which isn't something I've had for a long time.

I look at the front door of the house and remember when Fletcher carried me over its threshold. Was that the last time I felt it?

Can't be.

There's no way I've lived here for the past six years and not felt it. Is there?

Losing the baby was the first piece of hope I lost. A stillbirth at six months when the nursery had already been painted and would remind me of her every time I walked by was more than enough of a reason to lose some.

Then Fletcher bought Ruby, and I thought maybe we could do this. Live this life and make the best of it because . . . what choice did we really have? I mean a Thoroughbred with a Kentucky Derby winner in her blood was just what we needed. At least, that's what Fletcher told me. We could breed her and sell her foals and make a fortune. I was so ignorant to all the pitfalls in his plan when we bought her, I never considered just how much it would cost in stud fees to make that happen.

Then there was Fletcher's mass purchase of quarter horses, which unbeknownst to us, had been exposed to the neurological strain of the EVH-1 virus. We lost a third of them to it and the vet bills to keep the remainder alive drained a huge portion of our savings.

Another piece of my hope died with each of them.

The pressure mounted, and from what I know now, the bills did too. Fletcher's temperament changed and he had violent mood swings more and more often. The excuses. The secrecy.

Each and every one chipped at my hope until I was left with none at all.

Then he died. Died and left me to deal with a non-existent bank account, a mountain of debt, and my name on everything because his credit was ruined from what he said were mistakes with credit cards he made right after he graduated high school.

"Hey," Jack says. "You okay?"

"Mmm-hmm," I murmur and take another look at the ranch. The setting sun is lighting up the sky in oranges and pinks and casting a glow over the land I own, over the chaos I'm trying to manage.

"Tate?"

I shake my head and look his way, a soft smile on my lips, the wine making me sleepy and sentimental. "I'm good."

He gets out of the truck and opens the door for me, and for the briefest of moments, we stand there staring at each other. There's a neigh of a horse in the distance. A chirp of a bird. A rustle of trees.

But we just stand there, not making a sound.

"I have stuff I need to take care of," Jack says and hooks a thumb over his shoulder but doesn't move.

Come inside.

"Yeah. Sure. Me too."

Please, come inside.

"'Kay," he murmurs, taking a step in retreat without dropping his attention from my eyes.

I don't want to be alone right now.

"Good night, Jack."

"'Night."

We both stand there, though, facing each other, trying to navigate this newfound situation we've put ourselves in.

One I don't have the slightest clue how to handle.

When all you've ever known is relationships and the sex that results from those emotions, how exactly are you supposed to know how to handle the physicality without the rest of it?

Turn and walk, Tate.

One foot in front of the other.

I give Jack one last long look, taking in the sky at his back and the sincerity in his eyes, and then turn on my heel and start heading to my front door.

"Hey, Knox?"

"Yeah?" My pulse races as I turn to look at him, my stomach somersaulting.

"We did well today." His smile is wide, his eyes quiet.

"We did."

THE HOUSE IS SILENT, and my mind is preoccupied thinking of Jack.

Cleaning the kitchen table makes me think of him and what we did here last night.

Walking by the window and looking toward the stable has me wondering what he's doing.

But there's only so much picking up of the house I can do to avoid acknowledging the fact that I'm thinking way too much about a man who I shouldn't be.

It was just sex.

Incredible sex, but just sex all the same.

I blame my turbulent emotions on the fact that I hadn't had sex in over a year. Maybe a small part of it is because the only other person I'd slept with was Fletcher and that has me thinking about it—about him—more than I should be.

Now that I'm telling myself not to think about him, I open my laptop and enter Jack Sutton in the search engine to find out more information on him. The same things that I found when I originally searched for him after he submitted the resume come up, but I'm looking for information about him through a different set of eyes.

I want to know more about him, not just what skills he can bring to the table.

A LinkedIn profile that seems to have gone dormant since it says nothing about the real estate work he told me he did. There is no social media besides a private Facebook account that shows nothing other than his profile picture—an old one, at that.

There seems to be a million Jack Suttons in the world, but I can't find a single thing useful about the one I want.

"Well, shit," I mutter before navigating over to my old photography website. One that has about as many cobwebs on it as Jack's LinkedIn page. I flick through the old images of my portfolio, critiquing them even though years have passed.

"How you view the world through a lens should be shared."

I shove away the nagging thought and close my laptop to reinforce how much I don't need to think about it and pick up my book. But after reading the same page ten times and having no clue what it says, I close the book and stare out the window, allowing my preoccupied mind to wander.

Thoughts of the past and the future merge together. Worries about this new Steely prospect Jack has worked on when I had no clue he was even doing it. If I sell the foals I have when they are born, can I stretch those funds out long enough to last the next eleven to twelve months until the new batch of foals Steely wants are born?

How is that even possible when I already have collectors breathing down my neck? When I have Jack's ridiculous salary, which he's more than earning, to pay.

Ruby.

She has to be that bridge for me.

The thought pains me considering she brought me so much hope, but now hope is coming in other forms.

I press my fingers to my eyes and just hold them there for a few minutes and know that nothing is definite. Of all people, I know that.

How am I going to hold on long enough to make this work?

"Next time you won't give up everything you love for someone else."

The immediate anger I usually feel when I remember what Fletcher had written isn't as strong this time. The emotions don't feel as raw.

"How you view the world through a lens should be shared."

Jack's comment rings so loudly that it's screaming at me.

Click.

On reflex, I head to my studio and push the door open without giving myself a chance to think this through.

The disaster is still there—the shredded photos of a life I don't even remember living but have the emotional scars to show that I did are strewn everywhere, but there is so much more under it.

The urge to clean this up and purge the bad memories it represents takes hold like never before. One scrap of photo paper after another, one image after another, depict a life I no longer live and wouldn't want to go back to if I could.

Because I'm not the same person anymore.

I'm stronger.

And instead of diving into the pool and screaming in the deep end, I dust off my camera.

Twenty-Seven

JACK

"Lauren," I say for what feels like the millionth time since I called her back. The ten messages in my voicemail and five texts told me it was urgent, my ability to only put out one fire at a time making me pace myself. "Did you call your sponsor? You haven't answered that question."

"How am I supposed to know how to be a mom, Jack-Jack? How? Our mom didn't love us enough to stick around, so how in the hell did I think I could be one?"

I rein in my sigh of frustration and fight the droop of my eyelids caused by the couple of beers at Axe's and too little sleep.

The hysteria in her voice warns me she's on the edge again, and neither of us can afford to allow her to fall the fuck off.

"Did you call your sponsor?" I repeat the question.

"Why did I—"

"*Lauren.*" My voice is a little firmer this time, my directness about to be even more so. "Don't do this to yourself. You've worked too damn hard, only to pick up that bottle again." And I don't have time to come home and pick up the pieces. "The kids need you. Everyone at the ranch needs you."

I blow out a sigh at the silence on the other end and picture her. She probably has her long hair pulled atop her head in a messy knot and her glasses pushed high on her nose. There is probably one kid asleep on her lap and the other beside her on the couch because her need to prove to them she isn't going anywhere has created this codependence that is probably unhealthy.

But it works.

"And Mom did love us. It was Dad and his . . . *shit* she couldn't handle." I have no idea if our mom loved us, and the pain still stings regardless of how much I say it doesn't, but Lauren needs to hear this. She needs to believe it.

Fuck, I'll lie to her all goddamn day if this is what it takes to keep her sober.

"Did you call your sponsor, Lauren?"

"Tell me about you, Jack. What's going on with you? Is the job what you thought it would be like? Is she what you thought she would be like? Are you finding the closure you need? You better be because I'm telling you, when you get back, it's my turn to run from this place and find some myself."

"I understand."

And I do.

"Don't do it."

Her warning catches me off guard. "Don't do what?"

"Don't fall for her. Besides the obvious reasons, you can't do that. You can't fall in love with her and not come back home."

I snort at her absurdity, but at the same time, my eyes flit out the window and over to the light on in the windows at the main house.

"I'm not falling in love with her." I laugh and get up to grab another beer from the fridge.

"Said with such conviction," she teases, sounding a bit more like herself.

"We aren't doing this. We aren't turning the subject off you and on to me so that you don't have to tell me what's going on."

"I'll talk if you talk."

"Jesus. This isn't—"

"You've slept with her, Jack. You wouldn't be so defensive if you hadn't."

"I've slept with a lot of women," I counter.

"Yeah but then you move on. You aren't moving on just yet. That means it will give you enough time to fall for her, if you haven't already. Isn't this what happened with what's her name?" I can hear her snap her fingers on the other end of the call, but I don't offer up the name. I don't remind her of Becky Lofton.

"Why are we talking about me? I thought you were the one—"

"And you're the fall-hard type of guy. I've seen it too many times to count."

"I'm not the fall-hard guy anymore." Falling hard means I get hurt, which is something I've learned to avoid.

The last fall I took nearly broke me.

"And I'm not your alcoholic little sister either."

"Did you call your sponsor?" I ask yet again, but now with my mind preoccupied on the light in a window where there hasn't ever been one on before.

"God, you sound just like Dad," she says.

"Then don't call me acting like the world is going to end if you don't want me to make sure you're taken care of and are okay. I love you, kid, but . . ." Fuck if the constant management of you and your addiction isn't exhausting.

"But what?"

"I just want you to be okay."

Silence eats up the line. "I will be."

Christ, I despise the fragility in her voice. I hate myself even more for not understanding it or her better.

Is this how Dad felt?

Exhausted from wondering if she was serious or playing games each time she cried for help? Was he constantly on edge, waiting for her to relapse again?

"You sure?"

"For now, I will be." There's a shuffling sound on the other end. "Promise me you're coming back."

"I'm coming back."

I end the call and toss my phone onto the couch before blowing out a loud exhale. Then I pick it up and debate calling our longtime ranch manager, Evan, to check up on her.

With the phone in my hand, I walk toward the window and stare over to the main house. To the shadow that continues to cross in front of the window every few seconds. To the woman I parted ways with a few hours ago but who I can't seem to shake from my goddamn mind.

"Well, shit, son. Did hell freeze over?"

"Funny, old man," I say to Evan.

"If you're calling, there must be something wrong." His voice sounds like a thousand cigarettes smoked and crushed into gravel.

"Nothing wrong. Just checked in on Lauren and she seemed a little rough."

His sigh has me feeling guilty instantly. "It's been raining non-stop for five days. That's a lot of time to be cooped up in that house with two little ones. I'll see about getting them out with me tomorrow. We'll do something in the stable to give her a break. I'll pretend I need help or something. That might help."

"Evan . . ."

"Don't even think of it. She's family. You're family."

Always have been.

"Thank you."

"You coming back? You better not get any ideas about staying there."

"I'll be back, Evan; although I'm sure you can run that place blindfolded and with one hand tied behind your back."

"I can." He chuckles, and it's a sound I can remember as far back as possible. Evan and his gruff demeanor but huge heart, his big bushy mustache and the magic tricks he could mesmerize a young boy with, has always been in my life. The man probably spent more time with me than my own father did, but he never judged me. "But it's you they'll all be looking for direction from. They need a Sutton here."

"Lauren's there," I say and know that she doesn't quite cut it.

"Not the same."

"I know." I sigh and run a hand through my hair. "I know."

"See you soon."

On the way to the kitchen, the lights in the house pull my attention again.

Keep on walking by, Jack. Don't even think about heading up there.

Last thing I need in my life is a woman who provides anything other than a physical release.

Organize the paperwork for the Steely Brothers. Get caught up on your work.

Last thing I need is to fall for a woman when the last one nearly broke me.

Go check on the horses and make sure that Will got his list of tasks done.

Besides, I have a life to get back to. My promise has been kept.

But Tate, *this,* can't happen—no matter how good the sex is.

And if sex is that good the first time, it will only get better once we get to know each other's bodies. Imagine what it will be like when the nerves are gone.

I should head to the bar.

Gain some distance.

Get some space.

I grab my keys and figure it wouldn't hurt to see what kind of ruckus I caused with my reaction to the pricks at Axe's today.

Her light is still on when I walk to my truck.

Her shadow still moving back and forth across the window when I climb behind the wheel.

Twenty-Eight

JACK

S he opens her front door.

This is a mistake.

Those lips of hers shocked in an O.

Such a huge fucking mistake.

Her nipples are hard, and the darkness of them is just visible through the flimsy white of her tank top.

Fuuuuck. There's no walking away now.

"I was going to the bar."

"Okay." Confusion etches the lines of her face as she opens the door a few inches wider.

"Tell me to go to the bar, Tate," I demand.

"Go to the bar, Jack." Her voice is flat. Unemotional.

"Mean it."

"But I don't mean it."

"What?" I ask in reflex when I like her answer perfectly fucking well.

"I don't want you to go to the bar, Jack," she says and then does something completely unexpected. She pulls her tank top over her head. Those handful-size tits with pink nipples tighten when the breeze hits them.

Like a jackass, I just stand there and stare at her. At Tate. At the woman I want but have known since day one that I should walk away from.

I'm screwed.

With her eyes locked on mine, she pushes her shorts down until they fall to her feet.

The curve of her hips. The tight strip of hair atop her pussy. The shuddered breath she emits that tells me she feels every bit as fucking taken aback by this as I do.

So fucking screwed.

"You should go to the bar, Jack." The suggestive smile on her lips tells me she doesn't mean a goddamn word she says.

And I'm going to enjoy every unexpected minute of it.

"FUCK THE BAR," I mutter the moment we crash into each other.

We're a frenzy of lips and tongues and me pulling off my shirt and her undoing my pants as we crash into the wall at her back.

There is no time for patience. No time for foreplay.

Only an urgency to be buried in that tight, wet pussy of hers that feels like Heaven and tells me it will haunt me like Hell and will take me every goddamn place between.

There is only insanity in the desperation to feel her again, to have her again, to fucking claim her again.

Seconds pass in ragged breaths. Each one panted a second too long until I can be buried in her.

Her back pinned against the wall. My hands on her waist, lifting her so that she can wrap her calves around my hips.

She curls her hand around my cock, and as good as that feels, it has nothing on when she arches her hips and rubs it up and down her slit.

Wet doesn't even begin to describe how fucking drenched she is.

Tight doesn't explain the resistance I feel when I lower her down onto me.

Fucking ecstasy doesn't hold a damn candle to what it feels like to be buried in her balls deep.

"Christ, Tate."

"Soooo good."

She clenches her muscles around my dick and pulls me in tighter, and I swear to fucking God, any less of a man would have come on the spot.

It takes everything I have not to.

But that's only because this feels so damn good that I don't want to waste the pleasure.

"You do realize that, when you do that, it begs me to fuck you on every goddamn surface in this house, right?" I groan as my head falls back, and I fight the urge to fuck her into oblivion.

Her laugh rings out as her fingernails dig into my shoulders. "Then I guess I need to keep doing it."

Those storm-cloud-colored eyes of hers are dark with desire, etched with need, as she tightens around me again.

My jaw clenches—hell, every goddamn part of me clenches in response.

I lean in and kiss her. The kind of kiss that makes my balls ache and my eyes roll back. The kind of kiss that is soft and slow like she needs since it's all she's going to get. Because she feels so fucking incredible that, the minute I move—the minute my dick slides out and then pushes back in again—there will be no way slow is going to pass through my mind again.

Hell, thinking won't even begin to be an option.

With my lips on her and my hands on her waist, I begin that slow slide out. I hold her against the wall as I fight for every ounce of control when I push gently back into her again.

"Jack." A sighed moan.

"Jack." It's *my* name she's calling when I'm buried to the hilt so there isn't a single ounce of space between where our bodies meet.

"Jack?"

Another pull out.

"Mmm?" I lean back to look at her to remind myself what I needed from her last time that she didn't give me.

Her eyes open and on me.

Her lips moaning my name.

It's her needing me right now.

Not Fletcher.

Not him.

Those eyes pull me in as much as her pussy does. Lids heavy with arousal. Hair a mess falling around her face. Lips parted and swollen from mine.

"Fuck me, Jack." If her words were explosive, then the groan that follows them is a Molotov cocktail.

Restraint snaps.

Gentle. Soft. Slow—cease to exist.

Now. Need. Hard.

It's all I can think.

All I can feel.

Until I can't think.

Until it's just Tate and me and her pussy and my dick.

"Look at me," I demand as black eyelashes flutter open.

Until it's just her fingernails scoring lines in my skin and my teeth nipping her shoulder.

"Look at me, Tate." As sex-drugged eyes hold mine.

Until it's her panted cry as the orgasm slams into her and my own release hits me so goddamn hard I almost black out.

Instead of moving, we slide down the wall, my jeans still around my ankles, and her legs still wrapped around my waist.

We don't speak as our hearts decelerate. We don't acknowledge we had sex two nights in a row when technically this isn't really a thing. In fact, we don't do anything other than sit with her forehead resting on my shoulder and my dick softening inside her.

"We have to move at some point," I finally mutter as her skin begins to cool beneath my lips.

She chuckles. "You mean we have to do the unsexy part of sex?" she asks as she slides her hand between her thighs and cups herself as I slip out of her.

"The unsexy part?" I ask, knowing full well what she means but loving that she's talking about it. Loving that this woman is comfortable enough with me to.

"Yeah," she jokes. "The duckwalk to the bathroom part for me. The wash your dick off in the sink part for you."

"Well," I say through a laugh as she rises and I watch her head down the hall. "I guess I need to find that sink then."

"You probably should," she says over her shoulder looking to where I'm sitting. Her eyes roam to my dick, still semi-hard against my thigh, still coated in both of us. Her smile is shy when, after what she just did, there's no way in hell she's shy. "We'll need to use that again later."

And just like that, I'm left speechless for the second time tonight.

Twenty-Nine

"Holy shit."

It's my first and only thought as I look in my mirror above the sink in my bathroom.

My cheeks are flushed. My neck has red marks from where his goatee scraped against it. My eyes . . . my eyes are alive with excitement and pleasure.

And I initiated it.

Not only did I initiate it but I also told Jack Sutton that I freaking wanted to do it again.

My hands go over my face as I die of embarrassment, questioning what had emboldened me all of a sudden.

But I know what it was.

It was picking up the pieces of my old life off the floor. It was realizing each memory felt manufactured. Each one was hiding a lie I never knew about. Every piece held love, but it was deceptive and duplicitous. Yes, Fletcher and I loved hard, but he also lied harder.

It was as I was sorting the mess that I realized just how strong I am and how I don't recognize the woman I was back then.

It was hearing that knock on the door and knowing who it was and what I wanted, to lose myself in Jack for a while. To forget to remember, to bury the past, and to see that I have a future as Tate Knox, not Fletcher's wife.

It was hiding behind the realization of what I had done by using humor to do the walk of shame, only to find there isn't shame. There is only freedom in knowing what I want and not being afraid to express it.

That's all new for me.

I run a hand down my chest, over my breasts that Fletcher teased were too small but that Jack seems to have absolutely no problem with. To my hips that swell out. To the apex of my thighs still throbbing from the pounding he just gave it.

And I feel alive—scream-from-the-rooftops, dance-in-the-rain, flip-off-all-my-haters alive.

A giggle bubbles up in my throat as I try to figure out what in the hell to do next.

"You okay in there?" Jack calls out with a laugh as I hear a faucet turn on in the bathroom down the hall as he cleans up.

"Yep. I'm good."

And when I look back in the mirror at the goofy smile on my face, I know I just might be.

Thirty

JACK

The door is ajar.

Black trash bags, which look to be full of shredded photos, line one side of the floor. Framed photos are arranged in a gallery on one wall. There are black-and-white stills of the landscape, colorful ones of exotic places overseas, muted ones of the everyday on this ranch. The other side of the room has unframed 8x10s hanging from clips on a crisscross of strings. There is a small workstation with a laptop, camera parts, and accessories beneath a row of windows.

The studio is clean but cluttered, minimalist in décor because the items that make the biggest statement are her work.

I move to the clipped pictures. There are images of a hand on a coiled rodeo rope, some of the thumb and forefinger pinching the top of a cowboy hat, and still more of the nostrils of a horse with what looks like a smiling mouth.

Details.

That's the first word that comes to mind. She picks the tiniest detail, focuses on it, and lets the background become the canvas somehow. I'm sure there's a term for it, but fuck if I know it.

I run my fingers over them. I feel stupid doing it, but they call to me, and I can't help but feel as if I am meeting a whole different side of Tatum Knox while looking at these photos.

It's as if the hardened woman with a defiant temper and determined streak a mile long is also this introspective observer. She's someone who watches and waits and only clicks that button at the most perfect of opportunities.

The last image against the wall startles me. It's nothing like the others. Not animal or landscape or part of life. It's of a letter, and the words on it call to me to read it, to step deeper into this world of this woman I don't quite understand but want to. The sloppy handwriting reminds me of the last letter I received that pushed me to take some time to find myself again.

I know she's standing behind me. I can sense her—can smell the scent of her skin—but I don't turn to face her. I can't seem to take my eyes off the photographed letter in front of me.

So, I give her a minute to come to terms with the fact that I just invaded what I can only assume is her private sanctum.

"I was right. You need to start taking pictures again. Your work is incredible."

The floorboards creak as she moves closer, but I keep reading the words of a desperate man telling his wife he's sorry. The wishes for a happier future. The blessing for her to have a next time. His final goodbye.

I read the words with contempt. I see a selfish man who can't face the deeds he's done. I see a coward.

I stare at the scrawled writing reflected on glossy paper a few more seconds and finally understand the conflict of emotions Tatum Knox has lived with. How she could love her husband and hate him at the same time. How she heard the words and believed them, only to find out all the lies behind them.

When I turn to face her, I'm knocked astride momentarily.

Sure her cheeks are flushed and her hair is wild from the sex we just had, but there is an intensely raw honesty in her eyes that tells me she knows I know.

That tells her that her secret is out.

That tells me she trusts me when trust isn't something she gives freely.

Fucking everything.

"Did you love him?" I ask without hesitation, hating the wince she gives me but needing the answer all the same.

"What kind of question is that?" She sputters over her response, spine stiffening, and eyes narrowing.

"A simple one," I say, knowing a part of me is asking for selfish reasons considering I just had sex with her against the wall and hate the thought of her loving someone who didn't deserve her. "Did you love him?"

She opens her mouth and then closes it, her thoughts having to catch up with her mouth. "Of course, I loved him. Why would you even ask me that?"

"Not everyone loves their partner."

She twists her lips but keeps her eyes on me, not shying away from my directness that makes most squirm. "He was my everything . . . and then he wasn't." Her voice is a whisper that is tempting me to ask so many questions.

And then he wasn't.

"I'm sorry." It's all I can say. All I can think to say because I hate the fucker. Call me an asshole, call me judgmental, but the more I learn about him, the more I'm glad I didn't get the chance to know him.

Anyone who puts that look of love edged with regret, devotion laced with deception, in to someone else's eyes isn't worth my time.

"He wrote me a letter," she says, her voice scratchy and uncertain.

"So I see." I glance back at it, wishing I could shred it and add it to the pile of ruined photos in the bags. "And you took a photo of it."

"I only take pictures of things that move me."

I nod and hate that his words moved her. Fuck it. Let's face it, I hate everything about him that has to do with her from her last name to the photo of the hands on the reins that I sure as shit know are his, to her bed, which I want to lay her down in but that I know he shared with her.

"He left you a letter," I say.

"I took a picture of it because I was afraid the police were going to take it from me."

Her comment surprises me, but I take a few steps to my left and lean my hips against the workstation and wait for her to explain.

I've already connected the dots and pieced together what happened.

"How'd he die?"

"Car accident." She waits a beat, looking down at her fingers twisting together before looking back at me. "They said he was distracted with texting and hit a tree."

"Do you think it was an accident, Tate?" I ask what she's afraid to say.

"I don't know." Her voice is barely a whisper when she speaks.

"That looks like a suicide note to me."

The woman in front of me nods ever so slightly, her shoulders shuddering with her next breath.

And what the fuck do I say to that? How do I soothe her when I'm fucking torn over it myself?

A man so desperate to avoid facing his dire financial situation that he ended his life. I wonder how bad it has to be to get to that.

"Did the sheriff see this?"

"Fletcher didn't have any bags with him in the truck. If he was leaving—if that was a Dear John letter—then he would have had bags with him." She hiccups over the words and ignores my question.

"I don't understand," I say as I move toward her and hunch down so I can look her in the eyes. Why does it matter so much how he died? Why is she so upset by it other than the obvious?

"It isn't your fault." My hands are on her shoulders and move up to frame her face, my thumbs wiping away the tears that fall. "Regardless of what happened, it is not your fault." I could be speaking to myself but choose not to hear the words. "He's the one who did this. He's the one who left you to clean up this mess."

"I just . . . it all happened so fast. I didn't show Rusty. I didn't tell him about it. They ruled it an accident. They—"

"Why are you beating yourself up?"

Her lip quivers beneath my fingers. "Because the insurance company sent me money."

"For the car? For what?" I ask, trying to comprehend.

"His life insurance. I sent them his death certificate and they sent it to me." Another hiccup. "What was I supposed to do? I didn't even know he'd taken a policy out the year before."

I don't mean for the laugh to fall from my lips, but it does. "This is what you're upset about? You accepted life insurance money after he died and you're worried because the medical examiner listed his cause of death as one thing when you think it might be something else?"

Her eyes, pooling with tears, widen, and she nods.

And then it clicks.

It isn't solely about the thought of suicide. It's also about her integrity.

"You're afraid you scammed the system? Is that it? That you took money you wouldn't have gotten if his death had been ruled a suicide when you think it might have been."

Another tear slips over and slides down her cheek. "I used it to pay the overdue accounts so I could try to make this work. I swear—"

"Shh," I say, and when she goes to speak again, I brush my lips against hers to stop her.

"I didn't have a choice. I took the money to pay off his debt. I only wanted to—"

"Shh," I say again, my own guilt eating at me.

My own remorse simmering for so many damn reasons.

How easy would it be for me to hand her a check and take all this worry away from her? How simply I could pay this all off so that her worry and guilt and grief could be laid to rest? It would be as easy as putting pen to paper. It would make amends, but then what?

It isn't as if doing that would solve my own issues. It isn't as if doing that will stop the ball from rolling downhill when it is already on its way down.

"I know. I just—"

"In life, sometimes you have to do things you never thought you would to get by or to put one foot in front of the other until you can see straight again."

This woman who can hold her own, can threaten to shoot you if need be, has survived every hostility this town has thrown at her before and after his death, but is reduced to a pile of tears over a possible lie that most people wouldn't even blink an eye at.

Her honesty is astounding. The way it has wrecked her even more so.

"Tate." I pull her against me and wrap my arms around her.

She hesitates for a second, almost as if she doesn't think she deserves my compassion, but then she slides her arms around my waist.

And we take a moment to just hold each other in the middle of her studio that reflects a past she's been burned by, a future she has before her, and a man who isn't quite sure how to deal with any of this.

For a man who doesn't ever need shit like comfort or connection, her head under the curve of my neck, her arms wrapped around me, and the shudder of her hiccupped sobs against my chest feel pretty fucking good.

Thirty-One

TATE

"Can you stop the bank from having people show up here unannounced?" I growl at Sheryl the minute she picks up the call.

"What—why—hi, Tatum. How are you today?"

"The lender had an appraiser show up here like they already own the place. He tried to tell me lenders appraising the property their loans are for is standard practice. I call bullshit. Jesus, Sheryl. He walked around without announcing himself or saying a damn word."

The pure panic that hit me the moment I saw him talking to Sylvester comes back. How I sprinted across the pasture to prevent the appraiser from telling anyone the truth. How the anger rioted and shame washed over me in a violent wave when I pulled him away and told him he needed to get off my property.

Thank God Jack was at the hardware store and missed it.

"That shouldn't be happening. I'm in regular contact with them. They know we're trying to get you up to date on payments."

"Well, it's happening on a regular basis. Can you just assure them the land and ranch are still here and they haven't gone anywhere so they can stop checking? Besides, they sent papers over but haven't formally started proceedings so they have no right to be here. Hell, the paperwork said that it can take up to six months to begin . . . so let them know, this isn't theirs yet. They can't have it."

"I'll call them *again*."

"Do that," I snap and then sigh. "I'm sorry. I didn't mean to be a bitch. I just don't want the staff knowing."

Her throaty laugh fills the line. "Yes, you did mean to be a bitch, but I know it wasn't directed at me." The sound of papers shuffling fills the line. "I'll call them again. And I'll let them know again, that we're not just throwing our hands up and walking away."

"Thank you. I appreciate it."

I end the call, lean against the wall of the stable at my back, and exhale my frustration.

"You don't want the staff to know what?"

I jump at the sound of Jack's voice and a startled yelp falls from my lips. "Jesus Christ, Jack. You scared the shit out of me." I hold a hand to my heart to calm the panic of Jack overhearing any of that phone call.

"Just heading out to help Will." He holds up his tool belt to prove his point but then narrows his gaze and takes a step closer. "Is everything okay?"

I nod. "Yes. Great. Fine."

He glances around and then reaches out and runs his thumb over my cheek. "You know if you needed to talk to me, I'm here." He drops his hand when Will laughs close by.

"I know."

He offers a ghost of a smile. "You're saying the words, Knox, but I'm not one for lip service. You need to mean them."

"I'm fine."

"If there were a problem, you know you could trust me with it. I'd help."

My smile is tight as my guilt eats me whole. "No problem at all."

He purses his lips and nods a few times. "Okay then."

Jack walks down the path with a glance back before turning the corner so I can't see him again.

Sagging against the building behind me, I wonder how much longer I can keep this hidden. How much longer will I be able to hold on and play the part that nothing is wrong?

The second anyone in town catches so much as a whiff of this, the Destin twins will be out for blood while the rest of the townspeople I work with will withhold their services, afraid I won't be able to pay them. I won't be able to keep it from Jack then.

My reputation may suck in this town, but my payables in Lone Star are up to date.

And that is what's currently keeping this place afloat.

Thirty-Two

TATE

Something has shifted.

I'm not sure if it's me or if it's Jack, but after the night he saw my studio, something has changed between us.

I feared our little chat behind the stables might have changed that. That Jack would figure out I am keeping things from him, and it would shift our new dynamic.

But it didn't.

Everything feels the same and yet so very different.

It's as if I can finally breathe. His reassurances and the way he held me tight that night changed things, but I'm not quite sure if I can put my finger on how. Is it trust? Is it that I have someone I can confide in? Or is it that I finally have something to look forward to, like the little glances he sends my way when I least expect them.

"Will, when and if Steely wants to move forward, things are going to happen fast."

"Ten-four, Jack," Will says with a tip of his hat as he mucks out the stalls.

My hand runs down Ruby's flank, the brush right after it as I murmur sweet nothings to her, but my mind is on Jack. It's on what he just said and what might happen if the Steely Brothers want to take a chance on us.

"With the girls about to go in estrus, which will happen sooner rather than later, they'll send some guys out to stay here. We talked about logistics, and it's easier for them to bring the studs here for the month than for us to travel to them. And if Doc Arlington's right, the mares we have will start going into labor about the same time."

"It's 'bout to get busy around here." Will laughs.

"In more ways than one," Jack jokes. There's a clatter of pails against the concrete floor and the sound of a hose being turned on. "If it goes the way we think it will, I might be asking you to stay a few nights up here with me in the bunkhouse. All of that's a lot for Tate and me to manage on a normal day, but trying to pretend like we're ten times bigger than that for these Steely guys' sake means we need to look like it too."

My mind tries to calculate where the money is going to come from to feed hungry cowboys for a month. I think back to the bills when we had a full staff before money started getting tight and cringe.

I'll have to make a decision soon whether to use the money I'm saving by not having to pay Lone Star Feed toward trying to make up a mortgage payment, a show of good faith that I'm really trying, or use it for this new development.

Rob Peter to pay Paul.

Christ.

Maybe I need to lower my asking price on Ruby.

No matter what I decide, Jack's right. We have to appear bigger than we are because no operation as huge as Steely Brothers is going to sign on a rinky-dink operation.

"You good with that, Will?" Jack reiterates.

"With staying here a few nights? Not a problem at all. My old man's been hitting the bottle a lot lately, so I'd gladly take the chance to be elsewhere for a bit."

There's a pause of silence, and I wish I could see Jack's face because something tells me that little tidbit of information was new to him.

"Hey, Will?" Jack asks.

"Yeah?"

I peek my head out from the stall to find Will looking at Jack, his expression serious and hopeful and all things youthful.

"You're welcome to stay up here any time you need to," Jack offers. "You have a good future ahead of you. If you need to get away to keep your head on straight, know there's a bunk here any time you need it."

Will nods but averts his eyes quickly, but I catch a sniffle as he occupies himself with an already mucked stall.

Hell.

Why did I need to see that? Why did I need to know that Jack is not only kind to me but also good to others?

Why did my heart need to skip a beat?

Jack looks over to me with a somber expression. He may be standing there with a hose in his hand cleaning down the stalls, but I see the man who was standing in my studio two nights ago. The one whose jeans hung low on his hips and tugged on the desire he awakened. The lover who didn't judge me as I told him I cheated the system, who didn't blame me for not wanting to believe my husband committed suicide to escape.

The man who held me against his bare chest as we fell asleep on the couch after talking till the early morning hours.

"You good?" he asks, and I just nod.

But it's the crunch of gravel that pulls my attention away from him. His eyes narrow as I walk to the stable's opening to find

Rusty's cruiser pulling to a stop, the dust he kicked up swirling behind him.

"What is it, Knox?" Jack asks, and I'm not sure what bugs me more: knowing why Rusty is here or Jack calling me Knox.

"Nothing," I mutter as I stalk toward the driveway.

"Tate?"

I stop and look back at him, my smile slight and my anger simmering. My name back on his lips goes hand in hand with my need for this bullshit to go away because things might finally be looking up for me. "It's fine. I'll take care of it."

"Who is—*Christ*," he swears when he finally sees who the visitor is. "How about you introduce me to him."

Will glances our way, oblivious to what is about to happen, and I shake my head.

"No, it's just . . ." I can take care of it myself. I know he's seen how this town is to me, but I don't want him to see more of it. I don't want him to see me through a different set of eyes. "Let me. It's my . . . I can handle it."

Jack stands there, the muscle feathering in his jaw, but he nods without saying another word and moves back to helping Will.

My hands are on my hips, and my feet are on the edge of my driveway by the time Rusty steps out of the cruiser.

"Let me guess," I say as soon as he shuts his car door. "You finally found out the truth. I'm a fugitive who's been on the run for years. The stable is actually a meth lab, and I keep the horses as a cover. That's why I can't make a profit to keep this place afloat with horse sales . . . but, shhh, I do have a tank load of money over in the broken-down silo from all my drug sales." The smile I flash is sickeningly sweet and loaded with the same sarcasm that laces my voice.

He coughs out a laugh with a shake of his head. "Seems someone ate their Wheaties with a side of snark this morning."

"Nope, just sick of this bullshit." I shift on my feet. "What is it, Rusty? You've only come out this way for two reasons: to tell me my husband died and to tell me someone hates me or my ranch or both. The first one can't happen again, so I'm guessing it's the latter."

His smile is slow to spread, but when it does, it brightens his eyes. "I like this new you. Where has she been?"

"Good question." I snort, but I know.

And I hate that it has anything to do with a man, but it does.

Not that Jack gave me worth by befriending me or that a few bouts of sex gave me that a-ha moment about everything, but there is something to be said about finding someone you trust after feeling like there is no one you can.

"So?" I let the word stretch out as he eyes the two trucks in the driveway that aren't mine.

"Rumors are you're selling. That you're getting this all set up to pawn it off to some big rancher who's going to gut this land and make a circus of the town."

"Uh-huh. Big ranchers are knocking down the door to buy me out. The line they're waiting in is right there." I point to the empty lot on the side of my house. At least the rumors make sense since Jack used to deal in acquisitions. "What is the deal, Rusty, because I know you aren't here to chase down gossip."

"There is no deal," Jack says, startling me since I hadn't heard him walking up behind me. Rusty turns slowly, his thumbs hooked in the loops of his slacks, his shoulders squared. The look of surprise on his face probably mirrors mine. "Is there, Sheriff? You're out here chasing bullshit rumors and badgering Tate because it's ten times easier than confronting your old buddies from high school about shit they need to stop."

"And you are?" Rusty asks, his tone not the slightest bit amused.

"A concerned citizen who's having to connect the dots because it appears that you're not exactly doing your job," Jack says as he steps up beside me, arms folded over his chest, posture defensive.

"Name." There is no mistaking that Rusty's pissed.

"Jack, I'm the new ranch manager."

"Well, Jack Sutton—"

"Ah, see? You did know who I was when you rolled up. Let me guess, they've talked about me in the Lone Star rumor mill too?" Jack says and looks my way with a smirk. "At least I'm in good company."

"I'm not sure exactly where you come from," Rusty says, "but where I come from, we don't threaten officers of the law."

Jack's chuckle is low and condescending and the purse of his lips as he stares at Rusty says *you're a piece of shit* loudly enough for everyone to hear. "Not sure what I said could be construed as a threat, Sheriff, but in a small town like this, you have to be jonesing for something to do. So, instead of coming out here to bug Ms. Knox, why don't you chase down the real problem?"

Rusty's smirk holds no amusement. "And what might that be?"

"For starters, you should head over and see Jed at the Lone Star Feed. He's been stealing from Tate here for over a year now, taking her money and selling her a cheaper and shittier quality product than what she paid for. I think his business practices warrant a check by the law." Jack takes a step toward Rusty and lowers his voice. "But we both know you won't do that since he's your second cousin and all."

"I heard about that yesterday, and I also heard you've come to an agreement about how to settle it," Rusty says, donning his official voice for the first time since he showed up.

"It's settled, all right, but that doesn't mean he didn't break the law." Jack shakes his head as if Rusty is a joke. "And while we're at it, you need to chase down Gary Bolton and see exactly how he ties into these complaints that keep being called in to your office."

"Why's that?"

"Because Gary Bolton runs a side business with Harvey Hickman," Jack says, referring to the son of the owner of Hickman Ranch, the very ranch we might be stealing business from. "I would bet that Gary and Harvey are talking about how we might possibly be stealing away their most lucrative client. Gary has drinks with Jed every Monday, and they talk because Jed hates Tate because he's a fucking idiot. Then Jed turns around and sees the Destin twins on Wednesdays when they play their weekly poker game."

"I'm not following you," Rusty says with a little more snark than necessary.

But I'm not either.

"The Destin twins paid Tate and me a visit down at Axe's the other night." My eyes whip over to Jack's. That explains why everyone in the bar was staring at me when I came out of the bathroom. "They warned me to leave things alone, demanded I let Tate fail, and told me to get the fuck out of here . . . so you want to know how this little circle jerk of pricks fits together? They all want something Tate has or poses a threat to."

"You're reaching there."

"Am I, though?" He holds his hand up, and Rusty startles at the rebuke. "The Hickmans fear the business we might win fairly. The Destin twins want this land and think that because their great-granddaddy what's his name's family founded this town, they have a right to whatever land they choose. Their threats prove they're more than willing to do what it takes so long as they get this place in the end. And Jed? Well, you fucking know about Jed. It's a small town, sir. The goddamn gossip train is a million miles long, but it seems I laid out who it is you need to talk to in order to stop this nonsense bullshit. We aren't going to be run off. Tate isn't going to sell. And if horses don't work out, we're going to turn this place into a retreat for photographers. Make sure they know that because that will really piss them off. *End of story. Understood?* Now, I suggest you crawl back in that cruiser of yours and go deliver the news as if it's an official mandate or I'll be more than glad to do it myself."

Jack stops short of poking Rusty in the chest to prove his point, but even though he doesn't, I'm left dumbfounded as I stare at the two men and process all that Jack just delivered.

Rusty holds Jack's glare for a beat. "If you want to say something to them, you should say it yourself. I don't peddle rumors."

Jack's laugh rings out. "Seems to me that's the only thing you do peddle. "

They glare at each other, testosterone ricocheting between them until it feels as if they are one step shy of a fistfight before Rusty steps back and turns to me.

"You okay here, Tate? Is there anything you need from me?" His eyes are kind and his concern seems genuine.

The irony isn't lost on me. The one time he doesn't need to be concerned, he is.

"For the first time, Rusty, I actually am."

We're silent as Rusty walks to his cruiser and climbs in, but the minute he turns out of the driveway, I face Jack and stare at him slack-jawed.

"What?" He laughs the word out. The hardass who confronted Rusty moments ago has been replaced with a self-satisfied man.

"Where in the hell did you get all of that from?"

"The bar has other attributes besides being a way to keep my distance from you."

Thirty-Three

TATE

"What's that?" I ask as Jack strides into the backyard with a dog that's wagging its tail back and forth with every step.

"It's a dog." His smile is more than warm as he absently runs his hand over the dog's head.

"I know it's a dog," I say as the ball of fur takes note of me and hobbles slowly toward me. "But what is she doing here?"

His smile is sheepish, and his eyes are full of hope as he watches the multi-colored mutt who is currently licking my hands to death. "She's a rainbow dog."

"What's a rainbow dog?" I ask as I notice the peculiar scar in a ring around her snout.

"Someone used a metal can as a muzzle on her," he says as I lean over and nuzzle my forehead against hers, unable to comprehend the level of cruelty to which some people are capable. When her ears fall back and her tail tucks between her legs as I lift my hand to pet her, my heart breaks. "And a rainbow dog is an older dog that probably won't get adopted because everyone wants puppies . . ."

"So she'll be euthanized?" I know that is one of those harsh realities that no one likes to look too closely at, but with this sweet girl sitting in front of me, I can't help but acknowledge how reprehensible the idea is.

"Not sure. Possibly." He clicks his tongue, similar to the way he does with the horses, and the dog sits and looks up eagerly at him, as if she's been doing this her whole life. "Good girl, Gracie," he coos. "If not, she'll live in the shelter. Maybe do some stints in foster homes, but she's been there for a long time, and this town is so small that anyone who would've wanted her has already had a chance to see her."

"And you brought her here, why?" I ask, but I know why, and my heart is already lost to her. With her misshapen head, the numerous scars I can feel dotting beneath her short fur, and her timid brown eyes that love me already solely because I have a soothing voice and gentle hands, I knew I was hers the minute she wagged her tail for me.

Jack looks at me with the same chocolate-colored eyes as Gracie and smiles. "Because she kind of lives here now." He ducks his head like a little boy and wins my heart as if he hasn't already claimed a piece of it.

A piece of my heart?

There's no way that can be possible. There's no way this man I hated at first sight can be the same person I look forward to seeing first thing every morning.

Can it?

I mean . . . it's just the circumstances. I've been lonely and he. . . he . . . makes me feel good. It's his belief that I can do this when everyone else seems to want me to fail that is making me feel this way.

"You're mad?" Jack asks. To him it might seem that way, but

I know my face has gone bloodless as if I've seen a ghost for an entirely different reason.

It isn't possible.

Falling for Jack isn't part of this deal.

No way.

"No. Not mad." I shake the spooked look off my face and force the smile on my lips to be real, which isn't that hard when I have the most pathetically sweet dog's face on my lap and Jack Sutton staring at me like a little boy about to be scolded.

I turn to Gracie because she's much easier to look at than he is.

"I know she's another mouth to feed when you have plenty already, but I set up food delivery for her . . . on me. That way, she isn't a burden on you. I just hoped—"

"I do believe you are rambling, Jack," I tease with a laugh. "Do I make you nervous?"

He stops and looks at Gracie, who's patiently staring at me. "Only when I think you're going to make me take her back."

"I'm not going to make you take her back," I say.

"Good. Great, isn't it girl?" Jack says with another ruffle of the fur on her head. "I thought you could use some company." He winks. "Someone to talk to. Besides, I'm not too fond of you being here all alone at night."

And for the second time in as many moments, I have to cover the emotions he pulls out of me. I have to keep in mind that Jack's time here is finite. He has a life to get back to and a ranch of his own that he needs to go run.

I swallow the sadness the thought brings and know I can't hide the tears welling in my eyes as I look at him. Hopefully, he'll mistake them for happy ones over Gracie.

"Thank you." My voice breaks when I say the two words.

And I mean them.

I think I just might need Gracie more than she needs me in the coming months.

Thirty-Four

TATE

Ruby's coat glistens in the sun. The bangs of her mane fall over her eye as those deep brown eyes stare at me like she knows what I'm thinking.

Click.

"You're such a pretty girl," I praise as I hand her a slice of apple. She takes it and moves to trot along the worn path that circles the ring, hooves kicking up dust to contrast against the bright green of the trees beyond.

Click.

I close my eyes and picture my next shot. How it will look once I edit it on the computer. I would take a panoramic so I could capture the reflection of the sunset and then pull out all the vibrant colors with the computer program.

Now, if only I can capture what I need.

"They're negotiating." Will's voice is edged with a palpable excitement as I turn to him.

"Negotiating?" I ask, my pulse kicking up a notch.

"With Steely."

A smile fights its way onto my lips as I try not to get too excited over what exactly *negotiating* means.

"Does the negotiating sound like it's a good thing?"

Will's grin adds fuel to the hope beginning to bubble up inside me. "Jack's a hard man to please," he says, and I bark out a laugh.

Pleasing Jack—pleasuring him—doesn't seem very hard from where I stand. His groans from last night as I took him into my mouth and sucked him off while his hands fisted in my hair and my name on repeat on his lips are proof enough of that.

"Tate?" It's Jack's voice this time. It's his excitement that carries across the ranch.

It's my fingers crossed for luck as my hands hang by my side.

"At the house . . ." But my words fade as he closes the distance in a few strides, his face void of all emotion.

And just when my heart falls—when I think we've lost Steely and the contract that will keep Knox Ranch afloat—Jack lets out a riotous whoop before picking me up and spinning me in circles.

Gracie lets out a bark from where she's lying in the shade on the verandah as I shriek. "Really? We got it?"

"We got it, baby!" he says and then plants a kiss squarely on my lips.

And then we both jump back, more than aware that Will is standing there staring at us. We are both shocked but excitement is brimming beneath the surface.

Will emits the loudest laugh, which I swear echoes across the ranch. "Don't stop on my account. It isn't as if I don't already know you two are a thing."

I stare at him, shocked that he knows when we've done everything to act as if we aren't sleeping together. "Will," I say like a mom scolding her child.

He snorts and rolls his eyes before heading toward the stables.

"Your secret is safe with me," he tosses over his shoulder.

"Good to know," Jack says as he steps up to me again. This time, he frames my face with both hands. "Now, where were we?" he asks and gives me a proper kiss, loaded with every ounce of violent-edged desire that I feel in return.

When my senses are thoroughly put through every pleasurable wringer imaginable, he steps back and looks at me. His grin is wide, his eyes are alive, and every part of him vibrates with pride.

"We got the contract, Tate." He shakes his head as if he can't believe it. "It's on a probationary status, but we got it."

"I don't even know what to say." Emotions I can't describe hum through my blood. My head spins and heart races. "I—"

"Don't say anything yet," he says and runs a thumb up and down my cheek, "because you're going to hate me for the next forty-eight hours."

"What? Why?"

"They'll be here on Wednesday. Four men. Twelve stallions ready to stud."

"But I thought they wanted to wait till the next crop of foals were born before they made their decision."

He winks. "I talk a good game, baby."

"I know, but—"

"Are you saying you doubt me?" Another kiss pressed to my lips in the most casual of ways. It feels as if standing here and kissing in broad daylight is something we always do instead of our nighttime rendezvous behind closed doors.

"I don't doubt you. I just don't understand why an outfit like Steely would choose us over Hickman. I mean . . . I know that was the plan but now that it's a reality . . . I just—"

"Take a deep breath." He puts his hands on my shoulders and exhales loudly as if to show me. "This is what you hired me for, remember? To run the ranch and bring on a steady clientele. Yes, I oversold us a bit, but that's why we're going to work our asses off for the next two days so that we deliver."

"Jack . . ."

My excitement has slowly morphed into panic as my mind grasps everything that's about to happen.

Getting the contract is overwhelming, but Steely coming here brings a whole new set of problems, like four men living in the bunkhouse for the next month, a dozen more horses to board and feed.

"Don't do that. Don't start overthinking this. We'll figure it out. We'll make this work," Jack says, voice encouraging, eyes clear.

"It's just a lot, and what if we don't deliver? What if they get here and see we're nowhere in the realm of Hickman?"

"I sold them on our personal service and our attention to detail. That's why they agreed to it on a one-year probationary period. These four guys like what they see while they're here, then we'll be set."

"And they're okay knowing you won't be here the whole time? They know that, right?" I ask.

"Tate." He uses my name to soothe me. "Don't you trust me?"

Doubt tries to win a war I'm sick of waging so I push it back down and answer him with an even. "Yes."

And I do.

Only, I'm not sure if that should excite me or scare me.

Especially after realizing he never answered my question.

Thirty-Five

TATE

There's an excitement to the chaos that engulfs the ranch over the next few days. An organization to the madness as we work around the clock to make my little ranch look like it's bigger and better than it's ever been.

Sure, the doubt still reigns.

Of course, the worry over finances is never far from my mind. The fear that despite Sheryl's phone calls, the lender might send who-knows-who out here while the Steely employees are here, lingers.

Still, we work hard and we get the job done.

Music plays from somewhere in the far stables where Will is busy setting up each stall for the studs. It'll put them far enough away from the mares that it doesn't cause problems, but close enough for them to smell the females in heat.

Talk about a tease if I've ever heard one.

"Whose idea was it to have them bring all those horses?" I groan with a smile on my face as we repair the rails of the ring we stopped using years ago.

"Gotta get them ladies pregnant," Jack says with a smirk. His hair is plastered to the back of his neck, drenched through with sweat long ago. I'm sure mine isn't much better where I have it tucked beneath my baseball hat. He has a smear of dirt on his cheek, the stubble on his jaw is the length of however long we've been at this, and the tear in the stomach of his dark blue shirt is from where it caught on a nail as he walked by.

"What are you staring at?" he asks, still in great spirits despite how freaking exhausted we all are.

"Just thinking I might work a little faster if I had some motivation."

"Motivation?" He stops and turns toward me, tipping the front of his hat up and off his eyes.

"You without a shirt on is a good start." I'm only partially teasing him.

"And you on your back is a good start for me too," he says with a laugh that tells me his comment holds about the same amount of truth as mine.

My laugh is soft, and I just shake my head. "If this girl is on her back, I think the only thing she'll be thinking about is sleeping," I joke.

"We'll see about that." He hammers a nail, and I watch him. "Get to work, Knox." He glances my way and flashes those dimples of his, making my heart skip a beat.

We work side by side, sometimes in silence and sometimes singing to the song Will has playing. It's brutal labor, physically tiring, mentally draining, and so much more than I've ever done before, but there's something so satisfying about working hard to accomplish something.

With Fletcher, I was nothing more than a window dressing. I was present but shielded from everything he was hiding. I was sequestered in this house to prevent me from going into town and knowing the truth.

But right now? I feel like I'm a part of this. Yes, Jack negotiated this whole deal, but I'm helping to make it happen.

"I've seen you taking pictures," Jack says after we move onto the smaller pens where we'll put the female in estrus and add the stallion raring to go.

"Hmm?" I glance over to him and then back to where I'm grading the dirt with a rake.

"Nothing. Just something I noticed, and I wanted to say I'm glad. You should reach back out to that gallery."

"That was years ago." I reject the idea immediately.

"And talent is talent. It doesn't fade with time." When I start to refute him, he cuts me off. "At least consider it."

It's my turn to snort. "Yeah. Sure. Right after I get through entertaining four men and twelve extra horses for a month."

"Who knows, you might have some new subjects to shoot."

He stands to his full height so the sunlight casts him in a silhouette.

Click.

I'd kill to grab my camera and capture him like this. Sweaty and exhausted and sexy.

"What?" He angles his head when he catches me studying him.

"You're the subject I want to shoot."

Jack's laugh rings out, and Will looks over to us. He's too far away to hear our conversation but he's close enough to hear Jack's reaction.

"Only if I get to take some of you while you're, uh, on your back."

I roll my eyes and sigh. "Such a guy."

We continue hour after hour, completing task after task. My muscles ache, my eyes are blurry, and my body is so exhausted that I can't even think coherent thoughts.

"Take a break, Tate. We'll get the rest," Sylvester says. "Jack just gave me a rundown of what's left."

I look at Sylvester and know his old body is tiring, which makes me feel horrible that he's here. No matter how many times we told him we had it covered, he wouldn't take no for an answer. We couldn't hurt his feelings by telling him he was actually slowing our progress, so we gave him what tasks we could.

"I need to make sure the bunkhouse is all set up first."

"I can do that," Jack says.

"Nah. I got it."

I walk toward the bunkhouse, my head down, my mind so tired I have to mentally count the steps I'm walking as a means to keep my focus. I don't think I've ever worked so hard in my life, and yes, I'm beyond tired, but I'm also so very satisfied, which makes zero sense to me.

Voices in the paddock have me looking toward the sounds of Jack and Will razzing each other, and it's when I do that I notice them in my periphery toward my house.

The pops of reds and pinks and purples spilling over the sides of the galvanized planters on my verandah. The planters that have been filled with dead flowers and weeds since Fletcher died are now full of vibrant colored blooms. The *life* stops me in my tracks momentarily.

I know I have mountains left to do, but I'm drawn to the stark contrast against everything else around them. It's so simple that it's breathtaking.

Absently running my fingers over the petals, I walk from planter to planter.

When I turn and see Jack standing at the end of the walkway, his thumbs are hooked in his belt loops and his head is angled to the side just watching me.

"You planted flowers." I don't hide my smile. "They look good. They'll give the Steely guys the impression that we're put together around here. Nice touch."

"I didn't plant them for the Steely guys," he says.

"No?"

"No." His expression tells me he's trying to work through something in his mind. His lazy grin slow and lopsided. "They're for you."

"You planted me flowers?" Every skeptical part of my body melts into a puddle at my feet.

"They're wildflowers."

"They're pretty," I murmur as I lean over to smell them.

"I thought they fit you. I thought they fit your wild."

And if I had dismissed my earlier thoughts of how he had taken a little piece of my heart, blaming them on my exhaustion, I now know I was wrong to do so.

Now I know he has.

Thirty-Six

JACK

"I don't think I can move."

Her groan is as loud as the sky is colorful. When I roll my head on the grass where we're lying to look over at her, her eyes are closed, her hair is a tangled mess on top of her head, and she's covered in dirt and grime.

She's fucking beautiful.

"We're still not done," I murmur as I close my eyes and exhale. I need a beer. I need Tate beneath me moaning. I definitely need some food. And I fucking need my phone to stop vibrating text alerts from my sister.

But I don't necessarily need those things in that order.

"Almost through." She groans again. "Just a few more things. But, hell, I'm impressed with how much we've gotten done."

"This place looks incredible," I say and fight the urge to roll onto my side and kiss her soundly.

If I do that, there will be no stopping me, and the last thing Will and Sylvester need to see is us rolling around naked.

Her unexpected laughter bubbles up, delirium edging its sound. "Do you have any idea just how many Jack Suttons there are in the world?"

Internally I freeze and hope she didn't just catch the hitch in my movement her question caused. *Has she made the connection somehow?*

"You looking me up, Knox?" I ask, trying to make the playful tone drown out the sudden worry I have.

Another soft chuckle as she reaches out and grabs my hand, threading her fingers through mine. "You aren't exactly an open book."

"Says the woman who's more guarded than a goddamn vault." When I squeeze her hand, the cool grass beneath them feels nice. It's odd for me to even notice that, but I do.

"You've been here almost three months now."

"Mmm-hmm." Where is she going with this?

"We worked together for one. We've been sleeping together for the other two . . ."

"And?" I ask without looking at her. She wants to know what happens when the next three months finish and my contract is up.

When I have to tell her the truth about why I'm here and break her heart . . . and her trust.

"And nothing. Never mind. I'm just tired and hungry and thinking way too much."

"I told you who I was, Tate."

And I did.

I just never told her who I wasn't.

She laughs and waves her free hand in the air in indifference. "Jack Sutton. Rancher. Seeker of helpless females he thinks need help."

"You're far from helpless," I say as my phone vibrates, yet

again, in my pocket. "You hungry?"

"Starving."

"I need to run into town to get a few more things. How about you can ask me anything you want when I come back bearing food."

"Food?" she asks, and I allow the rare treat of eating out to change the subject I'm not ready to broach. A few hours won't change the inevitable that I'm not sure how I'm going to fucking deal with, though.

"Yep. Food. I'll pick some up. What do you want?"

"Anything. Everything. And chocolate. Definitely chocolate," she murmurs with a smile turning up the corners of her lips.

"Everything it is," I say and give in to the temptation at my fingertips. Leaning over, I brush my lips against hers.

"No! I'm gross," she says, pushing against my chest but then fists her hands in my shirt and kisses me back.

It takes every ounce of strength I have to pull away from her soft tongue and gentle sighs, but I have to take care of a few things before we can get to this.

"Food. You're distracting me," I murmur against her lips. "I need to go get food."

"And chocolate," she says, and I can feel her lips smile against mine.

"And chocolate."

"Lauren," I say and groan internally as I lean my head back against the seat of my truck. I'm parked on the shoulder of the road about a mile away from the ranch so I can have this conversation in private, but the smell of the Italian food next to me is making me hungry, and I just want to get off the phone so I can get back to Tate. "I've got to get back to work."

Tate is probably still busting her ass getting the bunkhouse ready while I'm out here trying to get my sister sorted out. My sister. My burden.

"Haven't you been playing this long enough?" she gripes as my niece sings shrilly in the background. "At what point are you going to stop playing this game, Jack? You did what you said you were going to do. You can say you fulfilled the promise. Hand over the check. Don't hand over the check. The only thing I care about is that you get your ass back home." Where her tone starts out playful, it ends angrily.

"Fulfilling the promise is more complicated than I thought," I murmur and wonder if that's technically a lie.

"I'm ignoring that you said that. I'm pretending that I don't hear the tone in your voice that, God knows, I've heard it before. You better not be—shit, Jack. There's so much wrong with this. Don't you know that?"

I do know it, and I don't want to fucking talk about it.

"How was your meeting tonight?" I ask, playing on her need to be the center of attention.

"I didn't have time to go. There—"

"Goddamn it, Lauren. Why the hell not? You promised me you'd go."

If I could crawl through the phone and strangle her, I would. She wonders why I took off? Between our dad needing to control my every move and her sucking all of the oxygen out of every room, there wasn't enough space or air for me to breathe.

"And you promised me you wouldn't fall in love with her."

"No, the promise I made you was that I'd be home in time for the calving season. My word is good. You know that."

"And so is mine."

"I love you madly, Lauren, but you also drive me up a wall," I mutter as I start the truck and shift it into drive. "I need to go back to work, and you need to call your sponsor. I'll be home when my contract here is up. Good night."

The bunkhouse is lit up like Christmas when I walk into it. The space is nothing fancy, with four bedrooms that branch off the common area. The kitchen is in the middle with a large table where I have binders that detail the history of each of our forty horses laid out. Old-school rodeo posters are framed and hung on the walls, and a television sits on the far side in front of a worn couch.

The binders are a visual reminder of what lies ahead of us in this coming month. All the hard work we'll have to put in and the schmoozing along with it to make someone believe in us enough to give us the contract.

I walk from room to room, looking for Tate. There's mine with my stuff strewn about the small space. The beds in the others are still unmade, but the fresh sheets sit folded atop of them.

"Tate?" I call out as I move about looking for her.

"She ran up to the house," Will says when I poke my head into the stable. He and Sylvester are sitting on the floor, backs against the wall, and a beer in their hand.

They look as exhausted as I feel.

"Pizza's on the table," I say. "I'm going to go bring Tate hers."

The house is quiet when I enter. Tate's boots are by the door, clumps of dried mud scattered around them.

"Tate?"

Gracie's tail thumps somewhere, and when I step into the hall, I see her lying on the floor, looking at me with her head cocked, her eyes eager.

"Hi, girl," I say as I walk toward her and am just about to call out for Tate again when she comes into view.

She's sitting on her couch, arm propped on the side, hand under her chin, and completely sound asleep.

And fuck if my chest doesn't constrict at the sight of her.

The dark fan of her lashes on her dirt-smudged cheeks. The curls of hair that have fallen out of her ponytail. Her full lips just slightly parted.

She's busted her ass the past few days.

When I first showed up here, I wondered how this place had stayed afloat. I questioned how this pixie-sized woman could be the one doing it.

Now I know she can.

Now I know she has the determination of a giant and the grit of a titan.

I'm not sure how long I stand watching her before I set the food down on the table. With her soft snores filling the house, I get Gracie some food and fresh water and take her out. I pick up the kitchen some and wash our coffee cups that were still sitting on the table from when we went over what was left to do before the delegation gets here.

Since when do I have cups of coffee with Tate as if we are a couple? When did that happen?

When I started spending most nights here, that's when.

"Convenience," I murmur, denying the truth to myself as well as the air around me.

It's only when I go to let Gracie back in that I see Tate's camera sitting on the table by the front door. I pick up the expensive piece of equipment with no other purpose than to put it in her studio so it doesn't get knocked off by a rambunctious Gracie.

But when I walk into her office and set it next to its case, I'm stopped by the stack of black-and-white images sitting atop the workstation.

Fletcher's face greets mine. His smile is wide, and his eyes are clear. There is a subtle dusting of freckles across his nose, and faint lines at the corners of his eyes.

The photo hits me like a sucker punch. The man who started all of this stares back at me, and I'm not sure how I feel about it, about him.

That's a lie.

I feel in droves: hate, uncertainty, spite, jealousy that he had Tate first. So many emotions and yet I want to feel absolutely none of them.

Bastard.

I can't bring myself to look away for the longest of times as I sort through them all and know it won't do a damn bit of good to me if I do.

Liar.

None. Because I can't confront him over what he's done and I can't make amends for the trail of hurt he left behind.

Cheat.

When my eyes blur from the rage, I force myself to flip to the photos beneath it. The ring finger on Fletcher's left hand and the light mark where a ring should be. At one of him from behind, just his cowboy hat and his hair curling over his collar. At another one of just his eyes staring straight at me, telling me to back the fuck off.

Telling me to leave while I can before I hurt her any further.

The pictures allow me to see him through Tate's eyes. The little details only someone you're with might notice like the nuance in your posture or the laughter dancing in someone's eyes when they don't think anyone is watching.

It fucking kills me to know he loved her first.

It's stupid to expect her to get rid of them just because she's with me. It's ridiculous to want her to throw away memories of her old life—even when that old life was based on lies and mistruths.

They were married for years. She was going to have his baby.

The lead weight in my stomach weighs heavily and forces me

to take a step back. I'm invading her privacy just by lingering in here.

"Fuck," I mutter, forcing myself to leave the images where they are instead of trashing them like I want to and walk from the room before shutting the door softly behind me.

Gracie's tail thumps again, but she doesn't move from her spot beside Tate.

I should leave.

I should head to the bunkhouse and finish shit up for tomorrow's impending arrival.

I should go take a shower.

Instead, I sink down on the couch next to Tate. When I put my arm around her shoulders, she turns into me as if it's as natural as breathing, to rest her head against my chest.

"I love you," she murmurs so softly I almost don't hear it.

Almost.

"I know," I murmur into the top of her head before I press a kiss there, knowing full well it's her sleep talking.

It's her dreams murmuring.

It's her wild speaking.

Thirty-Seven

TATE

"Y ou sure you've been here this whole time?" the head guy from Steely Brothers asks as he walks toward me.

I nod slowly, still playing the game. "Yes. We've been here almost seven years, Pete. I understand Hickman is more established, but I think our horses can offer the same, if not better, quality foals than what they're providing you," I say, hoping I'm saying the right things.

Be confident but not arrogant. That is how Jack told me I needed to be when I was speaking to these men.

"And, hopefully, some circuit winners in there too." He laughs.

"I only provide the quality," I tease. "It's up to you to train the rest."

His laugh rings out as he steps into the stable to look around and I hang back.

"Let them look without being their shadow."

He warned me that if I hover, they might think I'm trying to hide things.

I argued that he should be the one doing this, but he just reminded me that I was the owner so it had to be me escorting Pete around the property. It should be me selling the merits of my ranch, not my employee.

"It's the personal touch they are looking for. You doing this will give that to them."

The two monolith-sized horse trailers look so out of place and, yet, so perfect parked in the drive. I watch Jack and Will assist Pete's employees unload the horses and bring them to the stables opposite of our mares.

The constant dancing on their feet and the brays, which are loud and vibrant, tell me that the studs can smell the females.

"Your horses are beautiful," I murmur as I lean down and pet Gracie's head beside me.

"As are yours."

Across the distance of the pasture, I meet Jack's gaze. It's only for a fleeting second, but there's something in his expression—pride, maybe—that makes me stand a little taller.

"Shall we?" I ask.

We continue the tour around the ranch as the others finish unloading the studs and park the equine carriers in the empty field for storage. I patiently answer every question Pete has. I diligently find the answers to the ones I don't know without trying to be defensive.

The whistle that we're about to officially start this union pulls our attention to where the workers have gathered near the breeding pens, and we move in their direction.

"Everything to your liking?" Jack asks as we approach.

"Just like you promised," Pete says and then smiles when Will leads Cali into the breeding pen. She's antsy and fights him some, but only because she's caught a whiff of the scent of one of the stallions that Cory, one of the workers from Steely Brothers, is walking across the distance.

"Nothing like jumping right into things, huh?" Pete says with a laugh.

"Cali presented," Jack says as she dances some more on her feet before squatting a bit and urinating.

"Yes, she sure is," Pete says while Cory fights to control the sire, who had taken note of Cali. Pete reaches out and shakes Jack's hand and then mine as the gate is shut so the two horses are locked in together. "Here we go."

It's a delicate dance as the horses move around each other.

It's carnal and animalistic and, at the same time, clinical.

I catch Jack's glance and his slight nod as the stallion approaches Cali and she bucks away.

Almost as if she knows what is coming next.

Almost as if she knows she can't escape him.

Almost as if she knows after him, she'll never be the same.

Her life will forever be changed.

Thirty-Eight

TATE

The lights burn bright in the bunkhouse. Laughter rings out more often than not and floats through the still night air.

It's as welcome of a sound as it is lonely.

Because so long as it's happening, Jack's there. He's doing his job schmoozing and entertaining the men from Steely instead of being here at the house with me.

He's doing what I hired him to do.

I take a sip of wine and close my eyes as the cool breeze hits my cheeks.

I miss him.

It's why I'm sitting on the porch swing at eleven o'clock at night instead of sleeping.

Hell, maybe I've gotten so used to sharing my little victories with Jack that I'm just waiting here to share today with him like has become our norm.

Maybe, more than anything, I want to tell him that I finally *get it.*

The *it* being what it feels like to see something I've worked so hard for flourish. Sweat and tears and grime and grit and a whole hell of a lot of determination has taught me that I actually love this place. I haven't ever felt that before.

But sitting here with the men laughing, the night air around me, a little piece of my heart lost but found, and a small taste of success on my tongue, I now know what it feels like.

I now know it's a feeling that was and still is worth fighting for.

Funny thing, I thought there was only one *it* to get, but when a whoop over winning a hand in the poker game they're playing reaches me, I realize there are two. The second *it* I finally get is what it feels like to have someone at your side who wants you to be a part of every single victory no matter how small it is.

It's a foreign feeling to me.

I recall Jack's glances today. The soft touches he'd give me that went unnoticed. Little things to tell me he was proud while never trying to steal my thunder.

He wants me to be part of every step and involved in every decision. It's a heady feeling that is powerful and rewarding all at the same time.

My phone vibrates on the table beside me. I pick it up, not knowing who would be texting me so late.

JACK: You did well today.

PRIDE SWELLS within me and tears blur my visions. I really needed to hear his voice, but this is the next closest thing to it.

ME: Thanks to you. This is all because of you, Jack. Thank you.

I SEND the text and imagine him checking his phone while the beer and jokes flow around that table.

JACK: Good night. Tell Gracie not to get too comfortable.

I SMILE and know the dog is going to love getting to sleep in Jack's usual place in the bed beside me.

Standing, I take one last look at the lights burning in the bunkhouse before Gracie and I head inside.

Maybe them being here is for the best.

I'm getting a little too used to him being beside me.

In three months' time, he'll be gone, and I'll be, what? Devastated? Better off because of the time I spent with him? Heartbroken?

Maybe a bit of all three.

And definitely a lot of one.

Thirty-Nine

TATE

"So far, we've had six of your forty present. We've introduced them to their designated stud twice and let them do their thing," Cory says as he gestures to the whiteboard the men have set up to keep track of all of the combinations and pairings of our mares and their stallions.

"That's . . . great." My response is hesitant because I'm still trying to process all that has happened in the last week.

Nonstop.

That's the only word I can think of to describe it. I feel like I'm putting on a dog-and-pony show, and I'm the dog while Jack is the pony.

If the men go to the bar, Jack accompanies them so he can play defense against the Lone Star residents bad-mouthing the ranch or me.

It's as if we're on a constant vigil, and hell if I'm not expecting Rusty to come careening down the driveway at any moment to report another complaint. Even worse, I'm fearful of being served my notice that we are officially beginning the foreclosure process. Neither the complaints nor being served would look good to Pete.

And I really need this to look good to Pete.

Steely agreeing to a long-term contract would give me a steady income for the next few years. It would mean I'd be willing to possibly sell a few more things off if I knew I had some guaranteed income coming down the pipeline.

It would mean I would be able to keep this ranch, my house . . . this life I fell into and wasn't sure I wanted but now don't want to walk away from.

"Right?" Cory asks.

"I'm sorry, what was that?" I ask, hating that I wasn't paying attention.

"That all of this is looking rather positive."

"It is. Yes. It's just . . ."

"A lot." He shrugs unapologetically. "We can be a little overwhelming. The boys and I don't get out much, so fresh scenery to look at, some new bars to frequent, and some new horses to mate . . . hell, it's like we're kids in a candy store."

"Be my guest." I laugh and shake my head. "Enjoy yourselves while you're here." I take a few steps back and casually check the area to make sure no one is close by. "You mentioned you know Jack. Do you guys go way back?"

He snorts. "It seems like everyone goes way back with Jack but no one can really remember from where." He tosses the eraser he's holding onto the table and perches on the edge of a stool. "That's just Jack. He knows everyone and can convince anyone to believe what he needs them to in order to get the job done." He points to the board. "Case in point, us being here instead of at Hickman Ranch where we've done business for the past ten years."

"Lucky for me," I murmur. "I'm going to go check on a few things."

"You know where I'll be," he says with a wink.

Striding out of the stable with Gracie on my heels, I head toward the main house to grab the vet records that Pete asked for earlier. I cut through the mares' stables and bite back a yelp when a hand closes over my mouth and I'm pulled back into an empty stall.

Just as quickly as the stall door is kicked shut behind us, Jack has me spun around and his lips are on mine. They brand me with a desperation I feel so deep in my bones that all I can think of is how damn much I've missed him. Missed this.

The heat of his body and the strength humming beneath it. The taste of his kiss and the scrape of his goatee.

"Tate." My name is a long, drawn-out groan between kisses as his hand kneads my breast through my shirt while my hand cups his cock through his denim. "Do you have any idea how fucking badly I've missed you?" He might as well have growled the words with all the grit and heat they carry. "Do you know how hard I am every goddamn night needing you?"

A nip on my lips. A tug on the button of my pants. The grunt as he slips his fingers inside my waistband and slides them between my lips to find me wet.

And, hell, he hasn't done more than kiss me, but it's all I need. Jack Sutton has reduced me to a woman who becomes wet on command. Whose body reacts at the thought of him.

"Fuck, you're sexy."

His lips swallow my gasp as our bodies collide into the wall at my back, his fingers moving, my body thrumming. His teeth scrape over my collarbone at the same time he plunges his fingers inside me before sliding out to coat my clit. He repeats the motion over and over until my body is strung so goddamn tight that I feel a grenade detonating when the orgasm slams into me.

"Come for me, Tate," he commands not knowing it doesn't matter if he says it or not, because there is no stopping this.

My knees buckle. My hips buck into his hand as his other covers my mouth to muffle my moan that sounds like sex personified.

There's something about the moment and the desire that's too prevalent in his eyes, that makes repaying the debt all I can think about. All I can focus on is how I want to taste him. How I want to pleasure him.

When I drop to my knees, his groan fills the stall, and I haven't even touched him yet. But within seconds, his cock fills my mouth. Our eyes meet, gray to brown, as his face pulls tight with pleasure. Moments after that, his hand holds the back of my head as he slides all the way to the back of my throat. He keeps it there as long as I can hold it before gagging slightly on him.

The taste of his precum hits my tongue when I back off it. His fingers tighten in my hair, his restraint hanging by a thread.

"You seen Sutton?" someone asks right outside the stall, and I freeze in shock, stopping my own muffled gasp before it can escape around the suction I have on his cock.

But Jack doesn't let me move. His cock is thick and heavy in my mouth as a full-on conversation is being held outside of where we are.

"I thought he was in here somewhere," Will says.

He doesn't release the hold he has on my head.

"I just saw him come in here."

He doesn't move his hips back so I can let him fall out of my mouth.

"Yeah. I think he was grabbing something for Tate," Will says, their feet shuffling over the concrete floors.

He pushes a little deeper, and his thighs tense beneath my hands.

"Tate. Mmm. She isn't a hardship to look at," the other guy says as their feet stop.

Then he slowly slides back out until just the tip of him is in my mouth before starting the process all over again.

"C'mon," Will says, not responding to the other guy's comment. "He's probably over with Ruby."

As their footsteps fade, Jack begins moving a little faster, a little harder, until his controlled groans fill the stable.

Until the hot spurt of his cum shoots down the back of my throat.

"Jesus Christ, Tate," he murmurs when he looks down at me, hand beneath my chin tilting my face up to his. He leans over and presses a kiss squarely on my lips. "Next time, it's you who gets to be tasted."

Forty

JACK

"Pick up, old man," I mutter as the phone rings for the fourth time.

"You've reached Evan with Sutton Ranch. I'm out steering cattle. Call you back later." The beep follows after his voice.

"Hey, Evan. Just checking to see how everything is going with the ranch . . . and with Lauren. Last night, I had to beg her to call her sponsor. She was upset and frantic and I talked her off the ledge, but I wanted to see if you could check on her for me. I'm sorry I keep asking. I know it isn't your problem, but I'm still buttoning up the stuff I needed to do here. I'll be back before the season starts. You have my word."

I end the call and sink back into my bunk. The cigar smoke swirls outside my room. The ballgame on the television drones on. The outbursts from the guys winning a hand in the poker game they've got going come sporadically.

Shit, if I'm not exhausted.

Twelve days of all-out with these fuckers.

Twelve days of sneaking moments with Tate.

Twelve days of realizing I lied to Lauren. I am falling for Tate—hell, I might have already fallen for her.

There isn't a single thing I can do to fix this or save it.

Not one.

The only thing I can do is figure out how to walk away and leave the smallest ripple possible.

I've been lying to Tate since day one.

Fucking lying, and I know it's something she won't forgive.

"Christ," I groan, push up from the bunk, and slam my way out of the room.

"Shit. We woke the sleeping bear," Cory says with a slurred laugh and Pete looks my way from beneath his hat as he tries to hide his nonexistent poker face.

"Where the fuck you going?" Garret, one of the other helpers, shouts.

"You guys are killing my game. A man's gotta get laid some-time." I grab my keys as they hoot and holler.

"I bet it's that redhead down at the bar. Vivian? Violet? What the fuck's her name?" Cory asks.

I stop at the door and toss them a cocky grin. "Does it really matter? It isn't like I'm going to remember by the morning."

Their laughter and shouts of encouragement carry through the door when I shut it and strut toward my truck. I climb in and rev the engine before driving just beyond the gate of the ranch and parking on the road by the small grove of trees.

My jog back up the gravel path is quick, and my fist banging on Tate's door is even quicker.

The light flicks on in the hallway as her feet fall on the hard-wood floor within.

"Jack?" Her voice is surprised as she steps back to let me in.

I might have the same damn startled look on my face, but it's for such a very different reason.

How in the hell did this woman with her storm-cloud-colored eyes and bee-stung lips win my fucking heart?

"Is everything okay? I just heard your truck take off." She looks toward the empty driveway again, confusion etching the lines of her face as she reaches out and runs a hand down my arm because I'm just standing there and staring at her.

At her simplicity.

At her need to be in control and ability to give it to me when it's warranted.

At her wild.

"Yeah." I step into her and press my lips to hers in a kiss so very different from any others I've given her before. This time, there is a softness in it. A regret. A knowledge that I only have so many of these left to give. "I missed you, is all."

She doesn't respond with words.

Instead, she pulls me into her arms and kisses me back with the same gentle desperation I feel.

THE SKY IS TURNING GRAY. It's subtle hues as the early morning sky prepares for the sun to rise remind me of Tate's eyes.

I turn to look at where she's snuggled beneath the covers, hair fanned out on the tan pillowcase, one leg wrapped around the comforter's edge while her breast is partially uncovered by the opposite end.

She's beautiful.

Not in the typical sense. She's slight in stature with small features, perfect tits, and a great ass, but it's her unforgettable personality that draws me to her. Fire and ice when she needs to be and sunshine and storm clouds at other times.

It takes everything I have not to crawl back into bed beside her and curl into her warmth, spread her thighs, and taste her again.

My dick stirs to life as I think of the way she mewled and bucked beneath my tongue last night. When she tucked in close against me and her breath feathered over my skin as it evened out, I wanted to tell her the same three words she told me the other night.

But I'd be awake.

I'd know what I said.

She doesn't know she did.

I need to go get my truck and then drive up the driveway before the guys wake up. I need to go pretend I was out getting laid by Violet instead of Tate.

"Hey." Her voice is husky, eyes squinting as she pushes the hair out of her face.

"Morning."

She glances at the clock. "It's early." The two words are a groan that I couldn't agree more with.

"No. Stay in bed. Get some more sleep," I say when she begins to push herself up.

Bending over, I press a kiss to the top of her head as she grabs my pillow and hugs it to her before closing her eyes and snuggling back under the comforter. "I'll be up in a few minutes," she murmurs, her voice sleep drugged as she falls back asleep.

"I've got everything covered. Get some sleep, Tate."

I stride out of the room but look back one more time.

Somewhere along the line, I forgot I came here because of a promise I made.

Sometime over the past few months, I lost sight of the fact that I was supposed to be making amends with the universe. I'd forgotten that my purpose here was to right some of the wrongs I'd made in my real estate dealings when I took advantage of small ranch owners by trying to help Tate.

Both of those notions have become one hundred percent overshadowed and forgotten because of her. Tatum Knox. The unexpected woman I can't seem to get enough of.

I've definitely fucking fallen for her.

And hell if that isn't a hard one to swallow.

Forty-One

TATE

"Thanks for your help, Will."

"We're the ones eating it all," he says as he helps me carry the groceries into the bunkhouse. "It's the least I can do." He sets them on the table and then pauses. "Wait, you actually went into town and shopped? No delivery? What happened?"

"Nothing." I shrug. He doesn't need to know that my trip was to test the temperature of the town. The stares were still there, and some people were still frosty when I tried to interact with them, but . . . it felt much less daunting this time around.

"I just needed to take a mini-break. Go to town for a bit. Get an ice cream cone."

"Being around all us men has to get tiring." He laughs.

So says the eighteen-year-old.

"Nothing I can't handle. Things are going well?" I ask nonchalantly because I don't want to seem like I'm prying. "I mean . . . you're okay with being here and staying here? I don't mean to take you away from your family." I stumble over the words I'm not sure if I'm supposed to know about what he said about his father's drinking.

"Tate." I stop unloading the fruit from my bag and look at him. His blue eyes are loaded with emotion. "This is the longest span of time I've ever had where I haven't had to block a fist being thrown my way."

"Will." I don't know what to say other than his name to let him know I hear him and I feel horrible for him.

"He drinks to cope with my mom's death . . . but that isn't the life I want to live, so I'm trying my best to do better."

Emotion overwhelms me, and I have to force my hand not to shake. "Jack's contract is up soon. Maybe you should consider if you want to stay on after that. With a paycheck, that is. We can figure something out so you can still do school at night. Hire a few more hands, and I don't know, but we'll figure it out."

"Are you serious?" The hope woven into those three words lingers in the room.

"Yes. I'll talk to Jack about it and make sure he shows you what you need to know."

"I don't even know what to say. I just . . ."

"You're a good kid, Will."

He drops his head and nods before stepping out to grab more groceries . . . or to gather himself. I follow a second later to find he's gotten the rest of the groceries, so I shut the tailgate for him.

"Where's Jack anyway?" I ask.

"Down in the breeding pen."

"'Kay."

The sun is playing peekaboo with the clouds as I make my way down to the pens for what feels like the hundredth time in the past weeks. The sounds I've grown accustomed to—anxious mares whinnying, testosterone-fueled stallions revved—are a soundtrack around me.

My eyes are cast down, checking messages on my phone about upcoming food deliveries and times that Doc Arlington is available to come out to perform ultrasounds on the mares to see if any of this was a success, when a text from Sheryl pings, letting me know we might have a buyer for Ruby.

I stare at the message as I let it settle in, and I allow myself to believe the horse that was such a staple for this ranch, such a beacon of hope for me in the darkest of times, might be leaving.

My hands tremble as I dial her number.

"Sheryl. It's Tate."

"You got my message?"

"Yes. It breaks my heart a little if I'm being honest," I say as I bite my lip and lean back against the wall of the stable.

"It's going to break your bank account even more if you don't."

"Are you sure, Sheryl? I mean, even if we sell all the foals that should be born over the next few months along with the income we know is coming from this contract with Steely, I still have to sell her?"

"Yes."

"Sell who?" Jack's eyes are shadowed beneath the brim of his hat, and thunder begins to rumble in the far-off distance when I meet his eyes. "Sell who, *Knox*?" he demands when I just stand there like a deer in the headlights.

"Let me call you right back," I tell Sheryl and hang up without waiting for her response.

"What's going on here?"

"Don't you dare take that tone with me," I snip back, defensive over the secret I've kept from him.

"Tone?" he barks out. "How about you tell me what the fuck is going on here? I'm over here busting my ass to close this deal with Steely, who wants exclusivity. They want to know you're their breeder, which I promised them you would be, and now you're talking about selling a horse? Don't you think that should be something your ranch manager should know?" he asks. "Selling a horse to someone else is not considered exclusivity."

"You don't get to question me." I see the man who came to me the other night, the one who laid me down on the bed and took his slow, sweet time worshipping my body, but I hear the same man who walked in here on day one full of an arrogance and condescension that echoed my father's.

"I'll question you any goddamn time I want," he counters, the muscle in his jaw feathering, his hands fisting.

"No, you won't." My voice is part growl, part yell as the exhaustion of the past few weeks and stress of having to sell Ruby really mix with the guilt of keeping this from him.

When he steps forward and grabs my arm, I flinch. There's something about his expression that has me seeing Fletcher standing above me after he'd shoved me down into a chair, screaming about all the things I messed up for him. I feel that fear that hums beneath the surface and taste the bitter unsurety of whether he would actually hurt me.

But Jack doesn't notice. He's oblivious to how I just put him and Fletcher in the same category while inside I'm silently dying over it as he leads me toward the house. If I didn't know we had eyes watching us, I would have told him to fuck off and run the other way.

It doesn't help that Gracie isn't too fond of what's happening and is nipping at Jack's heels as he walks, no doubt drawing even more attention to us.

Our labored breathing and the clomp of our feet are the only sounds as we enter my house. The minute the door shuts, every ounce of anger I have for him parading me up here like a scolded child unleashes in a litany of words that probably don't even make sense.

Of course, my rant falls on deaf ears because his is louder, more resonating, and it dominates the small space.

"Don't you ever grab my arm like that again!"

"You want to fight in front of a man who's going to give you a big payoff next year? You want to let him see you act like a god-damn child?"

"A child? A—"

"What in the hell are you trying to sell, Tate? Did you just give up on this? On the ranch? Did you think things were too hard and decide you didn't want to do it anymore?"

His accusations hit me harder than expected. "After the past few weeks and all the work we've put in? How dare you accuse me of that!"

"Then what the hell is going on?"

"It's Ruby. I'm trying to sell Ruby."

"You're what?" His voice rises in pitch, the tone a precursor. "Are you fucking insane?" He takes a step toward me that has me stepping back. "She's your cash cow. She's the one you sell off when things are dire because you have no other option. What in the fuck is going on, Knox?"

"Do you think I would sell her if that weren't the exact case?"

He snorts and stares at me with a disappointment and disbelief that burns deep within. "You're full of shit."

If words could slap you, my face would be bright red.

"I am?" I shriek, feeling like every ounce of trust we've worked toward together fractures when he says those four words.

"You said things were tight but you had the insurance money to use. You have some foals coming to sell. You have this deal coming through if we can close this strong . . ." He scrubs a hand over his jaw. "Are you losing the ranch, Tate?"

"No." The lone syllable is loaded with a desperation that I try to pass off as me being offended he even asked.

But the minute the word is out, I'm already ashamed of the lie. I'm already dreading how this whole conversation has gone. I'm already on the defensive.

"So, because times are tough, you're just going to sell her? I mean, that's the only thing that makes sense." He snorts in disgust. "I never figured you for a quitter, Tate."

While his words might be meant to motivate, they are actually incendiary. It's the hurt that pushes me to retaliate. It's the shame that chooses the words it uses. "And I never figured you for a bastard."

"I should have fucking figured," he mutters as we stare at each other, faces red and words we can't take back floating into the air between us. Rather than dying in the tension like they should, they take root and dig deeper.

Jack stares at me, the muscles in his neck strained as his pulse beats frantically against his skin. He's taking a step back figuratively, but I take one forward. I take all of the pent-up hurt and exhaustion and everything between that I told myself I'd never put up with again, and I hurl it at him.

I know later I'll look back on it and realize that I'm in the wrong.

But in the moment, there's nothing stopping me. In the moment, I see Jack but am consumed by the thought of selling Ruby and the shame of losing my house. I see the man I'm falling in love with but fear telling him every last detail.

Because telling him means letting him in completely. It means giving him my absolute trust and giving him the tools to ruin me if he wants to.

That fear owns me and uses my temper to protect me.

"Just because I let you slide between my legs every night doesn't give you the right to make decisions for me or tell me how I should make mine." It's my turn to shock him with words. The double take of his head says as much. "How do you think we're getting by, Jack? How do you think I'm paying your salary and every other goddamn thing that has come up in the past few months?" I fight back the tears of frustration and only grow more mad when I lose and one slips down my cheek.

"Tate."

"No. Don't you touch me." I yank my arm back. My emotions are on overload, and now that the dam has broken, there is no stopping it. "Fletcher took every-goddamn-thing I had. What was in my savings from my trust. My credit. My reputation. He maxed out a home equity line I thought had a zero balance. The draw of the bet and the adrenaline rush of winning was stronger than his love was for me. He gambled away *everything* we had, Jack, and I've been digging myself out of the hole since the day he died. Is that what you need to know? Does that explain why I need to sell Ruby?"

He stares at me, lips lax but eyes hard. The man is the perfect picture of compassion for me and utter rage for Fletcher as he reaches out to wipe a tear off my cheek with the back of his hand. I step away.

"Don't," he warns as I cross my arms over my chest, closing myself off to him physically as well as emotionally. I'm hurt and just want to be.

"Please, leave me alone."

"Are you losing the ranch, Tate?" he asks again, and this time, my chin quivers in response. "Jesus fucking Christ!" He moves from one side of the room and then back as he processes. "You're losing this place and you didn't trust me enough to tell me? Talk about ironic. You throw words at me about sliding between your thighs . . . well, turn that around, will you? You let me sleep with you—*make love to you*—but you don't trust me enough to tell me this place is being foreclosed on?" He stops as he passes in front of me and grabs my shoulders and shakes them. "I can't help you if you don't let me! I can't make this work if you keep shutting me the fuck out!"

"That's not what I was . . ." I shrug out of his grip and move across the room to abate the onslaught of emotions racing through me. Maybe if I move far enough, I can outrun some of the fear of letting him completely in. When I finally turn back around, my chest constricts at the sight of him standing there so obviously hurt that I didn't trust him.

Trust.

My hands tremble as I draw in a breath. "The bank is process-ing the foreclosure papers on the ranch. I . . . I used the insurance money to pay off all the accounts and to keep them current, but that's completely gone."

"So, you took care of your accounts before taking care of you," he murmurs, his voice calm and understanding and warm and everything I need, but my own shame coats it a different color so that I can't see through it.

"It was the right thing to do . . . and—" I blow out a breath to combat the tears that burn in my eyes. "And I'm just barely keep-ing my head above water. I'm months late on the mortgage, but it's a catch-twenty-two. I use the little income I'm getting to keep this place running so I can attract and contract with a client like Steely with the hopes of securing a steady revenue stream *or* pay the mortgage." I can't meet his eyes so I stare at my fingers twist-ing together in front of me.

"Tate." He says my name and the broken way he says it screams that he's disappointed in me.

"I'm sorry"—I hiccup over the word— "I just . . . I thought if people knew, if this town knew, then they'd make things even harder on me until they succeeded in pushing me out."

"But you didn't trust *me* enough to tell me." There's hurt in his voice. Anger. "After all the work we've done, the time we've spent . . . you pegged me to be just like everyone else. You ex-pected me to try to hurt you too."

"Jack!" But my plea isn't enough to drown out the regret and pain in his voice. "I was afraid. I *am* afraid." I take a step toward him. "Trust is what got me into this mess in the first place!"

"Save it, Tate." He waves a hand at me as if he's writing me off. "If after all of this, you don't trust me . . . you never will."

"I trusted Fletcher," I explain in desperation. "That trust allowed him to run our finances into the ground, and I was the meek, mousy wife who let it happen. I didn't question him when he told me the late nights he spent in the bunkhouse were because he was working when he was really on the phone with bookies all night. I didn't realize that his highs were high only because he'd won a huge payout and that his lows weren't my fault but were blamed on me anyway. Hell, I didn't even question the trips he was taking to Montana before he died. He'd convinced me he was close to closing an exclusivity deal, but he'd come home empty handed, pissed at the goddamn world and refusing to talk about it. You tell me, Jack Sutton, how exactly does someone put trust in someone else again when the one person they should have been able to trust the most, screwed them?"

I'm embarrassed. I feel raw and vulnerable and just want to be left alone and hugged and fixed all at the same time.

"I'm not Fletcher, Tate."

"I know you aren't, but it's hard to believe it isn't going to happen again and even harder to admit that I'm in this position in the first place!"

He doesn't react, but instead stares out the window at the guys working with the horses. "How bad is it? Will this deal with Steely fix things?"

"Most foreclosures take about six months once the ball gets rolling. The ball is already rolling."

He chews his bottom lip, and I hate that he won't look at me. "I'm not letting you sell Ruby, Tate." His voice is calm and even. "That isn't the way to go. I'll get the deal. I'll finalize it and figure out a way to get Steely to pay you progress payments during the gestation period."

I shake my head. "And what if the foals don't go to term? Then what? Not only will I owe them stud fees but also I'll owe them for the amount they've paid toward the foal that died." I scrub my hands over my face.

"Then I'll float you the goddamn money until you get caught up to current. Christ, Tate. Quit being so goddamn stubborn."

"Absolutely not. I won't take your charity."

"Then I won't accept your half-assed apology about not trusting me."

"That isn't fair."

"Isn't it, though?" He blows out a breath in frustration. "You won't accept help. You kept this from me so that I couldn't help. *You didn't trust me.* What the fuck are we fighting for, Tate? So we can do all this, the everything"—he throws his hands out to his sides— "and you can lie down and die and lose it all?"

"That isn't what I said. I'm not giving up," I explain because I'm not. I've already decided that. My plan is to sell Ruby and do whatever else I have to do to get good with the bank again. I don't want to do it, but like he said, it's a last resort.

He finally turns to face me, but instead of speaking, he just shakes his head with sadness and disappointment pooling in his eyes before he heads toward the front door.

I suck in a ragged breath as the first sob hits me. Shame and grief and guilt mix and explode like a match to a powder keg in that first wave of tears. I'm mad at myself. I'm angry at the world. I'm furious at everyone but the man I just let down because I didn't trust soon enough.

"Hey."

He never left.

When I look up, there's the silent click of my camera's shutter.

"What are you doing?" I ask, feeling violated in the oddest of ways. There's no way I want my stupidity documented. "Give it to me." I grab for the camera in his hand, but he pulls it back so I can't reach it.

"This." It's all he says as he pushes some buttons and then hands the camera to me so I can see what he's talking about. "This is what I want you to look at. This is what I want you to remember about today. Not that we fought. Not that you were embarrassed that I finally found out the truth. Not that you finally learned to trust me and the sky didn't fall in. Not any of that."

"I don't understand—"

"Today is the day you stopped being under Fletcher's thumb. Today is the day you began mapping out your own future and started to break free from everything he weighed you down with."

The image on the screen is of tears streaking down my cheeks, stained paths of persistence on my makeup-free face. My lips are parted. My eyes are looking up beneath a veil of thick lashes. It's the look of shame coated in defiance, resolve winning over defeat, and determination mastering fear that stands out the most.

"Today is the day you *own your wild*."

I don't tell him he's crazy. In fact, I don't even look up at him because I'm too mesmerized by the picture and his declaration.

Jack's feet clomp on the floor.

The door opens quietly and then closes with a *thud*.

But I'm standing in my hallway, staring at an image I love and hate all at the same time.

Today is the day I own my wild.

Forty-Two

TATE

The water sluices over my skin with each stroke.

It's cool and refreshing and therapeutic.

One after another.

Again and again.

I count each one as a measure of time.

My head tilts to the side so I can draw in a ragged breath.

I've settled into a cadence to try to put distance between our fight tonight, the truths I finally told him, and the pain I caused him.

The exertion doesn't take away the sting that Jack hasn't answered my texts.

The emotions ate at me, every single one of them.

So, I came to the one place I used to use as my meditation to get through my every day. The place I haven't returned to since the first night I slept with Jack.

The sun is setting, and the pool is getting dark, but I don't get out to turn the lights on. I've done this enough times to know the length by heart. I've found solace here enough times that sometimes the darkness feels so much more inviting.

No one can see my shame then.

No one can see me wear the guilt.

No one can hear my screams underwater.

I do a flip turn and push off toward the other side, still trying to shake Jack from my mind.

When someone jumps into the pool in front of me, it's the last thing I ever expected, and it startles me so much that I choke on a swallow of water as I find my feet beneath me.

But the cough dies on my lips when I look up to see Jack in the pool with me. His body may be naked, but it's the apology and the regret and the love in his expression that holds me hostage.

There are no words as we step toward each other or as he pulls me against him or before our lips meet in a tender kiss laced with desperation. His hands roam over my body as if they are mapping every single curve.

We speak in actions. His kiss to my neck, my palms running up the plain of his back. His hands digging into the flesh of my hips, my wrapping my legs around his. His fingertips pulling aside my bathing suit bottoms and skimming over me, my teeth sinking into his shoulder in reaction. His cock slowly pushing into me, my accepting every single, thick, hard inch of him.

"Jack," I moan.

"Uh-uh," he murmurs when his lips find mine again. "I don't want to talk, Tate." He uses the buoyancy of the water to push my hips back so his crest slides over the rough patch of nerves within me. "I just need to feel you." He pulls me back against him roughly so I'm forced to take the pleasure. "Feel us." Another tantalizing withdrawal that has every part of me begging for him to fill me again. "Just this." And he fulfills my desire by thrusting back into me. "Just us."

We continue this slow, methodical pace until our nerves are as assaulted as our emotions were earlier, and our actions are as devastating to our senses as our words had been. Until we're left wanting to be together instead of wanting to be apart.

And so we make up.

And so we make love.

Forty-Three

JACK

"You're avoiding me."

"Lauren. Hello." All the tension of the day seizes up at the sound of her voice.

"I take it that means you've fallen for her?"

I snort and wonder how many times she's going to ask me before she realizes I'm not going to dignify the question with a response. "Evan said things are good there," I deflect.

"Have you told her the truth?"

"Not your business, Sis." I roll my shoulders and dig in for the long haul in this conversation. "He said that the heifers are healthy and doing well so we should expect a good lot of calves this year. It's always good news when business is good, right?"

"What's your end game, huh, Jack-Jack? Are you getting off on being the hired help? Is it a turn on to fuck the boss?"

"Have you been drinking?" I ask, her belligerence at an all-new level.

"Nope. This talk is coming to you sober, and sober Lauren isn't bothered if she hurts your feelings like drunk Lauren is."

I sigh at her lie but don't refute it. "Did something happen?"

"Did something happen?" She laughs. "Let's see. You aren't here doing what you're supposed to be doing. Dingo was bucked off a horse when it spooked while riding the fence line and was hurt."

"But he's okay." I know our wrangler is because I already talked to Evan about it.

"The weather's relentless. It has been raining for days on end, and I don't care how big this house is, it isn't big enough with kids and no escape."

"It's supposed to let up tomorrow," I tell her, my phone app still alerting me daily of the weather back home. "And?"

"And this is a lot to do on my own, Jack."

"What is? Being a mom to your kids? Watching out the window as Evan runs the ranch for me while I'm gone? Last I checked you've never really had a hand in the day-to-day there other than having the Sutton name . . . so am I missing something here?" I ask with a frustrated sigh, not caring that I'm going to hit a nerve with the comment. "You reap all of the benefits and don't have to do any of the work. Do you want to explain to me why any of that gives you the right to be the raging bitch you're being right now?"

She's silent, and a silent Lauren is almost worse than a drunk Lauren. "You have no right to judge me."

"Ditto."

A tense silence weighs across the connection, and I roll my shoulders in exasperation.

"Look," she starts followed by a shaky inhale. "I get you're out there supposedly keeping your promise to Dad, but that promise died the minute *he* died. That promise has already been fulfilled. So, yeah, I get you need to find yourself or make amends for the shitty things you did in your past business life, but at what point is it too much? He was a bastard, Jack. It isn't your job to find his redemption."

"I can't just walk away. I signed a contract."

She snorts. "So what? She'll get over it."

"That's enough, Lauren."

"You fucked her over the moment you slept with her, you know that, right? Women can't separate this shit like men can. You're going to make her fall for you and then you're going to break her heart. How exactly are you making things better for her by doing that, huh?

"I've got to go."

"The best thing you can do is come home."

"I said I'd be there in time."

"Even better, you can distance yourself from her now so you hurt her less then."

I end the call without saying goodbye.

My sister's already said enough.

And fuck if ninety percent of it wasn't true.

Forty-Four

TATE

The days trudge on.

Hours upon hours of our normal duties but then the added responsibility of keeping four men occupied and out of trouble as the boredom of a small town hits the Steely crew here at Knox Ranch.

Last night, tires crunched down the driveway and headlights were flicked off as not to light up my house at well past two in the morning.

With a five in the morning start time, that isn't a whole hell of a lot of sleep.

Maybe it's a good thing that Jack was occupied last night. Maybe the distance will help me to detach myself some from him and the inevitable that is starting to weigh heavier and heavier every time I see him. Sadness has started to creep in with every slash across the calendar day as it passes because each new mark marches us closer to him leaving.

The thoughts and emotions that follow soon after are all-consuming, and I hate it. Hate them.

At the same time, I almost feel as if he's avoiding me. He has gone from finding ways to pull me into the tack room and steal a kiss to going out of his way not to find the two of us in those situations.

Then again, maybe I'm just overthinking it.

But what he said and the picture he took of me have made more than an impression. I forced myself to print the portrait and frame it. It's the reminder of where I've been, what I've been through, and how I survived.

I force myself to focus on the grain I'm mixing instead of the inevitability of him leaving, and I manage to get two batches done before Jack's shadow crosses in front of the open doors.

"Hey, you got a minute?" I call out.

"Not really." His feet hesitate for a moment before he starts to walk again.

"Jack!" If my voice makes me sound desperate, it's because I am.

This time, he stops. His head is hung down for the briefest of seconds before he nods ever so slightly and turns to face me. "What did you need, Tate?" His voice is clipped with impatience as he looks at me from behind his sunglasses, and it bugs me that I can't see his eyes.

"Nothing . . . I just—we haven't talked much, and I . . . never mind."

"I've been busy." Impatience rings in his voice. "What did you need?"

"Nothing. I guess I wanted to make sure we were okay, is all."

"Perfectly fine. Anything else?"

I stare at him, tears burning in my eyes.

Blame it on PMS or on exhaustion, it doesn't really matter. "Nope. Not a thing." I retreat a step before turning on my heel and heading back into the stable to finish what I was doing, hating how stupid and insecure I feel.

"Christ." I hear him hiss the word and then the crunch of his boots on the gravel as he follows me inside. "Look, I'm sorry, it's just been a rough couple of days."

"What happened?" My mind fires to everything on the ranch that could go wrong, which is a long, long list.

"Just shit back home." He glances my way, and of course, now I feel like a complete ass. I've leaned on him, but I don't know that I've ever really let him lean on me. I don't think I'm a selfish person, but assuming that his distance was because of me sure as hell makes me feel like I'm the most self-centered person on the face of the earth.

"You want to talk about it?"

He looks anywhere but at me. "No. It's fine."

Interesting that we had a giant fight about my not wanting to talk to him about my finances and now he's avoiding telling me about whatever is bothering him. Pot, meet Kettle.

"Got it." I turn back to the counter. "Sorry I bugged you."

His sigh sounds like a curse when he emits it. His voice softens. "Don't be that way."

"Be what way?" I counter. "Wanting to know more about the man I'm more or less living with? I mean . . . I know you like your coffee black, your steaks medium-well, and you aren't ashamed that you like to cuddle, but that's about it. You had a dad you could never please so you left home, only to regret some of the reasons too late. You have a sister, who puts worry in your eyes more often than not, and a brother, who passed away and you don't talk about." My hands grip the edge of the counter as I struggle to control my emotions and the feeling of rejection hearing all of this awakens in me. "Is it sad that Cory probably knows more about your life off this ranch than I do?"

"It's complicated."

"Yeah, well, you've seen my life, right? Complicated is all I know."

And without another word, I slam the pail down on the counter and stalk past him.

I don't know if I'm upset or relieved that he doesn't grab my arm to set things straight.

That he doesn't let me in more.

Forty-Five

TATE

"Grab your camera. We're going for a walk," Jack says when I answer the knock on my front door.

"I don't want to."

"Grab your camera, Tate. Or I will. Either that, or I'll toss you over my shoulder and carry you across the field. Everyone will notice and ask questions. Your choice, Knox." His voice isn't warm, but it isn't frosty either. We haven't talked since our little tiff earlier, so I'm not surprised.

I glare at him. The last thing I want to do is *obey* and, yet, something urges me to believe that he's asking more than demanding. That if I dug my heels in and refused to go, he would relent and leave me be. That's the only thing that allows me the permission to do what I really want, which is to go with him.

Within minutes, I have my camera and Gracie and I are trailing slightly behind him. I don't want to give him the satisfaction of thinking I want to be with him.

When I actually do.

We walk across the property as the sun begins to set. Dragonflies dance around us in the warm evening air, and I can't help but stop to snap images of their wings glistening in the light like glitter floating in the air. Jack keeps walking when I stop, Gracie bounding beside him as if she doesn't understand the discord between us. Every once in a while, I aim the camera his way and snap a few shots.

His hand petting her head as the dandelions blow out of focus in the distance behind him.

Click.

His untucked red T-shirt against the starkness of his denim.

Click.

The strong line of his nose, the rough cut of his jaw, the hard set of his chin as he waits for me to catch up.

Click.

We walk in silence until we hit the edge of the pond. Jack takes a seat and stares at the ripple of the water as birds and more dragonflies dance across it to grab a drink.

I listen to nature's symphony of birds chirping, trees rustling in the breeze, Gracie panting, and the hum of everything else around me. The longer I listen, the less I sense the tension between us.

Maybe we just needed to step away.

Maybe we just needed to distance ourselves from the stress of it all.

"Jack?"

His sigh is heavy, and I hate that he doesn't turn to look at me—not once. "What are we doing here, Tate?" He plays with a blade of grass, pulling it apart and letting the tiny pieces flutter to the ground.

Click.

"You tell me. You're the one pushing me away. Being a dick. Closing me out."

"You're right. I am."

I wasn't expecting his blatant agreement, so it takes me a moment before I ask, "Why?"

"We're . . . we're us." He barely glances my way, but it's enough for me to see the pain in his eyes, and that causes worry to reverberate through me. "And pretty soon, I have to leave and be the man I swore I'd never be. I have to live the life that I promised myself I'd never live. It's what I want, it's what I need to do, but I don't know . . ." He shakes his head. "So, not only am I having a hard time figuring out how I'm supposed to be those things but I also know that it's going to hurt like a son of a bitch leaving you."

Then don't!

The words scream through my mind as the panic that's been slowly building bubbles up.

I can't tell him to stay, though. Jack has worlds to conquer. Things he needs to learn and become. There's no way I can hold him back from that.

There's no way I can tell him I've fallen in love with him.

There's no way I can burden him with that.

"I'm a man who falls hard, Tate." He picks up a rock and side-arms it so it skips three times across the water before sinking beneath the surface. "So, it's easier if I don't fall at all."

"Okay." I nod as if I understand, but I don't.

"It's just easier for me that way. In the past, the transient nature of my job made it easy for me. Moving on every few months."

Look at me, Jack.

"But you're heading home soon. You'll have somewhere permanent." Just getting the words out is half the battle because I'm secretly dying inside. Privately hating that I've let myself get so close to someone so fast. "What then?"

Let me see your eyes because your lips are moving, but I don't believe you.

He shrugs. His profile against the lake stoic and unemotional. "Then I guess I'll do what's expected of me."

I feel your kisses every night.

"Which is?"

I see the glances you steal of me.

"Get married. Have kids. Learn to be the man my dad expected me to be."

I feel you.

"Wouldn't he just want you happy?" I ask.

I know there's more here.

"Yeah. I guess."

Look at me, Jack.

"There are all kinds of versions of happy."

"There are." When he finally turns and looks at me, his eyes are miserable and his expression is pained. "But we live in two different worlds. I'd never ask you to walk away from this now that we're on the cusp of success and I can't walk away from mine. So, love and happiness don't exactly get to factor into the equation."

"You're wrong, though." I fight the desperation that laces the edges of my voice, but it's still there. I told myself I couldn't hold him back, ask him to stay, and yet that's exactly what I want to do. Ask. Beg. Plead. "Happiness and love should always mean something."

"I can't be your *next time*, Tatum." The despair in his tone mimics mine as our eyes hold in the waning light, and I see it. He doesn't have to say the three words for me to hear them.

And he knows I see it.

He just nods ever so slightly before wrapping his arm around my shoulders and pulling me against his side.

We sit like that for some time. Together. Alone. Quiet. Accepting the inevitable and fighting it all at the same time.

I take comfort in the heat of his body beside mine, in the brush of his lips over mine, and in the soft sigh of a kiss we slip into as he lays me back onto the grass beneath us.

He makes love to me in the twilight without any words but with every emotion pouring out of him through the gentleness of his actions. The reverence in his touch as he kisses away the tear that slips down my cheek is something I draw deep into me so that I can keep it with me once I no longer have the man who bestowed it.

Forty-Six

JACK

"You want to tell me what this is?"

I look up from the barrage of texts I've shared back and forth with my sister, same bullshit, different day, to find Pete walking across the stable with a stack of stapled papers in his hand.

"What's what?" I rise from my seat and accept the stack he holds out.

It takes me a second to realize what they are and for the dread to settle in. I count to ten, forcing the fight or flight to wane so I can keep my tone even and unfazed when I speak to him.

"This has been an almost flawless venture, but we're one day out from leaving, and when I went into town today, I was handed these and then given a warning. You want to tell me what the hell they are and why I shouldn't be concerned?"

I flip through the ledger as if it's something I've seen before. Lines upon lines of bets made, of bets lost, of an exorbitant amount of money owed in the balance line. "What was the warning?" I ask as my temper roils beneath the surface.

"That we were making a mistake investing in this venture. That Knox owes enough to bookies that she's going to take any money paid to her and bail. She has horses for sale. She has the ranch in general for sale, which is why you're here. What the fuck is going on here, Sutton?"

I huff a laugh as my hands grip the fucking papers. "I'm not selling the ranch for her, Pete. Why would I work so hard to negotiate the deal with you if I were going to?" I move to the opposite end of the bunkhouse and turn to face him. "These are old news." I smack the papers against my palm. "Just some assholes in town who Knox's husband shorted some cash when he died. She's straight as an arrow. I wouldn't be here or pushing her to you if I didn't know that for a fact."

"Then why those?" Pete juts his chin in the direction of the papers.

"For starters? The Hickmans are less than thrilled that you're here and not there."

"They got lazy and dropped the ball."

"But they only see her stealing you away."

"You said for starters. What other shitstorm am I walking into if we solidify this deal long term?"

"This land is desirable. The Knox's won the bid on the land and two brothers who didn't want to get into a bidding war over it have been harassing her since the day the papers were signed. She hasn't flinched once, and I don't see her doing it in the future." No way in fucking hell she will now that I'm going to button up this deal and save this place from going belly up.

"This is concerning, Jack. Investing money and trusting a partner is a little hard to do with someone when you fear they aren't going to be there from one season to the next."

"She'll be here, Pete. I'm telling you. My word is good on this. I haven't let you down yet, have I?"

He purses his lips, indecision etched in the lines of his face. "But what happens when your contract is up, huh? You don't stick around most places long. Rumor has it you'll be moving on soon."

Fucking rumors. I feel like a traitor uttering these words to him before I'll ever admit them to her . . . or even to myself, but he needs the truth, not some bullshit sales pitch. "Because I'm in love with her, Pete."

His startled intake of air is exactly how I feel—staggered by the admission.

"Come again?" He laughs around the words because he's known me long enough to have never heard them grace my lips.

"You heard me. I'm in love with Tatum Knox . . . and if you think I'm going to leave her here alone to fend off the wolves, then you don't know the man I am. That's part of the reason I proposed the progress payment plans. I know it isn't the norm in the industry, but you want these horses, Pete. Trust me on that. With your crew coming every month to check in, your presence will be noticed and, in turn, will give the ranch not only security with the payments but also help me keep these assholes from thinking they can push her out." I glance out toward the pasture where his men are slowly preparing for their departure tomorrow before looking back at him. "You know my word is good."

Pete just shakes his head. "I know it is. I know what you're made of. The question is, how are you going to take care of this little problem, Sutton? Because we can't leave here without it being resolved."

"It won't be a problem by the time you load the horses up in the carrier tomorrow afternoon."

He nods, and I toss the ledger onto the table before leaving.

It only takes me a few minutes to find Tate. Her strokes are carving across the water, one confident strong movement after another. I step toward the edge of the pool so when she reaches it, she'll notice me.

I told Pete I loved her.

She touches the wall and then looks up to me, lifting her swim goggles off her eyes to her forehead. "Hi."

But I couldn't tell her.

"Hi. Should I be worried that you're swimming laps?" I ask, afraid something is upsetting her enough to make her want to scream underwater.

"Funny." She rolls her eyes. "Just getting some exercise."

"Whew." I smile. "I, uh, have to head into town to take care of a few things."

Tate treads water but looks confused. "But what about the barbecue?" she asks, referring to the farewell dinner we have planned for the Steely Brothers crew to celebrate four weeks of hard work and, hopefully, pregnant mares.

"I know. I'll try to make it back in time." Her eyes narrow, and I know I need to go before she can look too closely and see the rage beneath the surface. "It's just some loose ends I need to tie up so that Pete can leave with all of the i's dotted and t's crossed."

"I'm sure he'd be fine if you took care of it tomorrow so that you could join us tonight."

"I'm sure he would, but I don't want to give him any reason to head back with doubt of any kind."

"Okay." She takes a deep breath. "Hurry back."

"I will."

And when I walk away, I hate that the lies keep piling up.

But is it really lying when I'm doing it to protect the person I love?

Forty-Seven

JACK

Luckily, Ginger's directions where to find the Destin twins are spot-on. The parking lot of the strip mall located in the next town over is well lit and void of any cars. I look at the storefronts for a dry cleaner, a pizza joint, and a silkscreen shop as I drive toward the alley that runs behind the structure.

The back lot is where I find all the cars as well as the door that leads to the hole-in-the-wall bar I'm looking for. The kind with windows painted black and a solid slab door with nothing but a padlock on the outside for security when the establishment is closed.

As if on cue, the dark, four-door sedan rolls up and parks right outside the entrance. Ginger said that one of the brothers stops by every two hours to take wagers and make payouts. I guess tonight is no different.

Before I can think this through rationally, I let the rage that brought me here spark to life as I climb out of the truck. Each step ratchets it higher. Each sidewalk panel I cross allows it to build.

When the driver's side door opens and the bald brother steps out, I don't give him a second to think before my fist plows into his nose.

The crunch of my knuckles on his cartilage is sickening and satisfying at the same time. But I don't revel in it. I'm too enraged, too focused.

Before he can recover, I have my hands fisted in his shirt and am slamming him against the car hard enough for his skull to bounce off it.

I don't care about the blood pouring out of his nose.

I don't think twice about it being just him and me in a dark parking lot or that he might be carrying a gun—it is Texas, after all.

My only thought is Tate.

My only goal is to stop this bullshit once and for all.

"Tatum Knox."

Those two words are all I have to say for him to know what the punch was for.

"So?" The asshole smirks, so I swing for the softness of his gut. My fist lands with a *thud,* and I can feel the whoosh of air come out of his chest in reflex.

I can smell the alcohol on his breath, the marijuana on his clothes, and I know that in and of itself is the only reason he isn't fighting back.

Thank fuck for that because I have a feeling all it would take is a whistle from him to get his customers in the bar out here . . . and then I'd be a dead man.

"Do you think the bets her husband made in that stack of spreadsheets are going to scare someone off?" I growl, my face inches from his. People from the bar stare as they come out on their own accord, and I just give them a glare to tell them to leave us the fuck alone. "Do you think that pathetic fuck's debts, which you let him run up only so you could nail him to a wall and try to get him to leverage his land, are hers to pay?" I slam him against his car again. "She is not selling. You are *not* going to run her off. And if you ever so much as say Tate's name again, let alone try to badmouth her or her business again, I'll kill you."

"Try it," he grits out, the blood pouring from his nose spraying me as he speaks.

"Give me a reason, and I will." My chuckle is long and loud and manic enough that, when I look in his eyes, I don't think he wants to find out if it's true or not.

He believes me.

Though, technically, I wouldn't kill him, but I'm the fucking great white in his goldfish bowl. There wouldn't be a minute of sleep lost if I used the ranch I inherited and my connections to swallow his whole operation.

And for some reason, a puzzle that had been mostly dismissed as unsolvable becomes clear. Tate's accident. Sylvester's comments about the dark sedan that ran her off the road in front of the ranch.

Perhaps the same dark sedan that I have this asshole pressed against.

Makes sense now why it seemed like no one looked all that hard for the person who ran Tate off the road. Perhaps it was because he was one of their own.

I look at this pathetic fuck and know exactly how to play this.

I'm going to call his bluff.

I'm going to scare the fuck out of him with lies upon lies so that he'll never know if they are true or not, because he'd never dare to flesh them out.

"You know Fletcher was an avid hunter right? He was a paranoid fuck, but an avid hunter nonetheless." I smile as I draw a connection between two things that have no connection, hoping the certainty in my voice convinces him. "He had trail cams everywhere on that property of his. All thirty acres of it."

"Why the fuck do I care?" he snarls.

"The best part about those thirty acres is they lined the main road going toward town. He'd catch footage of deer on the road, of kids playing homerun derby with their bats to mailboxes, and of trivial shit that no one cares about." I tsk. "Except, the one time it caught footage of a dark, four-door sedan." I lean back and make a show of checking out his car as his body stills beneath my hands. Motherfucker, I think my hunch is right. Thank god for that. "Much like the one right here. In fact, that footage caught what looks like it purposely running another car off the road. Tatum Knox's car to be exact."

He sputters something that sounds like bullshit, but it doesn't hide the sudden widening of his pupils or hitch of his breath.

"Who knew that footage was just sitting on Fletcher's computer all this time under the file name "Proof"? I bet he held on to it as leverage in case he needed it." I whistle. "You think it would cause a stir, Destin, if this security footage somehow ended up in the hands of the police?"

"You're lying."

"You'd like to think I was, but, hey"—I lean in closer—"I bet the police could zoom right in on that license plate too. Wouldn't that be nice? It isn't as if you were smart enough to cover it when you played chicken. I mean what do you think the charge would be? Hit and run? Reckless driving? *Attempted murder*?"

"Fuck you," he grits out.

"Ah, there's that stellar vocabulary of yours again. No wonder you have to resort to illegal activities to make a living." It takes everything I have not to plow my fist into his face again and make sure his nose is broken so badly that every fucking time he looks in the mirror and sees how crooked it is, he thinks of me. That he never forgets my threat.

Most of all, I want him to be a walking reminder to everyone in town not to ever fuck with her again.

"You're full of shit. If you had video, why was it never given to the police, *huh?*"

"Because Fletcher was a low-life chicken shit who was lying to his wife about how upside down he was." My fist pounds on the car. "If he turned it in, she would have found out all about his connection to you and the debts he owed. She would have made the connection that it was you who ran her off the road as a threat to get him to pay up."

"Get off me."

"What was that?" I say and lean in closer to him. "You want me to turn the footage over to Rusty because you're a stubborn fuck who doesn't believe me?" My grin is wide and taunting as I release his shirt, turn my back to him, and begin to walk away. "Gladly. I'll head straight there." I throw the last words over my shoulder.

"Don't you dare!" he shouts as his footsteps reverberate off the ground behind me.

I turn to face him just as he starts to cock back his fist. "Not a good choice, Destin. Not a good one at all." I point to all of the people now milling around outside the bar and whisper, "Witnesses," with a smirk on my lips as if I'm giving him sage advice.

Surprisingly, he isn't as dumb as he looks, and he lowers his fist.

Good.

"Oh, and if that security footage isn't enough incentive for you, I'll remind you that I also have copies of your books—illegal ledgers that show you're making money through illegal gambling—that you were enough of a jackass to hand over to my customer. Should I go over all of the ways Rusty can bring charges against you with those?"

Where my smile is wide, his scowl is startled.

I have him wedged solidly between blackmail and pressed

charges, and he knows it.

"This is your only warning, Destin. You or your brother ever go near the ranch, her business, or her in general, then all of this goes straight to Rusty. Possibly even the Feds since it seems you run a multijurisdictional operation here." I step into him so that there is no mistaking my threat. "There will be no *next time*. Understood?"

He spits a mouthful of blood onto the concrete and nods before I slide back into my truck and peel out of the lot.

Adrenaline courses through my veins the entire way back to the ranch, my body jittery from the high of knowing I did something that will protect her when I'm gone.

Christ. When I'm gone.

The thought eats at me just as potently as the events of the last half hour do.

Two things I can't control but tried to.

Fuck.

I park the truck and just stand there in the driveway to take a minute to calm myself before joining the barbecue. I have to pretend as if nothing happened when I feel like so much has changed.

From where I stand, I can see dinner is in full swing. A bonfire is burning in the pit, its orange glow lighting up the darkened sky, and everyone seems relaxed and happy.

But my thoughts go back to a man I never knew.

To someone who has affected the turn of events in my life.

Fletcher Knox.

Before tonight, I hated him with everything I had. His selfishness. His deceit. His sense of entitlement. The way he could convince people he was worthy of the things he stole from everyone else around him.

For putting Tate in a situation to be harmed.

But something happened on the way home. A part of me realized that in the end, Fletcher might have finally tried to do one selfless thing in his life. The man who was a selfish chicken shit, who lied and cheated and stole from his wife as he racked up debt and couldn't face her or the situation he'd created, might have tried ending this all with his death so that his wife wouldn't be harmed.

That is if Tate's hunch about his death is right.

Either way, he failed. He hurt her in so many ways that the pain lives on. It's in each day that she works herself to the bones to get this place profitable. It's in the fear that flits through her eyes every time she's asked to trust again, and it's in the screams she lets loose underwater.

Hell, yes, the fucker failed.

Laughter rings out across the ranch just above the soft twang of Thomas Rhett singing on the radio as I pace my way to the stables. As my feet eat up the ground, I debate whether to tell Tate about the ledgers or about the confrontation I got into with one of the Destin twins and the threats I made. And if I tell her that, then I'd have to share my realization that it wasn't a drunk driver who ran her off the road that night, but a warning from her husband's bookie to settle his debts.

My feet falter when I hear her voice carrying over to me. Her laugh is carefree and playful.

It tugs on the part of me I keep trying to pretend doesn't want more with her.

When I see her in the simple sundress with a glass of wine in her hand, it calls on me to figure out how to change it all.

But I can't.

I can't fix lies by covering them up.

Fletcher of all people taught me that.

"Jack!" Her eyes widen, and a grin lights up her face when she sees me walking across the pathway.

Don't shatter her happy.

Don't dampen her wild tonight.

Let her celebrate.

Let her enjoy the moment of hope that she's going to make it. That the ranch is going to make it.

Tell her it was nothing tonight.

Let her enjoy the beginning of her *next time*.

Hell, it won't be the first lie I've told her.

And it sure as hell won't be the last one.

Forty-Eight

TATE

"Tate!" Jack's tone makes my heart drop. "Tate?" It's loaded with an emotion I can't quite place, but I drop the bucket of supplements I'm mixing and rush to find him.

"Jack?" I clear the doorway. "What is it? What's wrong?"

We've been waiting to hear about whether Steely is planning to sign a long-term contract with us, on our terms, and it's all I can focus on.

It's too much to hope there's news.

It's too much to fear that the answer is no.

I'm about to call his name again when footsteps become faster.

"I'm nervous," I tell him before I see him, and when I do, when I see the grin that lights up his face and the pride that is embodied in his eyes, I know. "No way. You're serious?"

"They signed, Tate! They fucking signed!"

And before I can let the news hit home, Jack has me in his

arms and is whirling me around in a circle.

"Oh my god." The words repeat on my lips over and over.

I can't let go of him. My arms are wrapped around his neck, my face is buried into his shoulder, my feet are off the ground, and all I keep thinking is if I let go, this is all going to go away.

That this isn't going to be real.

"Every single thing they agreed to, Tate," Jack murmurs, his lips pressing a kiss to my cheek. "The progress payments to tide you over, a signing bonus to help pay a huge chunk down on what's late to the lender, another signing bonus for being their exclusive breeder . . . and on top of that, they have some interest in paying for a sire to breed with Ruby. Of course, they'd take their cut of the profits, but it's a way to keep Ruby and make some money off her."

"I'm afraid this is a dream," I finally say as the tears begin. Each one shedding a little piece of the worry and stress that has owned me for so long.

"Not a dream. It's a sure thing." He squeezes me tighter and bends his knees so my feet hit the floor. He physically removes my arms from his neck, frames my face in his hands, and leans down so we're eye to eye. "The ranch—*your ranch*—won't be in foreclosure anymore."

The sobs come harder now, and he keeps staring at me with a soft smile and an even softer heart before pressing the most tender of kisses to my lips. It's the kind of kiss that lacks violent passion but that makes up for it with heartfelt emotion.

It's the kind of kiss you never want to end.

But when it does, he keeps his hands on the sides of my neck and just leans his forehead against mine.

Relief has been an emotion I forgot how to feel, but today, I feel it in spades. Today, I feel love. And while I know the hard work is just beginning with Steely, I also know it's so much easier to do when you know your effort isn't going to be in vain.

"You did it, Jack. You really did it."

"No. *We did it*. You and me. Thank you for trusting me. Thank you for letting me help."

There are so many things to say to him, but words can't adequately express my gratitude or appreciation for him, so instead, I push up onto my tiptoes and kiss him back.

"To little victories," I murmur.

"This was a big victory, Tate."

"You told me we needed to celebrate victories," I say, as my hands run down his chest, my eyes darting down to his crotch.

"What exactly did you have in mind?" He leans back and lifts his eyebrows, suggestion owning his smile.

"You're the one who claims to be the sure thing," I tease.

His laughter dominates the air seconds before he kisses me again.

And then he shows me just how sure of a thing he is.

Forty-Nine

TATE

My feet move from one end of the deck to the other as I debate for what feels like the hundredth time whether or not to push the send button.

I look at the phone as if it's going to give me the answer, as if it's going to explain to me why ever since Jack told me Steely signed, I've wanted to call my mom.

It's stupid and silly and so out of the blue after all of these years, but every part of me yearns to hear her voice despite all of the unresolved feelings I know it would churn up.

Maybe it's just the emotions of everything I've been through and the possible success on the horizon that has my finger hovering over the send button.

I chew the inside of my lip and bite the bullet. I push the send button.

Each ring in my ear causes my pulse to skyrocket. Each foot of ground I cover, the only way I have to quell the rush of emotions rioting inside me.

"Hello?"

My heart skips a beat at the sound of her voice. At the sudden urgency I feel, the need I have to simply hear her talk.

"Mom?" My voice is shaky but there are also traces of hope woven in it.

"Tatum?"

My name, which is spoken with such reverence, such longing as if she's missed me and can't believe that it's me, breaks me.

The first sob comes. Then another and then the waves of them are so strong that I can't get a word out because as much as I resent her for not letting me be a part of her life, I also miss her.

"Tate. Please. Are you okay? Are you—"

"I'm okay," I say through the sniffle. "I'm fine." And really, I am. The ranch. Jack. Me. Things are looking up. "I—you—it's just so good to hear your voice."

"Oh, thank goodness. You scared me there for a second."

Even though the words are spoken, even though the reconnection has been made, silence falls on the line.

You were right about Fletcher.

Do you know how much I needed you but knew I couldn't call you?

You were wrong. I never came crawling back.

The resentment I have surges back up and overtakes the momentary forgiveness I granted her with. Her shame I can sense through the line seems like it swallows her words.

"Tate—I—I don't know what to say."

It's funny because there's so much to say, so much hurt and pain to work through, but neither of us know where to start. We only know that we have to.

"I wanted to call and tell you that I'm okay. I'm not asking for money. I'm not calling to tell you that you and Dad were right. I just needed you to know that I'm okay."

Her breath hitches, and I wonder what she looks like now. Is she still as elegant as before but with more lines etched in her face? Does she still hum classic rock songs when she cooks dinner? Does she ever think of me?

"I think of you every day."

The answer to my question has me fighting back another wave of tears. "That's good to know." My voice is barely audible and loaded with caution.

"Tate, honey . . . I'm at a loss for words."

"I am too, Mom. Like I said, I just needed you to know I'm okay."

A pause follows as we both struggle with the discomfort brought on by years of the unresolved. "How do we fix this, Tate? How do we . . ."

"I don't know." My hands tremble, my heart doesn't know how to feel, and my lips don't know what else to say. "This is a start." And it is. "At least now you have my phone number."

"Maybe we can talk again?" she asks timidly.

"Of course." I swallow, my mouth dry, my tongue heavy. "I have to go now. Goodbye, Mom."

I end the call and stand in my backyard with trees around me and Gracie at my heels and wonder if, in time, I can learn to forgive her and my father.

I can't wrap my head around that just yet. I can't open myself back up to the only other people in my life besides Fletcher who devastated me.

But I needed to know that I could.

I needed to hear her voice. So many things in my life are looking up, so many unresolved things are now being resolved . . . maybe I needed to know the last thing left out there—my relationship with my parents—might be able to be too.

Maybe I needed to know this so in my mind, I could move forward on a clean slate.

And now I know I can.

When I catch sight of Jack walking to the edge of the verandah, his head angled to the side, his expression curious as he studies me, I know that I can, in fact, open myself back up again.

Look at what happened when I did with him. My life changed for the better.

"Everything okay?" he asks as he holds out a glass of wine to me.

I nod with my phone clenched tightly in my hand, another piece of hope taken back that I feared I had lost forever, and smile.

Fifty

TATE

"Jack?"

My heart pounds in my ears as I walk through the empty house.

"Jack?"

When I see the light on out in the stables, the panic hits. That sudden surge of adrenalin—of instinct—that tells me something is wrong.

With the horses? With the ranch? With Jack?

I can't shake the feeling as I look for my robe. But I don't have the patience to find it. Something is wrong. I know it. In my cami and shorts and work boots slipped on over bare feet, I run through the warm night air at top speed toward the stables as an impending sense of doom fills me.

Things have been going too well.

We spend our nights making love with words unspoken but with emotions shown in touches and whispers of sweet nothings.

The other shoe has to drop.

The contract, the signing bonus, the guarantee . . . everything with Steely, all done with the complete absence of drama from the citizens of Lone Star.

"Jack!" My voice is a broken, breathy cry as I clear the entrance of the stables, expecting the worst, and skid to a stop.

Because what I see is something I'll never forget.

Fergi, one of our mares, has just delivered her foal. The baby is covered in blood and the fetal membrane still clings around his hind legs as he tries to stand and then slips back to the floor.

He emits the sweetest, most beautiful sound as he tries again, desperate to get to his mom, who's standing behind him, exhausted.

The dance goes on a couple more times before the baby finally stands and nuzzles against his mom.

I'm afraid to look away and miss a second of his first seconds of life. This is Mother Nature in her most perfect of moments.

Only, I glance away, and when I do, I find Jack watching me. Where my tears have spilled over my cheeks, his are still welled in his eyes.

His smile is soft, and his expression is inexplicable as he stares at me in a way that will be etched in my mind. Full of love, heavy with hope, and tainted with just a hint of sorrow.

Jack is cautious when he skirts the outside of the stall so as not to disturb the two. When he closes the gate, it's almost soundlessly.

There are no words spoken as he reaches out and frames my face before kissing each tear track in tiny motions.

When his mouth finds mine, it is nothing more than a brush of lips, but it's so painstakingly slow, so unabashedly tender, that I know I've never been kissed like this before.

I fear I never will be again.

His fingers link with mine as he leads me out of the stable and up to the house. We slip out of our clothes like a couple who's done this too many times before. As a couple who knows the other's body and doesn't want to waste time staring because they would rather take the time giving pleasure.

He lays me down upon the sheets, which have turned cold in my absence, and crawls over me, eyes never leaving mine. His body touching me at all times in some way or another.

It's almost as if he's afraid to lose this connection if his skin leaves mine or that if he speaks, words will ruin the moment.

Jack runs his fingertips down my left cheek, a featherlight touch that sends shockwaves through my body. His cock is already hard and pressing against my thigh, but there's no rush or urgency to this moment. It's this tenderness that threatens to undo me. It's the promise of more that begs me to let him.

My breath is a gasp with each touch, and I turn my face to press a kiss into the palm of his hand. I close my eyes and take a snapshot of the moment for my memory bank.

His forehead rests against mine as the heat of his breath fans over my lips. And we just lay like this—with his knees spreading my thighs apart, with his cock positioned at my entrance, and with my trust and heart in his hands.

There's a raw emotion between us, an acknowledgment that we just shared something special that had nothing to do with us and everything to do with us at the same time.

"Tate." My name is an exhaled sigh as he pushes into me slowly.

The pleasurable stretch of him burns through me but not as bright as the emotion.

Nothing can rival that.

"Look at me, Tate." A command. A demand. A plea. *An apology*.

My lashes flutter open, and our gazes hold as we become one.

Hearts and bodies.

"It doesn't fix it," he murmurs as he dips down to take a sip of my lips. "It doesn't change things." Another soft kiss that lingers as if he's fighting against pulling away. "But I can't not tell you anymore. I'm in love with you, Tate."

A push in. *My gasp.* A grind of his hips. A pull back out. *My heart breaks.*

"We were doomed from the beginning you and I . . ."

Another rush of sensation as his cock drags over the rough patch of nerves within.

"I fought it with everything I have, but I fucking fell for you."

His tongue dances against mine in a slow, sweet seduction that rivals his revelation.

"We'll figure this out somehow." Another push in. "We have to." Another grind of his hips. "Because I'm not ready to let you go." Another pull back out.

My orgasm is a slow build of pleasure.

"Six months isn't long enough with you," he murmurs against my lips.

My body tenses as his hips grind into mine again. As our fingers entwine on either side of my head.

"I love you, Jack Sutton." My truth a murmur of a confession that I've been too afraid to voice.

"Thank fuck." He groans as his lips claim mine again. As my body detonates into a million tiny fragments that I fear only he'll be able to put back together again.

Fifty-One

JACK

ME: Lauren, I need a few extra weeks. Something's come up that requires me to be here. Evan has things covered, so it won't affect you. Thanks for understanding.

I HIT SEND ON the text and then put my phone on do not disturb to avoid her wrath.

Something's come up, all right.

The something being I'm not ready to leave yet.

And when I do, I've decided to take my secrets with me.

Fifty-Two

TATE

"I just passed Doc Arlington. Should I ask?" Jack's hope resonates through the connection loud and clear.

I laugh. "I was just dialing you."

"Tate?"

"*Ten*, Jack! Ten out of ten pregnant mares so far." My words are part shriek, part exclamation. If I could reach through the phone and hug him right now, I would.

"And—"

"Doc said all the mares are healthy. The fetus' heartbeats are strong. Everything is textbook." I am talking too fast, but the excitement, *the relief,* is like a flood breaking a levee, allowing the hope that I've been holding back for months to finally spill over. "She'll be back next week to check the second batch of mares we bred."

"Whew." He sighs in relief, and I can hear his smile in his voice. "Things are looking up, Knox. Two foals born last week. The ten left from last year's heat to be born any day . . . and it looks to me like we're going to have a busy time next spring with all these new ones from Steely."

We're.

I hear the pronoun and even the parts of me that know it's unintentional seek to hold on to the hope that it is.

In reality, *I'm* going to have a busy time next spring, not *we're.* I'm too excited to go down that road, though.

"Things are definitely looking up." I feel like shouting my excitement to the open sky, but I settle for grinning so hard my cheeks hurt. "You should probably call Pete and tell him the good news about the ultrasounds."

"I think you should do the honors, Tate," he murmurs.

I open my mouth to refute him but then stop myself. He's prepping me for when he won't be here because, up until this point, he's been Pete's only point of contact, soon it will be me.

I won't let it dampen my mood. Can't.

Because he loves me.

He said so himself.

That has to be enough.

It has to be.

I let out a raucous laugh because I just can't keep it in anymore, and the sound is so powerful that it pulls one from him. God, it feels so good to have some of the worry gone.

The crunch of gravel at the entrance to the ranch draws my attention. It comes with a squeal of tires, but when I look across the field and see Will with the farrier, I know it isn't him.

"I think a delivery's here," I say absently, distracted by how fast the car is coming up the drive. By the skid of its tires on the gravel as the driver slams on the brakes.

"Delivery?"

"Not sure." I take a step toward the car and the person who

seems to have their head resting on the steering wheel. "I have to go check."

"'Kay. I'm just around the corner. Be there in five."

I take another step closer to the car, cautious and curious.

"Can I help you?" I call out to the woman at the same time as she flings the car door open so hard that it hits the fence rail she parked next to.

There is an almost listless laugh that's followed by some muttered curses as she half slides, half falls from the car.

"How can you live in this godforsaken place?" she shouts as she stumbles, the open door catching her before she falls. She steadies herself and shakes her head as if to clear it before taking her time to turn to me.

Dramatic, much?

"Can I help you?" I repeat, clearly concerned by how this woman, who appears to be three sheets to the wind, was able to drive a car. She definitely took a wrong turn, but thank God, she pulled in here. If she hadn't, she'd be on the road going head to head with Jack.

The crunch of metal from my own accident has me absently running a hand over my shoulder and shivering.

Her eyes narrow as she takes me in, and her laugh is as unexpected as it is loud when she throws her head back and emits it. "Jesus fucking Christ. It makes soooo much sense now," she says, each word a drawn-out slur.

"Miss?" I take another step toward her. "Are you okay? Have you been drinking?"

"What would give you that idea?" She gesticulates wildly, her smile wide but bordering on unhinged.

"How fast you zoomed in here. How you're slurring your words."

Another laugh that goes as unreciprocated as her first one did.

"Aren't you cute?" She scrunches her nose as she studies me. "And for the record, I don't slur my words. *I just prefer to talk in cursive.*" A lift of her eyebrows. A visual challenge for me to push her on this.

I will let her say whatever crazy things she wants so long as she doesn't climb back behind the wheel again.

She steps out from behind the door, her gait unsteady, but her eyes are sharp somehow. She looks like she stepped out of a fashion magazine with her designer clothes and Italian leather boots. Her blonde hair is pulled back into a fancy ponytail, and there are numerous diamonds adorning her fingers.

"Do I know you?" I ask.

Her smile is arrogant and looks familiar, but I can't exactly place it.

I breathe a small sigh of relief when I see Jack's truck on the stretch of road leading to the turnoff for the ranch. This drunk woman may seem harmless, but that doesn't mean she doesn't make me uneasy.

The cluck of her tongue and her scrutiny draws my attention back to her.

"He just had to have you, didn't he? He couldn't keep his hands to himself. *Like father, like son, apparently.* Expectations and tough love for one of them, unconditional and immediate love for the other. So, of course, he came here and made sure to leave his mark on you," she says as if I'm able to follow her crazy. "Of course, he had to have the ultimate *fuck you.*"

"He? Him? I'm sorry, but I think you're mistaking me for someone else."

Jack's truck turns onto the driveway, the dust that just settled from her arrival now stirred back up.

"Nope. I know exactly who you are, *Tatum Knox*. You're a sweet little thing, aren't you?" A smile. "My Jack-Jack," she says with a shake of her head, and for the briefest of seconds, I think

she's Jack's wife. But before the panic sets in wholly, she continues. "My brother comes off like a sheep, but don't be fooled, he's
a wolf underneath. Cunning, vindictive, and apparently, territorial
considering the way he's staked his claim on you. That's the one
thing our father never expected him to be when the promise was
made."

My head all but explodes when I realize she's Jack's sister.

"*Lauren?*"

She nods, her eyes assessing me and judging, her smile sliding
slowly. "Ah, so between your sweet lovemaking and the sordid
lies he fed you, he did mention me." She clutches a hand over her
chest. "Be still my heart."

"I'm sorry. I'm not following you. Did you hit your head on
the steering wheel by chance?"

Her laughter is back. The roll of her eyes follows right after
it. "Our brother had it, you know? Our dad gave it to him freely."

"What? Lauren—"

"Approval. Tatum. *Fucking approval.*" She snaps like a frustrated teacher. "I had it regardless of what I did because I was the
only girl. Jack never got it because he was the only son . . . but
when our brother came along out of the fucking goddamn blue
months before he died, he got it simply because Dad felt guilty.
He was the bastard love child my dad never knew about. The one
who tried to ruin each one of us in exchange for the money he's
now going to end up getting anyway."

The horn starts blaring as Jack gets closer, but I'm so lost in
what Lauren is saying, in the hairs standing up on the back of my
neck, that I don't turn and look his way.

That I don't heed his warning.

"I'm not following you."

"The Sutton household was a crazy place to grow up. Forty-
five thousand acres loaded with cattle and horses, and I never had
to lift a goddamn finger on that ranch. Not a one. Our father was

too afraid I'd run away the first chance I had, just like our mother did . . . but Jack-Jack? He had to work his ass off day-in and day-out regardless of whether he wanted to or not. The kicker? It was never good enough. Never fast enough . . . never fucking enough." She snorts.

"I'm sorry. Jack will be here in a second if you need him," I say around the dread beginning to trickle through me. Deep down, I fear whatever she's going to say next.

"Oh, but it's you I want to talk to." She scrunches her nose. "Our dad wanted to make a man out of Jack. Make him live by strict rules and hold him up to unrealistic expectations. Push him away and make him hard. And, of course, Jack bucked it all. He left to go be the man he wanted to be and flee the name he couldn't escape." Her laugh is anything but sympathetic and borders on manic. "When our brother turned up and daddy dearest, who was sick and lonely in his final months of losing the battle to cancer, couldn't see the forest through the trees. Nope. He sees this surprise as his chance to get a do-over as a father. This is his chance to fix all the things he did wrong when it came to Jack."

The honking continues, but I don't even spare a glance his way. My heart is in my throat and every part of me is bracing for an impact I can't quite begin to fathom yet.

Jack's halfway up the driveway.

"But the bastard son didn't want any love or approval. No. He only wanted *money*. He thought he could take advantage of his sick father who he didn't give a damn about, so he showed up in person and harassed him. He charmed him at first, conned a dying man into thinking he was sincere. He pushed and pushed until my father collapsed from his constant barrage and I banned him from ever coming back. Then he turned his conniving ways on me. Tried to tempt me with my vices so I'd force our father to just give him the money and be done with him. Didn't take him long to figure out that the person who held the most power over my father was Jack, and when he did, he set out to try to successfully blackmail him. You get a threat and you get a threat . . . you all get threats," she says dramatically *à la* Oprah Winfrey fashion as she throws her hands up. "As if spilling the big secret of his connection to the Sutton name even registered on our radar. He was too stupid to know that not a single one of us cared." She pulls a flask out of her purse and takes a long swallow of what is most definitely not water. "But then there's you. Look at you making out in all of this."

"Me?" I cough the word out as confusion reigns.

"You got Jack warming your sheets and saving your ass. Perfect storybook romance if you ask me. All you're forgetting is—"

We both turn to look as Jack's tires screech to a halt on the gravel much the same way Lauren's did.

"—the happily ever after," she says coyly, completely ignoring the first time he yells her name.

"Lauren!" he shouts again, warning thick in his voice. A shot over the bow as Jack jumps from his truck and jogs toward us. Each step he takes, though, I mentally take one in retreat.

"Isn't it funny how Jack fucked his brother's widow to get back at him? Isn't it ironic that Jack promised to make amends for the wrongs he's done in life, only to end up just as fucked up as his brother was? What better way to get back at your bastard brother than to sleep with his wife?"

Widow.

Brother.

Wife.

Her words hit my ears. I'm hearing them, but the understanding is fuzzy and sluggish—as if my brain is trying to block them out and physically reject them.

"*Fletcher*?" I . . . I don't understand. My feet move toward her as if that will give me a clearer understanding, but my head screams to run away. "Wh-what did you just say?" I stutter the words out as the bottom of my carefully reconstructed world falls out from under me.

"That isn't true," Jack shouts as every muscle in me freezes, including my heart. "Fucking hell, Lauren. I swear to God, Tate—"

"Fletcher's your brother?" I ask as I stare at his brown eyes, which are wide and spooked. The subtle stutter of his body gives me an answer before his mouth even opens.

Utter shock.

My stomach revolts.

Complete disbelief.

My body feels like time is passing in slow motion.

Unfettered anger.

My hands tremble and body shakes.

All three emotions stomp and pound through me like a damn wildfire, out of control and uncontainable as they burn and burn and burn.

"You're Fletcher's brother?" I screech, my breath hard to catch because I can't even remember to breathe with the rage that is robbing me of all senses, all reason.

He lied to me.

This was all a goddamn lie.

The *her wild* and him being *the sure thing*. The half-cocked smirks across the paddock and the pleasurable moans beneath the sheets. The breaking down of walls and building together of trust.

"That's not how it was."

"Get away from me!" I scream, my voice breaking right alongside my heart as he reaches out to touch me. I jerk back so hard that I stumble.

"Lauren, what did you do?" he shouts, his face a mask of fury, his voice as frantic as the look in his eyes.

"What?" she asks innocently, but her smile says she's anything but. "I was just telling her about our brother. About how you came here to get the final say."

"Are you fucking insane?" He's still screaming as he spins on her. "Get the fuck out of here. You disgust me."

But the fearful desperation that vibrates through his voice is answer enough to tell me it's true. All of it is.

I'm paralyzed by the truth, needing distance but unable to move.

"Jack . . ." I say with numb lips. "I don't . . . I—"

"I can explain," he says interrupting me.

"I trusted you." I can see each word reach out and punch him. I can see each syllable make impact.

But they don't hurt him enough.

Nothing can.

He lied to me. He made me believe him and then he lied when I trusted.

"I promise. There's an explanation. Everything is not what she said. That is not what—*fuck*!"

"But it is what she said."

I can't breathe.

Oh, God, why can't I take a damn breath?

"No."

"Was Fletcher your brother?" The question might as well be acid in my throat.

His nod is subtle, but the defeat in his eyes has me covering my ears and shaking my head, not wanting to know. Knowing that no matter what he tries to explain, it will never be good enough.

It'll never be enough.

It will never make any of this any better.

Everything we had was all a fabrication so he could get something he wanted.

I finally believed in my ability to trust again . . . and . . . and . . . I vomit the contents of my stomach on the side of the driveway. Over and over until there is nothing left in me but despair.

"Tatum." He puts his hand on my back and I jump away from him again.

"Don't you touch me!" I scream through clenched teeth as the shock gives way to anger, as the trust gives way to deceit. I double over, and my arms wrap around my midsection as I stumble a few more feet toward the house.

"Goddamn it, Lauren!" He's still shouting at the top of his lungs, and the horses begin to stir at the disruption. "It has to be about you, doesn't it? *Always about fucking you.* You didn't have my attention, so you had to make sure you stole it by coming here. You didn't like that, for once, I'd found my own happy, so you had to come here and ruin it. You . . ." It's the broken sound in his voice that breaks me further when I thought I was already broken enough.

My tears slip over.

"It's your fault you didn't tell her the truth. Not mine."

"Shut your fucking mouth! Shut it, or I swear to God, I will disown you as a sister, and the next time you fall into a bottle, I'm going to let you drown. I won't pick up when you call or bail you out or help you hire a lawyer when your piece-of-shit dead husband decides to take those kids from you!"

"You wouldn't dare." She laughs and is still laughing as Will comes barreling out of the stables to see what the commotion is about.

"Jack?" he calls out, confusion and concern ringing through.

"Get her to the bunkhouse," Jack orders Will, flinging his arm in the general direction of the building. "Get her out of my fucking sight."

But when Jack turns to look at me, when our eyes meet, all I can do is shake my head and reject the words he hasn't even spoken yet. Reject the apology and fear in his eyes, because he doesn't have any right to feel them when I'm the one who was just blindsided.

"No."

It's on repeat with the shake of my head as I step back up the verandah steps.

"Tate, let me explain."

"Get your shit and leave." Why does this hurt so badly? "I don't want you here anymore." Why do I feel like a grenade just detonated in my chest? "You're fired."

"Knox." My name is a weighted sigh.

"Exactly," I say, my voice steady for the first time. "I was someone else's woman once. Just like you, he wasn't the man I thought he was either."

When I step into the house, when I lock the door at my back, I finally allow my knees to give out, and I slide to the floor.

It's only then the gravity of the entire conversation hits me full force.

It's only then that I realize just how much I love . . . *loved* Jack Sutton, who is just as much of a liar as my husband . . . his brother.

Fifty-Three

JACK

"**D**amn it, Tate." I pound on the door, her muffled sobs just on the other side. "Open up. I need to explain. *This* was never supposed to happen. *You* were never supposed to happen. Fuck!" I give it one more pound and then lean against it as the weight of what Lauren did pulls me under.

My chest hurts.

My breath is harsh.

My eyes burn.

Fucking hell.

All I want is for Fletcher to be alive so I can beat the ever-loving shit out of him for the hurt he's caused my family.

For the hurt he's put Tate through.

For goddamn fucking everything.

But I can't.

I can't because he died and I lived and all I wanted was to see if his widow was worthy of the inheritance check my father left him.

All I wanted was to see the life he lived and remember why I was proud to be a Sutton when all he wanted was the money attached to the name, not the honor it held.

All I needed was to learn about the man he turned out to be and validate my hatred for him.

Hell if I didn't get all of that . . . *but I also fell in love with his widow.*

Every-fucking-crazy-thing about her.

"Open the door, Tate."

I pound the wood as I slide to the ground and rest my back against it.

"I'm not going anywhere. I'm going to sit here until you talk to me. And after you hear it all, if you want me to go . . . then I'll still go."

"Go away," she says, voice muffled and laden with hurt but still there.

At least she's still there.

It's something.

"A few months before my dad died, he found out he had another son. He ran into an old mistress somewhere, and when she heard he was sick, she told him about the son he never knew he had. To make a long story short, he contacted him and asked to meet. The son didn't believe him."

I remember being in Tennessee and the frantic call from Lauren, having to tell her to slow down, to explain what in the hell she meant by, *"We have a brother."*

"Apparently, Fletcher found out our dad owned one of the largest cattle ranches in the United States and decided to hear the old man out. At first, my dad was too blinded by his guilt to see what Lauren saw in Fletcher and then later would relay to me. He charmed the sense right out of our father and didn't give a rat's ass about him or that he was dying. All Fletcher wanted was his money. He convinced my father that a paternity test wasn't needed because, damn, didn't they have the same eyes?"

I snort, remembering how pissed Lauren was every time he'd come around or call. How I was too tied up with the Gerard deal to head back and pay this any attention.

Especially because every time I tried to talk to my father about it, he'd make excuses and avoid the topic.

"We tried talking to my father about Fletcher. We tried to tell him the sides we saw of this new family member and how it was odd that Fletcher kept asking too many questions about the ranch and its worth and laying the charm on way too thick, but my father couldn't see it. Instead, he bragged to me about whatever bullshit accomplishment Fletcher convinced him was true." My exhale is frustration personified. "The whole thing caused more of a rift between my father and me. Here is a man I'd spent my whole life trying to get any kind of approval from, any kind of compliment from, to no avail, and he gives it to this snake-oil salesman without flinching. He told lie after lie, and my father fell for each and every one of them when I couldn't even get him to congratulate me on being one of the top professionals in my field."

I lean my head back and recall the phone calls between my father and me. The relentless pressure he placed on me to succeed. The *fuck you* I felt deep in my bones after working endlessly for his approval and never getting it when Fletcher walked into our lives and had it without so much as a word.

"To say I resented Fletcher is an understatement. To say it shoved the wedge deeper between my dad and me, even more so. Fletcher stole time from me with my dad. Time I can never get back, and I'll never forgive him for that." I laugh.

I shift my position and listen for any sign of life on the other side of the door. When I'm sure she's still there, I continue. "Fletcher even went as far as to call my dad's attorney and ask point-blank how much was in the will for him. The executor—a smart man—told him the will hadn't been changed at all since it had been finalized years before. You can imagine how that turned out. Fletcher pitched a full-on tantrum over it, but he was smart. He was a con man. He first worked his way into convincing our dad that he was on the cusp of succeeding and needed some investment capital, angling for my dad to offer to help. By that time, my father had spoken to his lawyer and the bubble had burst. My dad finally saw the real Fletcher—the one we had all seen from day one with his thirst for money over anything—and wouldn't give him what he wanted. So Fletcher started in on Lauren. He knew she was a recovering alcoholic, so he sent her cases of wine every week. He encouraged her to drink the few times he was around and then threatened to have her kids taken away for neglect when she did. He pressured her until she begged our dad to pay him off so that she could hold onto her sobriety."

I sigh and pray that she's listening. That she hears me and can forgive me. That she realizes we were conned by him too.

"My father refused Lauren's pleas. When Lauren stopped allowing Fletcher to come around, the threats turned to me. He had the balls to tell me he would ruin my professional reputation if I didn't pay him off. I didn't budge, and so he began a smear campaign on me. He sent letters to my customers, to my bosses, to anyone associated with me, really. Hell, when our father died, he even threatened to file a lawsuit to stake a rightful claim on the ranch I stood to inherit. I never met him face–to–face, Tate, but I swear to God, I fucking hated him." I run a hand through my hair as something drags against the opposite side of the door.

"The whole thing was horrible. I hated my dad for not being able to keep his dick in his pants and for causing the situation that was beginning to destroy our family in the final days of his life. I was so angry at what he'd caused that I didn't want to go home and face him. The anger ate at me. His immediate acceptance of that piece of shit stung when I'd been busting my ass for years to get a tenth of that approval." I cough to push the goddamn emotion that burns my chest away, to shove it down so that it never sees the light of day.

"I never made it home to see my father before he died. I was so angry about everything with Fletcher that I didn't believe Lauren when she called and said the time was near. Even though we had our problems, my father was invincible to me, a giant, and I couldn't imagine him succumbing to cancer." Even now, I'm consumed by guilt, but I have so much to lose so I keep explaining. "I was in Kentucky, standing in the middle of the Gerard's family room when Lauren called. They were a nice couple who had spent their life savings trying to save a farm that had been in their family for generations. I remember I was standing there . . . amidst pictures and toys and evidence of a life lived . . . about to steal their farm for pennies on the dollar because it was what my boss wanted. I felt like shit for it, but I was the top agent and was so obsessed with the accolades and the praise over it, I was pretending not to notice the lives I was ruining in the process."

I blow out a breath and recall the punch in the gut I felt seeing Mrs. Gerard cry while sitting in the kitchen her great-great-grandfather had built with his own two hands. I recall my relief when I was able to step outside to take Lauren's call, and then the utter panic that followed when I did.

"When I answered the phone, she told me I had to get home and get home fast. I'd never heard her sound like that before and knew this wasn't a ploy. I knew he was dying. I raced to the airport and begged to be on the next flight out." I clear my throat and rest my head back against the door, reliving every damn moment. "You still there?"

She doesn't answer, but I hear Gracie's tail thump on the floor, and that gives me hope that she is.

"I called him before I got on the flight. He sounded so frail when he normally sounded like he could move mountains." The thought makes me smile as I close my eyes and relive the conversation.

"THAT YOU, JACK?"

"I'm on my way, Dad."

"I'm not going anywhere, son."

"Good," I say as tears threaten and guilt swallows me whole.

"Sometimes things happen in life that you aren't particularly proud of. In the moment, you do them because you think that's what's expected of you, but when you're looking at minutes left instead of years, you realize you screwed up. You tell yourself that, if you could do it all over, you'd make amends."

I nod and assume he is talking about our relationship. That he feels the same kind of guilt I do over not being closer. Over not trying harder. Over the stress he put on us with everything with Fletcher.

"I understand." I think.

"If there was one thing you'd want to make amends for in your life right now, excluding family and me, what would that be?"

It is an odd question, but I humor him. I am fresh from Mrs. Gerard and her tears, and the unsettled and unfulfilled feeling I have from the deal still lingers in my gut. *"I'd save a ranch, not ruin one,"* I murmur through the line. *"Help the small guy instead of the corporation for once."*

His laugh sounds off and then turns into a cough that ends up with him struggling to breathe. I'm in a city, hundreds of miles away, and I'm helpless to do anything for him.

"Dad? You okay?"

He coughs a few more times, a murmured yes in there somewhere. His breaths are shorter now, though. His breathing more labored.

"Promise me something, Jack."

"I'll promise you whatever you want when I get home," I say. *"Face-to-face."*

"Promise me you'll make that amends, will you? Promise me."

I laugh, but it dies as quickly as I emit it because I realize he's

355

dead serious. "I promise, Dad." I rise as my flight is called over the loudspeaker. "Is there anything you need me to do for you? Any amends you want me to help you make?"

"Yes." Another string of coughs as I get in line to board. "But I'll tell you when you get here. Face-to-face."

"Okay. I'm boarding. I'll be there soon." I pause, my father never one to accept any show of affection. "I love you." My words are soft and I fucking hate the tear that creeps down my cheek.

"Me too, Jack. Me too."

"So, SEE? I made my dad a promise that I'd make amends," I say when I finish relaying that last conversation with my dad to Tate. "I focused on it the whole flight home. How I'd find a small ranch in trouble. How I'd come in and help it to succeed instead of helping sabotage it so it would fail. Sound like a ranch you know?"

I shift and hope maybe that made her smile, but fuck if I know. I'm in the dark about what she's thinking, so I trudge on.

"By the time I landed, my father had died. Lauren's texts were all over my phone the minute I turned it on. I was devastated. Ruined." My voice breaks with emotion, and I pause for a moment. "What I didn't know was he'd left me a voicemail while I was in flight. It's still on my phone right now. One sec, I'll play it for you."

I pick up my phone and navigate to my saved voicemails, pushing the speaker button just after I push play.

"Jack." My father's voice booms through the speaker, and chills chase down my spine hearing it. "There's so much to say to you and not enough time to say it. It's something I should have said a long time ago, but I was too proud and you're too stubborn . . . I love you, son.

You were always my shining light. You never knew it, but you were. Yes, I was tough on you, and I hope you can forgive me for that, but this is a brutal business. I pushed you so that you would go out on your own and become your own man. I wanted you to harden and grow tough. I needed you to trust your instincts and rely on yourself.

Of course, I let you think I didn't want you to leave.

But I did.

I knew you'd step into my shoes one day, and I needed you to be taught the things I never was. That when the sun sets, it's you who has to lie in the bed with the decisions you make every day. It's you who has to be confident they are the right ones even when everyone else thinks they are wrong.

I'm proud of you, son. Of what you've accomplished on your own. Of what you'll accomplish when I'm gone. I'm sorry I didn't get a chance to tell you that face-to-face.

Time has a way of creeping up on all of us. Of running out on us when we only want one more minute . . . one more second. I wish I had those with you. I wish I had a do-over so I could see you live the day-to-day, knowing how proud I am of you.

Come back to the ranch, don't come back to the ranch—you do whatever's best for you. But the ranch is yours. Every last bit of it. There's more than enough set aside for Lauren and the kids, so don't you worry about taking care of them.

One last thing. You promised me you'd make your amends, and I'm holding you to that. I know your word is good . . . but I have one I need you to help me make too. The executor has an envelope for Fletcher. It's a payoff. I know, I know. You're mad at me for that, but I had a paternity test done anyway, and he's mine. If he takes the money, then he waives all rights to any claim of anything from the estate. The amount is small in the grand scheme of things and it gives me peace of mind that he won't be able to come after you or your inheritance—that my mistakes won't haunt your future.

So two promises, Jack: Make amends and pay the asshole off.

And remember I love you. I always have. I always will."

"I hope you could hear that," I say when the voice mail ends.

"I hope you're still there because there's more to tell."

There's a shift against the door, and I feel like that's her way of telling me she's still there. That it's her way of letting me know she's listening.

"My father died two weeks before Fletcher did, and after months in probate and legal channels, and even more time spent trying to track you down . . . well, you know the rest."

The lock at my back turns.

I scramble up as the door swings open.

Tate's cheeks are splotchy and her eyes are bloodshot, but at least she's standing there.

"I don't know the rest. How can I?" Her voice has so much hurt and betrayal woven within every single thread of it that I don't know how to answer her. "You came here to pay off your dead brother, and what? Saw me and thought you'd fuck over his widow instead? You thought you'd get back at him by messing with me?"

"Fuck her over?" I choke on my disbelief. "I came here to fulfill the promise I made to him and the promise I made to myself. I helped save this place. It was like kismet. You were struggling and looking to hire help. I saw the ad, and I swear to you I felt like my dad had set it all up ahead of time. How can you even begin to consider all that we did here on the ranch as me trying to fuck you over?" I try not to sound defensive because I'm more aware than anyone that I don't have a leg to stand on.

If I weren't aware, all I would have to do is look at Tate to know that.

"Not the ranch. Not the business. *Me*." Her chin quivers as she fights back tears, and it guts me. Absolutely guts me. "You let this happen, Jack. You caused this."

"Tate . . ."

"You made me believe you. You made me believe in me. You made me hope. You made me dream the dream that wasn't really mine." She hiccups back a sob. "You made me love you. Even worse, you made me trust you when I swore I'd never be able to trust again . . . so yeah, you fucked me over."

I watch a single tear slip down her cheek and know there's nothing I can say to fix this, at least not in the heat of the moment . . . maybe not even a few hours removed from my sister and her bullshit.

So I tell her the truth.

"You're right. I did all of those things. I saw you that first day on the porch with your hand on your hip and your threat to shoot me and I knew my brother didn't deserve a fucking ounce of your love. Not fucking one."

"It doesn't change a thing, Jack. You still lied. You still—"

"I was wrong." I run a hand through my hair to try to find something to say to get her to hear me. "I was determined to hate you at first sight. Sure, we'd talked on the phone and you had offered me the position, but I expected to look at you and know you were just as much of an asshole as your husband was. I thought I could show up and walk away and that might be enough to convince my conscience that I had tried to make good with what I'd promised my father." I itch to reach out and touch her. I crave any kind of connection with her but know she won't have it. I'll have to make it through words. "But there was something about you, Tate. I don't know if it was your beauty, the pain in your eyes, the defiance in your posture . . . but there was something about you that told me I should stay and see for myself exactly who you were."

Her hand grips the doorknob so tightly it creaks under the pressure, but I see her bottom lip quiver. "I meant what I said. I need you to go."

Tears course down her cheeks, the pain I caused in every single track they leave.

"You don't mean that."

She nods. "I do." But her eyes say differently. "Please be gone in the morning."

"I love you."

She physically rejects the words with the grimace on her face, a hitch of her breath, the shake of her head.

"I know," she whispers. "I believe you . . . but . . . but I lived a life with a man who thought it was okay to lie to me. It didn't start that way, but it morphed into it. When he died, I promised myself never again. I told myself I deserve better. So I can't . . . I *won't* allow myself to walk into a relationship that's been a lie since the beginning."

She hiccups over a sob.

"Don't do this." When I step toward her, she steps back into the house.

"You were leaving in a couple of weeks anyway. We were walking headfirst into a heartbreak as it was. This way, we just save ourselves a bit of false hope and whispered promises we'll never keep . . ." She takes another step back, the physical distance her way to reinforce the words she's telling me. "It's just better this way."

"I meant everything I said, Tate."

"There was a lot you didn't say that you meant too." Her breath hitches. "Goodbye, Jack."

Fifty-Four

TATE

I hear his protest when I shut the door.

I see the knob wiggle after I turn the lock.

And then, before I allow myself to change my mind, I'm running down the hallway and falling onto my bed as I succumb to the hurt.

To the betrayal.

To everything I thought we would have together—a today, a tomorrow, a forever. God, how silly those thoughts are, have always been.

Jack Sutton was never going to give up his life on his fancy ranch for a small-town life here.

Jack Sutton, the man who moves over and over again to avoid falling, wasn't ever going to stay.

I can repeat those truths to myself over and over, but that doesn't mean I wasn't still hoping they were lies.

Fifty-Five

JACK

L auren's soft snores come from the room opposite mine in the bunkhouse, but I don't listen to them.

I don't care about them.

The past hours replay in my mind. The hour I spent on the phone getting her set up in rehab followed by another one to her ex-mother-in-law who is currently watching the kids to ask her if she'll keep watching them while she sobers up. Just another revolution in a long list of repeats when it comes to my sister.

And I did all of that while fighting every goddamn urge I have to make Tate listen to me. To shake her shoulders until those storm-cloud-colored eyes of hers see the truth, see that I love her.

But I fucked this up. I fucked her over.

She deserves better than me.

Than this.

She deserves everything for her *next time.*

It doesn't mean the ache in my heart agrees with me, though.

Fifty-Six

TATE

I force myself to watch Jack load his two duffel bags into the back of his truck and keep watching as his sister walks out, sunglasses on and looking like hell, and slides behind the wheel of her car.

I make myself stand at the kitchen window so I can physically watch him go . . . as if that will help my heart and my head and my hope be on the same page.

Sleep came in bouts, but I spent most of the night staring at the ceiling as I tried to process how something so good could turn so very wrong.

How I tried to process how I'm going to watch the man I love walk out of my life.

"It's better this way." But even I don't buy the lie.

"Tate?"

I fight the urge to run and hide. I fight an even stronger urge to run into his arms and beg him not to go.

But I can't do that.

I just can't.

"I know you're standing there," he says as he pushes open the front door and walks into the kitchen.

Gracie's tail thumps at the sight of him, but I don't turn because I know it would hurt too much to meet his eyes.

"Can't you even look at me?"

Tears threaten as I stare at the floor and shake my head.

"Tate? Look at me. Please." The raw emotion in his voice begs me to do as he asks as surely as his words do.

When I do, it's as if my heart constricts in my chest. He looks tired and worn out. Maybe he got as little sleep as I did last night.

"When I came to Lone Star, it was to fulfill both promises I'd made my dad. I never thought I'd get a chance to do them at the same time. The first was to make amends for some poor decisions I made in my last job. The other was to find out if you were every bit the piece of shit my brother was. A liar. A cheat. Someone I was ashamed to have my name associated with. I figured that, if you were any of those things, I'd tell the executor that I couldn't find you. I'd get a copy of his death certificate to prove his demise and then turn Fletcher's portion over to charity. *But then you happened.*" He shakes his head ever so subtly and a ghost of a smile—one laced with regret and sorrow—curves up his lips. "Your grit and ferocity and devotion and love and your wild happened."

He blows out a breath and looks out the window toward the ranch we made new again. "Coming here, getting to know you? For the life of me, I didn't understand how fate crossed our paths, but I know I wanted you to fight for all of this." He waves his hand toward the stables. "I wanted to fight for it beside you. Hell, I wanted to help fix the things he broke in you. Maybe if I helped you, then I could figure out myself . . ." He emits a soft chuckle as he looks down and then back up to me. "But then you went and made me fall in fucking love with you, Tatum. *Then you happened.*"

It takes every ounce of restraint I have not to step into him and tell him to stay.

But I know I deserve better than what he did to me.

Both are painful.

Only one is what I'll allow myself to accept.

"This has been in my wallet since the first day I stepped on this ranch." Jack takes a step forward and sets an envelope onto the counter beside me. "Take your time. Figure out what you need to figure out. It's a lot easier to love through the hate than to hate through the love. I know that better than anyone. I just hope you choose to fight as hard for me and for us as you did for this ranch. I just hope you choose me."

Tears well in his eyes, and that muscle feathers in his jaw as he takes another hesitant step toward me.

I hold my breath.

I freeze.

And then he leans forward and brushes his lips against mine one last time. My tears tangle on his tongue as it slips between my lips. His thumb brushes back and forth over the line of my jaw. The wince on his face, as if it's physically hard for him to step back, to walk away, tells me this is as brutal for him as it is for me.

"Until next time," he murmurs.

He meets my eyes one last time before he turns on his heel and walks out of the door.

His feet clomp on the stairs, carrying him out of my life.

Tears course down my cheeks as every part of me wants to call him back.

As every part of me yearns for him.

But I glance over to the picture he took of me that's sitting on my counter. It's supposed to remind me of the beginning of my *next time*.

The one that represents my promise never to settle again.

And I know calling him back would be settling.

It would be allowing myself to accept things no one ever should. Deceit. Equivocation. Duplicity.

I pick up the envelope he left, and blink once and then twice at the check that is inside it.

His truck starts.

I stare at it, shove it back inside, and let it fall to the floor.

I follow the crunch of gravel as his sister's car and then his truck drives to the road.

When the sounds are gone, when I'm all alone, I walk out of the back door and step into the pool—clothes and all.

And I sink under water so that no one can hear me . . . and I scream at the world.

Fifty-Seven

TATE

One week later . . .

"Tate. It's me. I was hoping you'd want to talk by now. I've been trying to give you your space." His sigh is heavy. "Look, I know you're mad. You have every right to be mad, but I'm fucking miserable without you." His laugh is self-deprecating at best, desperate at worst. "Yeah, its selfish of me to care how I feel when I'm the one who made you feel how you feel, but I just want to see you again." Another sigh. "Call me back."

I look down at the screen of my cell and stare at it for a beat.

Then I play the message again.

Fifty-Eight

TATE

One month later . . .

"I'm assuming you're getting my messages but don't want to talk yet. I'm trying to be patient . . . but you know me, that isn't an easy task. I talked to Will, and he said nine of the ten horses tested last week are pregnant. That's nineteen of the twenty. Congrats. That's great . . . Christ, listen to me. Picking up scraps so I have a reason to talk to you. I miss you. That's all. I just miss you."

Fifty-Nine

JACK

One month later . . .

"Will?"

"Jack?" His laugh is surprised. "What're you doing calling?"

"How is she?" I ask.

"Don't do this to me, Jack. Don't put me in the middle." He sighs, and his voice lowers. "You mentioned me in a message . . . after Doc's last visit, and Tate . . . she unloaded on me. Said she needed to be able to trust me. Please don't . . ."

"Christ. Sorry, man. I didn't mean to get you tangled in this. I'm just . . ."

"Fucking miserable?" He asks. "Sounds like it to me anyway."

"Fucking miserable and then some," I murmur as I take in the view from my porch. Miles upon miles of green, rolling hills stretch in front of me, and dozens of heads of cattle dot the land. I'm far from alone here with the full-time staff, but fuck if I don't feel completely isolated and lonely.

"Then why did you give up so easily?" Will asks.

"I didn't. Look, I did what she asked." And I've regretted it every day since.

"Since when do you ever do what she says?"

Sixty

JACK

One month later . . .

"**E**very time I call, I think this might be the time you pick up and talk to me. Every goddamn time. You told me I'd move on when I got home. I haven't moved on, Tate. I don't expect to either. I love you. Plain and simple. I love you."

Sixty-One

TATE

One month later . . .

I arch my back, trying to stretch away some of the exhaustion that has set in. It's getting worse with each passing day, but there isn't much I can do about it. It is what it is, and having a fully functioning breeding ranch is what I wanted. It's what I got.

Now, I have to figure out how to do it.

"Harris is loading up the foal now," Will says, referring to the extra hand we've hired to help with the sale of this season's foals. "He'll be back in a second to help."

"What about this one?" I point to the fawn-colored colt walking in the ring. A bittersweet smile paints my lips as I think of the night he was born. The worry I felt and then the relief that coursed through me when Jack watched me from the other side of the stall.

I ignore the sting the memory brings. I've gotten good at ignoring the pangs over the past few months, but it doesn't mean it hurts any less when I do think about him.

"The owner's coming to pick him up today."

"Name?" I ask so I can put it in my records.

"Next time."

"What did you say?" I ask, my attention snapping up to meet Will's eyes.

"*Next Time*. That's the name of the ranch that bought the horse."

I blink back the tears that well in my eyes as I stare at the clipboard. Emotion swells within me at the coincidence.

Sixty-Two

JACK

"*Next Time*. That's the name of the ranch that bought the horse."

I hear Will say the words, but it's Tate I stare at as I stand just outside the stable.

She turns slowly to Will, as if she's in shock. There isn't any way she would know that I renamed the ranch now that it's mine to do with as I please.

Her back is to me, but that small frame of hers stands tall as her head hangs forward while she writes something on her clipboard. Her hair is swept up, exposing that neck I've longed to press my lips to. She has a flannel on to fight off the chill of the afternoon, and from what I can see over the gate she's standing behind, it looks as if she's swimming in it.

It's then that I realize it's my flannel. It's *my* shirt she's wearing.

And there's something about seeing it that steadies the ground beneath me.

But her—the sight of her, being near her—makes every agonizing minute of the past four months dissipate.

"Do you have a problem with the name of my ranch, Knox?"

Her body jolts at the sound of my voice. The hitch of her breath is audible as she turns to face me in what feels like slow motion.

Gray eyes meet mine. Her chin quivers, and her lips tremble before they curve up into a guarded smile. "Jack?" My name on her lips is like a goddamn knife to my heart.

"I didn't fight hard enough for you, Tate. I told you to fight hard for what you wanted. For this ranch. For the people in town to see the real you . . . but when the rubber met the road with you and me, I didn't fight hard enough for you. I didn't prove to you that I was worth it. That our love was worth it."

"*Jack*," she says my name again, and panic hits me when I see tears begin to slide down her cheeks. *Silently.*

She's going to push me away.

She's moved on.

She doesn't love me anymore.

"No. Don't, Tate." I take another step toward her, desperate to say and prove and do whatever the fuck it takes not to walk out of this stable without her knowing how I feel. Without resolving this somehow. "You have to hear me out. You have to—"

"Jack." She hiccups a sob and before I can think what to say or do next, we are in each other's arms.

She is right where I need her to be.

"I'm so sorry," I whisper. "I love you so much."

"I'm so sorry," she murmurs against my chest as her tears wet my shirt. "I couldn't tell you—I didn't know how to—Jack—"

Her words hit my ears, and I shock to reality because what I thought was going to be a reunion doesn't sound like one by the apology on her lips.

To the idea that . . . and when she steps back, when I see my flannel shirt unbuttoned, when I see her tank top . . .

When I see the soft swell of her pregnant belly, I don't even know how to process it.

"Tate?" My eyes flick up to hers and then back down to her tiny baby bump.

My hands go to the back of my neck.

My lips open and then close.

My heart . . . my goddamn heart explodes in my chest in the best possible way imaginable.

"I—Tate—what—how—Tate?"

"I'm so sorry," she whispers as her hands come up to frame my face. As her lips kiss the tears on my own cheeks. As they find mine.

And in that instant, I am home.

I am whole.

I am complete.

"I didn't know how to tell you." A kiss. "And then I didn't know what to tell you." Another kiss. "And then I didn't want to burden you with taking care of something I didn't know if you even wanted. We never talked about—this—"

"Tate." I lean her shoulders back so I can look at her, the woman I love, and the child I already love even though we've never met. "I don't even know what to say."

"I can explain." My hand slides over the small bump of her belly as every part of me right down to my bone marrow settles.

"You can explain later." My lips find hers to tell her I love her and that I plan to make up for lost time. "But it doesn't matter. None of it does. All that matters is you," I murmur against her lips. "And this." I pull her against me again, wrapping my arms around her as I breathe her in. "And the rest of our lives we have to spend together to figure it all out."

Who knew?

Who knew what I would find when I walked onto this ranch ten months ago?

That I'd find Tate Knox and fall in love with her.

That I'd want to make a life with her.

That we'd get to have a next time together.

That I'd never be able to live without her and her wild.

Epilogue

TATE

Five years later . . .

"Are you ready to do this?" I ask as I look across the kitchen.

It looks like a bomb went off. There are mashed potatoes all over the cabinets where Rein lifted the hand mixer too high and splattered them everywhere. The flour I'd portioned aside to thicken the gravy dusts one corner of the floor because I wasn't paying attention and Tack's little fingers pulled the measuring cup off the counter.

"Nooooo!" I yelp as I bolt across the kitchen to prevent him from pulling down the whole sack of flour this time. Saved in the nick of time, I push everything as far away as I can from the edges of the counter.

"You, mister!" I say and point the whisk at him, "are trouble with a capital T."

"Touble wit captl T," he repeats and then smacks his hands together so whatever flour is left on them flies in the air.

He giggles at the sight of it.

It's the kind of giggle that would make any mom surrounded by the chaos of preparing Thanksgiving dinner stop and stare. It's the kind that reminds you that this kind of craziness is good, worth it, because someone like Tack is a part of it.

His belly giggle is music to my ears and I lower myself on my knees to the floor. "Tack."

"Yes, Momma," he says, those eyes and dimples of his that match his daddy's win me over in much the same way.

"I love you."

"Kisses!" my two-year-old shouts, and in keeping with our typical routine, he runs full force into my arms for love.

After my cheek is covered in slobbery, little boy kisses, I squeeze him tight a little longer than usual. I relish the moment in a way I never thought I'd get the chance to. I take the second to adore my second child before my first catches sight, gets jealous, and demands twice as much attention in turn.

But the usual doesn't play out because Rein squeals in excitement at the exact same time the front door opens, sending a gust of snowflakes into the hallway.

"Smells good!" Jack says, and even amid all the other voices that follow suit, his is the one that still causes butterflies in my stomach. His is the one that still puts that automatic smile on my lips.

"It's utter chaos in here," I call out as I wipe my hands on a dishtowel, "but that's what you get when you let a two- and four-year-old help."

I turn the corner and stop in my tracks.

It's a simple sight that I'm certain is unfolding all over the United States of America tonight. My friends and family all just walked in, chattering away as they take off their coats and readying themselves for the good, the bad, and the ugly of family time during the holidays.

Click.

There is something about this snapshot of a picture that awes me.

Because it's mine.

"Hey." Jack's hands slide around my waist and pull me into him for a soft kiss. "Dinner smells good. You smell better." His hand squeezes my ass, and my eyes flash up to his. "I know a way we can work off those calories later," he murmurs with a suggestive lift of his eyebrows.

"I'm sure you do." I bat his hands away as if they annoy me when they do anything but.

Tack's squeals fill the air as he sees Will, his favorite of the group.

"If it's not my favorite squirt, Bridle," Will says, carrying on the running joke of our family and friends over our kids' names.

"Nope!" Tack yells.

"Oh, you're right. I forgot. It's Hoof. Nice to meet you, Hoof." Will holds out his hand to shake Tack's and receives a belly giggle in response.

"No way."

"Hmm. Let me think. Horseshoe?"

Another giggle. "It's Tack!" he shouts before Will picks him up and spins him around.

Rein runs into the room with a flying leap, her bouncy curls flying and new dress whirling around her as she waits for someone to take notice of her sparkly shoes.

"Fi will notice first," Jack says.

"Oh my god!" Fi says as if on cue and moves to hug our little drama queen.

"It'll be weird without Sylvester," Jack says quietly.

I nod, my chest constricting at the thought and knowing it's weird for him without Lauren here too.

But Jack and Lauren's relationship beats to its own drum as Jack controls the tempo. This year, he chose to forgo inviting her, but it was his choice, so I didn't push.

"Who's hungry?" I ask about the fray and get a raucous response in return.

"Alcohol. If we're going to eat your cooking, dear, we need alcohol first," Fi says before enveloping me in the biggest hug. "God, it's good to see you," she says into my ear. "And just wait till I tell you about the guy who got my number on the flight."

JACK

CHATTER FILLS THE HOUSE.

Laughter rings out more often than not, dotted with a few shouts of, "That's not fairs" from Rein over something Tack did to annoy her. They're so much like Lauren and I were together as kids it's scary.

Plates are empty or getting close to it. Glasses of wine have been refilled more times than not.

Tate's at my side, chatting away. Her curves are softer now, her smile wider, and the caution that used to own her eyes has been gone for years.

Everything has changed about her, gotten better with age but one thing hasn't.

Her wild.

That's something I never want to change.

She looks my way and offers a soft smile before going back to talking with Evan, our retired ranch manager here in Montana.

I just sit back and watch everyone.

We started with two ranches: one thriving and one dying.

We started out as two individuals: one who couldn't trust and one who was a little lost.

We started with nothing and ended up creating everything. This life we've surrounded ourselves with people we want to live with is worth more than any balance in any account.

Our new college graduate, Will, who moved here to be with us and help run things in Montana.

Our resident flirt and all-around center of attention, Fiona, who may have married and divorced again.

Our newest addition, Ashley, runs the photography retreat we set up last year in the newly renovated Knox Ranch. There are still horses being bred and the Steely contract is still solid, but behind what used to be the main house, we built cabins to facilitate the new retreat.

Nothing like saying fuck you to the town of Lone Star by building the one thing they judged Tate for.

Old man Evan, who is now retired from the Next Time ranch, sits at the other end and remains as quiet as can be with a ghost of a smile on his face.

My eyes meet Tate's as I slide my hand out to take hers beneath the table. I know this means the world to her too. The family we created and the love that we've fostered.

I catch Will getting flustered when Ashley starts talking to him, and the quick smile Tate wears tells me she sees it too.

We were there once. Falling in love and too stubborn to acknowledge it.

But damn it was fun.

So much has changed. So much is different.

And I wouldn't change a thing about it.

"Who's ready for the card exchange?" I ask, garnering a high-pitched cheer from the family room where Rein is off pretending she's a famous YouTuber.

"That's my job!" she says and runs into the dining room with a stack of cards in her hand.

"You know the rules," Tate says. "Each card was filled out by a member of the family. Each one says what that person was thankful for. And you have to guess who wrote it."

Rein is already halfway through placing cards in front of people when she yells, "Is there a prize for guessing?"

"You and your prizes," I say.

"These are PG-rated, right?" Fiona asks followed by a cackle.

"We can always count on you to ask that," Will says.

"Who's up first?" Tate asks and starts our Thanksgiving tradition.

One by one, our family reads their card and guesses. It doesn't matter if they guess correctly because there are smiles and more wine and more laughter.

"My turn?" I ask when all of the attention is focused on me.

I open the white envelope and pull the card out. "I'm grateful for sticky cheeks to kiss and tickly tummies to blow raspberries on."

"Mommy! Mommy!" Rein guesses as she jumps up and down, clearly all the sugar she's eaten taking full effect.

"It's your dad's turn, Rein. Shhh," Will says and pulls her into his lap to tickle her.

"Let me think," I play along. "I guess . . . Rein?"

"No!" Rein giggles out.

"Then, Tack?"

"No, silly," Rein repeats.

"Oh, it's Tate!" I say and lean forward and press my lips to hers. "I'm grateful for those things too. And you." I kiss her again.

"Get a room!" Fi shouts out.

"No!" Will says. "We might end up with a Saddle or Filly if they get a room."

The whole table laughs as Tate rises from her seat. "Next time," she eyes me, "I get to name the baby."

I snort. "There will be no more next times."

Tate's expression falters for the briefest of seconds as a coy smile plays on her lips. "You sure about that, Sutton?"

Everyone laughs and carries on, but there's something about the way Tate said it—the softness to it and the love in her eyes when she looked at me . . .

Wait.

What?

"Tate?"

"Mmm?" The dishes she's clearing clank as she begins to head toward to kitchen.

"Tate," I repeat as I blink at her in disbelief . . . thinking, wanting, waiting for her answer.

"Don't blame me that you're a sure thing."

ACKNOWLEDGMENTS

This book was a labor of love. I know I say that about every book, but Then You Happened was a struggle from the beginning, all the way to the end for me. Somewhere along the way this past year, I lost my creativity. No matter what I outlined, what I typed, what I tried to pour onto the page, it didn't feel right. For the first time in my writing career, the words just didn't come. I felt broken. But there were you, my readers. The ones who day-in, day-out, told me you were eager for my next novel. The ones who left messages and comments to encourage me. I want to thank you for your kind words, your patience, and the motivation you may not have known you provided me with, but did. I saw you. I still see you. I owe so very much to you.

ABOUT THE AUTHOR

Photo © 2017 Lauren Perry

New York Times Bestselling author K. Bromberg writes contemporary romance novels that contain a mixture of sweet, emotional, a whole lot of sexy, and a little bit of real. She likes to write strong heroines and damaged heroes who we love to hate but can't help to love.

A mom of three, she plots her novels in between school runs and soccer practices, more often than not with her laptop in tow and her mind scattered in too many different directions.

Since publishing her first book on a whim in 2013, Kristy has sold over one and a half million copies of her books across eighteen different countries and has landed on the New York Times, USA Today, and Wall Street Journal Bestsellers lists over thirty times. Her Driven trilogy (Driven, Fueled, and Crashed) is currently being adapted for film by the streaming platform, Passionflix, with the first movie (Driven) out now.

With her imagination always in overdrive, she is currently scheming, plotting, and swooning over her latest hero. You can find out more about him or chat with Kristy on any of her social media accounts. The easiest way to stay up to date on new releases and upcoming novels is to sign up for her newsletter (**http://bit.ly/254MWtI**) or follow her on Bookbub (**http://smarturl.it/KBrombergBB**)